THE RED HEIFER

New York City History and Culture

Jay Kaplan, *Series Editor*

THE RED HEIFER

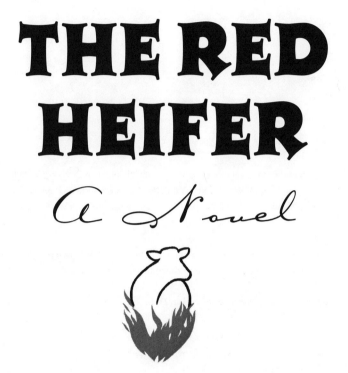

A Novel

LEO HABER

SYRACUSE UNIVERSITY PRESS

First Edition 2001
01 02 03 04 05 06 07   7 6 5 4 3 2 1

Some of the chapters in this novel appeared originally, in slightly different form, in *Jewish Affairs* (South Africa), *Literal Latté* (New York), *Midstream* (New York), *Pif Magazine* (Internet), *Serpentine* (Internet), and *The Southern Anthology* (Louisiana). Many thanks to the editors of these publications for their cooperation and support.

The paper used in this publication meets the minimum requirements of American National Standard for Information Sciences—Permanence of Paper for Printed Library Materials, ANSI Z39.48-1984.∞™

Library of Congress Cataloging-in-Publication Data
Haber, Leo.
      The red heifer : a novel / Leo Haber.—1st ed.
      p. cm.— (New York City history and culture)
      ISBN 0-8156-0692-3 (alk. paper)
      1. Lower East Side (New York, N.Y.)—Fiction. 2. Working class families—Fiction. 3. Jewish families—Fiction. 4. Immigrants—Fiction. 5. Boys—Fiction. I. Title. II. Series.
      PS3558.A257 R43 2001
      813'.54—dc21   00-047-097

Manufactured in the United States of America

Leo Haber, consulting editor at the monthly journal *Midstream*, was born and raised on the Lower East Side of Manhattan and educated in New York City at City College, Columbia University, and Herzliah Hebrew Teachers' Institute. He was the chairman of the Department of Foreign Languages at Lawrence High School in Cedarhurst, New York, where he taught English, Hebrew, and Latin. He has also served as adjunct lecturer in Hebrew at Baruch College, adjunct assistant professor of English at City College, and adjunct professor of Hebrew at Hebrew Union College. His poetry and fiction have won numerous magazine awards, and he has also written articles on current affairs, literature, and music for a wide variety of publications. Mr. Haber and his wife, Sylvia, live in Brooklyn.

CONTENTS

AUTHOR'S NOTE

THE TRANSLITERATION into English letters (romanization) of Yiddish and Hebrew words in the novel and in the accompanying glossary at the end of the book departs frequently from accepted scholarly practice for several reasons. The prevailing system reflects the pronunciation of European Jews of Lithuania and environs, commonly referred to as *Litvaks*. However, most of the older Jewish characters in this novel emanate from Galicia in southeastern Poland and parts of western Ukraine. They are commonly referred to as *Galitsyaners*, and their pronunciation of Yiddish and Hebrew differs appreciably from the "norm." An attempt has therefore been made to approximate their nonstandard pronunciation of these two Jewish languages. This also accounts for the fact that some Yiddish words and expressions appear in two different spellings in the novel and in the glossary (sometimes three, when the Israeli Sephardic version of a Hebrew term is included) to reflect two different speakers with two different pronunciations.

Another deviation from the norm acknowledges common American practice, as in the spelling of the holiday of Chanukah. The initial "ch" is pronounced like the final "ch" in "Bach." Scholarly practice prefers "kh" to "ch" in English to approximate this sound in Yiddish, and "kh" or "h" with a dot below the letter to approximate this sound in Hebrew. Nevertheless, the author of this novel has opted for the "ch" familiar to Americans. Also, in deference to practice in the English language, capital letters and apostrophes are used in the romanizations in the novel although neither exists in Yiddish or in Hebrew.

Finally, some Yiddish and Hebrew words have entered the English language and appear in American dictionaries in spellings that vary from the accepted standard for romanization. This novel, by and large, retains the American-dictionary versions.

The author of the novel assumes full responsibility for the choices delineated above. He wishes to thank all friends and relatives who helped him with the translations in the glossary and the romanization in the text, many of whom, with the best of intentions, advised stricter adherence to scholarly practice. Heading this list is Professor Joseph Sherman of the University of the Witwatersrand in South Africa, a scholar and a true friend, who devoted many thankless hours to this task and who is blameless for all the "errors" incurred by the author.

THE RED HEIFER

THE BLUE GUN

THE SUN like a splattered orange wandered over a dark cloud and once hidden began to cry. I did too because the droplets of water, not juice, splashed against my eyeglasses and made me not see the strange ways of the world. I dashed up four flights of stairs and slid my hand along the wooden banisters. My hand caught a splinter on the third landing and I began to cry again. The hallway smelled. Somebody on the third floor had not seen the orangy sun with bright rays that sped everywhere before the advent of the cloud and had left a pile of gray, smelly garbage in the darkened hallway between landings. I wrinkled my nose and forgot the wooden pain.

"Ma," I screeched, "it's raining on one side of the street and not the other!"

My mother was in the kitchen salting the meat. She rinsed and she rinsed and she hardly turned her head to me. "That happens," she said. I knew if she said that it happens, then I was telling the truth.

"My glasses got wetted up," I said by way of continuing the conversation while watching the meat. "I couldn't see nothin'."

My mother also smelled, but it didn't bother me. She smelled of onions and garlic and oregano that caused my tongue to push up to my nose and wipe away in both directions.

"So how did you see that it was raining on only one side of the street and not on the other?" she asked. She knew I was lying, and she always found out. The meat was dark and bumpy. It flipped and it flapped and it seemed very heavy. Ma pushed it and pulled it and turned it over and it went wherever she made it go. I had nowhere to go.

1

"I didn't see it, I felt it. I felt it near the candy store and then I went to the other side of the street and I didn't feel it."

"You crossed the street without asking anybody to cross you? That's a bad boy."

Even though I had no place to go I decided to go back downstairs because there was no sense staying here and watching the meat get salty and bloodless. I always said stuff I shouldn't, and then I always got caught. "I'm goin', Ma."

She left the meat on a wooden tray. She wiped her hands against her smock and finally turned to me. She pulled me by the ear and wiggled it. It didn't hurt. There was a window in the kitchen that faced the back yard, and when I looked down, I could see brightness return to the fences and the tufts of grass that lined the edge of the other building. It was time to go.

"Yes, *zindele,* it rains on one side of the street and not on the other. That's the way it goes sometimes. It's good in one place and bad in another place. We have a hard life here but we live, and on the other side of the ocean, your cousins and uncles and *tantes* they run for their life. Better you should stay on the side of the street where it's sunny and not on the side that rains. But ask a big boy at the candy store to cross you. Don't go by yourself."

I mulled over these words all the way back down to the street. I ran for my life but didn't catch it. It was with me all the time, but in running for it, I forgot about the splinter and I forgot about the smelly garbage in the hall and went from dark to light with no rain anywhere to be seen. I heard a loud noise like a bomb in the movies, and a man with a suit and a tie fell right in front of me and didn't say a word. I skipped over his end of the body and watched a very fast car speeding noisily off toward the park. It raced and screeched and turned the corner and disappeared.

"Run for your life!" somebody yelled. It was not my mother even though it was a lady's voice. So even here on this side of the ocean I had to run for my life. I ran across the street without asking her to cross me because I was afraid. From the other side of the street I could see where the rain had not fallen and where it was eternally sunny and where my mother told me to be always, so even though I got there the wrong way, I was there and that was all there was to it.

But now the interesting stuff was happening where I left. The man lay on the ground and from him came blood like from the meat with no mother and with no salt. He twitched and he twisted and flip-flopped without a wooden board underneath him. He picked up his hand and made with his pinky to the candy store, and Moysh who was big and fat and talked like a baby came out and bent over him. I could see all this even though Moysh was roly-poly and covered the man on the ground with his fat body. The man put his hand inside his pocket and took out a gun just like the gun that Chaim's uncle gave him on his birthday except that Chaim's gun was red and this gun was black. The man on the ground pushed the gun toward Moysh and it fell inside Moysh's pocket where it made a big bulge on the side of him right below the big bulge of his belly. Moysh got up and ran. I yelled to him to run to my side of the street where it never rained and people like Chaim's uncle and *tante* who gave him the gun did not have to run for their life, but Moysh ran on the same side of the street to the corner where a police car was waiting. A policeman jumped out and pushed Moysh up against a fence and tapped him and took his gun. Chaim kept his red gun for a whole day before it broke on the sidewalk when he dropped it. Chaim cried and his mother hit him. My mother never hit me. She only pulled my ear and that was when she wanted me to listen. But at least Chaim had his gun a whole day. Moysh's gun didn't even last a minute. My father said that Moysh never had any luck with anything, even while running for his life.

So my father also knew about running for his life! It didn't surprise me because he knew everything, every little thing. My mother knew when I was telling a lie, but my father knew when I was even just thinking about telling a lie.

"Don't tell me about guns," he said. "I don't want to hear nothin' about guns. Guns are for *goyim*. You better learn to say *Krishma* before you go to sleep so you won't dream about guns. That gangster had a real gun when they shot him, not a fake one like your friend Chaim. And don't tell me that

Chaim's uncle is gonna get him another gun. He can get him a hundred guns. You ain't gettin' a gun. You gettin' a *laptsedekl* to put on you to protect you from guns in this nasty world. *Ameyrike gonif!* A *tachshitl* you gave me here. Guns he wants, and he almost got killed."

My father said all this later, after an ambulance came and they took the man away on a long wooden tray. I think it was wood. The sides were wood. Maybe the middle was softer like a carpet or like a bed. One policeman went into the ambulance with him. Maybe he wanted to give the man back his gun that he took from Moysh, who took it from the man. That would have been fair.

I didn't say about the screaming and yelling that went on the whole time. It made me deaf. The funny part is they screamed and they yelled from all over and I couldn't see anybody. It was like there was a big crowd screaming and yelling but the crowd was hiding. Only my mother's face was not hiding and not screaming. She looked out of our window on the fourth floor and saw me on the far side of the street. I saw her too because I was also looking up, and my heart bumped in me, not because of the bloody man in the street, but because my mother was looking to see how I crossed the street. I wiped my glasses. She was laughing and crying. That made me feel better because when Ma laughed and cried it meant she was happy and she was going to hug me sooner or later.

Hot summer months we sometimes slept on the fire escape. The iron was rough and rusty, and Ma put a soft cloth and a sheet all over so we wouldn't get rusty too. It was just like the carpet underneath the man going into the ambulance. The sides of the fire escape were like the wooden sides of the tray that carried him.

Nights were heavy with smells and screeches of all sorts. I listened for the cats down in the yard that scraped along the fence. Sometimes they screamed too, a kind of crying that maybe meant it was going to rain. And sometimes it did rain, and I had to scramble inside the window before my eyeglasses got wet again. But most of the time it didn't, and it remained hot even under a dark sky and no sun and no brightness. I counted stars because Ma said I knew how to count, but I lost my way among the stars and counted them over and over again.

Sometimes we slept on the roof until I got up and started walking and Ma started screaming. She screamed sometimes even though she didn't scream when the man exploded from the bomb they shot him with. But she didn't slap me for walking. Chaim's mother would have smacked him four times in the tush and two more times in the face, but I was lucky. I almost walked off the roof and only got yelled at.

Chaim told me that Moysh was in jail, and I started to cry. In Vinnie's candy store I had seen the comics in the paper over Mates's shoulder, and when Dick Tracy caught the bad guy, he always ended up in jail. How could Moysh be in jail? He didn't do nothing. Maybe he bombed the man with the suit and the tie. Maybe he came over and put his fat body on him in order to see where the bomb went. Maybe he took the gun from the man because the man was his uncle running for his life and was giving Moysh a birthday present. There were lots of maybes that I always liked to think about even though I never finished deciding on one maybe over another.

Everything smelled good in Vinnie's candy store. If the telephone rang and I got lucky, Vinnie would ask me to run up to the fifth floor and call Mr. Weinberg down to the phone. If Mr. Weinberg got a call from his son in California, he would give me a whole nickel for calling him down, and I would buy a chocolate candy with jelly in the middle and have money left over for a glass of seltzer. But I didn't like seltzer because the bubbles jumped all over inside my throat and my belly, so I saved the leftover money for another piece of candy tomorrow. The candies had bright papers on them. They sparkled like stars in the night, and I took a long time to unwrap them. I didn't throw the papers away. I saved them in little balls in my pocket to protect the leftover money from falling out.

Mr. Weinberg told me that California was always sunny and I wanted to go there until he told me that it never snowed in California and then I didn't want to go there. Once he let me talk on the telephone to his son. He said say hello Leybish Weinberg, and I said that. Then the other voice said who are you and I said I was me and he laughed and told me to be a good boy and Mr. Weinberg took the phone away from me even though I was a good boy, and he said to his son: Leybish, you should have a son like that and what are you waitin' for, you shlemiel.

Maybe he called him that because the son in California didn't know who I was until I told him, and maybe he called him that because he wasn't in the candy store with all the paper-covered candies, and maybe he called him that because the son in California wanted a gun even though he wasn't a *goyim*.

Mr. Weinberg was a giant and had a long gray beard that grew from one side of his black hat to the other side. When he met my father in the street and spoke to him, his beard would fall down on the top of my father's head, where he also wore a black hat. The gray beard would rest there and take it easy. Mr. Weinberg's mouth moved a lot when he talked, but the beard didn't move. It just rested on my father's hat.

My father kept his hands behind his back when he spoke and tied them up there. He leaned forward a little bit and said his words into Mr. Weinberg's chest. Sometimes he spit. I tried spitting too, but I couldn't do it too well. I also tried to whistle, but my father put a stop to that. "*Goyim* whistle. *Feh.* It's not nice to whistle. You wanna be a goy?" No, I wanted to be a *goyim* because they got guns for their birthday. I got candy for my birthday, and that I could get myself by calling Mr. Weinberg with the gray beard to the telephone in the candy store.

When would it snow again? Tell me when? My father looked into a book and made wrinkles over his eyes and sang a little tune. It will snow, he sang over the book, when the *moshiach* comes. It never snows in Jerusalem, but it will snow when the *moshiach* enters the holy gate. Our sins will be white as snow, and a blanket will cover the earth like the blanket of water in Noah's time, not to wipe out the whole creation this time, but only to wipe out a Hitler, *yemach shemoy*, may his name be erased, who reddens the snowy world with innocent blood.

It snowed just before Yom Kippur and I was happy that I wasn't in California and that the *moshiach* was coming. This time I didn't see a man in a suit and a tie fall in the snow and bloody it up like Hitler, but I saw the people and the cars make the snow dirty and brown. Only in the park across the way, in the baseball field where nobody was playing, did the snow stay white and clean. My sins were as white as that snow.

Pa brought home two chickens, which he put in the bathtub. They jumped and they cackled and they drowned out the screech of the cats in the back yard. They looked very big even through the tiny crack between the bathroom door and the wall, and they fought with each other all the time. My father waved them over our heads and sang and sang and then explained to me that these chickens would die instead of us and that we would live to see many more snows and the chickens would live to lie on our plates. I started to cry.

"What are you cryin' for?" my father said.

"I want the chickens to see more snow," I said.

"Did you ever see a kid like this?" my father asked. "What do Yom Kippur chickens have to do with snow?"

"I want the chickens to see the *moshiach* come."

My father was beside himself with joy. "I have a *tzaddikl* here. He wants the *moshiach* to come for the chickens. The *moshiach* don't come for us. He don't come for my brother in a concentration camp, for my sister, for my brother's wife and his children, but he gotta come for the chickens. *Mahn zindele,* from your mouth to God. May the *moshiach* come for the chickens and in the meantime come for us too before it's too late."

※

That winter the snows came without the *moshiach* and the sun went into hiding. Colors changed. Overhead everything was gray and even inside our house the black banisters and the brown garbage turned green. I looked for the chocolate candies and their multicolored wrappers, but Vinnie hid them away and the boxes were white and empty. Chaim turned blue.

My mother tried to keep me from going to Chaim's room on the second floor. She asked me to stay with Mates, who was older and would take care of me. I didn't like looking over his shoulder all the time as he sat in the candy store reading the paper for nothing. I always thought he read the paper for something, but Vinnie always yelled at him, "You wanna read the paper for nothin'? This ain't a liberry." Mates told me that there was war in the newspaper. No more pictures of ladies on the front page but words of war. He was a good reader but he stayed on the front page and on the second page so long that he never got to "Dick Tracy," and I lost interest in looking over his shoulder. I sneaked up to see Chaim.

Chaim was blue. His face was as blue as the summer sky even though I almost forgot what the summer sky looked like. Chaim's mother didn't let me near the bed and I didn't take off my coat. I wore a heavy coat with a buckle and I also had a hat on with ear flaps that made me not hear but kept me warm. I even wore big boots that my mother had to put on me because she knew how to push on one end and pull on the other end since I couldn't do that. But I pulled the side zippers up after she finished. On the floor by themselves, the boots looked like my father and Mr. Zukerman talking to each other. Not Mr. Weinberg because he was taller. On me, the boots didn't look like people. The leather smelled like squash mixed with *knubl,* which was garlic, my mother said. I stood at the opposite end of the bed that had a gate, and I leaned my hands on the gate without taking my clothing off and looked at blue Chaim.

Maybe Chaim's mother hit him so hard that she knocked the blood out of his face into his belly and left him black and blue. Maybe he stayed outside in the summer so long that he became the color of the sky. Maybe he got a blue gun from his uncle running for his life, and Chaim was dumb enough to press the blue gun to his face and kiss it all day and all night.

I asked Chaim what color his new gun was even though I didn't even really know if he had a new gun, but he didn't answer.

"Don't breathe on him," I heard Chaim's mother say from the kitchen.

I didn't know if she was talking to me or to Chaim. Chaim seemed to be breathing a lot, but the breathing went up to the ceiling, not on me. I breathed only a little bit, and to make sure, I breathed into the gate at the end of his bed and waited to see if the breathing would bounce back at me. It did. "I'm not breathing on him," I said. "I'm breathing on myself."

My father who was not working came into the room and didn't even get angry when he saw me. He sat down near Chaim's bed and took out a prayer book and started praying. He moved his whole body from the tush to his head back and forth like he always did in shul, and he closed his eyes on both sides of his nose and shook his head this way and that as if he disagreed. I saw droplets of water trickle out of his eyes. It was snowing outside, not raining, and my father didn't have eyeglasses to collect the snow.

Chaim's mother came in and scowled. "It won't do any good," she cried out. "You and your foolishness. There ain't no God. He don't look after His people. He leaves them alone to die before their time."

My father continued shaking and praying and crying. The snow continued to fall at the window behind Chaim's blue face.

My father got up to go. He motioned to me. "Go over to your friend," he said, "and say goodbye. Wish him *a refiye shelayme.*" My father walked into the kitchen to talk to Chaim's mother, maybe to tell her that God don't look after chickens either. I went around the side of the bed to Chaim's blue face and said, "*A refiye shelayme.*" Chaim stirred. Under the covers there was movement. His face remained straight and blue, and his lips did not part into an answer. But under the covers there was action, and slowly, slowly I saw his elbow stick out from the covers and then his hand and then the blue gun. He gave it to me. I was right all along. He had a new blue gun. No maybes this time. And he gave it to me for keeps. I took it and stuffed it into the pocket of my heavy overcoat. You couldn't tell it was there because everything bulged in my coat with my hands in the side pockets. It was for keeps because I never saw him again, just like the chickens.

"Why do people die?" I asked my father.

"People die," he said, "because if people didn't ever die, they wouldn't believe in God and they would be worse to each other than Hitler."

I decided that if I ever saw Hitler in the street in front of our house, I would put real bullets into my blue gun and shoot him down like I was a *goyim* so maybe my father's brother and sister wouldn't run for their life so much and maybe Chaim's mother would believe in God and maybe Mates would skip the pictures on the front page and get to "Dick Tracy" fast.

⹊

Where does the sun go in the winter? I knew it was there because the snow was the sun's tears frozen in the cold on the way down to us. But I couldn't tell in which part of the sky. I looked east in the morning and west in the evening and sometimes it was there and most of the times not. It was a dodger and tricky and it failed to keep us warm when we needed it most. My mother stoked the coals in the furnace in the basement and my father told me not to tell anybody that we lived for free in our rooms because of my mother's work. He left every morning and came back every night, sometimes happy because he found a day's work, and sometimes sad. He was even sad when he was happy because the mailman came and didn't bring the right letters.

The mailman didn't talk very much. He hated everybody, and his cap wasn't as nice as the firemen's cap, which was so big and so black even though their fire engines were redder than Chaim's first gun. Once the mailman spoke to me. He said, "Tell your father to pray for me and my relatives too. Does the crazy old coot think that only Jews die in this here world?"

I wanted to tell him that chickens die also and that my father prays with the chickens over his head and that Chaim died too and he was a Jew whose mother didn't believe in nothing, but I didn't because the mailman never looked at me when he spoke and it was hard to answer a back without eyes.

Squirrels didn't look at me in the park either. They scurried so fast from tree trunks to a little grassy hill at the other end of the park, and they didn't look when they crossed the street. They were faster than cars, but I spoke to them anyway. Where are you runnin'? I asked. I run to the park to see you run and to see the guys play baseball in the summer when the sun is shining, not in the winter when the snow is white all over the field, and I run to the candy store in the winter when it's too cold to stay outside and I want to read "Dick Tracy" over Mates's shoulder if there is no war that day, and I run home in the evening to find my father happy or sad and sad when he's happy to see if he brought the *moshiach* with him, but if there is no *moshiach* for chickens, why should there be one for squirrels? So why do you run?

They didn't answer me all winter, just as the sun didn't shine, and the war didn't finish, and Hitler didn't appear in front of our house for me to shoot. The only sure thing was Chaim's blue gun in my pocket. I didn't lose it or break it or find bullets for it. I kept it in my coat and waited for spring.

It took so long in the cold city, but *Paysach* meant that it was spring. I had an idea that the Seder would finally come because the days got warmer and when I looked for the sun all day it was there. My coat came off and I hid the gun in Ma's china closet behind the Seder plate because nobody touched that part the whole year. Mates told me that Chaim was hidden in the ground in a box and I thought I might find his hiding place and see him again, but Mates said you can't breathe in the box and I started to cry and didn't look for him anymore.

I looked for my father and also for my mother, who was getting very fat and who lowered her eyes a lot. My father stroked her cheek and told her not to worry because God will help, and my mother read a book like my father. "We will be fruitful and we will multiply and we will defeat the wicked designs of that murderer, with God's help," my father said.

The night before the Seder we searched all over the house for bread. I held a candle and my father followed me as if I was the sun and he was looking east and west all winter. He had a brush of feathers in his hand and he found a crumb here and a crumb there and brushed it into a thick handkerchief. We made the leavings into a nice bundle and tied it up good. The next morning we burned it outside in the street, and the warmth of the fire helped a little bit because it was still pretty cold in the morning hours.

"When you grow up," my father said, "you'll be a scholar and you'll get married and be a husband and your wife will also have a child and you will burn the *chumets* with your own son in a happy hour."

"What does a scholar do?" I asked my father. His hands were behind his back and he was leaning forward as if I was another man like him to speak to.

"A scholar studies *Toyreh,* the five holy books, and *Shas* and *Gemoore.* Maybe a little arithmetic, maybe a little geography, maybe a little history, maybe some music—would you like to play a violin?—maybe some books with poems and stories like Goethe and Schiller, maybe even some science like Einstein, even though I don't believe in it."

I never heard so many maybes in my whole life. "I want to play on a comb with tissue paper like Mates does," I said to my father.

He couldn't believe it. "A Heifetz you'll never be. That's for sure. Maybe it's for the best. You'll study *Toyreh* day and night. The *goyish* world kills us in more ways than one with the movies and the baseball and the short dresses and the guns."

I thought my father had found my gun but it was still there behind the Seder plate in the china closet.

That night my father came to the Seder table with tears of joy in his eyes. His mouth was a perpetual smile that made creases in his cheek, and his forehead was flushed with red. I didn't get scared because the red wasn't blue.

He held a letter in his hand. His hand was black and rough with hair but the under part was soft and still pink like mine. He looked at my mother, who was very fat, and at me, who was very skinny, and he waved the letter in the air like he was saying goodbye.

"*Danken Got,*" he said. "Thank God. A letter from my brother, the *shoychet* in Radom in Poland. He and his wife and his children are all alive and well. He has been saved so far from *chamas ha-maytsik,* the anger of the oppressor, *yemach shemoy.* He escaped into the Russian part and though they don't let him be a *shoychet* there and they don't let him teach *Toyreh,* at least he's alive and well with his family, thank God. Now we can have a good *Sayder* and a happy *Paysach.* And you can bring us another *kaddishl* or maybe a girl to keep up our family without worrying."

Only one maybe, my father said. Maybe a girl. I didn't want a girl. I saw the Seder plate on the table in front of my father with a potato on it and a chicken wing and other things and I wanted my blue gun.

"What is a *shoychet?*" I asked my father.

"A *shoychet* like your uncle in Poland is a man who slaughters animals, mainly chickens, so that we can eat them."

We were sitting in the center of the room like on Friday night, and all the candles were aglow. My mother wore a long dress, not a short one, and she didn't go to the movies. "Your uncle is a scholar," my mother added. "At your age he was already learning holy books."

"How does he slaughter animals?" I asked.

"The Four Questions are becoming ten questions," my father said. "This is not the time or the place. He slaughters animals. Better they should die that way than with guns. Thank God he's alive and well."

After many prayers and much singing without a violin but with screeching from the cats down in the yard and after the horseradish and the soup, we came to the chicken on the plate. I refused to eat it. My mother urged me to put some skin on my back and to eat, but I wouldn't do it. My mother felt my head and asked my father to feel my head.

"He's not sick. He's all right. Why won't you eat the chicken?"

"I don't want an uncle to slaughter the chickens," I said, "before the *moshiach* comes for them."

My father burst out laughing, and my mother laughed and cried. She wiped a tear away. "Foolish child," she said, "to make a fuss. It's not a sin. A *shoychet* observes the holy law of kindness to animals and delivers painless instant death."

I began to choke without having swallowed a bone. My mother punched me in the back, but not like Chaim's mother when he wasn't in the ground.

My father raised his hands to heaven. "He's choking without even eating. He won't even survive to say *kaddish* for me, the little *bandit,* and yet a nephew of a gentle genius who would not hurt a Jew or a goy. My *tzaddikl.*"

My mother began to sway back and forth as if she was reading the prayers. Her hand was on my shoulder, and she caressed my cheek. "He's a good boy," she said to my father. Then she turned to me. "My little son, *mahn zindele,* from slavery in Egypt and Moyshe Rabbaynee's time till now we were never the slaughterers of the world, only the slaughtered." She hugged me.

That night when my father and my mother were asleep, I crept out of bed and got dressed by myself. I sneaked into the living room where the Seder table was still standing with Elya's cup on it filled to the brim. Elya had not yet come, and the *moshiach* who would follow him was therefore delayed indefinitely, maybe till next *Paysach.* I didn't want to add any more maybes. It was bad enough that Moyshe Rabbaynee was still in jail. I climbed up on a chair to the china closet door and opened it. The blue gun was still there in the dark, although hard to see behind the Seder plate. I took it out and walked quietly out of the house. Down the four flights I went without sliding my hand on the wooden banisters to catch a splinter. Outside, I walked slowly past Vinnie's candy store, which was closed because nobody was buying anything late at night for *Paysach,* and I smelled the candies, which had miraculously reappeared on the other side of the glass in all their splendor of the colored wrappers. I crossed the street by myself and glanced up to the fourth floor to make sure that my mother wasn't looking out of the window. If she wasn't, I prayed, I would even let her have a girl. I climbed a short fence and went into the park where the squirrels I think were still scampering across the black grass but without even looking at me. I didn't speak to them this time. I had things to do. Behind the grassy hill, I dug a little hole in the ground and buried the beautiful blue gun in the hole I myself had made with my own hands and sent it on its way back to my friend Chaim whose mother didn't believe in anything. I recited the *kaddish* prayer for the buried gun even though it was only a gun. I returned home without being caught and without shooting Hitler, *yemach shemoy,* and decided to be a scholar like my uncle in Poland who was now in Russia even though I refused to be a *shoychet,* a slaughterer, or a slaughtered running for my life.

AUNT GEETY

NEXT YEAR I was seven, maybe eight, and Lepke's gang was after me even though Lepke was dead in the electric chair, which was like the chair in the barbershop except that you couldn't read the comics in the electric chair while you were being made dead. I myself never read the comics in the barber chair because I had to take my glasses off for the barber to cut my hair on the side near the *payes,* so I couldn't see the paper in front of me. It wouldn't have mattered anyway even if I could have kept my glasses on because I couldn't read yet, and Mates, who was older and explained the comics to me, wasn't even allowed to sit in the chair next to me and read the comics out loud while I was getting a haircut. The barber said no, and no was no. He was an ugly man, almost like Lepke except he didn't wear a slouch hat and was alive.

So many people were dead. Some people were dead in a hurricane that came to Avenue C and knocked down all the pushcarts on Sunday morning and made the old men with beards cry from their eyes to the hair on their cheeks that got matted down like wet grass in the park across the street in the early morning. Three old men were dead and didn't cry, and that was bad dead because they were good old men.

"They're good old men," my mother said to my father. "They work hard for a living selling *shmates* and don't go on home relief. God should show pity on them."

Some people were dead in the big ocean when their battleships got killed in Pearl Harbor, which was very far from Avenue C, so I didn't have to worry about the war as yet. I saw the pictures of those ships on the front page of the

15

Daily News before Mates got to "Terry and the Pirates," and I looked for Lepke's boys at the bottom of the ocean, but their faces were smudged and I couldn't be sure. So if they weren't Lepke's *banditn* who died in the battle but our brave sailor boys, then that too was bad dead.

I also remember the zeppelin that blew up in New Jersey, which is very close to New York. Every place named "New" is probably close to us because we're a "New" too. Though I wasn't afraid of the faraway war, I was afraid of zeppelins. But the dead people on this zeppelin were German dead, so I didn't know if that was a good dead or a bad dead.

My father couldn't help me out on this one. "Not all German people are bad people," he said to me when I asked. "Only German Nazis are bad people and those who help them kill."

When I asked him if the people in the zeppelin were German Nazis or German not-Nazis, he said he couldn't be sure. What kind of answer is that? Fathers become fathers because they're sure; otherwise they're children. But my father said that you have to be like Rashi who wrote the greatest commentary on the *Toyreh*. Rashi says in three or four different places, "I don't know the answer." So that means that all fathers have permission not to know. When I don't know something, my *rebby* gets angry at me and sometimes gives me a very light slap on the fingers of my hand, but I never saw him hit my father. He stands up and bows a little when my father comes into the room. I wonder if he knows that my father don't know sometimes. I don't think I'll tell him.

Lepke's gang was after me because maybe they thought I still had that gun I sent back to Chaim's grave under the sand in the park. Lepke's guys had guns and they used them for real. I wanted to tell them my blue gun was fake, but then Mates read me a story from the *News* that told about one of those gangsters in jail who carved a fake gun out of a bar of soap and colored it black with shoe polish and got out of jail that way. So it wouldn't have done any good anyway because Lepke's gang wanted fake guns too, even blue ones.

I protected myself from being shot by them in two ways. I said *Krishma* twice every night before I went to sleep. My *rebby* told me that *Krishma* protects me from dying when I'm asleep. It protects everybody. You say the Lord our God is one and only, and He takes care of your soul while you're dreaming. So I decided that if I said it twice, it would protect me asleep and awake, at night and also in the day.

The second way was an even better way. My mother said to my father one day, "I think your *kaddishl* has a talent for music. He sings to himself all the time like a *chazn,* and it's on tune all the time. He picks up every *nigun* in shul and even makes turnings on them that I never heard before."

"So what?" my father said.

"So what?" my mother said. "Your son has a God-given talent maybe, and all it is is 'So what?' I think we should get him lessons on the violin or the piano."

My father looked surprised. He made many wrinkles over his eyes and even in his nose. "What do you want to make of the *tachshitl,* a klezmer, God forbid? I expect him to be a scholar, an *oyker hurim,* an uprooter of mountains in *Toyreh* and Talmud, like his grandfather, *ulev ha-shulem,* and his uncle my brother in Europe, God should help him escape from evil."

My mother didn't seem surprised like my father. Her face was wrinkled like his but beautiful. She looked like a shriveled angel who would protect me when I'm asleep. Even though her belly was fat, her neck was tall and skinny. Her hands were red from washing so many dishes, and her cheeks were even redder from the summer heat, but her throat was white as snow down to her pumping heart up down, up down.

"So what's wrong with a klezmer?" my mother asked.

"A klezmer? A musician?" my father gasped. "A klezmer is worse than a *gonif.* A *gonif,* God help him, has to steal because he's poor and his family needs bread. But a klezmer don't want to learn *Toyreh,* so he becomes a klezmer and associates with actresses and *kurves* and lowlifes of all kinds and he wanders from town to town and lives in hotels with strange women and becomes fierce and devious. The murderers in the world should be afraid of *him,* not the other way around!"

So I decided to become a musician to make the murderers afraid of me. My mother took me for lessons to the Settlement House and then to practice on a piano in Mrs. Gottlieb's apartment who had four daughters and a piano and no sons and everybody said that was a disaster, which I can understand because who wants girl daughters who are going to be fierce and devious klezmers? But I thought that Mrs. Gottlieb's daughters knew what they were doing.

"Nobody will rape them, thank God," I assured my mother. "Lepke's gang will be afraid of them all the time."

My mother was shocked. "Where did you learn that word?" she asked in dismay.

"I learn all about fierce in the *News* from Mates before we get to 'Terry and the Pirates.' "

My mother sighed and laughed at the same time. "God protect us from this golden land," she said like a prayer, but I didn't need the prayer for protection. I told everybody in the candy store including Lepke's gang that I was going to be a musician and they better watch out.

At about the same time, somewhere between the zeppelin and the dead boys at Pearl Harbor, maybe before, my mother gave birth to my younger brother Noosn, or Nathan in English, and my Aunt Geety came to live with us forever.

♥

There's good and there's bad in this world, my father would always say, and you gotta learn to live with both. I agree. Noosn was badder than bad. He cried all the time, by day and by night. Naturally, he didn't know how to say *Krishma* or how to play the piano, so I suppose he couldn't protect himself and had a lot to cry about. But it was a pain. It hurt my ears. He never cried in tune. He cried in between notes, in between two keys on the piano, even in between the E and the F on the piano where there ain't a black key in between to go in between.

But Aunt Geety was good, even though she wasn't really my aunt. She gave Noosn a few drops of wine from the Passover bottle and he stopped crying. My mother would never do that. She picked Noosn up and patted his behind and whispered secrets to him that she never told me until he stopped crying. I liked Geety's way much better.

Aunt Geety was really Cousin Geety. My mother said that her father was her brother and this made her my cousin, but she was too old to be my cousin so she became my aunt. I didn't really understand how Uncle Oosher could be her father and also Ma's brother at the same time, but my father said I was a foolish boy and wasn't I his son and Noosn's brother at the same time? Even though that didn't make much sense to me since they were two different things, I was very glad that my father finally knew something again.

Aunt Geety. She sat in front of the big mirror in the bedroom and twisted her hair this way and that way for an hour. Her hair was gold with flecks of brown, and, unlike my mother, who tied her hair up in a pile on top of her head, Aunt Geety let it all fall down to her belly button, or to the other side of her belly button in her back. She curved her body on the seat and sang to herself all the time that she looked into the mirror. She sang in tune—a sweet Yiddish *lidl* that didn't have any words and that made me close my eyes even though I always wanted to look at her. She was like a goldfish in the water bowl that looked at my face and parted its lips open and closed, open and closed, in an underwater song of love.

"She gotta come live with you here on the East Side," Uncle Oosher said one day to my mother who was his sister. "If she lives in New Haven, she'll marry one of them and then where will we be?"

My mother looked at my father, who looked at Uncle Oosher, who gave me a candy bar.

"Eat it later after dinner so it won't spoil your appetite," my mother said to me.

"Them boys in the streets of New Haven," Uncle Oosher continued, "whether they're street bums or high class from Yale University are all the same. They hate us and love our girls. And if she falls in love with one of them, will she wait until after dinner to eat the chocolate? *A nechtiker tug.* Impossible. She'll run away with one of them, and I'll lose her forever. You take her in here, she'll help you with the children, and you teach her. Find a boy for her from a *yichusdik* Jewish family. Save my life."

So that's how Aunt Geety came to live with us. I thought she came from far away, but New Haven is also a "New" and must be very close. That made me worry that she would go back to New Haven any day now, and I didn't want her to go back because I could be the boy from a good family that they found for her. Not Noosn, since he was still a baby.

Aunt Geety dressed me and tickled me in my special part, and I laughed and said tickle yourself, and she laughed and said that I knew too much, but I didn't know anything. I wasn't even a father yet. When she bent down over me, I thought her chest was split in two with an ax, and I started to cry, and she called me silly, like my father sometimes does. Geety took off her blouse and her chest protector and showed me that there was no blood from an ax on the edges of her splits. She made me touch them all around to prove to me that they were smooth and shaped like that from the beginning, and she said that when I grew up I would remember that moment. I haven't ever forgotten it. When my father picks up a knife to cut the *Shabes* challah-bread, I lean away so that he won't cut my chest in two and make the two sides swell up like balloons from the accident. My uncle in Europe, my father's brother, is a *shoychet* and cuts the throats of chickens, which Ma and Pa force me to eat. Who knows? Maybe my father cuts chests.

The summer heat was unbearable day after day. We made fans out of cardboard boxes and waved them all the time, but it didn't help. I went to the neighborhood playground with Aunt Geety and jumped around in the kiddie pool because the water was cooler and made me feel better. Aunt Geety strolled off to the tennis courts to talk to people, and I came running after her to make sure she didn't catch a train to New Haven.

"Go back to the water," she said. I think she was angry.

"All the big girls," I said, "have balloons like you. I can see them now. Did their fathers split their chests too?"

"You're a stupid kid," she yelled, but she laughed this time. "That's what all girls have, not boys, and that's what boys like." She turned to three men who were standing next to her and pushing her. One of them touched her balloon. "Lay off," she said. "Private property."

That's what my mother said it said on the grass in front of the big house in Brooklyn we once went to when Noosn was very sick. "Private property." I didn't know that Aunt Geety was also rich. I expected her to be rich when she would be eighteen because Uncle Oosher said that next year when she will be eighteen she will with God's help and his sister's help, get married and inherit the riches of family life which she lost when her mother died, but not now. "That's why it's an emergency," Uncle Oosher said to my mother and father. "You have to save her before she gets eighteen and has the legal right to run away with one of them."

So when she said "private property," which meant she was rich already, I knew that if I didn't save her immediately, all would be lost for Uncle Oosher, and I would never see him again and never get a candy bar to eat after dinner when it don't spoil my appetite, and to tell the truth, I didn't feel like eating it anymore anyway.

I made my plans on how to save Aunt Geety from running away to break Uncle Oosher's heart. I got my ideas on Friday night when winter came and it was cold enough outside to sit at the *Shabes* table with Ma and Pa and Geety and not feel like going out into the ice-cold to escape the heat, which had already gone away. From my seat alongside the kitchen window I could see the white snow on the ground glittering under the street lamp. Nobody was walking across the street near the park, and the snow was clean and flat and without footsteps of little children or old ladies and men or elves or *shaydim* or even the angels that came home with us after the *Shabes* prayers in shul. We ate in the kitchen because we didn't have a living room. Since Geety came to live with us, my father got a bed for the living room and sold the dining table to a neighbor who lived upstairs and was eating off the floor before he got our table. I slept on a cot in the bedroom curtained off from Ma's bed, and Geety slept in the living room on the new bed.

So we ate and sang *zmires* in the kitchen. Three rooms and a bathroom in between are enough for a small family. Once we lived with a bathroom in the hall for everybody, but that didn't seem to give us more room in the house. I forgot to mention Noosn. Noosn the nuisance. He slept in a cradle alongside Ma's bed, the lucky guy. Sometimes it's good to be a baby.

After the *Shabes* meal, Pa read us from the *sedra* of the week in the *Toyreh* on the cold winter nights, and that's how I found out about Yankev and the ladder and how he got rich by working seven years many times and how he was afraid of his brother Aysev, who hunted and used guns and killed and was like a Lepke. But I forgot the best part. I also found out about how Yankev was at the well and kissed Ruchl before he knew her and decided to get rich for her. It was then I decided that I would get rich for Aunt Geety and marry her and keep her home so that Uncle Oosher could visit her and me whenever he wanted.

She was beautiful even when she cried. Even when she yelled. She never yelled at Ma and Pa just like I didn't, but she yelled at Uncle Oosher one Sunday before he gave me a candy bar. She cried and she screamed and she yelled so loud you could hear her in Canarsie.

"I don't want to be a prisoner! I don't want to be religious. The guys like me because I got what it takes, and you keep me locked up like a murderer. I never murdered anybody, but you murder me!"

I should have gotten angry at Geety because Uncle Oosher was so disturbed that he never gave me my candy bar, but I had to forgive her because Uncle Oosher was too busy murdering her to think about my candy bar. It was not her fault. I never murdered anybody either, even when I had Chaim's blue gun, and I never screamed at Uncle Oosher, who was like my mother and father, but to tell the truth, Uncle Oosher never tried to murder me.

When Yankev in the *Toyreh* kissed Ruchl in the learning at the Friday night *Shabes* table in the kitchen, I said to Ma and Pa and Aunt Geety, "So fast?"

Ma got red in her wrinkled face, but Aunt Geety and Pa laughed out loud, even though Pa never did that before.

"Your *tachshitl* is worse than a klezmer," my father exclaimed. "Already he's looking at the girls."

My father really knows everything. He was never with me and Geety in the park, but he already knew that I looked at every girl to see if they had split chests. The girls my age didn't, but the girls that were ladies sure did.

On Sunday night I stood next to Aunt Geety while she was sitting in the fat chair in the living room that wasn't a living room anymore and while Ma and Pa walked Uncle Oosher to the subway station. I wiped one of her tears away and whispered into her ear. She had on earrings that looked like jelly candy rings except they were silver, not chocolate in color.

"Don't worry, Aunt Geety," I said. "I'll get rich and I'll marry you. I'm not going to be a scholar or a *shoychet* because they're poor people and they can't get married to beautiful ladies like you who don't want to be prisoners. I'll be a piano player in a band at night, and by day I'll sell ice cream from a truck in the summertime and I'll be a writer in the wintertime when you can't go out and you have to stay inside and work with a pencil or a crayon and paper drawing Terry and the Pirates. My band will play at our wedding and that will save us a lot of money and we'll be even richer."

Aunt Geety tickled me under my arms, but I didn't let her go any further. Still and all, what I said made her stop crying, and she hugged me until I couldn't breathe. I didn't yell this time but held my breath because I wanted her to hug me some more. She smelled of bathroom soap.

I was going bum-bum-bum-bum-bum-bum-bara-rara-rara-rara-rara-rara-rara-rop-bop-bop-bop on the piano in Mrs. Gottlieb's house when I realized that I couldn't wait until I had my own band and got rich to save Aunt Geety. That would take longer than seven years and I'd be older than Father Yankev in the *Toyreh*. I cut my practice short before Mrs. Gottlieb's daughters got home and called me a sissy, and I ran to the candy store below our apartment opposite the park to find Big Red, the guy my father and mother called *der Royter*.

He was a giant with fat arms. If he played the piano, he would have broken all the keys, especially the faraway ones that you have to lunge at to hit on the button. But he didn't play the piano. He didn't do anything during the day except hang around the candy store and buy me ice cream cones. By night it was a different story. He was one of Lepke's boys.

"Big Red," I said, "I wanna be in the gang. I gotta get rich quick."

He lifted me up and put me on his shoulders near the sky with my legs hanging over his hairy chest. His shirt was always open, and the hair tickled my bare legs, which wouldn't have happened if Ma had let me wear knickers.

"Why do you gotta get rich quick?" he asked. "You owe the loan sharks a bundle from crummy bets with the bookies?"

"I don't bet with my father," I said. "I study with him. He's a *booky b'-Toyreh v'Shas*."

Big Red laughed so hard I almost fell off his shoulders. "He's a what? Your little old man with the prayer book always in hand—a real honest-to-goodness bookie?"

"He knows the whole *Toyreh* by heart," I assured him. "Take me in the gang, but don't tell my father. He won't let me become a robber because in the *Toyreh,* it says—"

Big Red interrupted me and put me down on the ground with a thump. I felt it from my heels to my head through the yarmulke.

"So why do you need alotta loot, kiddo? Tell me, why do you need greenbacks, moolah, the almighty dollar?"

He was a Big Red, but he wasn't too smart. "The Almighty is not a dollar," I insisted. "He's the *Reboynesheloylem,* the Chief of the World, and He'll save our little children from Hitler, *yemach shemoy.*"

Then and there I felt terrible because I remembered the old man with a gray beard from Lemberg who came to my father's house last week and said that Hitler now was killing little babies, and even though Noosn was a nuisance, I didn't want him to be killed by Hitler. My mother brought the old man to Aunt Geety in the living room, but she started to cry again, and the old man ran away. I hope he didn't run back to Hitler.

"I can't tell you," I said to Big Red. "It's a secret."

My giant friend who was called *der Royter* grabbed me by the collar with his left hand and stuck his right hand in his pocket and pushed the gun against my head. My head was as tall as his pocket, so the gun touched my brain.

"You better cough up the goods, kiddo, or I'll shove you off to kingdom come."

"My father says there's no kingdom come. There's only the time of the *moshiach,* and there's a *machloykes* between the rabbis if robbers will have *techiyas ha-maysim* when the *moshiach* comes and share in *oylem-habe.* My father believes that when all the dead get alive in the-world-to-come, which means *oylem-habe* if you wanna know, the robbers won't. They'll stay dead."

"Are you threatening me?" Big Red asked.

"That's what the holy books say. I can't change it."

Big Red let me go. A crazy smile appeared on his face. "You're lyin'," he snickered. "I can tell when anybody lies. But with you it's even easier. You're lyin' because if robbers didn't get their share of what is it? *Oylem-habe?* Then how come you wanna be in the gang?"

I hesitated. I didn't really want to tell him my secret. But I had to. "It's—It's—It's for Aunt Geety. I—I have to get rich quick so I can marry her."

Big Red heaved a sigh of relief. "And you think, kid, that if that's the reason for robbing, then God will forgive the robber and give him eternal life in the-world-to-come in the time of the messiah?"

"I—I think so."

"Good."

"But I'll have to ask my father."

"Don't ask your father. You ask a rabbi, it's never kosher."

He grabbed my hand and led me into the candy store. He bought me a giant egg cream because in the wintertime Mr. Vinnie Supervia didn't have any ice cream to sell since people didn't want to buy it when it was so cold outside.

"I'll make a deal with you," Big Red said. "What time do you go to sleep every night?"

"Eight o'clock," I said.

"You know what eight o'clock is?"

"Sure," I said. I showed him eight o'clock with the thumb and forefinger of my right hand.

"Smart kid. When you go to sleep tonight, when you're already in your pajamas, you give this piece of paper secretly to your Aunt Geety. Don't let anybody see. Tell her it's a secret note from Big Red. If you do that, I'll talk to Lepke about taking you into the gang. Okay? Got it?"

I scratched my head under the yarmulke. "Before I say *Krishma* or after?" I asked.

"What's *Krishma?*" Big Red asked.

I couldn't believe it. Did he go to sleep every night after robbing the whole world without saying *Krishma?*

"*Krishma,*" I said "is what you say in the *siddur* in Hebrew before you go to sleep so God won't make you dead when you're asleep."

Big Red nodded. "Now I lay me down to sleep and all that crap. I get it. Kiddo, I need all the prayers I can get. You say the *Krishma* for me and for you. Say it twice, once before you give the secret note to your Aunt Geety and once after. God help me! I'm gonna be reformed by the prayers of a little runt."

❧

And that's the way it was. I gave the note to Aunt Geety that very night and said the two *Krishmas* like I always did anyway, but this time it wasn't only for me staying alive in the night and in the daytime. This time one was for me and one was for Big Red.

Early in the morning, before anybody was waked up, I went out of the bedroom to pee, and Aunt Geety grabbed me from behind and spun me around like a dreidl and hugged me to death. She had very thin clothes on, not like my heavy pajamas, and I could feel her whole skin, from her belly button to her legs when she hugged me. I wasn't tall enough to put my head against her balloons, but I could see them right through the silk pajamas when she let me go.

"You're a darling," she whispered to me. "You're my boy forever."

She always said forever, which was a very long time, I think. She didn't have any lipstick on, so I even let her kiss me. She gave me a little bite on the ear, and I yelped.

"Sh-sh-sh," she cautioned. "You'll wake up your Ma and Pa. Put your ear closer. I want to tell you a secret."

So many secrets. Everybody has secrets. I thought I was the only one who had secrets. Grownups talk so much and so loud and still they have secrets. Aunt Geety showed me a new piece of paper.

"This is a letter for Big Red. When you go downstairs to the candy store in the morning before I'm finished helping Ma clean the house, you give this letter to Big Red. Don't tell anybody, okay?"

I nodded. Then she plopped the piece of paper over her silk pajama in between her split balloons. She leaned over, her face almost down to my face and said, "Come and get it." When I hesitated, she insisted. "C'mon, *tachshitl*, take it out from the hiding place like a big boy."

I stuck my hand in between the big balloons and tried to grab the paper. She shivered with delight—she almost laughed, but she didn't want to wake up Ma and Pa. I pushed my hand further down in search of the secret letter. It was a tough job because the paper was wedged in between her big balloons.

"Is your weenie standing up?" she suddenly asked me.

I was surprised by the question. "Why should it stand up?" I asked. "I don't wanna pee on the ceiling."

She put her hands to her beautiful smooth face with the starry eyes and the white teeth as if to push the laugh back into her throat. "You'll want to. Someday you'll want to. I promise you that, my darling little boy!"

From that day on, I brought notes back and forth, back and forth, from Big Red to Aunt Geety and from Aunt Geety to Big Red. He always handed me his note in a plain way, into my hand, and I stuck it into my pocket. But Aunt Geety always played games. Sometimes the note went where it went the first time, into the balloon basket, and sometimes if she was sitting down, she put it under her dress between her legs far up toward her belly. That's when I found out that she didn't have a weenie. She was smooth all over, no sticks.

"How do you pee?" I asked her.

"I don't," she said.

"I see you go into the toilet," I said.

"That's only for number two. As for peeing, God made it so that a boy when he becomes a man, his weenie stands up and pees into me."

"So when I'm a man I won't have to go to the toilet for number one?" I asked.

"You still have to. But you'll save some for a girl you love," she said.

It all sounded crazy to me, but Aunt Geety never lied. She kept secrets, but as far as I know, she didn't tell lies. What I didn't know was why she and Big Red were sending so many letters to each other every day. They saw each other every day when Aunt Geety took me down to the park in the afternoon to play with all the other children or to take a trip to faraway. Big

Red was always there. When I played in the dry pool in the winter or in the wet pool in the summer, he snuck off with Aunt Geety to the park ministration house, maybe to the toilet there to pee into her. So why did they have to send each other so many letters? I never asked my father that question because I didn't want him to tell me that once again he didn't know.

⬮

One day in the summer—I think it was after my father came running into the house crying that Hitler had marched into Vienna and had taken over Austria—it was very hot again, like last summer. My father didn't really know how to run. He leaned forward and walked fast like other old men did. He didn't run like boys with legs flying. And he didn't really cry. He gulped and swallowed a lot without eating anything, but he looked like crying.

My mother said, "What difference does it make? Austria is Austria. They're all the same."

"No," my father said. "Kaiser Franz Yozef was good to us, not like the Nazis. And now Austria is dead."

On that summer day when Hitler marched right over Kaiser Franz Yozef, or maybe much later when I tripped over a chain in front of the grass and cut my hand and Aunt Geety had to take me to Bellevue Hospital where they put a stitch into my skin and I cried too, that summer I think, Aunt Geety took me in Big Red's car to a faraway park that was much bigger than ours. You couldn't see the other end of the park it was so big. Cars drove right through the middle of the park, and it had hills and mountains and lakes and boats and lots of sky and many many people besides grass and children and a playground.

Big Red's driver left us in the middle of the big park and went away, and when we walked on the hills, I held Aunt Geety's hand and Big Red held her shoulders. Aunt Geety ran off and climbed a tree. She held on to a heavy branch and leaned down from the sky so that her body almost fell out of her dress. Big Red looked up at her and put his hands over his face. Maybe he was crying too, like me for my stitch and my father for poor Austria that was also dead.

"I'm dying," Big Red yelled. "I can't look. You're driving me nuts. Beautiful! Beautiful! I can't take it anymore."

He walked away with his eyes covered. At that second, another man came over and touched Aunt Geety and pulled her down from the branch. She screamed. Big Red didn't turn around right away until the man said, "Hey babe," and kept his hands on her.

Aunt Geety pushed him hard and yelled for Big Red. The man tried to push her back, but he stumbled. "Heeb slut," he said, "go back to Germany where you belong and get what's coming to you."

Aunt Geety didn't come from Germany, she came from Kaiser Franz Yozef with Ma when she was a baby. That's what Uncle Oosher said many times. Big Red came from the Wild West. He punched the other man and knocked him down and bloodied his lip. The man ran off, and before Aunt Geety could straighten out her dress and stop crying, the man returned with four other men and they all jumped on Big Red. But Big Red was a giant and very strong. He punched all of them until one guy pushed a knife into Big Red's side and made him fall on the slanty grass of the mountain. Aunt Geety screamed again and again and people came running including two police.

Big Red called me over with his finger, and I was afraid that he'd make me take his real gun that was in his pants pocket, but he didn't. He said, "Tell me the *Shma Yisrool* to say if I die."

Big Red didn't know anything. He could never be a father this way. So I taught him how to say the *Shma Yisrool*. I whispered in his ear until the cops came: "*Shma Yisrool Adonoy Elohaynee Adonoy Echud.*"

Then I said, "Drag out the last word *Echud* until your *neshume* leaves your body and you're dead. *Echu-u-u-u-ud!*"

But the cops interrupted his last word, and Big Red didn't die. One of the cops asked me, "You okay, sonny? What happened?"

And I said, "It was just like in the movies except they weren't dressed like

Indians and Big Red didn't put a cowboy hat on his red hair and there wasn't any music when they were fighting."

"Is he your father? Is she your mother?"

"No," I said. "They just take me places, and I deliver letters. Aunt Geety is my cousin. Big Red is one of Lepke's boys."

They didn't ask me any more questions, but our pictures were in the *Daily News* before "Terry and the Pirates" and after bombs on London and Miss America, who I think was Jewish, and after Joe DiMaggio, who got another hit.

Uncle Oosher screamed at Aunt Geety even though it wasn't Sunday and he was not supposed to be visiting. Naturally, since he came in a surprise visit, he didn't bring any candy bars with him. Once he promised to bring me candy bars every Sunday. Today he just screamed.

"I leave you here to save you from the scum of New Haven, and you run around with New York gangsters?" Uncle Oosher also started to cry. Everybody in our family cried once in a while except my father. Jews have been crying for two thousand years, my father told me, since the destruction of the Second Temple and ever since they wandered over the face of the earth and were killed mercilessly by the Talkingmarders and the Hitlers.

Uncle Oosher turned to me and yelled at me. "You stupid little boy. You go with them all the time and you don't tell anybody?"

"It was a secret," I said. "Where we went and the letters."

"What letters?"

"That's also a secret," I said. "If I tell you, Big Red won't ask Lepke to make me rich quick so I can marry Aunt Geety. So I can't tell you."

Uncle Oosher slapped his hand to his forehead, maybe to the top of his head, because it was all skin and you couldn't tell where his forehead ended and the top of his head began.

"Rivkele," he said to my mother. "You're raising a lunatic here. Send him to Bellevue. Or send me. I'm going crazy."

I wanted to tell Uncle Oosher that I was already in Bellevue for a stitch, but that happened on one of my trips with Aunt Geety and Big Red and was part of the secret that couldn't be told, so I didn't tell him.

Uncle Oosher grabbed Aunt Geety by the arm and yelled, "You're not seeing that *bandit* anymore when he gets out of the hospital. I'm taking you back to New Haven and locking you up in a room."

I started to cry. I didn't want Aunt Geety to go back to New Haven and be locked up in a room. How could Ma and Pa let such a thing happen? They never did that to me. They did the opposite. They kept Noosn in a room in his cradle and sent me out all the time with Aunt Geety. I was free with her. I was not locked up. And now she would go away and never see the grass on the mountain with me and Big Red. I would never see the stars in her eyes.

Who was Rivkele? That was my mother, I think. My father also called her *Ayshes Chayil* and *Ahavas N'ooray* and sometimes Rivke. Aunt Geety called her Aunt Rivkee. Looks like she had many names.

But Aunt Geety did not go to New Haven after all. Also, I didn't get into Lepke's gang and get rich right away. And I didn't marry her.

She jumped to my side when it looked like Uncle Oosher would hit me for delivering secret letters, and she put her arms around me to protect me from the slaps of Uncle Oosher.

"Papa," she said, "leave the kid alone. He's a good boy. He has a good heart. He loves me, and I love him, and I'll help Aunt Rivkee take care of him forever. Meanwhile, I can't go to New Haven because I'm pregnant, and I want to have the baby in a good hospital in New York like Bellevue, not in a dump like New Haven."

Uncle Oosher screamed. "Pregnant? What did you say? You say that word? Pregnant? My daughter? My own daughter? *Ich chalish avek.*"

That meant he was going to faint, but he didn't faint. Instead he yelled, "Get the *m'sader k'dishin.* Get the *chipe.* Get *der Royter gonif* out of the hospital and in a tuxedo. Put a *yarmike* on his head. Invite the relatives before she gets too fat. Does that gangster know how to say the *Haray Ot* in Hebrew at the marriage ceremony?"

Aunt Geety jumped from a corner and shouted gleefully, "He's a quick study. Big Red picks up Hebrew real fast."

Since she also smiled at me, I said, "Don't worry, Uncle Oosher. I learned him how to say *Shma Yisrool* when he was gonna die."

"You—You little *bandit!*" Uncle Oosher continued yelling, pointing to me. "You were the *shadchn!* You were the marriage broker. It's all your fault. You brought them together. I can't believe it. You taught him Hebrew and you delivered letters. So you'll continue delivering and teaching. You hear me? You'll deliver the ring at the ceremony, and you'll teach him what to say there. That gangster Big Red with all he robbed in his life should be able to come up with a fancy diamond or I'll kill him. If you were older and a doctor, I'd make you deliver the baby also, you little *mamzer.*"

Mates told me that *mamzer* meant bastard and that Ma and Pa weren't married, but I knew that was a lie because Ma wore a ring just like the one that Big Red gave to Aunt Geety when he got out of the hospital. He still had a bandage on the side of his belly under his shirt and pants—he showed it to me many times—but that didn't stop him from getting married in a tuxedo. That also didn't stop him from taking Aunt Geety across the river to Canarsie to start a new life a million miles away.

Aunt Geety didn't stay with us or with me like she said she would. Maybe she didn't exactly lie, but nobody in this world keeps all their promises. Big Red didn't keep his promise to speak to Lepke, who was dead anyway a long long time. Uncle Oosher didn't keep his promise to come every Sunday to visit Rivkele and bring me a candy bar. Even Ma and Pa did not keep their promise to save the chickens in the bathtub from the hands of the *shoychet* and not give them to me to eat on *Shabes* and holiday meals. And God didn't keep his promise made in the *Toyreh* to save the Jews, including my uncle in Europe from Hitler.

Everything changes. Nothing keeps its promise and stays the same. Summer becomes winter, the leaves disappear, Big Red buys me a stupid suit for his wedding instead of ice cream cones and egg creams, even the notes on the piano if you play them a long time they begin to sound a little under or a little over so that you get a little unhappy, and Noosn the nuisance not a baby anymore becomes a real walking boy and a brother that says things and you have to listen. Everything changes.

But I continued loving Aunt Geety forever.

CHOIRBOY

"YOU DON'T understand me, Mr. Miller—Mahler—Mehler. You make me all mixed up. I'm not an official from the U.S. government, God forbid. I'm not askin' you to send your boy to school. I'm not a truant officer. I'm a musician, an artist. I'm a choir leader, a singer, that means a musician. No, my name isn't Mr. Singer. I'm Berel Braverman. I want your boy for my choir. My choir sings with the greatest cantors in the best synagogues. I lead a big symphonic liturgical choir. I want your boy to sing with me. That's what I want, Mr. and Mrs. Mehler."

The man never took off his hat, even to put on a yarmulke. He stood near the door of the kitchen that opened on the hall, never sat down. His fat wife was almost hidden behind him. Not completely hidden, since he was skinny and she was fat. My mother and father didn't sit either. They stood near the stove and near the sink and looked at this man and his wife as if they were Cossacks bursting in upon a home to bring fear and devastation. Only I was sitting, in a seat near the window that let me see the man and the outsides of the woman but not the middle because she was behind him. I didn't see her face either since she was shorter, but I saw her fluffy hair because it flew away from her face. The hair was blond, not like a Jewish woman, maybe like a Cossack.

My father started to sing a tune without real words: "Deedl-dum, deedl-dum, deedl-dee, ay-yay-yay." Maybe he did it to throw away the fear, maybe to wait for more explanations from the guests, maybe to make my mother laugh with joy.

33

"You sing good too," the visitor said. "I think you have a tenor voice, maybe a high baritone. You wanna sing in the choir too, Mr. Mehler? I can make a package deal if you want."

My father waved a hand as if pooh-poohing the whole idea. He scratched his ear and said to my mother, "Rivke, let the man and his wife sit down. What kind of people are we if we make our guests stand in the hall? Maybe they'll take a tea with lemon while we talk."

He just looked at me, and I jumped up from the table to make room for the guests. I didn't need words. I didn't need a tune. A look was enough.

My mother turned to the stove. The guests sat down. At first I wondered why my father mentioned the hall. They weren't standing out in the hall. Our door was completely closed. They were standing near the hall with a door in between. My father didn't lie very often, so this perplexed me. But then I came to the conclusion that my father's eyesight was very bad, and maybe he didn't see in the distance if the door was open or closed. My father couldn't lie. Even though it says in the Ten Commandments that you shouldn't lie only when you're a witness in a court, it also says you shouldn't steal, and my *rebby* once told me that if you lie at anytime, you steal the truth from the world. So this shows you shouldn't ever lie.

Mr. Berel Braverman's wife came out from behind him, and I saw her from top to bottom for the first time, and then I almost forgot Aunt Geety who was with Big Red in faraway Canarsie and married to him and not interested in me anymore anyway.

She was big and fat and beautiful. Mrs. Braverman, that is. She wasn't skinny with big eyes and a little smile like Aunt Geety. She was fat and round and had stuff sticking out all over her, and her eyes were painted with dark colors and her hair was bright yellow, a light color, and her smile opened up big and wide like the mouth of a lion and spread from one end of her face to the other not like a lion. She gave me a little pinch on the cheek. I didn't scream. When my *rebby* pinched me, I screamed because he hurt my cheek with the pinch, but when Mrs. Braverman pinched me, she did it light and easy.

I knew that the guests wouldn't be eating supper with us because my mother didn't have enough chicken for them even though I didn't eat the chicken. I was glad about that. If the fat lady started eating in our house, we probably wouldn't have enough to eat for a week. Abraham in the *Toyreh* served the angel-guests a ton of junk, but he was a rich man for believing in one God, and my father was a poor man for believing the same thing. I couldn't figure that out because maybe I was too young.

I touched my forehead and dreamed of being a big scholar who would understand these things and maybe explain them to other people. But it didn't help. I was only a runt in a *rebby's* class, with a small brain, and a big world that I couldn't fathom. I wanted to grow up fast the way my baby brother was growing fast, but you slow down growing up as you grow up, and sometimes you don't grow up at all, and that's not such a good thing.

When dumb Moysh was not in jail, he once showed me that you can still grow when you're a big man and not growing anymore. He took out his weewee and pressed it and it grew and it grew and it grew.

I was amazed. He asked me to press it too, but I told him that there's a dybbuk in his weewee and I would have nothing at all to do with it. Dybbuks were not Jewish. They weren't even Christian. They were controlled by gods and goddesses made of stones that Abraham in the *Toyreh* smashed up when he was a kid. So I wouldn't get near them either because I wasn't strong enough to break idols. I could see that Moysh was disappointed, but I ran away before he could force me. I often looked at my weewee and wondered if a dybbuk would get into it too. There were so many things that I didn't know and that the *rebby* or my father and mother never explained to me even though I think they knew everything.

"He's not strong enough to go to too many schools yet, the *boychik*," my father said to Mr. and Mrs. Braverman. "He was a very sick child with double pneumonia, and the doctor will only let him go to one school, not two. So he goes to a *rebby* in a store."

Mrs. Braverman looked agitated. "A sickly child? Berel, let's go. Let's go from here."

Her husband, Berel, didn't move. "I say singing will make him healthy," he said. He put a skinny hand on his wife's titties and held her back from moving. "Your son goes for piano lessons, don't he? I know that. He's strong enough to play the piano, then he's strong enough to sing in my symphonic liturgical choir before the holy ark that contains our holy *Toyreh*. It will make him better. He won't be sick anymore."

Mrs. Braverman smiled broadly. My mother put a glass of tea in front of her and in front of the mister. Mrs. Braverman asked for milk and put some into her tea. My mother was astonished by this. She had put lemon on the table and pieces of sugar shaped like a box, but the blond lady didn't use them at all. My mother didn't say anything. She just put a heavy mat on the table and gave her a new cup of tea and a small container of milk.

"Where did you hear my boy sing?" my father asked. "You got spies all over?"

Mr. Braverman smiled in a crooked way so that three drops of tea plopped out of his mouth on one side. Maybe he didn't have teeth there to make a wall.

"Spies?" he said. "Definitely. I gotta make a living, no? So I send relatives all over, to all the shuls in New York to find the best singers. My cousin, may he rest in peace, went to your shul a few weeks ago, and he heard your *boy-chik* sing along with the cantor. That's all I needed to know."

My mother was aghast. "Why may he rest in peace? Your cousin is dead suddenly?"

Mr. Braverman shook his head to mean yes. "Yeah, he passed away. He went to hear Kwartin sing *Rozoo D'Shabbos,* on a Friday night at the Rumainisher Sheel on Rivington Street, and he got into an argument with another guy who said that Cantor, I mean *Chazn* Pinchik, sings it better than Cantor, I mean *Chazn* Kwartin. They yelled and yelled at each other, and my cousin got a heart attack and poof, he went like this." Mr. Braverman hesitated, looked around the kitchen, and hastened to add, "You don't die from singing, certainly not from praying in a shul. But you can die from yelling and screaming about cantors. Now that's dangerous. But your son's singing, my cousin loved."

Then he turned directly to my mother and said, "I promise you that I'll watch over your boy like he was my own boy. Me and my wife, we won't let him out of our sight. He'll learn more music from me and how to pray with devotion and deep feeling. He'll become a real *tzaddik,* a righteous man. You'll see."

My mother smiled at me, her little *tzaddikl,* and I turned away to watch the shadows on the wall creep higher and higher as the sun got lower and lower, another thing I didn't understand. I also didn't understand how Mr. Braverman's cousin got a heart attack in shul and poof, went like this, and then later told Mr. Braverman that I had a nice voice. Maybe Mr. Braverman got secret messages from dead people. Maybe Mr. Braverman never studied with a *rebby* about not stealing the truth from the world and so he lied.

"Don't speak nonsense to me," my father said. "Don't speak foolishness. The cantors these days are not religious people. They're actors. They make moving pictures like Moyshe Oysher. They run around with women. Who can trust them? Rosenblatt was a pious Jew. He wouldn't even sing in the opera for the biggest amount of money without a hat on, and on the Sabbath too, God forbid. But that was twenty years ago. Not today. Today, the cantors are looking only for the money. So don't tell me stories."

Mr. Braverman got nervous and began to bite a nail on one of his fingers. Mrs. Braverman knocked his hand out of his mouth.

"A *tzaddik* you'll make of my boy?" my father continued. "He's a *tzaddik* already. He don't wanna be a *shoychet* like his uncle in Poland because he don't wanna slaughter an animal even the good kosher way for food. He worries about little squirrels in the park. He worries about some neighborhood bum who went to jail by mistake because another gangster put a gun into this stupid's hands and he kept it. He's a little *shadchn* and makes pairs, which is God's work. That is, he brings two people together in marriage, my niece with another bum who hangs around the candy store and the poolroom even though he's Jewish. My little son don't wanna play with any guns anymore. He hates guns now, thank God. He got the whole world's troubles on his shoulders at his age. He asks me day and night about my brother the *shoychet* and about the war in Europe."

My mother lowered her eyes. Mr. Braverman bit another nail. Mrs. Braverman let him.

"For twenty years since I came to America I tried to get my brother to also come here with his whole family. I don't make so much, but I would help him. I used to have day-to-day work in a shop before I became a *melamed*. But my brother didn't wanna come. He had a good position in the Jewish community in Radom in Poland, and he was an honored scholar, a genius in Talmud studies since childhood. But there were other reasons. He wrote to me that he wanted his children to stay Jews, and he was afraid that in free America they would run after everything that's free and forget where they came from and who they are. My little son, thank God, still remembers. He worries day and night about his uncle in the territory of the Nazi plague, God help us. By this child's merit, may my younger brother and his family in Poland be saved from the terrible conflagration. I heard from my brother only once after the war started and no more. Who knows where he is with his dear wife and children. But maybe if my little *tzaddikl* son will pray a little more and with more devotion and deep feeling by singing in *sheel* in your choir next to the cantor, even if he is an actor, then maybe my brother and all the Jews will be saved."

And so I became an alto, one of five other boys all older than I was, along with men sopranos, tenors, and basses, in Mr. Berel Braverman's symphonic liturgical choir that sang on the *bima* right next to the *chazn* during the High Holidays in September and sometimes even in October, the Days of Awe.

The *rebby* had so much hair on his face from his mustache and beard and long sideburns that hung in ringlets, that I couldn't see his lips except when he opened his mouth to yell or to eat a whole tomato. His head under the large yarmulke was bare. I think the *Toyreh* ideas that bumbled around in his head day and night made all his hair fall out one day. Even though he was very fat with a big belly, he was only a little bigger than I was. Maybe that's why my father called him by a little boy's name, *Reb* Duvidl. But his arms and his fingers were very long and very strong. When he took the *kantshik,* the stick with many straps attached, into his hand, I trembled. I called him the *rebby.*

"Yankev, our father," the *rebby* said, "dressed up like a hunter that Aysev was, with a fur coat that had hair on it so his arms could feel like the hairy arms of his nasty older brother, and so his father, Yitschok, whose eyes were very bad thought that Yankev was Aysev, and he gave Yankev the top blessing that goes to the oldest son."

"Yankev was a crook," I said.

"What?" asked the *rebby.* His eyes popped up from the holy book that had part of the *Toyreh* in it.

"Yankev stole the blessing from his brother Aysev. If my kid brother Noosn stole the blessing for the oldest son from me, he'd also be a crook."

"What? A crook you call our father, Yankev? *A gonif?*"

"Yeah. He stole."

The *rebby* made a motion with his hand. "What kinda language is that? How can he be a crook if he steals what belongs to him? Yankev made an agreement with Aysev when he gave him the bean soup to eat. That was in exchange for the birthright."

"You can't sell the birthright," I said. "I'm the older brother in my family. My kid brother Noosn is younger than me. My mother told me that he will always be younger than me. He will never catch up. That's the way it is if you're born second. He can never be first."

The *rebby* began making noises with his nose as if some pieces of snuff were stuck up there.

"But—But—But Yankev was supposed to be born first. The *Toyreh* says that he came out second holding on to Aysev's heel. That's why they called him Yankev which means heel. Aysev was a *gonif* himself and stole the first position and jumped out first, and Yankev tried to stop him, but he wasn't strong enough since he spent his nine months learning *Toyreh,* not doing exercise for hunting and killing, and so the only thing Yankev could do was try to stop him a little bit. So he grabbed his heel on the way out."

"On the way out from where?" Shloymy asked. He sat right behind me.

"*Feh!*" the *rebby* said. "Don't ask such questions. It's not nice."

"I think," I said, "that Yankev was holding on to Aysev's heel because in the mama's belly there ain't enough room for two kids, and he was close enough to touch Aysev all the time. But there wasn't room in the belly to change places. Aysev came out first because he was first all the time, and Yankev was always second."

The *rebby* jumped to his feet. His hands were flailing. He couldn't control his breath. His hands went for the *kantshik* on the wall, the piece of wood with three straps on it. I closed my eyes.

"You talk like that? That's the way you talk to the *rebbe?* You say dirty words and you make dirt from our fathers, the fathers of the Jewish people? I'm fainting."

He dropped back into his seat in front of the class like my baseball plops into my glove. The *kantshik* fell to the floor. My eyes were open. I looked through the store window to the street. Two boys from the next class were playing with pennies up against the wall of our store. I couldn't see where the pennies landed when they pitched them or which one was closer to the wall or who won. I could only see the looks on their faces, and from their looks I decided who was the winner and who was the loser. You could always tell from the looks.

This time with the *rebby* I won.

❖

My mother brought me to the Essex Mansion where Mr. Braverman's symphonic liturgical choir learned how to sing the prayers.

"You should grow up to good deeds," my mother said, "and to marriage in a place like this. People get married here on Saturday night and Sunday and especially Tuesday because God saw that it was good two times on Tuesday when he created the world, not one time like on the other days of creation. I always wondered what the owner of the wedding hall does with it during the week when it's empty and when it's not Tuesday. Now I know.

He rents it out to choirs and cantors to practice. My little son is gonna be a singer, a sweet singer of Israel. Like King David. Now isn't that nice?"

Mr. and Mrs. Braverman took me into a big hall with a stage and a piano, and my mother stayed in the office with the owner of Essex Mansion. My mother told me later that he showed her pictures on the wall of his family. There was no *kantshik* on the wall, only tons of pictures. He was older than my *rebby*. His hair was gray, but he didn't have a beard.

Five other boys who were bigger than I was stood near the piano in the empty ballroom. They looked at me and laughed.

"You're laughing?" Mr. Braverman said. "Laughing I'll give you. I'll give you guys a belt in the head so you won't laugh anymore. Peewee, go to the piano and show them."

I didn't know who he was talking to, but he said it again and motioned to me.

"Play something. Show these smart alecks what you know. They know from nothin'. Music they think they know. They ain't seen nothin' yet. Play something."

Mrs. Braverman was beaming. She led me by the hand to the piano and sat down next to me. She had such a broad bottom that she almost took up the whole bench. But I was pretty skinny, and I found a little place right next to her. She touched my knee and smiled. I played.

What is that?" Mr. Braverman said. "You hear, boys, how he can play? The two hands go in opposite directions. He's a genius of music. What is that piece? What are you playin'?"

"An invention by Bach," I said.

"A what? Bach was an inventor? Well, boys, the kid don't know everything. Bach was a composer. He wrote music. He didn't invent nothin'. Play something else, Peewee. Play something with a nice melody to it. Play something by Rumshinsky or by Shulem Secunda, like—like you know, '*Bei Mir Bistu Sheyn.*' "

Mrs. Braverman nudged me in the side. My hands were off the keys, and she put one of my hands on her leg close to her body. I finally realized that

Mr. Braverman meant me again, that he was calling me "Peewee" as a name. I played.

"Now that's nice, very nice. You hear that, boys? This kid's another José Iturbi who plays in the movies. This kid can play up a storm. What is it? What are you playin'?"

"*Für Elise,*" I said.

"Who wrote it? Maybe Mendelssohn, a Jewish composer? Maybe George Gershwin who was also Jewish?"

"Beethoven," I said.

Mr. Braverman told me to get up from the piano.

"Very nice," he said. "They know how to write good stuff too. So remember, boys, you be nice to Peewee here. Teach him everything you know. But don't be nasty to him. He can play stuff by Bach and Beethoven together."

I went to Essex Mansion every week for a long time, but my mother stopped taking me. She took me to piano lessons at the Henry Street Settlement House, and she even sat in the room with me and the teacher for the whole lesson every week and even on the days the teacher wasn't there and I practiced, but she stopped taking me to the Essex Mansion herself. That was because Mrs. Braverman came every time to our house and took me instead of my mother. Mrs. Braverman hugged me in front of my mother and told her she loved me.

Sometimes the cantor came in to practice with us. He wore a heavy coat and a white shawl around his neck even though it was very hot outside and inside because it was summer, and he practiced with us without taking them off. His voice was very loud and it shook back and forth on every note as if he was gurgling water or like it was coming out of a leaky faucet. He also sang so high, way above us, and once he broke a glass on one of the tables with his voice. He also yelled at Mr. Braverman and said we were all flat. I knew that all the time because I had the piano notes in my head, but I didn't yell about it. I wasn't a cantor.

Another time he yelled because he noticed Mrs. Braverman sitting with the sopranos.

"What the hell is she doin' singin' in the choir? They won't let a woman up on the *bima* in shul on Rosh ha-Shawnaw. Get another male soprano in her place. What are you, a cheapskate?"

"Don't worry so much," Mr. Braverman said. "We dress up in robes, don't we? They won't even know she's a lady. No lipstick, a black wig under her yarmulke, and big fat robes that cover you-know-what."

"It won't work," the cantor grumbled. "She got such big you-know-whats that everybody in shul will know who she is."

"It'll work. It'll work. Believe me, it'll work. It worked last year in the Bronx on Nelson Avenue with Cantor Cooperman."

"Him you call a cantor? He's a wagon driver, a lowlife. He can't sing for beans. The Nelson Avenue Shul you call a shul? It's a little room with old, blind, deaf people in it. They don't know from nothin'. Where I sing, where you assist me—now that's a shul. The public knows all that. They understand what's a prayer and what's a cantor. They're connoisseurs. They know the real article. They got good ears and good eyes. And they're very religious. You'll never get a female broad past them. It'll be a disaster. Get another man to fill out the section. Women should stay in the women's section where they belong."

Mr. Braverman motioned to his wife, and she got up from her seat among the grown-up men who sang soprano. All of them watched her as she walked away toward the door. She wiggled and she twitched. She pulled on her dress near her titties, not up but down, and faced the cantor with a funny look on her face. I watched her too.

Then she came back to the choir. "Peewee, come with me for a second," she said. She turned to Mr. Braverman and the cantor who were standing in front of the choir. "I need him for a second. You don't need him for a while. He don't have a solo until '*V'chol Ma'ameenim,*' so you can go on without him for a while. I'll send him back soon."

She led me by the hand, but she didn't take me into the office where the owner of Essex Mansion was sitting by himself looking at the pictures on the wall. She took me into another room, a smaller hall than the one we practiced in that also had some seats and a piano but no stage. She locked the door from the inside as we entered. We sat down next to each other. She started to cry.

"I'm so insulted," she bawled. "They don't appreciate me. Without me the soprano section will go haywire. They need me, but I'm a woman, and what do they care. It's not fair."

She cried so hard that her body shook. Suddenly she grabbed me and hugged me tight. She pressed me close up to her so that I felt every hill and valley. Then just as suddenly, she pulled us apart.

"You see my titties?" she said. She put one hand in and pulled them both out completely. They weren't titties; they were big tits, the biggest I ever saw in my life.

"I'm cryin' so hard," she said, "that they're liable to fall off. Put your hands underneath them and hold them up strong while I cry so that they won't fall off."

She placed both my hands underneath her tits and told me to press upwards. She cried and she cried and finally she stopped. I sat back down on my seat.

"Are you a little man yet?" she asked, wiping away her tears. "Does your weewee stand up yet? Maybe it did when you kept my titties from falling down on the floor. Let's see."

She opened the buttons in my pants and looked at my weewee. It was resting.

"So Peewee's weewee has a ways to go yet," she laughed. When she laughed, her tits shook the same amount as when she cried. I went to hold them up without waiting for her to ask. She laughed harder and harder. I didn't laugh. There was nothing to laugh about. She was a lady, and they wouldn't let her sing in the choir just because she was a lady person. She wanted my weewee to stand up, but it wouldn't listen. What was there to laugh about?

"Looks like I'll have to wait a while," she finally said. "You're a little angel," and she hugged me some more. "Button your pants," she added. "Let's go back to choir practice. We have to prepare good for the High Holy Days. We have to sing God's praises, without women, or with women behind the curtain or upstairs where they're not seen. You know why that's so? Because, when you're a man, if you see a woman's titties, you stop praying. Your wee-wee stands at attention and you gotta pay attention to *it,* not to the prayers. There's something to that, I gotta admit. Next week we'll come a little early, and we'll sit in the other room together and you'll watch me cry and laugh, and maybe my little *tzaddikl* will not take the world so serious and will laugh a little too."

So that's the way the practices went, and that's the way I think I learned how to laugh in addition to sing.

💠

Snow fell outside the store window while the *rebby* showed us how Jacob dreamed about angels going up and down a ladder on his trip from his father's house out of the country. The *rebby* said that in the hot Middle East, there was no snow to speak of, so we were lucky to have what even the country Israel didn't usually have, although it had a lot of milk and honey. That's why they called America a golden country, the *rebby* said, but that didn't make any sense to me, because gold was yellow and hot like the sun, not white and cold like snow.

Each flake of snow was different. I could see them clearly when they landed on the window and melted fast. They took many shapes, like people, big and small, fat and skinny. But all of them melted away no matter what shape they took. Fat or skinny, big or small, they all melted away. If you wiped them or just touched them, the snowflakes disappeared. Sometimes I felt like crying, but my father told me that no matter what, everybody dies.

Then Yankev came to the well. Ruchl came too, with the flock. Yankev saw her for the first time and got so strong that he rolled the big stone from off the top of the well so that all the shepherds including Ruchl could water their flocks. Then he kissed her. And then he cried.

"Did Ruchl cry too?" I asked the *rebby.*

"Could be. A woman always cries."

"Did Yankev hold her titties up from falling to the floor when she cried hard?" I asked.

The class roared with laughter. I thought maybe all the other boys had once been in Berel Braverman's choir and learned how to laugh so loud from Mrs. Braverman.

The *rebby* didn't seem to understand. "What should fall on the floor? What floor? Whose what?"

I tried to explain. I pointed to a girl outside the window and pointed to my chest. The *rebby* screamed in disbelief. He jumped to the wall and grabbed the *kantshik*. Then he grabbed me and turned me over his knee. He pulled the back of my pants down. He didn't ask me to hold up anything. He just whipped away, once, twice, I don't know how many times. I cried bitterly.

They carried me home on a stretcher like the one on which they took the gangster who was shot by a passing car in front of our house a few years ago. There were no cops in the taxi with me, not even the *rebby,* only the *rebby's* wife.

The next day or maybe the next week, my mother and father took me to the store. We were early. None of the boys were there, only the *rebby* and us. It wasn't snowing anymore. It was raining. The cool of the rain did not make the hurts in my tush any better. It still burned when I sat down. I slept on my tummy.

"What did you do such a thing for?" my father asked. "You're a learned man of the *Toyreh.* You know that a Jew is supposed to show kindness even to animals. How much more so to an innocent child."

The *rebby* didn't look at my father and mother and me. He remained seated, since he had not gotten hit with straps on his tush, and spoke while looking straight into a holy book. I think a Talmud book.

"An innocent child!" he grumbled. "What kind of innocent? He is a little devil, an *apikoyres.* He don't believe in nothing. He says Yankev shouldn't of stolen the birthright and that he was a crook and a liar for fooling his aged blind father Yitschok, and then he talks about—about—about the you-know-what of Ruchl, that is Ruchl our mother, that only a *bandit* would say.

Where does he learn these things in your house? Your brother in Europe was a genius in *Toyreh* and Talmud at his age. He never spoke about girls and you-know-what. Your little *bandit* will grow up to be the father of *banditn* all over the world. An innocent child!"

My father looked at me. "You said these things, my son, to the *rebbe,* to *Reb* Duvidl? Tell your father the truth."

My mother jumped between us. "I don't wanna hear. I don't wanna discuss. A *rebbe* who hurts my child without mercy and don't apologize and don't say a word of regret is not a *rebbe.* He's a monster, a—a Hitler, you should excuse me. My sick child could have died from the beating. Tomorrow we send him to public school and in the afternoon to the Hebrew School with the modern teachers who teach Hebrew on Houston Street. You're lucky I don't send the police to arrest you. You better be careful from now on with all the other children. You hear?"

I never heard my mother raise her voice in anger. I couldn't believe it. She marched me straight out the door, and my father trailed after us. He didn't say another word.

When I come to think of it, I realize that my mother saved me from maybe even worse. If I had to answer my father's question, I would have had to say yes to everything, yes to calling Yankev a crook, yes to mentioning Ruchl's you-know-whats. I would have had to say yes because you're not allowed to lie. It says so in the *Toyreh,* if you interpret the Ten Commandments correctly the way the *rebby* taught us. So if I told the truth, which I would have had to do, then I would have really got it, maybe worse than before, although my father never hit me with a strap. But my father's looks and my mother's tears would have made me almost die.

So she saved me for public school and lessons in Hebrew after school with modern teachers while I still continued playing the piano and singing in Berel Braverman's symphonic liturgical choir. I never again went into the room alone with Mrs. Braverman because I didn't want to think about such things until I was older and my weewee stood up all the time by itself. I didn't care anymore if her tits fell to the floor or not when she cried or laughed a lot. I just wanted to concentrate on singing the holy prayers and making sure that I didn't get hit anymore or cry anymore, although not crying was very hard to accomplish all the time with my uncle and my aunt and my cousins still wandering somewhere in the lands far away where the Nazis hit every Jew all the time and wiped out people like my uncle, the genius of *Toyreh* and Talmud, with all his family as if they were only snowflakes.

THE SACRIFICE

I LIKED cowboy-and-Indian movies when I was a kid though I never saw one in my whole life. My father didn't let me go to real moving pictures so I listened to the Lone Ranger on Vigdor's radio since we didn't even have a radio in our apartment, but that was enough for me. I don't know exactly why my father said no to the movies. Vigdor said it was the Depression, which meant that nobody had any money, even a dime for the 3rd Street movie theater, but another time he said it was for religious reasons and that my father was a fanatic, which meant he was very religious and didn't like movies that showed things I wasn't supposed to see.

What wasn't I supposed to see? According to my father, I was supposed to see everything. "Open your eyes," he said to me. "Open your heart. Open your soul. Look deep into the *Toyreh*." That was the way my father pronounced "Torah," the five books of Moses, who was Moyshe Rabbaynee in Jewish. "Look deep into the holy book," my father said. "Turn it over and turn it over because everything is in it." So Vigdor couldn't be right, and I didn't like it when Vigdor said bad things about my father or my mother. But I let him get away with it this time. When another time he gave me a third reason and said my parents were cheapskates, I got angry and refused to play with him.

I really wanted to go to the movies to see Tom Mix or some other cowboy riding on a horse, but I didn't like it when they shot Indians. Maybe this is what my father didn't want me to see. It wasn't so bad on the radio because the Lone Ranger never shot Indians. His best friend Tonto was an Indian. He only shot crooks, and that I could take because it was on the radio and I

49

didn't see it with my own eyes. I heard the shots—they were much louder than the tinny sound made by the blue gun I had when I was littler that I buried in the sand in the park for my friend Chaim—but hearing isn't like seeing. You can imagine what you want when you just hear and you don't see. Sometimes when my father read me Torah stories at the table on Friday night, I would close my eyes and imagine Abraham breaking his father's idols with an ax in my own mind. This didn't violate my father's order to open my eyes to the Torah because my father said that this story wasn't really in the Torah at all but in the *medrish,* which means in the legends. And so I imagined that all the shots on the radio were explosions on the Fourth of July and not shots at all. Then I thought they had to be real shots that kill because I didn't want the crooks to get away and hurt other people. In this world, it's pretty sad because you have to sometimes hurt people in order to stop them from hurting people.

"My mother ain't a cheapskate," I said to Vigdor. "She puts all the money I make singin' in Mr. Braverman's choir in Uncle Don's bank on the radio, just for me when I grow up and go to college or become a rabbi or a baseball player in the Polo Grounds. And still she gives me a nickel for a Melorol on a stick because the doctor said the ice cream would build me up strong enough to hit the ball out of the park."

Vigdor didn't answer. After all, he was Jewish too, so maybe he knew that *kibbud ov vo-eym,* honoring your father and mother, was in the Ten Commandments, and that he had made a mistake, even though my mother and father were not his mother and father so he didn't have to honor them so much. But my mother and father were pretty old, and the Torah also says *mipney seyvaw tawkum,* you should stand up before old people, and my father said that though it did mean real standing up on your feet, it also meant standing up for them in an argument out of respect. I didn't really know if Vigdor knew this part of the Torah since he never studied anything with his father and he went around everywhere without a hat on. But there are some things you learn from the air around you, not necessarily from a person, and I felt that Vigdor must have learned that it was wrong to say nasty things about anybody's father and mother without his father ever telling him this.

And without him being able to read Hebrew. That was really funny. I could already read Hebrew, first with my father's help and then from hour-and-a-half lessons with a modern teacher in the afternoon Hebrew School on Houston Street called the Talmud Torah. My mother had put me there after she took me out of *Reb* Duvidl's school in a store. But the doctor didn't let me go yet all day to public school because I was very sick when I was a baby. This meant that even though I could read Hebrew pretty good, I couldn't yet read English too good. But with Vigdor it was the other way around. He was high up in public school and could read English very fast, faster than Mates who read the comics to me in the candy store every day when Vinnie the boss wasn't looking. Still and all, Vigdor couldn't read a single word of Hebrew. Everything is topsy-turvy, but still you can't turn upside down respect for fathers and mothers.

So when Vigdor kept silent after I got angry at him, I forgave him for insulting my parents and began to play with him again.

Summer was hot and winter was cold, but it was all the same to me since I wasn't allowed by the doctor to go all day to school. To Vigdor and to Mates and to Chaim, who was dead in the ground, when he was alive, summer and winter were altogether different things. In the winter they went to school and couldn't play except late in the afternoon, but in the summer they could play from early in the morning until early at night without stopping. Even in the summer, I had to stop playing during the day because I had to rest. The doctor said so. And next to a father and a mother and a rabbi and a teacher and any very old person, you had to listen to a doctor.

I liked summer play better than late-afternoon winter play because in the summer, Feygy Grossman, Vigdor's kid sister, and some of her girlfriends would hang around in the vacant lot next to the synagogue and even play with us. In the winter, they never hung around there, and if once in a while, they did come by, they never played with us. Vigdor said that was because girls in the wintertime studied all afternoon and evening for school and did lots and lots of homework, while boys went out to play and didn't do any homework.

"So why is it," I asked, "that when they do come around once in a while in the winter when they finished their homework early, they still don't play with us?"

Vigdor shrugged his shoulders. He was very tall and his shoulders were way up high. "That's because they wear nice dresses to school, and they don't want to get their dresses dirty."

That didn't make much sense to me. They could come home and put on an old dress for playing just like Vigdor put on old pants and boots and a torn shirt too.

"Why do they do so much homework?" I asked.

"They want to be smarter than us," Vigdor said.

"Are your two sisters smarter than you are?" I asked Vigdor in astonishment.

"Never!" he said angrily. "Girls are never smarter than boys. No matter how much they try, they can never be smarter."

"My father is smarter in Torah and Talmud than my mother," I said to Vigdor, "but my mother is smarter in everything else."

"That don't count," Vigdor said. "Mothers aren't girls. They're wives. They gotta take care of the house and the money, so they learn to be smarter."

Vigdor always had a reason for everything, even when his everything was very stupid. I think he was jealous of his sisters because they got better marks in school and because he was funny-looking compared to them. He always bossed Feygy around and I didn't like that. I never bossed my kid brother Noosn around, even though he wouldn't listen to me anyway since he was so small and didn't have any brains yet, and just because Feygy was a girl didn't mean Vigdor had a right. Whenever I played with Vigdor, and Feygy was there too, I always made sure he wouldn't boss her around. I told him that I was responsible for her in the game and that he should lay off.

So early in the spring, I prayed for the summer to come so I could play with Vigdor all day with a few rests in between and with all the smart girls who did homework in the winter and wore beautiful dresses to school, especially Feygy.

Summer was not only hot. It was also ice cream and baseball scores and a whole bunch of flowers that came up in the corner of the vacant lot between the rocks and without anybody planting them or looking after them. They had no father and mother. They were orphan flowers, very small, resting on thin stems, waving in the summer breeze like children looking for a home. How they were created I don't know. No human being had anything to do with it. But since God created the world out of nothing, I suppose He could create flowers in a city dump out of nothing too, only out of rocks.

Summer also meant that sundown was late because the earth was closer to the sun and turning, turning all the time. The earth was sweating a lot from being closer in the summer to the rays of the sun. And when you're very hot and you sweat a lot, you can't walk so fast or run so fast, and I suppose the same thing happens to the earth. The earth turns slower, and so it's daytime much, much longer than in the winter. Nevertheless, it's still the same twenty-four hours for a full day and night because at night in the summer, the earth makes up for lost time during the day and turns faster and faster. I would sometimes wake up in the middle of the night and see my father sitting at the kitchen table, his head buried in a holy book. There would be almost-tears in his eyes and droplets of water on the holy page. I did not say anything to him—I didn't want him to even know I was up—but to myself I said: *What are you crying about, Papa? You never cry in the daytime. The night is soon over. The earth is turning faster and faster and faster. Soon it will be day again, and a very long day in which to play and in which the sun will surely dry your tears.*

❧

All the time, I was the Indian and Vigdor was the cowboy. This wouldn't have been so bad if he didn't shoot so much. Vigdor was crazy about guns. My mother told me that when he was two years old, he pointed a toy gun at her and said. "Bullets, dead." She thinks those were the first words he ever spoke. Vigdor would pull imaginary guns out of both holsters and shoot with both hands—bang, bang, bang, bang—so you couldn't escape. If one gun missed, he told me, the other gun would hit the target, which meant me. So I always had to fall down dead.

"Why don't the Indians win sometimes?" I complained to Vigdor.

"They can't win, you dope," he said to me, "because they're the bad guys."

"Good guys don't always win," I insisted. "Dillinger killed a lot of good guys."

"How do you know all that stuff?" Vigdor grumbled. "You can't even read the papers."

But I wasn't happy with my first answer. I should have told him that Indians have to win sometimes because there are good Indians too and there are bad cowboys. I remembered a bad cowboy once on the Lone Ranger who got him into a lot of trouble. But I missed my chance to say this to Vigdor, and so I had to stick to saying that bad guys sometimes shoot and kill good guys. And then there is Hitler, who wants to kill every Jew in the whole wide world. And he's the baddest of the bad guys. So I decided that I'd continue being an Indian and fall down dead all the time because I didn't want to be a Hitler.

Then something got into Vigdor, and he decided one fine summer day to switch places with me. I would be a cowboy and he would be an Indian chief. Maybe he did this because Mates came to play with us, and Mates was smarter than everybody even though he was a little chubby, and Vigdor wanted Mates to be on his side.

"I'm gonna be an Indian," Mates said definitely, and Vigdor couldn't argue with him. "I'm gonna be an Indian because they worship nature and they're not like stupid cowboys, who worship cattle."

This was altogether new to me. I never heard of anybody worshiping either nature or cattle. You worshiped God, and God made nature and cattle. How could you worship something that somebody else made? That Somebody Else had to be greater than the worshiped thing. So the thing shouldn't be worshiped. But if Mates said so, then it was so. He also never said lies.

"I can't be a cowboy or an Indian," I said. "I'm not allowed to be a worshiper of nature or cattle or anything like that. My father won't let me."

But since Mates insisted on being an Indian, Vigdor decided to be an Indian too in order to have Mates on his side in all the battles, and that meant that I had to be a cowboy whether I liked it or not. I almost decided to refuse forever until Vigdor assured me that I wouldn't be a grown-up cowboy but a boy cowboy. This meant that I wasn't Bar Mitzvah yet and wouldn't be responsible for my sin of worshiping cattle. He talked me into it.

Then Feygy came along since it was summer. She was wearing a nice dress and clean white sox and had a gold pin in her hair that sparkled in the sunlight. She was dressed as if it was still winter and she was still going every day to school.

Mates blocked her path and got down on one knee.

"Some day," he sang to her, "when I'm awfully low, and the world is cold, I will feel aglow just thinking of you, just the way you look tonight."

Feygy blushed and turned away.

"That Mates is so smart," Vigdor whispered to me so Mates wouldn't hear. "He only goes to grown-up pictures with Fred Astaire and Ginger Rogers that all the grown-ups go to. He never goes to cowboys and Indians." Vigdor thought for a moment, then added, "But how smart can he be if he always wants to be an Indian. That means he always wants to be with the losers."

"My father told me," I said, "that us Jews have always been persecuted by everybody, and that means we're losers too."

This really got Vigdor angry. I never saw him lose his temper before. "Well, I'm not gonna be a loser," he yelled, "even if I have to stop being Jewish. But if I have to be an Indian now, then watch out cowboys, I'm gonna be an Indian winner for a change."

And that's how I got tied up.

⸙

"Mates," Vigdor said, "take your little Indian son, your only son, the one you like so much, and leave your squaw Feygy behind—don't tell her a damn thing about what you're gonna do—and go to the place I'll show you behind the lot next to the synagogue and up the hill to that little sandy mountain in the back which the big guys use as a pitcher's mound when they play stick-ball here."

"If Feygy is my mother, I want her to come with me," I said.

"Shut up," Vigdor replied sharply. "It's not in the story. If she sees what's gonna happen to you, the mother'll drop dead right away, and that's not the right time in the story. So do what I say. It's my story, ain't it?"

I couldn't argue about that. Vigdor always made up the stories even though they almost never were like the stories that went on in my own head. I let him anyway, because he was older and knew how to read and write English, and until I could do the same, my stories had to remain in my head. But it surprised me that Mates did what he was told to do since Mates not only knew how to read and write English, but he could also say some words in French that he must have learned from all the lovey-dovey pictures he saw. I couldn't figure out how Mates got to go so often to the movies. His parents weren't really religious, I admit, so they let him go, but they lived down the block in the same kind of apartment house we did, and while we lived on the fourth floor, he lived even higher on the fifth floor, which Vigdor said cost even less. So that meant his father and mother had less money for movies than my father and mother. Still and all, he went so many times and saw so many pictures with Fred Astaire and Charlie Chaplin and the Duke of Windsor and Judy Garland that I got all the stories mixed up together whenever he told me the story of a movie he saw. Could it be that his parents were not cheapskates at all and mine were? I didn't want to think about that.

"Then Feygy is not Mates's squaw," I said. "Then she's my servant girl, and she could come along."

So that's how it all got started.

We walked up the hill slowly. Vigdor led the way and egged us on by wiggling the index finger on his right hand. In baseball, he always batted lefty and threw the ball with his left hand. Mates and I were behind, and Feygy behind us. I looked back every now and then to make sure Feygy wouldn't run away. She was very pretty, and her dress wasn't really a dress. It was like pants with a different part for each leg, but from far it looked like a dress because it was short like a dress. My mother told me that in the Torah it says that a man should wear men's clothing and a woman women's clothing and not switch. But the Grossman family was not religious just like Mates's family and didn't care much about such things. My mother told me the law in the Torah by luck. She almost never told me Torah laws. She left that to my father. But this time, I saw a picture in the Yiddish newspaper that she borrowed from our next-door neighbors the Zukermans of a giant ship sailing on the ocean. When I asked her if she came to America on a ship like that, she said no. She came on a much smaller ship that didn't go so fast. The one in the paper took five days to get to New York from Poland, but the one she came on took three and a half weeks. And then my mother told me, even though I didn't ask, that she had only one dress to wear all the time and one day it got torn and a man offered her an extra pair of pants to wear. But even though the man was the same height as my mother and his pants might fit her, she refused because of the law in the Torah. That's when I learned all about that. Feygy's dress that was like pants wasn't torn and she certainly didn't wear it for three and a half weeks straight. I suppose she was born in America and didn't have to go on a ship back to Poland.

At the top of the hill, Vigdor walked a little bit over it toward the back of the shul to a corner under a fire escape facing another street and found large pieces of wood. I think he knew they were there all the time. He came back with all the wood above his arms, and he wasn't even sweating. He placed the wood at the top of the hill in a square like a bed and told me to lie down in the middle. Then he changed his mind and told me to stand up again. He took long pieces of wood and a rope he had in his back pocket and began to tie me up with the wood against my back.

"What are you doin'?" I asked.

"This is for the sacrifice," he said.

"What sacrifice?" I asked again.

"You'll see," he said.

"I don't see nothin'," I said.

"I gotta wait for God to show me what to do," Vigdor replied.

This was ridiculous. I never heard Vigdor talk about God. He only talked about cowboys and Indians and worms and wild animals and how he couldn't stand his sisters. Mates talked about many gods, but not Vigdor. Also, I didn't like the idea of waiting for God to show him what to do.

"How does God show you what to do?" I asked. "God don't speak to you direct. You never go to shul, and you don't even know how to read Hebrew. So tell me, what language does God speak to you in?"

Vigdor grew impatient with me. "I don't hear direct from God. I hear voices."

Mates grew even more impatient, I think because he was left out of all the action for the time being. Even though he was much shorter than Vigdor and almost as short as I was, he was pretty fat and pretty strong for a kid, and he actually pushed Vigdor aside after Vigdor had tied me up with the wood. Mates put his hands on my tied-up shoulders.

"I heard the voices first," Mates said with his face turned away from me and in the direction of Vigdor, "and they told me what you were gonna do. But first I gotta say some prayers to the gods in Indian language before the sacrifice."

He started whooping and hollering around me and doing a dance at the same time. He put his palm to his mouth a dozen times and made an in-and-out sound. At one point, he tried to pull Feygy into his dance, but she refused to go and broke his hold.

"What did the voices tell you?" I asked Mates. I couldn't tug on his shirt to get his attention because my arms were tied up tight to my body and the wood. But I could move my feet, so I got next to dancing Mates and pushed him with my behind. "What did the voices say?"

"You're not allowed to talk during this dance. It's a religious dance. When Indians are getting killed all the time by cowboys, they gotta make a special sacrifice to the gods to make them change their minds and give a victory sometimes to the Indians. And before the special sacrifice, I have to say special prayers."

"Where did you learn Indian language?" Vigdor asked. It looked like he was as surprised as I was at Mates's words.

"It's easy," Mates said. "You take the English word and you lop off the first letter and you put it at the end in front of 'ay.' When you sing 'O say can you see,' you're singin' the first word in Indian. 'O say' is really 'So' in Indian. The Indians made up English, and we stole it from them and took every last 'ay' syllable and put it first in the word without the 'ay.' So that's how our English got started. O say that's how it got started. Now let us pray."

He continued singing in Indian and dancing around me. Finally, Vigdor made me lie down on the ground. From his back pocket he came up with a penknife that he opened up and that was very, very long. He gave it to Mates, who was bending over me.

"Now you gotta do the sacrifice to your son, your only son, the one you love so much who was supposed to be the next chief of the tribe when you die. But he won't be because you gotta sacrifice him so that the gods will let you kill white men for a change instead of the other way around. Then you won't be killed by a white man who steals your language and turns it around."

He thrust the long knife into Mates's hand. Mates's face turned whiter than the edges of the *Daily News* where there was no printing and no "Dick Tracy" or "Terry and the Pirates." I thought he was going to throw up.

"*You* do it," he said to Vigdor.

"You wanted to be an Indian chief, not me," Vigdor said with a scowl. "I always knew that Indians ain't got no guts. Take the knife."

I thought Vigdor wanted to be the Indian chief this time, but apparently he changed his mind. Mates held the knife in a shaking hand and raised it high. His eyes started to water. His Indian chant became fainter and fainter to the point of being without words. It was a high up-and-down wailing scream like the sound of an ambulance racing down the street. I was very scared.

Feygy jumped between us. "Don't send your hand to the kid," she yelled, her dress/pants whirling half way around and back like a dancer's costume. "Don't do him anything!"

Mates's shaking hand stayed up in the air. Vigdor didn't answer his kid sister.

"What kind of idiots are you guys anyway?" she continued to yell. "Indians don't sacrifice their children to the gods. You gotta eat a sacrifice, and the Indians are all vegetarians. They sacrifice wheat and barley and corn and cereal and vegetables and things like that. They are one with nature, not against it. You guys are so dumb. You never do any homework or study anything."

Mates finally spoke up, but in a small, small voice. "The Incas in Peru sacrificed human beings to the gods," he said in defense of his story.

That's when I spoke up finally. I didn't know much about Indians or cowboys or movies or even the exact meaning of the word "sacrifice," but I knew other things they didn't know. " 'Peru' means 'have a lot of healthy children' in Hebrew," I said firmly. " 'Peru u-revu' it says in the Torah. 'Make kids and multiply.' It don't mean 'kill your children,' so it's impossible that the Incas did such a thing."

"Peru is the name of a country in South America," Mates said. He sighed as if I was an idiot too. "It ain't a Hebrew word. It's like the United States. It's just a place where Indians lived. You think everybody in the world speaks only Hebrew?"

"When Adam and Eve were everybody in the world," I said, "they spoke only Hebrew to God."

"Well, Peru ain't Hebrew," Mates grumbled, "and this ain't the Garden of Eden. But Feygy over there is right. American Indians didn't sacrifice kids. And we're playin' in America so we gotta do it the American way."

He lowered his wavering hand with a look of relief and closed the knife. The color came back to his face, and I think he really looked now like a red Indian.

"But we gotta sacrifice something else in place of the kid," he exclaimed. He didn't want to give up his share of the game. He dug into his back pocket and came up with a sandwich that his mother had given him for lunch. It was two pieces of bread with lettuce and tomato in between. "This'll do the trick," he said. "Bread and vegetables are closer than anything to nature."

This time he began giving orders. He sent Vigdor looking for two good solid rocks, and Vigdor, who hadn't hardly said a word in the last few minutes, just nodded and went on the trail. He came back almost immediately with the two rocks. Mates put them aside for a while and spread out the napkins his mother also gave him along with the sandwich. His mother had cut the sandwich into two parts, and Mates put one part on the napkin. He began eating the other part. He seemed very hungry.

"While I'm eating the holy meal," he said to Vigdor, "you untie the kid."

Vigdor did what he was told. He looked longingly at the other half of the sandwich on the napkin, but he didn't say anything. Feygy had her arms on her hips and was glaring at both of them.

Finally, Mates finished his half of the sandwich. He licked his lips clean like a wily cat and rearranged the loosened pieces of wood on the ground where I had just been lying. He put the napkin and the half-sandwich on top of the sticks of wood. Then he crushed the two rocks together underneath the napkin until a spark came out of them and lit the napkin all up. The sandwich caught fire too, and then a small stick of wood and then a bigger stick and a bigger. It was soon a giant fire on top of the hill behind the synagogue.

"Halleluyah!" Mates exclaimed.

"Halleluyah!" Vigdor imitated him.

"You're all so stupid," Feygy said. "Both of you dummies are playing Indians speaking Indian language only, you make fun of the kid because he thought 'Peru' was a Hebrew word, and then you make an Indian sacrifice and say 'halleluyah,' which is a Hebrew word after all. That shows how much you guys know."

I think Feygy knew more than any of us about lots of things. Most important of all, she knew how to save my life.

❖

I never told my father or mother about what happened. I was afraid that they would never again let me go out to play with Vigdor or with Mates if I told them. For my part, I wasn't afraid to play with them again. Even if they wanted to tie me up for a sacrifice another time, I knew what to expect, and I wouldn't let them play that game with me. So I didn't tell my parents. Silence was not a lie. Silence was keeping the truth to yourself, I think. But I did ask my father about voices.

My father looked peculiarly at me. "What kind of question is that?" he asked.

"A plain question," I said. "I just want to know."

"You're thinking of being a prophet or something when you grow up?" my father asked or maybe said. "No more a baseball player? You hear that, Rivkele? Our *kaddishl* here is gonna be another prophet like Yechezkel and hear voices."

Then he turned directly to me, away from the holy book on the table that was now dry of all tears because it was daytime and very hot, and added the following:

"In the Talmud it tells that Rabbi Eliezer gave an opinion on the law and the other rabbis disagreed with him. So Rabbi Eliezer, to make a long story short, said in front of all the sages, 'If I'm right, let the heavens prove it.' At that moment, an echo came from the sky, a heavenly voice, and said, 'Why are you disagreeing with Rabbi Eliezer? Don't you know that we always follow his opinion when it comes to the sacred law?' But Rabbi Joshua refused to listen to the heavenly voice. He quoted from the last book of the *Toyreh* where it is written, 'It is not in heaven.' Another rabbi explained what Rabbi Joshua meant. He meant that since the time we got the *Toyreh* from God on Mount Sinai, we do not listen anymore to heavenly voices. The *Toyreh* said that we are to decide on the law by majority vote of the scholars and not by heavenly voices anymore. And we are bidden to follow the *Toyreh*. There's a funny ending to this story in the Talmud. One of the rabbis in that group later met the old prophet Elya on the road on one of his sojourns among people and away from heaven. He asked Elya what was God's reaction to the rabbis repudiating the heavenly voice by quoting the *Toyreh* given by God to the Jewish people. The-Holy-One-Blessèd-Be-He smiled, according to the prophet Elya, whose full name is Eliyahu in Hebrew and Elijah in English, and said, 'My children have conquered Me.' "

My father looked down at the tractate of the Talmud that was in his hands. He didn't even look at my mother in the kitchen, who was smiling at the story that my father had told. She always liked my father's stories from the Talmud.

"You must learn this book and many others like it, my *tachshitl*, and not listen to any voices that tell you what to do. Heavenly voices have misled our people all through the generations. Outside of a few prophets whose heavenly voices just told them to follow the *Toyreh*—and that age of prophecy is over—we don't listen to voices anymore. We follow the *Toyreh* and the learning that comes from it. Voices can do more than shatter the eardrums. They can kill our people."

I knew that my father was right about people getting killed because I came pretty close.

THE *SHIDDUCH*

THE GROSSMAN FAMILY lived downstairs on the second floor in our tenement house on the Lower East Side when I was a kid. We hardly knew them before I began to play with Vigdor. They were physically imposing figures who ordinarily could not go unnoticed—mother, father, three grown sons plus Vigdor, who was almost a man, one grown-up daughter, one younger daughter, the men all over six feet, the grown-up daughter a head taller than all the other women in the building. If we did bump into them in the hallway or up and down the narrow stairs, we marveled at their size and conjured up fanciful notions of ancient heroes from Hercules to Samson to King Saul. We wondered aloud sometimes how all of these giants managed to live together in a three-room apartment with one toilet in the hallway shared by two families. My father guessed that the parents slept in the bedroom, the unmarried daughters in the living room, and the four awesome unmarried sons in the back of the hardware store they operated two blocks away even though nobody seemed ever to see their sons leave for the night to that appointed venue. But we hardly ever spoke to the grown-ups.

The reasons were never mentioned. Mrs. Grossman had the habit of opening her second-floor door whenever anyone was traipsing up or down the stairs, which meant that she opened her door dozens of times each day. She'd nod to neighbors, say hello and sometimes add another bit of conversation, but nothing more. My mother didn't especially like this intrusion. She felt that her every move in the building was being watched by Mrs. Grossman, and she once mentioned the name of another neighbor she recalled from her childhood in the old country in Europe who spied in a similar way and was even as folksy and familiar in a similar way only to betray them to local marauders during a pogrom attack by neighborhood toughs or maybe Cossacks. My mother didn't expect this kind of behavior from the Grossmans in America, where pogroms didn't take place and where Jews didn't have to pose as gentiles during such times of danger, but it left a bad taste in her mouth about nosy neighbors and spying and aggressive greetings.

My father had religious reasons. The Grossmans were nonobservant. Their radio blared away during all of the Sabbath, loud enough to be heard in the hallway and on the stairs. As a kid, I longed to go to their apartment to hear some of the famous radio programs since we didn't own a radio until I was eleven years old, but I didn't dare ask. I heard summaries of Jack Benny and Fred Allen and Jack Armstrong, the All-American boy, and the Lone Ranger and Tonto from my friends in school, but I dared not admit that I hadn't heard the programs myself or that we were too poor to own a radio.

The Grossman boys and even the old father walked around with heads uncovered summer and winter, and this was unheard of among religious Jews. The women knew that Mrs. Grossman bought kosher meat for the table, but they weren't certain if meat and dairy dishes were carefully kept apart within their home. So inevitably, relations between the Grossmans and people like my mother and father were coldly cordial and minimal. On Sundays I stood on the stairs of the second floor on my way down from our fourth-floor apartment and strained to listen to the opening lines of "The Shadow" as I had heard them imitated by my school chums. If Mrs. Grossman opened her door at my shifting footstep, I ran.

It was therefore with elation and not a little surprise that I came home from Hebrew School one evening to find old Mr. and Mrs. Grossman seated at our kitchen table in the same seats that Mr. Braverman, the choir leader, and his wife had occupied some years before. My parents were standing close by, as in the previous time, and glasses of tea and slices of honey cake were also on the table as for all guests.

"I hear your older daughter Celia is making a trip to Poland," my father said.

The two Grossmans nodded.

"Is it just for pleasure," my father continued, "or maybe for your sons' business or something?"

They were tall even in their seats, the Grossmans. Mr. Grossman was even taller than usual because he had come up to my parents' apartment wearing a slouch hat that added six inches to his height, undoubtedly in deference to my parents' religious sensibilities.

"*Vos mir* business?" Mrs. Grossman said. Her husband kept silent. "*A shlok zol es trefn,* the business. The hell with it. It ain't worth a nickel. We should spend hundreds of dollars to send Celia to Europe for that *shtikl* business? Crazy we're not. Believe me you."

Her voice was strangely different from her hall voice. In the hall, the natural resonance of that space magnified her every tone. Here in the apartment, she sounded tweety, high-pitched, thin as a reed, without body, but the intensity was there and the self-assurance and even the aggression.

"So she's going just for pleasure? It's a lot of money to spend," my mother intervened to say. "Such a beautiful girl, she deserves it for sure, but it's still a lot of money, the boat and everything."

Mr. Grossman continued munching away at the brown honey cake with nuts. He sipped his tea through a solid piece of sugar held between his teeth, or perhaps between his gums, since he didn't seem to have teeth to speak of. His cheeks had fallen in because of the toothless mouth, but in eating they blew up and inflated and deflated like little balloons. His churning mouth left no room for speaking.

"Such a beautiful girl," Mrs. Grossman tweeted in sarcastic approval. "So beautiful she ain't married yet at twenty-eight, and me with a burden of a younger daughter and three *loy-yitsluch* grown-up sons who can't find girls for themselves to marry and eat up everything in the icebox even though the store don't bring in a penny. That's what beautiful means. It's a curse, not a blessing."

"*Zindik nisht,*" my mother hastened to add. "Don't say words of sin. Your children are strong and healthy and very nice looking, *kanehore*. God will look after them. God will help."

Mrs. Grossman slammed her glass of tea to the table. Luckily, it was only half full, and the liquid jumped high but stayed in the glass. My mother's word against the evil eye must have worked.

"So God will help. Who? When? Where? That's all He gotta do is pay attention to a plain Grossman family in an East Side with a million people? He can't even stop a Hitler from marching into Austria, He's gonna march my daughters and sons to the *chupe,* the marriage canopy? *A nechtiker tog.* It won't happen so fast unless I do somethin' about it. So I send my daughter Celia to Europe with all the money I can borrow or steal, God protect me. I woulda sent her to Vienna to find a high-class husband between the Jews there, but how can she now go to Vienna with the Nazis there and the Jews hiding in cellars? So I have to send her to our old shtetl in Poland and hope that one of the lazy nogoodniks who still lives there gets interested in her and also thinks she's beautiful which she ain't."

My mother looked at my father, who sat down slowly at the table at the one remaining seat. His head was slightly bowed and his brow furrowed in deep thought, the way he always looked before beginning to recite a prayer.

It was spring, almost a month before Passover. The window opened on distinct breezes that had a twinge of warmth to them. One could not know if they heralded a summer of heat or a return of the stark cold weather that had assaulted us for so many months. It was this way with everything—problematic, an enigma, a point of wonder whose solution required time and some patience.

"Mrs. Grossman," my father said finally. "Our home town of Sambor is not too far from Kalush where Mr. Grossman was born and lived. If your Celia is in Kalush, she can also go to Sambor in less than a day."

Mr. Grossman stopped swallowing.

"We have a young second cousin there who is maybe twenty-five, maybe thirty. A fine boy. Not so religious, but a fine boy. His whole family is still there—mother, father, brothers, sisters—like yours. Just like yours. He's even educated. He went to a technical high school in Poland and to cheder too for religious learning. He's even nice looking. I don't have pictures, but I remember when he was five or ten years old, he was the nicest looking boy in the whole family. And a calm disposition. He wouldn't hurt a fly even though he was in the Polish army. He's strong too. And the whole family there is worried about him because the other brothers and sisters are all married and he's the youngest and he's not married."

Mrs. Grossman began guzzling on the half-filled glass of tea. My mother refilled her glass immediately.

"We can write to him right away, and I'm sure he would meet Celia at the train station and show her around for a few days. Who knows? Who knows what would happen? I mean nothing would happen. He's a good boy. But maybe something good would happen. What do you say?"

Mrs. Grossman burst into such laughter that she sprayed all of us with droplets of hot tea. She slapped her husband on the back, and the tall man with the tall hat let out a yelp through mounds of brown honey cake that showed he had a voice and maybe even an opinion.

"You hear, Yankl?" she said to her husband. "Not only are they learned and religious and *erliche Yidn,* righteous Jews of the highest type, this family, but the mister is also a *shadchn,* a marriage broker, and he and his wife together wanna make a *shidduch* for our Celia with even a member of their own family in Poland. A match made in heaven. Can anything be better?"

My mother bowed her head. "It's the greatest mitzvah in the world," my mother said softly. "Maybe we can make another Jewish family, and maybe we can save a life too."

Mrs. Grossman slapped my father on the back the same way she had previously slapped her husband's back. My father was much shorter and weaker. He almost fell to the floor.

"*Mentshn,* it's a deal!" she shouted. Her voice suddenly sounded like the hall voice, loud, determined, self-assured, aggressive, and I in my corner marveled at the unforeseen turn of events in our tenement house.

❧

Celia Grossman was not beautiful. She was tall and could have carried beauty like a robust pine towering over a forest of lesser trees, but her face was sallow and pockmarked, her lips fallen in without ever having lost her teeth, her eyes squinty and colorless, her form out of proportion at every turn. Celia Grossman left for Poland a month after Passover and returned just before the High Holidays in September alone, without escort, but officially married to our cousin Harry, who was called Hershl by my elated parents. At the beginning of the following year, in February, Hershl himself arrived to join his new bride, and we went to greet him along with Celia and along with the whole Grossman clan at shipside on 46th Street in Manhattan. The following September, war broke out in Europe as Hitler's hordes attacked Poland, and all connections with Hershl's family in Poland, with the Grossmans' distant family in Kalush, and with the cousins of my father and mother in Sambor, Borislav, Dobromil, and Radom, where my father's brother was a *shoychet* and a *dayan,* a judge, in the Jewish community, were broken almost irrevocably. But Hershl was safe in the United States of America and Celia had a husband. A *shidduch,* a match, had been made on earth, if not in heaven.

I'm getting ahead of myself. Things happened after their marriage, exceptional things, months before the war broke out in Europe.

Celia's younger sister by perhaps a dozen years—Celia was the eldest sibling, her sister the youngest, with the four boys in between—was the girl named Feygy who had once saved my life from the binding and the sacrifice. She actually was much shorter than the general run of her family, an exception to the rule, so much so that she seemed to be from another clan. She was thin, wispy, fragile like a bird, which is what her Yiddish name meant. My mother always referred to her as Feygele, Little Bird, a diminutive of affection that fitted her very well.

She was very pretty, very sweet-looking, not in the teasing way of my Aunt Geety, but a charmer nevertheless. She certainly was not physically imposing like her tall elder sister or like chubby Mrs. Braverman, the choir leader's wife. But she generated feelings of pleasure in everyone with a winning smile and a demure way of moving around, wiggling under and over and side to side with a surprised look of delight on her face that absolutely arrested attention. It didn't take long for neighbors to realize that her new brother-in-law Hershl had begun taking undue notice of her. I even heard Mrs. Zukerman from next door whispering about the two of them to another neighbor while she was waiting to use the toilet in the hall. Mrs. Zuk-erman sometimes took care of me and almost never talked about the people downstairs. She talked mostly about food, since her husband was a waiter on Second Avenue, and sometimes she talked about God. So this whispering she did was a very curious thing.

Hershl looked much younger than his bride Celia. He was much shorter than she was, half a head shorter, and definitely much better looking. He had a shock of rust-colored hair that always flopped over one eye no matter how many times he shoved the strands backwards. And since he didn't ever wear a hat—my parents' original comment to Mrs. Grossman that their young cousin in Poland wasn't particularly religious being close to the truth—he was always working his hair. It was not in the least annoying to onlookers. It was, in fact, a winning trait.

Feygy would visit her sister often. By luck, an apartment in our building in the back of our fourth floor had become vacant just before Hershl's arrival from Europe, and the Grossmans jumped at the opportunity to rent it for their daughter and their new son-in-law. "Vacant" is not the most accurate word. Its previous tenant, a widow named Gussie, had actually been evicted by the landlord for nonpayment of rent. The widow and her few sticks of furniture were placed on the street one fine day, and Celia Grossman, as yet without her husband from Sambor, moved in.

My mother found a place for the widow Gussie in New Rochelle in the house of our Uncle Oosher, whose daughter Geety had vacated a room upon her marriage to Big Red before moving to Canarsie. I had always thought that Uncle Oosher lived in New Haven, but I must have gotten the "New" cities mixed up when I was younger. Uncle Oosher didn't live in a five-story tenement like on the Lower East Side of Manhattan. He actually had a house, a separated house in a northern suburb among gentiles, a house with many rooms and a toilet inside. My mother had to suppress her aversion to putting a widow woman into a home with her widower brother. Though both were fairly well advanced in years, it wasn't, after all, particularly nice. But in this instance, as in so many other instances with my mother, the desire to help another lost soul overcame any social or cultural or religious qualms.

The widow Gussie went suburban, and Celia Grossman, now called Celia Frimmer, had her own bridal suite on the fourth floor of a five-story walk-up, in the rear of the same floor where we lived in the front facing the street, but luckily two floors above her parents, who were too tired to walk up to her door with any consistency.

Feygy did walk up, frequently at night and many times by day, and many times after Hershl's arrival, when he was home and Celia was not. It was this way. Celia went out to a job by day—she worked as a finisher in the garment district where dozens of women sewed clothes and men ironed them. On the other hand, Hershl soon got a job as a night watchman at a matzoh factory on Rivington Street. Though he was nowhere near as tall as his brothers-in-law and even his wife, he was uncommonly strong, with arms bursting with muscles, and in spite of his invitingly handsome baby-face looks, he also looked fearless. That stuff about his service in the Polish army must have been true. End result—a watchman's dangerous job, which was not bad for a new arrival whose English learned long ago in a Polish school was spotty, to say the least.

So by day, Hershl was consistently home, alone. And Feygy came to visit.

My father left our apartment every afternoon to go to work at his new job as a *melamed,* a teacher in the local yeshiva also on Houston Street opposite the park, a yeshiva I never attended. He was home every morning and must have become aware of the shenanigans on the floor. He rose early to go to the neighboring synagogue for morning prayer and returned home for breakfast within the hour. Sometimes, he would see Feygy barrel up the stairs in a housecoat, sometimes in a flimsy skirt and blouse that was already half unbuttoned. Sometimes he heard what he didn't want to hear though he looked at nothing and hoped for nothing. He didn't hear it from Mr. or Mrs. Zukerman or any other neighbor because they wouldn't have dared to ply him with *looshn-hore,* evil gossip, that he avoided at all costs. He was not a meddlesome man, in spite of his major act of arranging the *shidduch,* the match between Celia and Hershl, which he considered a sacred mitzvah.

But he could not help himself in this case. He saw and heard it himself. Not only was Hershl an ember saved from the frightful conflagration soon to engulf all of Europe, but he was also a newly found son to my father. And

though Hershl was inevitably a newly found elder brother to me whose sudden appearance from inside the European cauldron could never offend, he
represented a massive problem of heart and soul to my father, for major prin-
ciples of another sort were at issue here.

My father did not know the ways of subterfuge or false diplomacy. He
only knew Torah law and Torah tradition.

"Hershl," he said to the young man who was drinking the inevitable cup
of tea at his side. This time my mother was nowhere to be seen. The matter
was too delicate for her ears. But I was at the door, my open book at the
ready if I was discovered. "You're like my son. *Mahn* Hershele, *si shtayt
geshribn b'fayresh,* it clearly states in the *Toyreh* you can't take a wife and her
sister together. It will crush the wife even more than any other secret relationship and destroy the family. It's in *Va-yikro,* the Book of Leviticus. We
read it again by *Mincheh* on the afternoon of Yom Kippur before the closing
N'eeleh service. Do you know why we read it on Yom Kippur?"

Hershl Frimmer, now called Harry, did not ask for an answer.

"We read it then because it's one of the worst sins, along with all the others mentioned there of family promiscuity. We read it then because at the
final moment of judgment, on the awesome day of Yom Kippur, we must
cleanse ourselves of this brutish inclination. We read it then because, to our
sorrow, many Jews only come to *sheel* on Yom Kippur, and they must hear
these words before it's too late. Hershl, my son, before it's too late."

Harry wavered between talking and not talking. "It *is* too late," he finally
said bluntly to my father.

My father did not show emotion or give up talking. "It's never too late,"
my father said. "You must break the relationship now before it's too late."

"I can't," Harry said. His words were like his physical body—short, to the
point, and iron-strong. "I won't, Uncle." He always called my father uncle,
even though he was simply a second cousin once removed of my father, but
my father was much older and enjoyed the status of uncle with him just as
cousin Geety, much older than I, was always Aunt Geety to me.

"I don't understand such talk," my father said. "Do you love that child so
much you can't think straight? You're married less than a year, you're six

months in America, and you're already carrying on without control? It's beyond understanding."

Harry crossed one leg, uncrossed it, then crossed the other. He wiped his
mouth with a flowing handkerchief. Then he adjusted the brim of his slouch
hat which he wore, I'm sure, to our apartment, like Mr. Grossman, just to
please my father. He looked like a handsome Dillinger before the FBI shot
the gangster in front of the movie theater.

"I married Celia without love. I did not love her. I don't think she loved
me. She loved marriage. I loved getting to America with her help and with
yours to save my life from Hitler. I didn't save my life in order to die an old
man in America without love."

Suddenly my father stormed at him. My father jumped up and pounded
on the table. His face went white. The benign look in his eyes turned cold
and piercing. I had almost never seen him act this way before.

"What kind of stupidity is this? What kind of foolishness? Has America
with the movies and the naked women in the papers scrambled your head?
Di bist a Yid! You're a Jew! You're not a heathen. You're not an animal. You're
Gots bashefenish, God's creation. You were meant for higher things. Yes, the
body must be served. It is God's creation too. A man must love. A woman
must love. But is there only one woman in the world, and that one gotta be a
sister, not a wife? Celia is a good woman. The way God made her is the way
God made her. She will give you children and a home and love, if you let her.
She's big, she's strong. She'll give you *a bintl kinder,* a bundle of children."

My father's next sentence he said slowly, out loud, emphasizing each
word one at a time. "*You will have a family again.* A big immediate family
again, Hitler or no Hitler. Is that to be thrown away for a man's foolishness? I
expected more from my young cousin, from almost a son of mine."

Harry put his face into his cupped hands. The long fingers covered his
eyes and pushed the slouch hat up so that the errant shock of rust-colored
hair plopped out and down. His fingers were far longer than mine, long
enough to span a tenth on the piano. I could only manage an octave, and that
with some difficulty. My teacher at the Henry Street Settlement House who
had escaped from Germany years before taught me to arpeggiate octaves

with my small hand. It made a nice rippling effect, and I thought of this while peeking out at the broken face of Harry Frimmer and the long fingers covering them in my father's house.

Harry began to pout like a child in a voice that approximated a whine. "Jacob married Leah and Rachel. It's not against Jewish law. It says so in the Torah. You're a scholar. You know all those things."

My father's patience finally gave out completely. "You're now giving me instruction in *Toyreh? Herst azoins?* Do you hear that, Rivke? Our Hershele is teaching me *Toyreh uf der elter,* in my old age."

My mother was not within earshot and probably did not hear her name mentioned. She was in the bedroom doing something or other, reading the *Tsenerene,* the Torah translation in Yiddish. I was in the living room in our railroad flat, at the door facing the kitchen where the two men were sitting, and I heard it all.

"Don't be such a wise guy," my father cautioned Harry. The plain American words we always said to other kids in the street sounded funny in the mouth of my father.

"The Patriarchs lived before the giving of the Law at Mount Sinai," he continued. "Some of the pre-Sinai injunctions against certain relationships did not apply as yet to them. But after Sinai, no self-respecting Jew would carry on with both a wife and her sister, *chas ve-cholile,* God forbid. That's the law until the *moshiach,* the messiah comes."

"I can't wait that long," Harry said impetuously. He got up as if to go. Though of average height, he towered over my father.

My father must have thought that he was losing. He straightened up tall so that he grew several inches at once, in my feverish estimation. He put both his hands on either side of Harry Frimmer's cheeks, squeezed them gently, and spoke in a much softer voice. The shouting was at an end. I breathed deeply in relief though the moment of deeper truth had not yet arrived.

"Hershl, listen to me. Maybe you think there is a God, maybe you think there isn't a God, may I be forgiven for even mentioning the last possibility. This modern world, the one you grew up in over there in Poland and the one we're trying to bring up good Jewish children in over here in America is beyond my understanding at times. But I know this. God may be looking for a sign from *us*. Most of the people in the world always look for a sign from *Him*. But in this time of terrible danger for our people in Europe, God may be looking for acts of goodness and morality and devotion from *us* to see if He should save the Jewish remnant from the coarse and terrible violence of the evil tyrant."

Hershl's face, his cheeks under my father's hands, clearly changed colors from tan to deep red to stark white to red again.

"Your family is still in Poland. Your mother, your father, your sisters and brothers, uncles, aunts, and cousins. My younger brother, the *shoychet* in Radom, is also there with his family—all of them in the greatest danger. The tyrant stands ready to attack, and if he makes a war and even if our dear relatives all escape destruction in the coming military battles, they will then surely face agony and death in the terrible concentration camps made for all Jews and for others too. The consequences of Nazi rule for the Jews in Europe we have already seen on that night of the broken glass, that *Kristallnacht* last November. Those optimistic people who closed their eyes in the past to the possibility of the worst happening cannot close them anymore after that night of a national pogrom against the Jews. Do you hear me, Hershl?"

Hershl nodded.

"Who knows? Maybe small acts of goodness and decency by us here will push the scales to the side of survival. Maybe these pious acts will be the sign God is waiting for. God may listen to *us,* Hershl. Yes, He may listen. In fact, He *must* listen to us. We will force him to listen to us by our righteous deeds. Maybe the ultimate decision is not, God forbid, His to make, All-Powerful and All-Merciful as He is. Maybe the decision to save the Jewish people from the archmurderer lies in *our* hands."

My father squeezed his own hands more tightly toward each other on Harry's discolored cheeks. He held on to Harry's face like someone holding a precious vase.

"In our hands," my father added. "Our fate is in *our* hands. In *your* hands."

Within a month, Hitler invaded Poland, and my father almost went berserk. Every day, upon his return from teaching at the yeshiva, he turned on the little, secondhand Philco radio we had recently acquired and pushed the dial from one news program to another. He could not stand still. He marched up and down the living room, doing miles of road work in a constricted area of fifteen feet by ten feet. He mumbled to himself constantly, something I had never seen him do. My mother did not try to stop him. She watched him out of the corner of her eye, brought him a cup of tea the moment he sat down, and tried to comfort him.

"Your brother is a scholar, a wise man," she said. "He'll know what to do to get himself and his family away from the Nazis. Don't worry so much."

And sometimes she invoked God. "Your brother is a *tzaddik*. God will watch over him and his family. Don't worry. Have *bituchn*. A Jew must trust in God."

I was so disturbed by my father's reactions that I had almost forgotten about Harry Frimmer and my father's conversation with him. I had even forgotten to snoop around the hallway to see if Feygy Grossman was still making her trips to his apartment when Celia wasn't there. It dawned on me that Harry might be just as worried as my father about the fate of his remaining relatives in the hometown in Poland. After all, Harry had left parents there in addition to brothers and sisters. And they were cousins of ours too. A crazy idea came into my head that if I mentioned Harry's relatives to my father, it might get his mind off his own brother, and he might even calm down a little in talking about somebody else's fate. It was a ridiculous mistake.

My father quickened his pace across the living room floor. "My brother, my cousins, *all* the Jews," he said, "they're all in trouble, in the worst trouble ever. Nobody is exempt. No matter if religious or not religious, with a head covering or without. We have sinned. We came to America, and we sinned. We began to live like all the others, violating the Sabbath, drinking, gambling in pool rooms, allowing the *yaytser-hore,* the evil inclination, to rule us, running around with other women, even with a sister, God forbid. It says so in *Yechezkel,* in chapter 22. Because of their sins against the poor and their immorality, the House of Israel will be like brass or tin or iron or lead in the middle of the furnace, like the impurities of silver. In the furnace, in the flames. Oh my brothers and sisters! My brother was right. Free America will destroy us. It kills us slowly, but Hitler, *yemach shemoy,* will kill us quickly because we have sinned."

About a week later, I saw Harry Frimmer downstairs at the candy store. He was making a lot of calls on the candy-store phone, and Vinnie the owner was annoyed because he was expecting a call from a candy distributor who was going to give him a better deal.

I told Harry what my father had said without mentioning running around with a sister. Harry nodded, blew his nose into his knuckles, and didn't say anything.

And a week after that, Harry was gone. My mother said that he had taken a train up north and had joined the Canadian army to fight Hitler. Since Harry had been in the Polish army, he undoubtedly knew all about military matters and was an ideal candidate for service in the war.

My mother cried a good deal. Harry was family and she feared for his life. She prayed for Hitler's defeat, but she wanted Harry and all other boys safe at home. The two hopes didn't go together, but my mother never thought about contradictions like that.

A month after Harry had left, Celia told everybody that she was pregnant with her first child. My mother was elated.

"God works in strange ways," my father said. "Maybe this is the beginning of the repentance, the *ge'ulo,* the redemption."

"*Halevay,*" my mother said. "Would that it were so." She thought for a moment, as if debating with herself whether to say something that might disturb my father or not. She spoke softly, slowly. "But do so many people have to die for the *ge'ulo* to come?" she asked.

Naturally, I didn't have to snoop around the hallway to know that with Harry having gone to war, Feygy Grossman stopped going upstairs secretly except to see her sister Celia and help her out in her pregnancy. Feygy was so beautiful and alive, and she found boyfriends elsewhere, but that's another story.

ELYA AND THE PROPHETS OF BAAL

ABOUT THE FIFTH TIME that Vinnie in the candy store told me to run up to Mr. Elya Weinberg's apartment to call him to the phone, I finally noticed that there wasn't a *meziza* on his fifth-floor door. I didn't ask Mr. Weinberg about it because I was thinking of the nickel or dime he would give me for letting him speak to his son in California on Vinnie's store phone and all the candy that I would buy with it. But I asked Vinnie after I had stuffed myself.

Vinnie shrugged his shoulders. "What's a *meziza?*" he asked.

This amazed me. Everybody knew that a *meziza* was on everybody's doorpost filled with all kinds of good prayers like *Shma Yisrool* to protect the apartment from *shaydim*. So I told him.

"What's *shaydim?*" he asked.

Vinnie, apparently, didn't know too much. All he knew was candy and newspapers and magazines and egg creams and other drinks.

"*Shaydim,*" I said, "are little bad angels that run around in the woods and scare you in the middle of the night."

"Are you guys Jewish or Irish?" Vinnie asked. "Only the Irish believe in leprechauns. When they guzzle two drinks they begin seein' things. But you guys don't drink. I don't get it."

Anyway, Vinnie said that maybe Mr. Weinberg didn't give a hoot about a *meziza* because he wasn't Jewish.

This idea perplexed me. First of all, everybody was Jewish. Second of all,

Mr. Weinberg had a long beard that rested on my father's hat whenever he discussed things with my father. Third of all, he spoke Yiddish to my father. So how could he not be Jewish?

But Vinnie said that didn't prove anything. In fact, since Mr. Weinberg was twice as tall as everybody—he had to bend down when he came into the candy store in order not to bop his head—that proved that he maybe wasn't Jewish since Jewish people were very short. I couldn't understand Vinnie's point because the four sons of Mr. and Mrs. Grossman on the second floor of our house were almost as tall as Mr. Weinberg. And they were all Jewish because my mother and father would not have let our cousin Harry Frimmer get married to their sister Celia if they were Italian or Irish or something.

So I asked my father. "Why doesn't Mr. Weinberg have a *meziza* on his door?"

My father said that Mr. Weinberg was a goy.

I knew that some of the guys from the church on Pitt Street who came to play baseball against our candy-store team were goys, but I never knew that Mr. Weinberg was one of them. I never saw him go into that church, and he certainly never played baseball in the park across the street.

Boy, did I like that park. When the summer was hot, I could go across the street and watch the guys play baseball in the concrete field that had bases marked out in paint. Big Red once hit a ball over the left-field fence and into a window on the third floor of the school on Sheriff Street even though he batted lefty. I think that's what made my Aunt Geety who was also my cousin like him so much. Big Red was such a great hitter.

But if there wasn't a game, I could go to the side fence of the baseball field that separated it from the two pools in the middle of the park and watch the guys and girls splash around in the water and dive off the board in the deep pool and run after each other. This happened only in the summer when the mayor of New York put water into the pool. Once when I was very little, I saw a guy catch a girl and put his hands on her chest. When she screamed, he pushed her into the pool. She came out and pushed him. Then he pushed her. I think it was a game I didn't know yet how to play.

So I asked my mother. "Ma, how come Pa says that Mr. Weinberg is a goy just because he doesn't put a *meziza* on the door even though he has a long beard and talks Yiddish to Pa even though he talks English to his son in California who once talked to me on the phone and told me to be a good boy?"

My mother thought for a while. It seemed to be a very big problem that took a long time to figure out. Finally, she said, "Mr. Weinberg is a communist. That's why your father calls him a goy. He don't believe in anything except in communism."

"Vinnie thinks he's a goy and goes to the church," I said.

"No, no," my mother assured me. "*Chas ve-cholile.* He don't believe, but he's still a Jew. A *goyish* Jew but still a Jew. A Litvak with a funny pronunciation in Yiddish, but a Jew like all of us. Someday he'll be a good Jew."

This answer definitely baffled me. And if I needed anymore bafflement, I got it when my mother added that Vinnie didn't know anything about Jews because he was a real goy, an Italian. She said *Talyener,* but Big Red told me that meant Italian in Yiddish.

So now I knew two kinds of goys, Jewish goys and real goys. I actually liked both types—Mr. Weinberg for giving me dimes when I called him to the phone and Vinnie for giving me candy for the dimes. Everybody, my father once said, has a purpose in this world.

▼

Once my father and Mr. Weinberg began yelling at each other. They were standing just outside the hall toilet on the fourth floor where we lived. Mr. Weinberg had come down from his fifth-floor apartment and bumped into my father just as he was getting out of the hall toilet and I was getting in. Though I had to go badly, I didn't. I wanted to hear things.

"What's that newspaper you're reading, *Chaver* Mehler?" Mr. Weinberg asked.

I could've told him myself that my father always went into the toilet with any old newspaper. It didn't matter which one he found in the street or on the subway train or on the bus. He took it home for toilet reading so that he wouldn't be able to think of holy Torah words in the profane toilet. So the correct answer was that my father didn't even know what newspaper he was reading. It wasn't the one with "Terry and the Pirates" because I sneaked a look at it before my father went. It was filled with print and almost no pictures even though it was in English. I thought only Hebrew books like the Torah and the Talmud didn't have any pictures, but I was wrong.

"What?" Mr. Weinberg continued. "You read an English paper printed by plutocrats and gangsters who steal from the poor? You should be ashamed of yourself, *Chaver* Mehler. A man like you. But what should I expect from a man who speaks the people's Yiddish but still reads a reactionary religious rag like the *Morgen Journal*. He should be reading our paper the *Freiheit* that is a Yiddish call to action against the imperialists and the exploiters. The Mrs. Grossman tells me that you won't even read a halfway socialist rag like the *Forverts* because it has dirty stories by Bashevis Singer in it. So if you read in English, you don't even read PM, which is also a chicken-socialist rag which makes compromises with the ruling class. But *The Times noch!*"

Mr. Weinberg waved a finger over my father's head. He would've waved it in his eye, but he was too tall to reach down to my father's eye.

"*The Times* is honest," my father said. "I don't read *tereetsim* there, false reasons to defend the evil Stalin for making a pact with Hitler, *yemach shemum v'zichrum,* may their name and their memory be erased. If not for Stalin and his vicious pact with Hitler not to make trouble for him, Hitler maybe wouldn't have invaded Poland so fast, and my brother would not be in danger of his life with his whole family. So don't call me *Chaver* Mehler. I'm not a comrade."

Mr. Weinberg was seething. "Mehler, if not for Stalin, your brother who got away to eastern Poland occupied by the Soviets wouldn't be alive today."

Pa lowered his head. His eyes closed slowly, and I don't think he saw much when he did that. He was looking inside, at things and times and places I couldn't see. He moved away from Mr. Weinberg and spoke to himself, it seemed.

"With God's help," he said, "England and France will maybe stop the Nazi murderer. Maybe my brother in Poland will escape to the West and come here to live with me, *mit Gots hilf, im yirtse Ha-Shem,* God willing."

I already knew that my father made mistakes in English even though half his words were in Yiddish. He should've said the times *are* honest, not *is* honest, but even that way it didn't make much sense because I thought only people and animals could be honest, not things like the times.

"You're a fool, Mehler," Mr. Weinberg suddenly yelled. "You expect England and France and other capitalist countries to fight Hitler? *A bobe mayse!* An old grandma's tale! Impossible. A fable. What are they doin' now since the war in September? Nothing. They're playin' games, that's what they're doin'."

He had as big a voice as he was. He was so loud that even though we were all standing along the stairs of the fourth floor, I fully expected Mrs. Grossman to peek out of her second-floor apartment in order to listen to the whole argument and tell all the other neighbors and her silent husband and all her sons and daughters including beautiful Feygy Grossman.

"You call this a war?" the giant Mr. Weinberg yelped. "It's a phony war! Capitalists don't fight capitalists. They only make out like they're fighting so they can fool the socialist world. Soon, soon they'll both of them all of them—England and France and Nazi Germany and Fascist Italy—they'll all get together with the United States to fight the Soviet Union and to exploit Africa and the Arabs and the poor people of India and Argentina together. You'll see. If you gotta thank God, and I don't believe in God, thank God that your brother is in the Soviet Union where everybody is equal and the *goyim* love the Jews like equals and the Constitution says so *b'feyresh,* in clear detailed explanations, better than the *Toyreh* and the Talmud put together, which are the opium of the Jewish people."

So Mr. Weinberg also knew about *goyim.* Did he know that he himself was a goy, a Jewish goy? I wasn't sure about that. I *was* sure that my father would yell back at him for saying anything is better than the Torah and the Talmud. But I was wrong. I think my father got tired listening to so many loud words. I never heard Mr. Weinberg talk so much, even when he talked to his son in California on the phone in Vinnie's candy store.

My father spoke in an extremely quiet voice. He didn't get angry. He was still talking to himself. "My brother, *tsi lange yoorn* with all his family, was a *shoychet* in Radom, a ritual slaughterer, a high religious official in his community, a *Toyreh* scholar, a genius from childhood on, before Hitler invaded Poland. Thank God he escaped from the Nazi part of Poland to the east. But it's not a picnic there under Soviet control. The communists will not let him learn or teach the sacred subjects or make food *koosher* for eating. How can he live that way? How can this beautiful *neshume,* this lovely soul, survive under a communist *dictatoor* that is against all religion?"

Mr. Weinberg spit on the banister and washed it down with his giant hand. "Your brother is a parasite!" he yelled. "Does he deserve to live? For what? He don't have a decent occupation to help his fellow man. All this kosher nonsense—just *narishkeyt,* that's what it is. *He's* an opium of the people all by himself. If he don't get a worker's job and make an honest living, he don't deserve to live."

My father recoiled in horror. "Bite your tongue," he said, a little louder than usual. "May your words never reach the heavens. You are a hard man, Weinberg. Say you regret it before it's too late."

"I don't regret nothin'!" And he waved his wet finger not toward my father's eye but toward heaven itself.

"Do *tsheeva,* Weinberg. Say a prayer of repentance."

"I don't waste my time in prayers, in stupid words of *teshuva* to a God who won't listen and who don't exist and who lets man exploit man."

I forgot about going to the toilet. I was very scared. I had never heard words like this before in my life. I closed the toilet with the key my father gave me. He led me toward our apartment by the hand because I think he didn't want me to hear anymore.

My father turned back to the giant with the Jewish beard just as we were going into our apartment.

"Pray, at least, that England and France should defeat Hitler. If the beast ever wins and comes here, *chas ve-cholile,* Weinberg, you will still be a Jew in his eyes whether you believe in God or you don't. You won't be better off than me."

Inside our house my mother also yelled at my father. This too was a surprise because my mother rarely yelled at anybody, let alone my father.

"Why do you fight with the Litvak?" she said, her face getting red with the effort. "Mr. Weinberg isn't really a bad man. He wants everybody to be equal. He wants the poor workingman to make a decent living in this Depression we had so long. So he says he don't believe. Don't believe everything he says. Everybody believes even when they say they don't. You can't live without believing. He says he ain't a Jew. Let him say it till the *moshiach* comes. A Jew is a Jew. A goy is a goy. You have to get a heart attack over him? Think of your children."

My father spoke softly again. "He said that my dear brother don't deserve to live. Weinberg will only give my brother the right to live if he's a communist."

It didn't seem to bother my mother as much. "God, not Weinberg, will look after your brother. Leave the old fool alone. What do you expect from a Jew with a beard like Karl Marx. Pray that the *goyim* in Europe will be kinder than this Jewish goy."

Again the *goyim,* but this time in Europe. I didn't even know that there were *goyim* in Europe. I thought the Jews were spread to the four corners of the world and were everywhere. So live and learn. And I learned other things too. My mother said that Mr. Weinberg looked like Karl Marx and I knew only three Marx Brothers, maybe four, but nobody with a name like Karl. Aunt Geety couldn't help me with that either. But Big Red said that Karl Marx was the captain of the communist team, not a movie star or a comedian, and Big Red should know because the communist team color is red. So I learned a new thing.

I even agreed with my mother about my father, though for a different reason. I didn't want my father to fight with Mr. Weinberg, not because the giant was a Jewish goy, or because my father might get a heart attack and die, but because if he fought too much with Mr. Weinberg, Mr. Weinberg might get angry at all of us and not give me any dimes anymore when I would call him to the phone, and then I would have a real problem because I wouldn't want to call him anymore, but I would have to because my mother always said that I must do that not just for money but because it was a mitzvah, a good deed, even to help a sinful man like Mr. Weinberg, and what a fix I would then be in.

I said to my father, "Ma says a Jew is a Jew and a goy is a goy. What's the difference?"

My father looked at me with narrow eyes the way he always looked when he was trying to figure out things. It took him a long time to give me an answer.

"A goy," he said finally, "has to obey only seven commandments given to the sons of Noah—not to murder, not to steal, not to follow idols, not to curse God, not to eat flesh cut from a living animal, to make courts of justice, and something else. A Jew has to obey 613 commandments, mitzvahs, 248 positive that you should do and 365 negative that you're not allowed to do. That's the difference."

"I thought you would say that the Jews are good and the *goyim* are bad," I said.

My father sighed. "Some Jews only, *zindele,* some *goyim* only, my little son."

"They got a better deal than we got," I said. "They got a lot less to do and a lot less to watch out not to do."

My father laughed. He laughed so rarely. If he wasn't with his face buried in a holy book, and you could therefore see his expression from the front, he always seemed ready to cry.

"We got a better deal, *zindele.* For a Jew it's always a pleasure to do mitzvahs. The poor *goyim* can gain their share of *oylem-habe,* the-world-to-come, only by doing seven. But we, thank God, gotta do 613 to enter the-world-to-come. Wonderful! It keeps us busy and out of trouble day and night, *yoymum vaw-loylaw.* That's why the *goyim* drink so much and get into so much trouble with the police. They don't have enough mitzvahs to do."

"Is that why we say a *brooche* every morning thanking God He didn't make us a goy?"

"That's why. That's the only reason why. We thank Him for so many mitzvahs to do, for giving us the burden of good deeds. And that's why we even thank Him He didn't make us a Jewish woman because they are free of most of the mitzvahs that take too much time away from their home obligations."

"Do ladies who are rich and have servants who take care of the house for them have to do all the mitzvahs because they got alotta time to spare?"

"I can't believe this boy," my father said. "He's a Talmudic scholar. He asks the most unbelievable *klutz kashes.*"

I knew that this meant stupid questions. My father told me that many times before. I was the king of *klutz kashes.* But my father never stopped me from asking.

"Also girls over thirteen who don't wanna help their mothers," I persisted, "do they have to do 613 mitzvahs?"

My father turned away. "Soon he'll be asking me questions about big girls. What'll I do with him?"

"What is *oylem-habe,* the-world-to-come?" I asked some more. "Is that when the *moshiach* comes, the messiah, or is that immediately after you die?"

"*Danken Got,*" my father gasped. "He didn't ask. He didn't ask."

Then he turned to me the way he always did when he wanted to make sure I understood. He looked through my eyes into the middle of my head. His answer was like a song, notes up and down.

"The-world-to-come is a mystery. We don't know what it is or when. If we did, we wouldn't look forward to it so much. Some things even your father don't know. But it is permissible to ask."

I didn't have any more questions, so that ended that. I would have liked to please my father and ask him about big girls like Aunt Geety or Feygy Grossman, but I didn't even know what to ask. I didn't know answers and I didn't even know questions. I had to grow up some more.

And then when I grew up a little more, something else happened. My father used to take me to three different *shuls* on the Sabbath. On Friday night, we strolled down Willett Street past Rivington toward Delancey and climbed up the many steps to the entrance of the Raysher *Sheel* to hear a good *chazn* welcome the Sabbath. He wasn't as good as the cantors I sang with in Mr. Berel Braverman's choir. After all, they were famous. Everybody knew their names: Leibele Waldman, Moyshe Oysher, Kapov-Kagen, Zavl Kwartin; but the Raysher *Sheel* cantor was pretty good for a local guy. My father swayed from side to side during the standing prayers, unlike all the other older men who swayed back and forth. I think the cantor's vibrato made him do that.

Sabbath morning, my father went to his own shul, the one on Clinton Street on the second floor above a shoe store. All the *davners* in this shul, the men and women praying, came from my father's and mother's home town in Galicia, Poland, the town of Sambor, and neighboring towns of Dobromil, Borislav, and so on. My father was the *chazn* in his own shul on most Saturdays and even read the Torah portion from the scroll.

I liked Clinton Street because it was a busy shopping street. Almost all the stores were open, even the shoe store below the shul, even the stores owned by Jews, but mostly *goyim* went in to buy things on the Jewish Sabbath. Still, I liked passing the stores and looking at the display windows and inside at the salesmen and ladies hanging around or doing things. In the fancier stores, they looked like they were dressed up for a Bar Mitzvah party. Smells of food from many stores and sidewalk carts mixed with smells from new patent leather shoes and smoking tobacco and whiskey and oiled wooden furniture and a dozen other things, and over everything mixtures of different music from a hundred radio stations on a hundred store radios, the spiraling sound circling up high like a thousand birds in a heavenly choir. Even Berel Braverman's choir that I sang in never sounded like this. I almost didn't want to continue on to shul with my father to hear him *davnen farn umed,* leading the prayers, chanting in front of all the hometown people from Sambor, Dobromil, and Borislav. But I went anyway.

Late afternoon of every Sabbath, my father took me back to Willett Street, but this time short of Rivington. Next to the empty lot where the big boys played stickball was the Bialystoker *Sheel.* My father went there Saturday afternoons because he wanted to participate in the Talmud lesson that the Bialystoker Rabbi gave before the *Mincheh* service. My father and I also took part in the *Shalesheedes,* the third Sabbath meal between *Mincheh* and *Maariv,* which were the afternoon and evening prayers. I also ate at the men's table with no women around—gefilte fish, *arbes,* nuts, honey cake, *lekech,* lots of good stuff—and I even sang along with the old men when they began the *zmires,* the Sabbath hymns. One time they made me sing some of the *zmires* solo because they heard that I was in Berel Braverman's symphonic liturgical choir accompanying Cantor Waldman at a wedding later that night. I got paid fifty cents for each wedding, a whole dollar if I did the "*Vee-maley*" solo, but I got only food for singing in the Bialystoker *Sheel.* I didn't complain.

Did I say how much I liked Willett Street even more than Clinton Street? On Sundays, Willett Street and also Rivington Street were filled with push-carts in all the gutters alongside the sidewalks. You could hardly walk from the sidewalk to the gutter except at the corners because the pushcarts were so close together. When I went to shul Saturday afternoon, I could almost see the pushcarts in my mind that would be stacked up so close early the next morning. When I got older, my parents let me go out Sunday morning alone, so I was able to run along all the pushcarts for blocks and blocks and look at all the goods and smell them. I didn't buy anything because I gave the fifty cents or the dollar that I earned singing in the choir at the Saturday night weddings to my mother.

But one Friday, which we call *Erev Shabes,* Sabbath Eve, my father got sick. In those days, I thought that normally only kids like me got sick and old folks died, but that medium-old people never got sick. My father was cough-ing and sneezing and he had the chills. My mother stopped him from going out and made him lie in bed under the covers.

I can't recall exactly when this happened, but I think it was after the first Passover of the war when my father received the long-awaited letter from his brother in Poland that he read to us with such joy at the Seder table. I'm also inclined to think that my father's illness took place when Hershl Frimmer came in the following summer on a month's furlough from the Canadian army, or to be exact, the Canadian air force.

Hershl was not in uniform. He claimed that he had already been overseas as a bombardier and that his plane had been shot down over Dunkirk. He told us that he had broken a leg on his parachute landing but, luckily, had been rescued by the British army and was evacuated with the British forces from Dunkirk in the nick of time. Then he was shipped back to Canada to recuperate from his injuries and now was given a long furlough to be with his wife who was soon to give birth to their first child.

Hershl's return surprised my parents, but perhaps as surprising was the fact that he went back almost immediately to his old job, even if on a temporary basis. My mother was overjoyed by his return. My father, as one would expect, had many questions to ask that he didn't ask—about Hershl's civilian clothes, about the absence of a limp, and about his taking a job in New York while still in the Canadian armed forces.

When my father got sick, Hershl Frimmer, Harry to all the young people, showed up almost immediately in our apartment before sundown on that Friday afternoon, on that *Erev Shabes.* How he got to hear of my father's illness so fast, I don't know for sure.

"Hershl, my son," my father said. "You shouldn't take off from work just to visit me. I'm not dyin' yet. You can't afford it, you with a wife to support and a child on the way and a short time before you have to go back to Canada."

My father always called him "my son" even though *I* was his son, but that was because Harry always called my father his father. My father and mother saved Harry's life from the Nazis in Europe long before the British army did. They did it by arranging for Celia Grossman to meet Harry where he lived in Poland before the war, marry him, and bring him to the USA as her husband before Hitler could get him. Consequently, my parents considered him a son and he considered them his substitute mother and father.

Harry waved his hand at my father. "Don't be foolish, *Tateh,*" he said, using the Yiddish word for father. Sometimes he called him uncle and sometimes father. "The Fur and Leather Workers' Union can fight the bosses without me for one day. That's called solidarity. All for one and one for all. And this is solidarity too. I owe it to you to be here when you need me."

I thought Harry had a night job in the matzoh factory on Rivington Street, but apparently he had changed jobs.

"Yes, I need you," my father said. "Take my *zindele* to *sheel* tonight and tomorrow for the *Shabes* prayers. I know you don't go *davnen* so often, Hershl, but go tonight and tomorrow so the boy won't miss praying even one *Shabes* while I'm sick in bed."

I don't know who opened his mouth wider in astonishment—Harry or me. But I knew that Harry could never say no to my father. He would take me to shul. I really was able to go alone—I was not a little kid anymore, but maybe my father wanted to find a reason for getting Harry himself to go to shul again. My father sometimes had reasons for things he didn't tell me.

Harry Frimmer took me that evening *to* shul but not *in* shul. Next door to the Raysher *Sheel* was the poolroom where all the *goyim,* Jewish and gentile, played pool all night and did other stuff too. Harry led me straight to the many rows of steps leading up to the shul. But he wouldn't go in with me. At the bottom of the stairs he said that he was going into the poolroom. He promised me that when he would hear us singing *Yigdal* through the walls of the poolroom, he'd know it was the end of the *Maariv* service and he'd come out to find me and take me home.

When the service was over and I got outside, he wasn't there. So I walked into the poolroom. Guys were chalking up their sticks and shooting at the balls. They didn't pay any attention to me.

One fat guy with his pants unbuttoned leaned over a pool table to make a shot. He used two sticks, one resting on top of the other. "The friggin' eight-ball into the friggin' side pocket," he said. Then he got off the table before he even hit a ball and waddled around to the other side. He bent down to the edge of the table and closed one eye. The other eye stared at all the balls. Squatting like that, he looked like a toad on a toilet seat. "Friggin' hard shot," he added. "I gotta line it up good."

A black soldier in uniform leaned against the wall. "Man, you're the slowest poke I ever did see. Any ole broad comes before you do."

"For chrisesake," the fat man said standing up straight and fat, "let a guy play, goddammit. And what do you know about women, bein' as you was so far away for two years in Adak in the Aleutian Islands without a civilian human being, let alone a woman, around. You're a friggin' pansy by now, for chrisesake."

I was hypnotized by the click of the balls on all the pool tables when they hit each other. Thwack, thwack, thwack. The best was when a player put all of them in one big triangle within a piece of triangular wood and broke them all apart with a giant thwack. Then all the balls sped in every direction at once like ants running from all sides of an anthill, racing for the corner holes and the side holes but getting in each other's way with smaller thwacks. I almost forgot to look for Harry Frimmer.

He didn't look for me either, it seemed, because I didn't find him at first. A chalkboard at the front of the poolroom listed all the baseball teams including my favorite, the New York Giants. A man came over to me when I was looking at the board and watched me for a minute.

"Who do you like, kid?" he asked.

"I like Aunt Geety and Feygy Grossman."

The man burst out laughing. "We got a real lady's man here," he yelped. Nobody paid any attention to him or to me.

"Play with your pecker yet, kid?" he asked.

"I don't know how to play pool," I said. "The peckers are too long and too heavy for me to hold."

The man almost doubled over with laughter.

"I mean who do you like on the board?" he asked. "Which teams do you like in baseball."

"I'm a Giant fan," I said. "I like Mel Ott and Carl Hubbell."

"Okay, so you like the Giants," he said. "But I don't mean that. No baseball team wins every day. I mean who do you like to win tomorrow afternoon? For instance, the Giants are playin' the Cubs. The Cubbies got a good team with Gabby Hartnett. Who's gonna win tomorrow?"

"I'm not supposed to pay attention to baseball games on *Shabes*," I said to the man. He had red hair like Big Red, but he didn't have too many of them, just a few scraggly red ones that waved over his head like a few skinny trees on an empty hilly field. The man scratched the big empty spots between the trees.

"So you're a rabbi's kid," he said.

"No," I said, "a teacher's kid. My father teaches *Chimish* and *Rashi* and *Gemoore* and *Toysefes.*"

"What? What? Is that like geometry and algebra?"

"No," I said. "That's religious books and commentaries."

"Religious stuff?" he yelped. "Your old man is a religious teacher? Great!

That's the same thing as a rabbi. A swami, a guru. Tell you what. Just tell me tonight who's gonna win in tomorrow's games. You don't hafta follow the games tomorrow. I'll follow them for you. Just ask God. You speak to Him regular, don't you?"

"No," I said.

"No?"

"No." Then I added, "I never speak to Him. Since we got the Torah, we're not supposed to listen anymore to heavenly voices. God is too busy making matches, I mean couples, you know, guys and girls to come together to get married, like Celia in my tenement and Harry in Sambor so far away near the Nazis. It's a hard job for God. But sometimes, every now and then, He whispers to me."

The man almost fell down to the floor. He held on to the edge of a pool table, straightened up, and swallowed hard. The two black circles in the middle of his eyes almost popped out, grew big like the black ball on the pool table among all the other balls of so many beautiful colors.

"You're my man," he said. "My main man. Just pick a team that's gonna win. Pick one. I'll give you a quarter."

A quarter was more than the dime that Mr. Weinberg used to give me, but I wouldn't take any money on *Shabes*. I picked anyway. First I picked the Giants to win. The man seemed a little disappointed. But since they were playing a doubleheader, I picked the Cubs in the second game. His eyes popped out again. He made a high sound with his voice like an ambulance siren in the distance. Then I picked team after team in both leagues—ten games counting doubleheaders. He patted me on the back. A minute later, Harry Frimmer came out from behind a locked door to take me home. He scowled at the man with the small amount of red hairs on his head. They whispered to each other, but not too happily.

The next morning my father was still chilly in bed, and Harry took me to my father's shul on Clinton Street. This time he came into the shul, and they called him to the Torah for an *aliya*. The older men had to help Harry with the *brooches,* the Torah blessings, because he forgot how to say them since he never went to shul. That made him pretty angry.

In the late afternoon, Harry took me to the Bialystoker *Sheel* on Willett Street next to the empty lot. Again he refused to go in. Once up there at the Torah scroll to say all that Hebrew was more than enough for him for one *Shabes*. He didn't want to be honored with another *aliya* at the *Mincheh* service by a new gang of old men who thought they were doing him a favor. I went into the shul by myself and Harry skipped.

When I came out into the dark street after the finish of the *Maariv* service, I didn't expect to find Harry there waiting for me. I thought I would have to go up toward Rivington Street and then toward Delancey to the poolroom to find him and pick him up for the trip home. But there he was in front of the Bialystoker *Sheel* on time, and with him was the poolroom guy with the skimpy red hair.

"You're an angel!" the man shouted softly. "A prophet from God! A goldmine! Ten outa ten! A perfect score! I never hit such a blockbuster in all my life. I cleaned up and made a bundle. It's after *Shabes*. You can handle money now, kiddo."

And he stuck paper money into my hand. I took a quick look and it looked like a five-dollar bill. I had never touched so much money in all my life. I saw him also put some money in Harry's hand. Then he spread out a big piece of paper under the light of a lamppost. All the teams were listed on the paper and all the games for the next day, for Sunday. Again two double-headers. I studied the sheet and made ten picks. Harry himself wrote them down on a small piece of paper of his own.

By Sunday, my father was much better. My mother let him get out of bed and let him sit in the living room in front of the better radio she had temporarily borrowed from the Zukermans next door during the time of my father's illness when he couldn't concentrate on a page of the Talmud. He listened with some degree of concentration to Zvee Scooler giving a funny summary of the week's news in Yiddish and in rhyme and later to the *Yiddisher Filozof* telling stories and deep ideas on WEVD. Ma gave him a lot of hot tea to drink with lemon and with a cube of sugar.

Harry came by to visit my father again. About five minutes after the beginning of the visit, Harry took me aside and pushed me into the bedroom that my father had vacated. He told me that I didn't do so good. I only picked nine winners out of ten, but he let me try again for Tuesday's games. All the teams were traveling on the train on Monday from one city to another, and there wouldn't be any games that day. But there was a full schedule on Tuesday. I made eight picks this time. Since my Sunday picks weren't perfect, Harry gave me only three dollars from Red Baldy, but I didn't complain. I hid all the money.

And so it went. I don't remember how long. I picked and I picked, and sometimes I got all the games right, and sometimes I missed one or two. I never missed three. The best I did was on a Sunday that was also a holiday with six doubleheaders. I got the winners in all fourteen games. Red Baldy gave me ten dollars for that day. After a long time, maybe a month, maybe two months, I had hidden away so much money I thought that we were all rich.

Until my father found out about it just before the World Series. He began screaming in a voice that came out of the top of his hat and that I had never heard before.

"A gambler?" he hollered. "A *bandit?* In my house? Under my roof? *Vay iz mir!* Woe is me! Soon he'll have a gun again like the fake one when he was a child and be a gangster like the one that was shot in front of the house and go to jail for life. God, what have you made us here in America? My brother the *shoychet* was right. That's why he didn't want to come here. He said this golden land will make rust out of my children. My children will stop learning *Toyreh*. They will stop being Jews. They will be *goyim, goyim, goyim!*"

I found out later that Vinnie the candy-store owner, an Italian goy, had snitched to my father. Vinnie heard the rumors from the gangsters hanging around his candy store and spilled the beans. He wanted to help my father, my father said, but I knew that you couldn't trust *goyim* to keep a secret.

The next Friday night, when my father without Harry Frimmer took me for services to the Raysher *Sheel* next to the poolroom, I was shocked to find the giant Mr. Weinberg walking along with us. He didn't speak a word to my father the whole way, but when we got to the shul, Mr. Weinberg took me by the hand while my father went up the steps to the shul alone.

Mr. Weinberg walked me straight into the poolroom. His beard was full and round and long and steel-gray. His eyes were flashing. When he walked in, he had to stoop his head to avoid hitting the top of the doorpost because he was so tall. He marched right up to a bunch of pool players and guys who hung around. He towered over all of them like Moses on the mountain, like King Saul in battle, like Samson. His black coat and black hat stood out among all the colored shirts and army uniforms in the room. I noticed Red Baldy in a distant corner near the ticker machine that gave all the baseball scores.

Suddenly giant Mr. Weinberg spoke up in a voice that was a blast from heaven. The high-flying birds outside must have scattered at the sound.

"Give me your attention, all of you *mamzeyrim!*" he bellowed. Every single person stopped as if paralyzed. Even Red Baldy who was racing toward me from the corner came to a sudden halt. Mr. Baldy's face turned white.

"Listen to the word from up high," Mr. Weinberg proclaimed. "If anybody in this here poolroom or outside anywheres else exploits this here little kid in gambling and other capitalist atrocities, if you involve him in nefarious games of chance and any other worthless pursuits, you will be judged an enemy of the people and a counterrevolutionary vagrant, and I personally will put a curse, a *maledizione,* on you and you and you so that you'll all burn in hell forever and ever and God Himself will not save you from His righteous wrath. *Sh'foch chamaws'chaw el ha-goyim asher lo y'daw'oo'chaw.* Pour out Thy wrath on all the lowlife *goyim* without gainful employment, the false prophets of Baal, the capitalist god of money, who exploit your little children, O God! That's final!"

Mr. Weinberg strode vigorously to the back of the poolroom right up to the ticker machine. A mound of thin strands of ticker tape was lying alongside on the floor. He stretched out his hand in a sharp movement, and a stream of fire came forth from his fingers and ignited the strands of paper on the floor. As he walked back in my direction, the guys in the poolroom unfroze and began to yell. Some of them stomped on the fire to put it out. Others ran to the toilet and came back with pails of water. Mr. Weinberg turned me around and walked me out the door. I could hear the yelling and screaming behind my back, but they didn't touch us. I could also see the small cigarette lighter hidden in the palm of Mr. Weinberg's giant right hand. He led me to the steps of the Raysher *Sheel.*

"Go to your father," he said. "It's all settled. Be a good boy. Listen to your father. Learn from him. Don't be a boss. Don't be a gambler. Work for a living, even if you have to be a *sheychet,* or a scholar. But not a gambler. Go, go. Go now to your father in shul. Say *Kaddish* for me when I die. My son in California don't believe in such things so I can't depend on him when I'm dead."

"Where are you going?" I asked him. "Are you goin' to die now?"

"Where am I goin'? I'm goin' home. Where else should I go? I don't go to shul. It's a waste of time. I gotta call my son in California on Vinnie's phone and ask him how the strike of the West Coast longshoremen is gettin' along. My son's a union organizer for Harry Bridges. Not like your stupid cousin Harry Frimmer who works for a solid red union and gambles like a capitalist on the side and skips out on his army service. Go to your father. Tell him to thank God you're safe now."

My father did ask me what Mr. Weinberg had said in the poolroom. I told him everything he said, but I didn't tell him what Mr. Weinberg did because you're not allowed to set a fire on the Jewish Sabbath or even carry a cigarette lighter.

As for Harry Frimmer, our cousin who escaped from the Nazis in Europe with the help of my parents and who led me to the poolroom in the first place, he never took me there again, and the guys there including Red Baldy never came looking for me again. Naturally, I never went there again myself. I thought if I sneaked in there, maybe Mr. Weinberg's curse would come on me too. In fact, every Friday night, when I accompanied my father to the Raysher *Sheel,* I averted my eyes from the poolroom as we walked by, going and coming. When the mourners in shul said the *Kaddish* prayer after the *Awleynu* prayer, I practiced it silently for the time when Mr. Weinberg would die.

That Saturday night after a big block party to sell war bonds and for soldiers on leave to dance with the girls in the middle of the street with big lights strung across from our fire escape to the fire escape on the other side of the street, I gave all the gambling money I won to my mother. She gave the money little by little to an elderly goy, not an Italian goy but a Polish goy, whom my father hired to help my mother with her janitor's job in the tenement. This goy smelled from whiskey all the time, but he was steady enough to stoke the furnace and sweep the halls since my father wouldn't let Ma do such things anymore. My mother couldn't give up the janitor's job completely because she needed it in order not to pay rent. So Ma kept the job by getting the goy to help out and paid him herself. She paid him from my winnings. I think my mother was pregnant again.

⬇

A few weeks later, one Friday night, my father was exceedingly quiet at the Sabbath table meal. He ate silently and then sang the *zmires* hymns in a softer voice. He didn't even test me on the Torah portion of the week like he usually did on Friday night. He seemed to be thinking hard again. My mother, standing at my side of the table, caressed my face.

"*Lebn zul Ameyrike,*" my father said finally. "Long live America." Yes, he was immersed in his deep-thinking mood. "Who can understand this country? In Europe the *goyim* are killing all the Jews, old people and children alike, in the concentration camps. I read it in a small article on an inside page of the *Times* like it was a secret, but also in the *Morgen Journal*. Even the lying *Freiheit* admits it. And here in America, where there are also terrible anti-Semites on the radio and even Nazi Bund meetings in Madison Square Garden, my son is almost like kidnaped by gamblers and gangsters, and who saves my son? An Italian goy like Mr. Vinnie and a Jewish goy, a troubler in Israel, like Mr. Elya Weinberg who still dawdles between two opinions and is a foolish communist and sometimes don't believe in nothing. Also a Polish goy, a drinking man, a *shiker,* but a good man, helps out my wife, my *ayshes chayil,* in this difficult time. *Mo rabu ma'asecho, Ha-Shem!* How manifold are Thy glorious deeds, O God!"

It was the first time that my father called me "my son" instead of "*zindele,*" "my little son," as if I was now a grown man and, like Harry Frimmer, his adopted son from Europe, also saved from a terrible fate at the hands of cruel Nazis.

JACOB'S DAUGHTER

AFTER HITLER'S ARMIES invaded the Soviet Union and we didn't get any letters from my uncle in Russia or in Poland, my father became inconsolable. Our Philco radio, bought used off a pushcart, had gone dead weeks and weeks before, and my father began spending hour upon hour in the Zukerman apartment next door listening to the news on their radio. He ran back and forth between apartments as if his own life depended on it, and my mother's constant concern for his health increased with every move he made. Since he insisted upon hearing the news reports at least twice a day, my mother decided to save up some hard-earned money to buy a new radio.

It worked out well for me as a kid because I didn't have to stand on the stairs anymore opposite the Grossman apartment on the second floor to hear my favorite programs. We had a decent radio of our own at last, and even though my parents listened predominantly to the news about the war and to the Yiddish programs, I managed to sneak in Stan Lomax giving the sports results on WOR and all the exciting stuff from "Amos 'n Andy" to "The Shadow" and to "Jack Armstrong, All-American Boy," from beginning to end. I even got my mother to listen to the "Lux Radio Theater" on Monday nights at nine, and she often cried when the stories were very sad.

I promised my piano teacher at the Henry Street Settlement that I would also listen to classical music on WQXR and WNYC, the city station, and in fact, I did for two hours each evening. At 6:30 P.M., it was the Gambarelli and Davito program—or some advertiser with a name like that—on WQXR presenting short musical pieces, instrumental and vocal. And from 7:00 to 8:30, it was "The Masterwork Hour" on WNYC, which didn't have any advertisements because it was a public station, presenting longer works like a full symphony.

I frequently missed some of the second program because it conflicted with the news and the sports reports beginning at 7:00, but still I managed to hear Felix Weingartner conducting Beethoven symphonies and Toscanini conducting the Tchaikovsky Piano Concerto with Vladimir Horowitz at the piano. The opening of this latter piece was actually the opening theme of the WQXR program, and when I was new to all this stuff, I thought that Gambarelli and Davito, the advertisers, were the names of the two composers of the work. Later on, I heard the full work on WNYC and told my piano teacher all about the wonderful performance without mentioning my early childish mistake.

Among other things, I also heard Beniamino Gigli sing "O Paradiso" from a Meyerbeer opera. As nice a voice as I had as a boy alto in Mr. Berel Braverman's symphonic liturgical choir, I couldn't ever sing like Gigli. Nor could I play the piano like a Horowitz for Mr. Edelstein, my piano teacher, who had conducted the Berlin Opera before Hitler came to power and who was a well-known pianist before he was a symphony conductor. But it didn't matter. The music was thrilling, and that's all that began to count for me. My parents didn't really listen to classical music, but they seemed to respect it. They may not have been as anxious for me to advance in musical knowledge as in sacred subjects, but they were glad that I often searched for good music on the dial instead of listening all the time to the adventure and comedy programs I loved that were frivolous in their eyes and a sign of the degradation of American culture.

After Harry Frimmer married and went to live with the Grossmans' elder daughter Celia on our fourth floor in the rear, I took advantage of the family connection to visit the Frimmers on our own floor and also the Grossmans, their parents, in their apartment on the second floor, with regularity. In truth, I wasn't looking for Celia or for Harry, our cousin Hershl, who sometimes was in the city, supposedly on leave from the Canadian air force, and sometimes wasn't. Actually, I wanted to see the youngest son Vigdor, who was several years older than I and whose baseball prowess I admired without reservation. I also went there to see the youngest daughter Feygy, who wasn't sneaking into Harry Frimmer's apartment by day anymore. She was very pretty, much nicer-looking than my friend, her brother Vigdor. He was tall and tough, and she was small and lovable.

Vigdor hung out at the candy store downstairs, and he was the star of the candy-store softball team that played on weekends in the park across the street. Once it was Big Red, but not after his flight to Brooklyn with his wife Aunt Geety. Boy, could Big Red and Vigdor hit! The fence beyond the outfield was up against a street that faced a public school building. It was not the school I went to. I think it was only a school for the first six grades, and I was in another neighboring school that included grades one through nine, officially a junior high school by title. But a school it was, and it was beyond the outfield, and a good target too for the best hitters like Vigdor and Big Red.

We didn't dare mess up the walls or the windows of the school with our own hands. We were scared of the police, whose station house was also nearby. But Vigdor messed it up but good many a time without one single twinge of conscience. I must have seen him hit two dozen home runs over the fence and over the street and break a window on the second floor of the school the way Big Red used to do. It was awesome. Nobody hit it as far or as hard so often. In fact, if some others occasionally did hit a home run, their shots barely cleared the distant fence, landing on the adjacent sidewalk. They almost never landed in the gutter or hit a passing car. But Vigdor's best blasts cleared everything and would have sailed to Canarsie had the school windows on the second floor not been in the way.

I was the team mascot because Vigdor liked me. He bought me candy and ice cream and protected me from neighborhood bullies, perhaps to compensate for taking advantage of me in childhood games when I was much younger. He was a good guy. He died in the war, I think in the Pacific theater on Okinawa just before the war against the Japanese ended.

❦

The oldest of the Grossman boys, Fayvl Grossman, also never came back. He was the first one to be drafted, being the oldest, and though he spent some years in Orlando, Florida, dishing out the payroll in a cushy job, at the last minute the army must have realized how big and strong Grossman boys were, and they sent him overseas to Europe. He landed on D day on the beaches of France a large inviting target, but I'm almost sure he got through those initial battles without a scratch. The stories I heard about why he never came back are conflicting. One version had it that he got hit in the Battle of the Bulge the winter before the Nazi government finally crumbled. Another version is that he dodged every bullet in every battle with success and died of a heart attack after entering one of the concentration camps our American armies liberated at the tail end of the war. This version is a possibility. He was the oldest of the Grossman boys and he had seen much more than the other three and understood much more and maybe suffered much more.

The two middle guys, Joe and Shmo, weren't drafted for reasons that I never found out. Their real names were Joseph and Samuel. Their parents called the older one Joey, but the younger one they called by his Hebrew/Yiddish name Shmeel. So we kids nicknamed them Joe and Shmo since these two always palled around together. But we never dared call them by those two names to their faces. It was Joey and Shmeel, lest we got our ears pinned back to our skulls. They were giants, even bigger than Fayvl and Vigdor, almost as big as the bearded Mr. Weinberg on the fifth floor, and they were mean. Not only did they hang around the candy store; they also were regulars at the poolroom down the next block where they consorted with gamblers and pool sharks and card players and dice throwers and all those other dangerous types that my mother and father continually warned me against.

My father, in fact, despaired of the Grossmans because of the antics of Joe and Shmo. "We married off Hershl Frimmer to a *prost* family," he said once in a depressed way. *Prost* meant low-class, vulgar, unlearned, even gross.

When I told my father the meaning of the English word "gross," he nodded in approbation and said, "*K'shmoy kayn hee.*" The latter part of the first Hebrew word *K'shmoy* did not refer at all to Shmeel Grossman's nickname. The word and the prefix were the beginning of a Hebrew saying that meant, "Like his name, so he is." It comes out clumsy in English, but the sense is that this particular family has a name whose meaning approximates its character. A man named Stone might have a heart as hard as a rock. A woman named Diamond might have a glittering personality. Then one uses the expression. And to my father, the Grossmans were gross.

"*Sha, shtil,*" my mother cautioned. "*Shvag.* Be silent, you two. Don't talk so much *looshn-hore,* evil speech. It's a sin. Itsik, you're a religious man. It's not nice."

Though my mother cautioned my father often enough, it was rare that I heard her pronounce her private name for him based on his middle name. My father's first name was Moyshe. Moses Mehler. I knew that he was called to the Torah as *Reb* Moyshe Yitschok *b'Reb* Aron ha-Layvee, but since I had left his hometown-society congregation to pray in the Hebrew School synagogue during the year and since I had been singing for years in Braverman's choir during the High Holy Days at other synagogues in the city, I hadn't actually heard my father's first two names plus his father's name being announced to say the blessings over the Torah scroll on the Sabbath or holidays for the longest time. The few others who addressed my father familiarly called him "*Reb* Moyshe." So it was strange for me to hear my mother addressing him as "Itsik," which was a personal way of saying "Yitschok," my father's middle name. She never called him by his first name, Moyshe. "Itsik" was something special between the two of them.

For a moment, it perplexed me. Perhaps she called him "Itsik" because there were so many Moyshes in the world. I once mentioned the many Moyshes to my father in passing jest. Not only was there Moshe Rabbeynu, the greatest of them all, who liberated the Jews from slavery in Egypt, and Moses Maimonides who was Rav Moshe ben Maimon, the smartest Jew who ever lived before Einstein, and Rav Moshe Isserles and Rav Moshe Feinstein, famous scholars and legal minds in Ashkenazic orthodox Judaism, and another Moshe whom I hesitantly mentioned to my father—Moses Mendelssohn, the grandfather of the great composer Felix Mendelssohn and a formidable Hebraic scholar of the Enlightenment whose children and grandchildren in Germany many years ago left the faith, but also, sadly enough, the dumb Moysh of my childhood who took the rap for carrying a gangster's gun that was thrust upon him near our candy store and spent years and years in jail for nothing.

With my mother's cautionary word in his ears, my father became silent. As in many other things, he respected my mother's delicate wishes. She was gentle, forgiving, and uncritical of all the world except Hitler. I never heard her say a bad word about anyone. I always marveled at her control. Perhaps a bad thought about others never entered her head at all.

Whatever the reason, I came to realize my own shortcomings early on. I could never sing like Beniamino Gigli, I could never hit a baseball like Vigdor or Big Red or Mel Ott or Hank Greenberg or Joe DiMaggio, I could never play the piano like Vladimir Horowitz or Arthur Rubinstein, or my teacher Mr. Edelstein, and I could never be the saintly soul that my dear mother was. I was a sinful boy who questioned everything, saw faults in every explanation, loved silly programs on the radio, admired baseball players above Torah scholars, and began one day looking at the girls and all that.

❦

Feygy Grossman was everyone's little darling. She, the younger sister of Celia Frimmer, née Grossman, was the youngest child and the remaining girl at home in the family, and as a consequence, fawned over and cherished in special ways. But she was, unsurprisingly, the little darling as well of all the neighbors in our five-story tenement house on the Lower East Side of Manhattan and of the tenements nearby. And after Aunt Geety and Mr. Braverman's wife, who at various times in the past engaged my confused and yearning attention to an extraordinary degree, Feygy Grossman, six years older than I, became my darling too.

She never moved slowly. She skipped, she ran, she turned cartwheels as if she were eternally practicing for the high-school cheerleading squad. She seemed always to be breathless, her cheeks aglow, her lips moist, her eyes wide and watery. Her long brownish-blond hair flew in all directions with her flight, and when she came to a stop to speak with someone, the thick strands of hair settled on her shoulders and over her brow to frame the face of an angel. Her bosom panted with anticipation, burst through her flimsy blouse, or pressed against the sweaters she wore that outlined ecstasy and unremitting joy to all who beheld her. Her skinny legs bent this way and that as she undulated under and over, side to side, head forward, head thrust back, never stationary, never frozen like a stick, the words tumbling out of her mouth so fast and so musically that she seemed to be on a permanent stage, not simply conversing, but singing and wiggling to the accompaniment of an unseen swing band.

The boys watched her all the time. She stopped games in the park with her wild entrance. Batters stepped out of the batting box and began rubbing their bats as if to get a dryer grip before hitting away. Pitchers stopped looking into the catcher's mitt for signs. They turned their heads to stare. If she stood along the first-base foul line where the parallel bars were situated up against the back fence, the second-baseman made sure to stroll over to the first-baseman, ostensibly to discuss who would be covering first on a bunt. If she wandered to the outfield and leaned against the distant fence, the outfielders suddenly began to back up as if the hitter were Vigdor himself or Babe Ruth.

Many a time, Vigdor got annoyed at her presence, especially when he was at bat. He couldn't stand the pitcher's delaying tactics and the shifting of fielders to get a better view of his sister. He wanted to hit away as soon as possible, and he wanted the fielders to stay put where they were supposed to be. He would yell at her and tell her to go on home. But she laughed at him, delighted in the effect she made on one and all, and if he ran after her, she acted as if she was racing out the gate of the playing field, only to return a moment later to watch the arc of his blow and to applaud her heavy-hitting brother.

On one occasion, Vigdor's team was playing a gang of guys from the Polish-American Catholic Church on Pitt Street. The game had actually been arranged by leaders of a neighboring Boys' Club after a fight had taken place between some of the Catholic guys and some of the guys who hung out at the candy store. It seems that the star of the Polish team, a tough-looking weight lifter called Mugger had strolled into the store to buy something or other, a rare appearance from the enemy on this turf. One of the guys in the store apparently said something to someone in Yiddish, and Mugger took it as a personal insult. He left and came back ten minutes later with five pals, and a free-for-all broke out. Result? A few split lips, some sore fists, and a blackened eye or two.

But it didn't end there. Mugger wasn't used to fair fights and standoffs. The following night he came by with a dozen friends carrying metal pipes and baseball bats. The guys at the store scattered in time, but Vinnie, the Italian storekeeper in our Jewish neighborhood, had to beg and cry real tears before he convinced the mob not to bash his whole store in. He swore that he was Catholic, that almost all Italians are Catholic and that there was no such thing as an Italian Jew. They didn't believe him at first because they knew that they were Polish and Catholic and that there were strange creatures around in the old country spoken about by their parents who were Polish Jews. They must have knocked half-a-dozen boxes of candy to the floor and ripped up mounds of the daily newspapers before Vinnie finally convinced them by reciting the Rosary from beginning to end. Luckily, they didn't get around to smashing the windows or the fixtures or the heater in the store, vandalism that would have undoubtedly pushed poor Vinnie into bankruptcy.

But Vinnie did go to the priest, and the priest went to the Boys' Club. The chief official there arranged for a softball game between the church gang and the Jewish candy-store guys as a kind of peace treaty with symbolic use of the baseball bats in a friendly game instead of as weapons in a vicious brawl.

That's when Mugger saw Feygy Grossman for the first time.

Three weeks later, Feygy disappeared. She was expected home from high-school cheerleading practice a little later than usual, so her family didn't think much of it as the afternoon hours passed by without a sign of Feygy. But by nightfall, they were worried. The eldest son, Fayvl, was already in the armed forces at Fort Dix, and the youngest boy, Vigdor, was in night school to make up some courses he had failed in high school the previous years. Consequently, the parents went running to the hardware store around the corner where the middle brothers, Joe and Shmo, were doing business. The older one, Joseph Grossman, left the store in charge of Shmo, and went out to scour the neighborhood for his kid sister Feygy.

To no avail. No sign of her anywhere, and nobody seemed to have a single notion about where she might be. The parents were distraught. Mrs. Grossman came up to the fourth floor, but not to visit with her daughter Celia who was home from work alone while her husband Harry was away at his night job as a guard at the matzoh factory on Rivington Street, a job I thought he had given up in favor of being a union organizer for the fur and leather workers. Mrs. Grossman went directly to our apartment and accosted my father just as he was returning from his job as a teacher at the yeshiva on Houston Street and just as he was about to go back down to the shul on Willett Street to say the evening prayers with a *minyan,* a quorum of ten men.

"*Rab* Moyshe," she screamed, "my little daughter is missing. She didn't come home yet from school, and she shoulda been home three hours ago. Help me! Help me!"

My father and mother were astounded by her vehemence, but very moved.

"What daughter?" my father asked. "Feygy? Little Feygy? Not home? Gone away?"

"She's not gone away, *Rab* Moyshe. She disappeared. She ain't anywhere. No Feygy, no note, no letter. I think she could be kidnaped, like the Lindbergh baby." And she started to cry.

My mother went immediately to her side to calm her down. My father seemed to be torn. He wanted to do something, but did not know what, and he had to go to shul.

"I—I'll say a special *t'filleh* in *sheel* for the safety of your child," he said finally.

But she was not consoled. "I don't want your prayers!" she screamed some more. "I want action. I want you to look. I want you to ask. I want you to scream at God for what he's doin' to me. Do I deserve it? So I didn't keep so kosher all the time. I got a good heart. I help people. My Feygy loves everybody and everybody loves her. Why her? Why me? God gotta run a fair world, not a Hitler world."

And she almost sank to the floor in agony. My father whispered to my mother who helped Mrs. Grossman up and walked her into our apartment where she gave her something to drink.

"Why don't they notify the police?" I asked my father. He scratched the back of his hair just below the hat. He was lost in thought for a moment.

"They don't wanna, I think," he said. "They're afraid she ran away by herself to live with bad people, *zoynes* and people like that. That's a big shame, a big big shame for a Jewish home. They don't want everybody out there in the world to know."

I had learned enough in the sacred books to know what kind of women my father was talking about. Though the *rebbys* in the yeshivas skipped over the parts that mentioned prostitutes, the modern teachers in the advanced Hebrew School I went to not only taught us the biblical word but also the fancy English word that was an accurate translation. I was astonished to hear the Hebrew word come from the mouth of my father.

One of the older men in the choir, who spoke a mix of English and Yiddish, had, in fact, recently asked me if I wanted to go to a *kurve*. He used the Yiddish word, instead of the ancient Hebrew. I acted like I didn't know what he was talking about, and he laughed his head off at me.

"*Sheyner boychik,*" he said to me. "Pretty boy, so you're still an innocent little kid. Wait till you get a little older. The chicks are gonna go nuts over you. You're gonna have a free ride for a good part of your life. You won't hafta go to *kurves*. Take advantage of it. I was once like that."

I didn't tell him that I had no intention of ever going to *zoynes* or *kurves*. I had decided to wait for Feygy, and now I despaired of ever seeing her again.

"Feygy is too good to do things like that," I suddenly blurted out to my father.

He looked at me in a peculiar way. "How do you know of such things?" he asked. "Too good for what? Things like what?" It was as if he hadn't even realized that he had himself brought up the subject. But he recognized the passion in my voice and my barely controlled anguish. He was anguished too, but in a different way.

"A daughter of Israel," he mumbled to himself, but not loud enough for my mother to hear. "Is it possible? In our building? Among our relatives by marriage? Even though they're *prost*? My son," he suddenly turned to me. "*Got vet helfn*. God will help. God helps the *prost* as much as the *aydle mentshn*. He even helps the *prost* more than he helps scholars and religious people and *tzaddeekim* because *a proster mentsh* needs the help more. He don't have the learning, and God forbid, he sometimes don't have the *emeeneh*, the faith to pull him through. He needs more help. How old is Feygy exactly?"

I was taken aback by his sudden question. I had always been used to his wandering meditations. They made me think of many extraneous things very often. But I rarely expected him to address me directly when he was so lost in thought and so sorrowful about the world.

"I think she had a birthday last month," I said.

"What birthday?" my father persisted.

"I think she was eighteen," I said.

"How did you know about it?" he continued.

"There was a big party for her," I said, "in front of the candy store on Sunday after the baseball game. All the guys from both teams and even some of the girls who watched the game chipped in and bought her a malted from Vinnie and other presents."

My father's face clouded over.

"The boys on the team come from here?" he asked slowly.

"Our team, yeah. The other team no. They're from around the block, from the Polish church."

"God help us!" my father exclaimed. "She is of age." Then he shook his head from side to side as if he was praying. "America can't be like the shtetl. Can't be. The *purits* has no rights here. God help her."

It was sometime later that I found out what *purits* meant. It referred to the lord of the manor in Poland. My wise father, whose only fault was that he did not look too kindly at the gentile world he had migrated from for obvious reasons, was not too far from wrong.

⬩

Marek Wojehowicz, alias Mugger, accompanied by an older man, came to the door of the Grossman apartment two evenings later. Mrs. Grossman was in bed, tended to by my mother, and Mr. Grossman was in the kitchen with me as I tried to read the Book of Psalms aloud to him from beginning to end.

I answered the door and the two strangers identified themselves and asked to come in. Mr. Grossman hesitated for a moment, then rose to the strangers. He towered over them, the one a young muscular workingman type, the other, who turned out to be his father, a gray-haired man much shorter than his short son, almost my height.

"Your daughter is safe," the old man said in heavily accented English to Mr. Grossman. "Go tell your wife not to worry and to get up from bed."

I ran into the bedroom without knocking and blurted out the news to my mother and Mrs. Grossman. Mrs. Grossman sat up in bed, let out an unearthly scream, and fainted right back into the pillow. But a bit later, my mother led the sobbing woman out into the living room in the railroad flat where she sank into a heavy sofa. She could not go any farther, and the men in the kitchen had to come from the other end into the same living room to be with her and my mother.

"My daughter!" Mrs. Grossman wailed. "Feygy, my little darling angel daughter."

"She's awright," Mugger's father said. "She sends regards to you."

"Regards?" Mrs. Grossman yelled. "*Ich chalish avek!* I'm fainting again. *Tsu a mamen* sent *min* regards? She should live so long! Tell her to come home right away before I take a stick to her!"

The old man didn't bat an eyelash. "She don't wanna come home. She likes it where she is."

"What does she like?" stormed Mrs. Grossman. For a fainting woman she seemed very loud and very determined. "She likes killing her mother? She likes driving her whole family crazy? Where is she? Bring her back this minute or I'll—I'll call the police on you."

Mugger pushed his father aside. "I love your daughter, Mrs. Grossman. I wanna marry her. I took her away. She wasn't kidnaped. She went with me willingly. I'll take care of her. You ain't got no choice. She ain't comin' back. She's stayin' with me for good."

Mrs. Grossman tried to scream, but her voice wouldn't come out with any force. She spoke a violent scream in sounds that were grating though low in volume: "What? *Heyratn a goy?* Get married with one of them? Over my dead body. I'll die first. Yankl, Yankl, you're a man. You're a Jew. Say something already."

Mr. Grossman's Hebrew name was Ya'akov, Jacob in English, Yankev in Yiddish, but his wife and others called him Yankl, a more personal Yiddish version. He stirred as if stung. He looked the young man in the eye, disregarding the young man's father, his contemporary. Then he walked over to his wife sunken into the sofa and looked at her as she simpered over my mother's protective arm. He walked back to the two men, the older and the muscular younger one. He towered over them. Again he stared at the young man. He lowered his eyes to meet his. Finally, he spoke softly, as if he didn't want to be heard, but that's the way he always spoke.

"My two sons will be home soon from work in my hardware store for supper. I hafta wait to see what they say. So you'll hafta wait." It may have been the first time I ever heard Mr. Grossman say anything more than a word or two all at once.

But Mrs. Grossman would not be squelched. She pushed my mother's arm aside and spoke up again. "I have two other sons," she said, with some pride. "The oldest one is in the army now, a soldier for the United States of America. He's fighting that sonofabitch Hitler, may he drop dead, and also fighting that Tojo, another *bestid*. My youngest son still goes to high school, but he's almost finished. All my four sons are big boys, giants, like cedar trees. You'll see."

Her voice did not sink on the last word to end a sentence, and she sounded as if she would go on forever, or until her waning strength gave out. My mother patted her brow with a handkerchief and fed her a glass of water to quiet her down.

The old man, Mugger's father, spoke too. "I also got other sons and daughters. Marek is the youngest. I got four other boys who are tougher than he is, built like a brick wall. My four girls are all beautiful and married a long time. They got four husbands that are almost like my sons, heroes, strong, afraid of nobody. You should see."

I wondered if any of Mugger's brothers and brothers-in-law could hit a baseball as far as he or Vigdor could or if they used the bats to knock heads all over the place and bust up boxes of candy too.

But my thoughts were interrupted by Mrs. Grossman who suddenly asked me to go upstairs to the fourth floor and her daughter Celia's apartment and call her and her husband down this minute.

"Hershl didn't go to work tonight. He has a little tiny cold, but he can come down here just the same. Tell Celia and Hershl the news about our dear little Feygele. Go, *yingele*." And she became tearful again.

I ran up the stairs two at a time. I didn't want to miss anything that might happen in the Grossman apartment while I was gone. It was maybe the first time in a long time that I was called *yingele*, little boy. Did Mrs. Grossman not know my name? I wasn't a little boy anymore, whether they liked it or not. I understood everything. I knew that Mugger, who could hit a baseball a mile, was doing things with Feygy. It got me a little angry, not because he was doing stuff with her—all the guys did that with all the big girls—but that Feygy let him. He said that she went away with him willingly. I couldn't believe it. Mugger was not even smart. The guys said he never graduated high school and that he was in the dumb class in junior high like 9B5 all his grown-up life. He must have repeated the grade four times. But also he wasn't Jewish and he never broke a glass at the end of their wedding. So how could she let a guy like that do stuff like that to a nice girl like her? So I didn't understand everything.

When I told Celia and Harry Frimmer the news about Feygy being safe and all that, Celia almost fainted, just like her mother downstairs. I didn't really explain everything clearly. I just said that Feygy was away somewhere with Mugger, the Marek guy. I tried to pronounce his full Polish name, Wojehowicz, but I got stuck on the last part of it.

Harry Frimmer began to shake when he heard the full name. "I'm not goin' down there," he said. "You go alone, Celia. They don't need me."

Celia started yelling at him. "They need you, they need you. Maybe they need you to translate the Polish. The father of the boy speaks Polish."

"He's speakin' English," I said.

"I ain't goin'," Harry said. "I seen enough of them. I lived in Poland all my life. I don't wanna see them no more."

Celia didn't know what to do. I wanted to get downstairs fast. So I took Celia by the hand and picked her up from her chair and led her outside to the hall and down the stairs all by myself. She was much taller than I was, but I was pretty strong.

When we came back into the room, it looked like nobody had said anything at all during the time I was away. Everybody was standing or sitting without a sound exactly where they were when I left. Maybe Mrs. Grossman was sniffling a little with her nose.

Celia fell into her mother's arms on the sofa in their living room. I thought she would crush her mother to death and also my mother, who was wiping Mrs. Grossman's brow, but Celia fell sideways toward the arm of the chair so she could continue looking out of the corner of her eye at Mugger. She looked at him very sharply, and for a very long time.

There was a knock on the door. None of us knew who could be knocking since Joe and Shmo wouldn't knock on the door of their own apartment. It was my father. I was happy to see him. He would protect us. But my mother was not happy to see him and perhaps a little afraid. She gasped audibly. Still she would not leave the side of Mrs. Grossman. My father had apparently been told by neighbors that his wife and elder son were in the Grossman apartment in the presence of unusual guests. I have no memory of where my younger brother Noosn could have been at this time. My mother would never have left him alone in our apartment. Was he being watched by another neighbor, Mrs. Zukerman, maybe, who always was willing to help out? Was he old enough to be in some school at night? Quite possible. I was older. My mother was still young, but my father was subject to all sorts of ailments. My father's face was drawn and all-seeing.

Mrs. Grossman piped up: "It is this lady's husband, *Rab* Moyshe, a scholar, a teacher of holy books. Maybe he'll say what to do."

Mugger's father removed his hat and bowed toward my father. "*Pan Rabin*," the gray-haired man addressed him. "*Pan Przewielebny.*"

My father shook his head. "I am not a rabbi, and I am not Your Excellency. Put your hat back on your head."

"His nasty son kidnaped our Feygy!" Mrs. Grossman screamed. "He took her away and God knows what he's doin' to her where. My little Feygele!" Again she cried.

"The elder of the two guests spoke again directly to my father. "My son did not kidnap the girl, *Pan Rabin*. We do not make *oblawa* in America. In America we are all friends, neighbors. My son loves the girl and wants to marry her. We have dowry money enough. She went because she wanted to go, *Pan Przewielebny.*"

My father's eyes scalded young Mugger. The tough baseball player turned his own eyes aside under the riveting gaze.

My father then looked at Mugger's father. "In our religion," he said to the old man, "we're not allowed to marry off a girl against her will. If she is over twelve and a half, she has reached the age of consent. We must ask her opinion first. And we cannot take anybody else's word for it, even yours, even mine. And to make sure that she isn't answering against her will, she must be free to speak her mind. That means that you must get her out from hiding and bring her back to her parents. She must tell her parents, her mother and her father, without you or your son around to—to influence her—what she wants to do. Then the family can come to a decision. You must bring her back immediately."

Mugger grabbed his father's arm and tugged on it with force. "Let's get the fuck outa here. They're gonna trick us. They don't believe me that I wanna marry her fair and square, then I don't believe them. Let's scramez-vous. These fuckin' Judases are too fuckin' smart."

The old father was reluctantly dragged toward the kitchen and the door. At that very moment it burst open, and Joe and Shmo entered quickly to block their way. The two giants almost pushed the thin reed of an old man and his slightly taller muscular son back into the living room.

"Who the hell are these guys?" Joe asked sharply.

"What are they doin' here?" Shmo added.

They knew, they knew. They must have been told by neighbors about the visit, like my father was. They changed the air in the room—it was like a wild wind of anticipation.

"Why are you on the sofa, Mama?" Joe asked abruptly.

"They kidnaped my baby!" she screamed. "They took Feygele away!"

"They what?" Joe asked, his voice rising.

"*Pan Rabin,*" the old father said to my father, "explain to the two brothers that we didn't kidnap. My son and his brothers have no patience with lies. The girl is safe and free and where she wants to be. The mama over there makes up stories all the time. She likes to scream and to cry. Tell her to stop, *Pan Rabin.*"

My father did not speak. My mother glared at him for a split second as if to say—don't mix in, and he remained silent. I think he whispered a prayer. Perhaps he was saying *Unu Ha-Shem, hoyshiyu nu,*—Please God, save us—from the Hallel prayers we had recently sung in shul on the *Sikkes* holiday.

Mrs. Grossman was not silent, but her voice was subdued. "*Byut a plakata ne dayut,*" she said.

Later on I found out from Harry Frimmer, who spoke Polish and Russian and Ukrainian, that these words were an old saying and that they meant—"They hurt you, but they don't let you cry." Everybody on the Lower East Side knew so many languages.

My father did speak up finally. He whispered to Joe and Shmo and explained the whole situation to them, and he also said that Mugger and his father were about to walk out because they wouldn't let Feygy come home. Joe whispered back, and Shmo suddenly left the room and went out the door. They talked some more quietly—my father and Joe, and then Shmo returned and took Joe aside and said things that even my father didn't hear.

Joe turned to Mugger and his old man. "If you wanna marry our sister, you gotta do certain things in our religion."

"What things?" Mugger asked.

"You and your father and all your brothers and brother-in-laws gotta get circumcised."

There was a moment of silence. Joe must have figured that Mugger didn't understand. "You guys gotta cut the foreskin off, like all Jews do."

Mugger burst out laughing. "Get that, Pop? The fuckin' Jews want us to cut off our cocks for them. Get that?"

I thought he would walk out immediately as he tried to do before, but he didn't. He and his father stayed put. Mugger laughed some more without moving except for turning toward his father. He even slapped his father on the back so hard that his father fell forward a few steps. I never would have done that to my father.

"It's a deal," Mugger said. "Hey shmuck, don't you know that everybody gets circumscribed these days with a clamp when they're born in the hospital? I'm circumscribed already. It's the fuckingest thing that ever was done to me. It cuts off pleasure. Pleasure, pleasure, pleasure. If I knew what they was doin' when I was a baby in the hospital, I wouldn'ta let them. But it's done, and you can't put it back. So I'm circumscribed like you said. I'm a good Jew. I can get hitched with Fay with all the blessings. Yeah, man!"

"*Pan Rabin,*" the old man asked. "Is that enough? Does it satisfy you?"

My father stirred. He seemed torn. He shook his head sadly. "It's not enough," he said. "If a proselyte is already circumcised in a medical way, but not according to the law, *k'das v'k'din,* then a drop of symbolic blood must be taken in addition. But I must hasten to add, even *mileh,* circumcision, isn't enough. One must study and not just take on conversion for the sake of marriage. One must—"

Joe interrupted my father. "*Rab* Moyshe, one must also fast a full twenty-four hours like we Jews do on Yom Kippur, the Day of Atonement. You get it?"

My father looked disturbed, but Joe would not let him speak. He turned back to the two men.

"You and your father," Joe added, "gotta fast a full twenty-four hours, let's say from sundown tomorrow night until sunset the next night. No, twenty-five hours. I made a mistake. Until one hour after sunset the next night. And you know what a full Jewish fast means? No eating and no drinking either. Not like that guy Gandhi in India who only drinks orange juice every day and calls it a fast. You can't touch nothin'. Not a thing for twenty-five hours. And you can't get laid. You just sit and pray. You don't even sleep. Got it, buster? That's the rule. That's the deal."

Mugger didn't seem to know what to say. His father looked at my father longingly, but my father turned away.

"And another thing. We don't trust you that you'll do it right. After all, it's only your word that Feygy went willingly with you. And you won't even tell us where she is or let us speak to her. So we're suspicious. Understand that? Suspicious. We could go to the cops and get her back, but we don't do things like that around here. We test our neighbors ourselves. So this is a test. You wanna prove you're tellin' the truth, you gotta do it our way."

Shmo shook his head up and down vigorously. He took off his jacket for the first time. His arms had muscles too. I think he was even bigger than Joe. He was a powerful giant, and tough little Mugger didn't look so tough next to him.

"Here's the whole deal," Joe said. "You know our hardware store on Pitt Street between Stanton and Rivington. Not too far from the church. In your territory. We got beds in there where we sleep, me and Shmeel and our other brothers when they're around."

For a moment I didn't even know for sure who Shmeel was. Then I realized that he never called his brother Shmo.

"You come to the store tomorrow afternoon with your father and all your brothers, and even your brother-in-laws, if you like. All you guys stay with us for the full twenty-five hours. We got beds in the back storage room for everybody. It'll be a big party on us. We'll monitor the fast. And we'll have a *moyhl* there, that's a religious doctor who does circumcisions, an expert, to take the symbolic drop of blood too. That's the deal. You stay with us from tomorrow evening until the day after tomorrow night."

Nobody had ever heard of such an arrangement in all our lives or of such religious laws. Mrs. Grossman wanted to scream, I think, but she couldn't. Mr. Grossman who had slunk into a corner all this time and hadn't been heard from remained attached to his corner like an errant schoolboy. My mother continued ministering to Mrs. Grossman, but my mother looked this time at my father yearningly as if to ask if all this made sense to him and if we could believe what we were hearing. My father did not return my mother's looks. He took me by the hand the way he did when I was still a little kid and began to lead me out the door not with pleasure but as if he had given up all hope for this world.

I did not hear the end of it in that room although I suspect that nothing more took place. I'm almost sure that Mugger and his father left soon after without much more being said. I don't know if the Grossman family said anything else to each other. I lingered at the door of our own fourth-floor apartment just like Mrs. Grossman did so often downstairs, with the door partially ajar to hear what I could hear. Soon enough I heard a lot of tramping feet, and I guessed that Mugger and his father and Joe and Shmo left together, so Joe and Shmo didn't have time to explain things to their distraught parents.

As for my parents, they didn't say anything about it in my presence as we walked up the stairs. My mother came along reluctantly. She wanted so much to stay with Mrs. Grossman, fearful that the unhappy woman would hurt herself in some way. But my father persuaded her that Mrs. Grossman would be all right and that my mother would be better off spending some time with me and with my kid brother Noosn, wherever he was. I think my father was actually protecting my mother. We trudged up the two flights of stairs to our fourth-floor apartment. My mother did not say a word; nor did my father. Maybe they spoke about delicate things when I was asleep. I never heard.

🎔

I did hear the end of the story pretty fast. Apparently, Shmo had sneaked up to Celia and Harry Frimmer's apartment in the rear of our fourth floor during the discussion downstairs and had prevailed upon Hershl, his brother-in-law from Poland, to wait at the street level and follow them all when they would leave the building at night. I don't know how Shmo got chicken-Harry to do this, but he did. Harry was to wait for the four men—Joe, Shmo, Mugger, and Mugger's father—and watch them waltz down the street. This way he would know what Mugger and his father looked like. When the two Polish guys split off to go in another direction, he was to follow close up and listen in to any conversation in English or Polish. Then if Mugger headed off somewhere else, he was to follow to the very end.

That's what Harry Frimmer must have done. The next evening, Mugger and his father and his four brothers and his four brothers-in-law came to the hardware store and began the amazing fast. Later that night, the *moyhl,* the ritual circumciser, came by. Much later that night, Shmo left the hardware store and went to another apartment on the Lower East Side where he found Feygy, the angel Feygy, waiting for her paramour. He pulled her out of the hideout and took her away somewhere and returned by himself to the hardware store some hours later.

The next day, the day of the full remainder of the fast, the hardware store was closed to customers. But late that evening, the ambulances arrived, and Mugger and his four brothers and his four brothers-in-law were carried off to Bellevue Hospital with their arms broken, their legs crushed, their faces bashed in, and some say to this very day their eyes blinded. Only their father wasn't touched. But the old man didn't utter a word, neither to the ambulance drivers and the emergency medical men, nor to the cops who arrived on the scene at almost the same time. The old man remained silent as if struck dumb, as if he could only speak to *Pan Rabin,* my father *Rab* Moses Mehler, who was inevitably not there.

Joe and Shmo were taken to the station house for questioning, but twenty-four hours later, a full day after the extraordinary fast and the unbelievable violence, they were let go. All of the five Wojehowicz sons and all the four sons-in-law must have stayed in the hospital for weeks, maybe months. They didn't die, but they didn't live very well either.

My mother and I were with the Grossmans when Joe and Shmo came home from the police station a full day after the fast was over, after the *oblawa*. They were not welcomed as returning heroes though we kids at the candy store spoke of their prowess as if they were Hercules and Samson and Superman combined.

Mr. Jacob Grossman opened his mouth for the first time in days and days. "What have you done?" he screamed at the top of his lungs at his giant sons. His voice was astonishingly strong and loud. "You have given me trouble, only trouble, all of us trouble. You have made me hated by all the people living here, even the Jews who don't do such things, but especially the *goyim*, the gentiles that we gotta live with. Who do you think you are, Shimin and Layvee?

He struggled for breath, then continued breathlessly.

"We are few in number. They will get together against me and kill me and you and you and you, and I'll be finished, me and my whole family forever. I curse you two! On my deathbed I'll curse you! You have brought shame on my house."

Joe and Shmo did not flinch before their father's shocking imprecation. They looked squarely at him.

"Are we gonna let some stranger make a whore out of our sister?" Joe said. Shmo mumbled as if repeating the same words.

♥

The Wojehowicz family and all the other gentile neighbors never got together against the Grossman family to kill them or even hurt them, but our older guys at the candy store below never played another baseball game with the guys from the church, and I never saw Feygy again either. I heard that she was sent to a relative in another city the way my beautiful Aunt Geety was sent by her father to us on the Lower East Side some years before to be away from the dangers of her own hometown and to find among us a proper husband.

Harry Frimmer, who never revealed to me how he had managed to find Feygy's hiding-place, told me that she was dragged away kicking and screaming. According to Harry, when the family—Mr. and Mrs. Grossman, Joe, Shmo, Celia, Harry, and Vigdor before he was drafted—went to visit Feygy in a distant city some time later, she almost spat at them in front of other relatives who were looking after her.

"A man dies for sex," Celia said to her little sister, trying to smooth her silken hair and to mollify her, "but a woman is wiser and lives for sons." Her heart bled.

"I let Mugger's glances dart at me," Feygy said ruefully, "because I wanted him. But your sons," she screamed at her parents, "two bullies, would not have it so. My brothers!"

They did not respond. Feygy looked at her haggard elder sister. "I shall grow old without love as you do," she said bitterly. She walked away from them all, spoke to the walls of her new house that would never be a home for her.

"What is this new style," Mrs. Grossman said, "that America and the movies and the books have brought to our family? What, then, is this love you have learned in this golden land that we thought saved our lives and Hershl's life and still kills us? A death little by little! My grandfather just taught us to be Jews and to have sons and daughters and build a family for the future. That's love. What is this love you speak of?"

Feygy snarled. "Jacob loved Rachel. He knew what love was. But your brutal sons, my brothers, spring in the night like murderers to crush my heart. We are special they rave, chosen by God to be apart from everybody else. I crave togetherness, Mama. That is love."

I was also told years later that Feygy never married, never had children. Her sister Celia did raise four children with Harry, but in a relationship that was almost as loveless. Her two brothers who ran the hardware store and survived the war struggled to make a living in a decaying quarter of the Lower East Side. They managed. But Feygy, the two other soldier brothers who were killed in the war, including my friend Vigdor, and the parents, Mr. and Mrs. Jacob Grossman, inadvertently received the full measure of the father's curse.

THE BLACK PRINCE
OF THE HEBREW SCHOOL

VIGDOR GROSSMAN was a lot older than I was and twice as big as I was when I was a kid, so my mother let him take care of me when she had to do janitor's work in our tenement. All that time, she never let me cross the street by myself, but if Vigdor was with me, she let me do anything.

My baby brother Noosn would soon be as big as I was now, and my mother promised me that I would be much bigger by then too. This should have made me happy, but all it meant was that I would have to cross him and take him places and take care of him just the way Vigdor was doing now. That was one of the advantages of being the baby brother in a family. Noosn wouldn't have to take care of anybody, unless the mother of another boy in another family would ask him to take care of a son who didn't have an older brother. I didn't really want ever to take care of Noosn. But I was lucky because Vigdor Grossman always wanted to take care of me.

He told me things. "Do you know," he said once when we ran back home to go to the toilet, "that everybody got worms in their stomach and when you go number two, the worms crawl out?"

I did a lot of looking from then on in whenever I went number two. And even though I never saw any worms, I worried a lot about what those worms were doing while they were in my stomach.

Another time, Vigdor took me all the way up to 34th Street on the subway and to Macy's Department Store so that we could look at Santa Claus in his red uniform, and that was when Vigdor told me another story.

"Do you know," he said, "that Santa Claus is Jewish?"

I wasn't shocked by this bit of information because all of the old people with beards around the block were Jewish. But Vigdor told me much more.

"Your father who's a Hebrew teacher," he said, "don't let you go to see Santa Claus because Santa Claus married a *shikse,* which is a non-Jewish girl. From that time on, he was kicked out of the Jewish club, and he became an Eskimo. Now whenever Santa Claus *davns* in Hebrew, he don't face east to Jerusalem, he faces north to the North Pole. That's why Jewish kids don't get presents from him. We don't want 'em. He's a traitor. He faces the wrong way."

How did Vigdor know about *davnen* in Hebrew? That was because of me. His mother and father never sent him to Hebrew School, and he never got Bar Mitzvahed either. But once when I had to go to Hebrew School after I didn't go anymore to *Reb* Duvidl who beat me with a *kantshik* and my mother couldn't take me, she sent Vigdor with me to watch me cross the streets. My mother told him to stay near the school and wait an hour and a half until my class was finished and then take me home.

But something funny happened. While Vigdor was hanging around outside in the street, the Hebrew School janitor came out to watch him. Vigdor had begun a game of "Johnny on the Pony" with some of the older kids who were waiting to go to the next class in the Hebrew School. Vigdor was the roughest and toughest guy in the game, and his team won every jump because of him.

But the janitor, a man with a beard named Mr. Slomowitz, got very angry. He grabbed Vigdor by the ear when Vigdor was hunched over another guy on the pony line. That was the only way that Mr. Slomowitz could reach Vigdor's ear since my friend was really too tall for him.

"What kind of a Jew are you?" he said to Vigdor. "You play a stupid game called 'Johnny'? What are you, a goy? You should play a game called 'King David,' or 'Joshua at Jericho,' or 'Jacob at the well.' That's what you should play. 'Johnny' is for *goyim.* Are you Jewish?"

Vigdor nodded.

"You go to cheder, to Hebrew School, to yeshiva?"

Vigdor shook his head no.

"You had a Bar Mitzvah?"

Again no.

"You know how to *davn*, how to say prayers?"

Another no.

"Come with me," said Mr. Slomowitz.

He took Vigdor by the hand and led him into the Hebrew School and downstairs into the boiler area alongside the school's synagogue. He sat Vigdor down near all the pipes and gave him a *siddur*, a prayerbook. And he began teaching Vigdor how to read Hebrew.

I heard all about it directly from Vigdor when I finished my class. My mother and father had to pay a dollar a week for me to learn all that stuff in the upstairs school, but Vigdor was getting it all for nothing downstairs from the janitor of the school. So the two of us started going together to Hebrew School on a regular basis. I went upstairs, and Vigdor went downstairs.

Soon enough, Mr. Slomowitz found some other kids in the street who never went anywhere to learn Jewish stuff, and soon enough they joined Vigdor in a little class in the boiler room.

The principal of the Hebrew School, another bearded man named Dr. Shulman, must have heard about it when he looked out the window and didn't see kids playing "Johnny on the Pony" anymore. He came downstairs to investigate and found Mr. Slomowitz teaching kids in the boiler room. He started yelling at Mr. Slomowitz right in front of us when we were going home from class and when I was looking for Vigdor to take me home.

"You're not a teacher here," he yelled. "You're an ignorant janitor. You don't have a teacher's license. You don't even get paid for it."

"I'll get paid in *eylem habaw*, in the next world," Mr. Slomowitz said. "I don't wanna get paid here for teachin' *Teyreh*. If you get paid here, you don't get paid there."

It was the same Torah as my father's *Toyreh*, but it sounded different in Mr. Slomowitz's voice. Even the giant Mr. Weinberg didn't say *Teyreh* though in many other words he spoke just like Mr. Slomowitz. Were they both Litvaks, not Galitsyaners like Ma and Pa? One Litvak teaches kids how to *davn* from a *siddur,* and another Litvak don't believe in *davnen* at all. Strange world!

"You can't teach on our premises. It's not your classroom."

Mr. Slomowitz shrugged his shoulders. "If the boiler room is not my room, then I can't work here and make the heat."

Dr. Shulman didn't say anything else, and as far as I know, he didn't come downstairs ever again into the boiler room.

When my father came in once to pay the small tuition for my Hebrew School studies, he spoke to Mr. Slomowitz who told him about the principal.

"Aren't you afraid they'll fire you?" my father asked.

"Ich hob im tif in drerd," Mr. Slomowitz said, *"mitn job tsuzamen. Ich vil nit vern raych fun aza shmutsike meluche far eyn Yidn."* All of that meant that Mr. Slomowitz had Dr. Shulman deep in the earth along with the job because he wasn't gonna get rich from such dirty work for a Jew.

My Hebrew teacher Mr. Himmelfarb told us about the Jewish settlement in Palestine, the *yishuv,* and how they built whole cities like Tel Aviv.

"Mr. Himmelfarb," I asked, "who does all the dirty work in the Jewish cities? Stuff like making the boilers give heat or like cleaning up all the *shmuts* in the shuls and in the street. Outside of Mr. Slomowitz and my mother, nobody who is Jewish wants to do this work."

Mr. Himmelfarb didn't know what to say. First he looked angry, then he looked sad, then he laughed. "When the Jewish people have their own country again in the Land of Israel," he said, "not only will there be Jews who clean the streets and stoke the boilers, but there'll also be Jewish policemen and Jewish crooks and Jewish showgirls and Jewish playboys. We'll have everything, just like every other respectable nation!"

I told Vigdor that I didn't believe that for a minute. Jewish crooks, okay. We had them hanging around Vinnie's candy store already. Jewish playboys—well, the guys from the candy store did play softball in the neighborhood park, and Vigdor was the best at all kinds of games. What was so extraordinary about that? But Jewish policemen? I never saw one in my life.

And Jewish showgirls? What would they show? They never showed me any-thing.

But Vigdor said I was still a kid and that he knew some girls who showed him everything. On all our trips together, he never showed me those show-girls. Some things you never find out in this world. And some things you gotta keep quiet about. I never told my father what Mr. Himmelfarb said about crooks and showgirls in Israel because I kind of knew that my father wouldn't like the idea at all. Then he might take me out of the Hebrew School where we sang and danced and played Hebrew games and acted in plays, and he might put me back with an old *rebby* with a *kantshik* like *Reb* Duvidl who beat me up once. Sometimes you gotta protect yourself even from your own father!

My father didn't always try to protect me. I forgot to tell about the year be-fore Mr. Himmelfarb became my Hebrew teacher. That was when Miss Morgenstern was my very first teacher in the school. She taught me how to read Hebrew in a new accent that made my father laugh even though he hardly ever laughed. She was so fat that when she laughed, her whole body shook so much that I thought everything would fall off. But she was also the one who taught me how to dance and play Hebrew games and act in He-brew plays that were sometimes in Yiddish. She didn't have to teach me how to sing. I was already in Berel Braverman's symphonic liturgical choir for a long time where I sang a few solos on special Sabbaths when the choir per-formed in a big shul with a famous *chazn* who is a cantor.

"He sings like an angel," Mrs. Braverman said one Sabbath noon as we all stood around the tables filled with food for the *kiddush,* ready to eat a ton. And she gave me a full swat on the tush as she praised my singing. I ran away from her because I didn't want her to touch me anymore but also because I was more interested in the creamed herring that was out on the tables and the honey cake with nuts. I skipped the tiny cups of wine set on each table for the *kiddush* prayer that the chazn was about to sing because I only drank wine on Friday nights and at the Pesach Seder. Too much wine upset my stomach. I certainly didn't go for the little cups of golden schnapps that were on separate trays alongside the wine. Some of the men and even ladies preferred the schnapps to the wine even though it forced them to say a different *brooche,* not the blessing on the wine.

Once the big fat heavy-chested tenor in our choir said that, as a boy, he sang with Jan Peerce and Richard Tucker, and he tried to pour some of that stuff down my throat. He said the schnapps would make me roar like a lion instead of sing like an angel. He also said it would give me balls. But I twisted out of his grasp because I preferred to sing like an angel and I already had balls. No *chazn* ever praised a tenor in a choir. That was against the rules. But the rabbi in this shul who didn't like the chazn because he repeated so many words in chanting the prayers told our tenor that he had a golden voice. I concluded that his beautiful sound came from drinking so many little cups of the golden schnapps.

Mrs. Braverman was almost as fat as the tenor in our choir but not as fat as my first Hebrew teacher, Miss Morgenstern. She could sing too. It seems that fat people have strong voices. But what amazed me most was that Miss Morgenstern could also dance. She had spindly legs, and I always expected her to collapse on the ground whenever she showed us a few dance steps. But her skinny legs never buckled. For us, that was the real miracle of Chanukah, not the story she told us about the oil in the Temple.

On the Sunday of Chanukah, my mother and father came to the school with all the other mothers and fathers to watch us act in a play and spin the dreidl in holiday games. My mother carried my little brother Noosn in her arms. I didn't dare tell her to put Noosn down for a while and let him try to walk, for two reasons. First, because all my classmates would think I was jealous, and second, because whenever Noosn tried to walk, everybody laughed and said what a cute kid he was and they wouldn't pay any attention to me anymore.

I had a part in the Chanukah play. I was dressed up like a dreidl, and every time Miss Morgenstern and all the kids sang the dreidl song—*Sevivon, sov, sov, sov*—I turned around and around like a real dreidl showing all four Hebrew letters on four sides of me. There were five other kids also dressed like dreidls, but I was in the middle of the line right in front of the audience.

The people clapped. My mother couldn't clap because she was holding Noosn, and my father never clapped for anybody. He just sat there.

When we were going home, my father took us into the principal's office along with Miss Morgenstern.

"When is he gonna learn *a poosek chimish mit Rashi?*" my father asked angrily. That meant that he wanted me to learn the Torah with the famous commentary written by Rashi, like he did all the time, and not fool around with dancing and spinning like a dreidl.

Dr. Shulman smiled. He always smiled at parents. He never smiled at the janitor, Mr. Slomowitz, and he only yelled at kids.

"In God's good time," Dr. Shulman said. "In a happy hour."

This didn't satisfy my father.

"What good is all the singing and dancing?" my father asked. "That's for girls. A boy should learn the holy books."

My mother freed one hand from Noosn and put it on my father's arm.

"Show respect, Itsik," she said to my father. "You're talkin' to the principal."

Dr. Shulman jumped in. "*Reb* Mehler shows me enough respect, Mrs. Mehler. Don't worry. I'm not insulted. I have to show respect to *him*. He's a *gaon* in the Torah, a genius. Would that we had more like your husband in *klal Yisroel*."

My father scowled. Either he was not impressed or he was very embarrassed by all the compliments.

"I'm sure," he said, "that Mrs. Morgenstern is a fine woman and a good mother and wife. But she shouldn't be teaching dancing in a religious school. She shouldn't even be singing in front of so many men. A woman's voice is an enticement."

Miss Morgenstern did not smile. She stood up. She wasn't so tall, but she was very wide. She looked at Dr. Shulman and then at my father.

"When Miriam sang and danced at the Red Sea, you would have told her to stop singing and stop dancing? And when she repeated holy words from the Song of Moses at the Sea, "*Shiru la-Shem ki gaw'o gaw'aw, sus v'ruchvo rawmaw va-yum,* would you have told her not to say such things? Moses didn't."

"*B'vakashah, g'veret,*" said Dr. Shulman. "Be respectful."

"I won't be silent," Miss Morgenstern replied sternly. "And I can only be respectful to someone who shows respect for me. And I'm not Mrs. Morgenstern. I'm not married. I don't have a husband. I don't have children. These are my children. Your son is my child. And I must educate him in Hebrew and in Torah not only to understand these things but also to love them and to love the Jewish people and the ancient land of Israel. In the *Sh'ma* it says *v'awhavtaw,* and you shall love God, even before it says *v'shinantom,* you shall teach the laws to your children. The two go together, but first you must teach a child to love."

My father lowered his head. "*Yasher koyech,*" he whispered. "You have honored me with a good word. You are the mother of all the children."

He rose, and my mother with Noosn rose with him. I did too, as I always did in front of my father and guests.

"Stay for the party," Dr. Shulman said. "There is cakes and other goodies. All a hundred percent kosher."

"We must go home now," my father said. "The baby is tired, my wife is overworked. I must help her put the child to sleep and then I have my *sefurim* to study. My *tachshitl* here can stay for the party instead of us. Avigdor Grossman, your unofficial student, is also here in the auditorium. He lives in our building. He's a good young man. He'll take my *kaddish* home. Come, Rivke."

My father turned to me and gave me some change. "Here are a few cents to put into the *Keren Kayemes* box for the Zionists in *Erets Yisrool.* I saw the blue-and-white boxes on the tables in the auditorium."

But Dr. Shulman wouldn't let my parents escape so fast.

"Tell me, *Reb* Mehler," the principal said. "I need a moment's help from a man of your learning. I have to make a speech this week to a teachers' group. I want to quote from the Talmud, the statement that a teacher is even more important than a mother and a father. Where can I find it to get it exact?"

My father whispered to the principal as if he didn't want others to hear.

"In the *Gemoore Sanhedrin, daf keef-alef,* near the bottom of the first side of the page. The words of Rabbi Elazar Ben Azariah. Your mother and father give you this world; your teacher gives you this world and the-world-to-come."

Dr. Shulman beamed as everybody moved to the door. "We are important people, you and me, *Reb* Mehler. We guide the children of the next generation. I knew I could depend on you."

My father shook his head. "The same page says that every *tzaddik*—the most righteous man or woman—does sins in his life. And the other side of *daf keef-alef,* the second *umed,* tells of King Menasheh, son of the righteous and learned King Chezkiyeh. Menasheh worshiped idols for fifty-two years and did the most evil things in spite of the best and holiest education given to him by his parents and by his teachers. It didn't help. So we shouldn't praise ourselves so much."

"I stand corrected," Dr. Shulman said. "We sometimes fail. We are not God."

My father did not stop. Just a little while before, he looked like he had wanted to leave. But once he was in a Talmudic discussion, all of time came to a halt.

"King Menasheh did repent finally, the *Gemoore* tells us, but only because of *yiseerim.* You would say *yisoorim* in your pronunciation, Mr. Principal. I don't speak modern Hebrew."

"*Yisoorim?*" I asked. "Troubles? What troubles?" They were the only words I spoke at this meeting. I didn't want my father to stop.

"Yes, my little son," my father said. "Troubles. When Menasheh was conquered by Babylonia and went into exile and maybe suffered serious personal illness and great losses in his family and in the Jewish people that he did not rule anymore, then he repented and called out in anguish to the God of his forefathers. Only then did he give up foreign gods and the ways of the world. Only then. Not his father or mother or teachers could succeed the way troubles succeeded in opening his eyes. Let's go home."

Dr. Shulman led my father to the door. Miss Morgenstern led my mother. I followed them all, thinking of all the troubles that had already come in Europe.

"One more question, *Reb* Mehler," Dr. Shulman said. "Why didn't you put your son into your yeshiva next door? After all . . ." He didn't finish the sentence.

My father was silent for a moment.

My mother spoke up. "He's a sick child. He can't go till half-past seven o'clock at night like all the other yeshiva boys. The doctor won't let. He can only go a little. So he goes here."

My father shook his head in agreement as he headed toward the door. "It's also not such a good thing," he added, "for a son and a father to be in the same school together. The father when he's a teacher in the same school must not play favorites."

He motioned to my mother, who followed him out the door. I went past my mother quickly because I thought Miss Morgenstern would hit me for all the rotten things my father said to her earlier in the meeting, but instead she grabbed me and hugged me and held me tight for a long time after my parents left the principal's office. Only my mother always hugged me like that. Maybe Miss Morgenstern really *was* the mother of all the children, like my father had said.

▼

I saw three parades in the street with Vigdor one day soon after. Ma let Vigdor take me for a long walk on a Sunday morning. She even packed up sandwiches and cookies for the two of us. I liked a roll with lettuce and tomato in it, but Vigdor ate peanut butter and jelly inside two pieces of plain bread. Ma made two sandwiches for Vigdor because he was so big and strong and needed a lot of sandwiches to fill up his belly.

Vigdor said to me: "You're a sickly kid. You had triple pneumonia when you were a baby. You can't play baseball like me, or touch football, or paddle tennis with the girls on the other side of the park, or even jacks, which is a real girl's game, and you're not allowed to run too much, so you gotta walk for exercise. Walk with me."

So Vigdor took me far, far away from our tenement where we lived to-

gether, he on the second floor with his parents and only two of his big brothers because Fayvl was in the army fighting Hitler and without his two sisters,
one being married and the other, his little sister Feygy who was very pretty,
having disappeared, and me on the fourth floor with my baby brother Noosn
who was almost always in the arms of my mother and couldn't walk anywhere with us on a cold Sunday morning just before winter came.

We walked past Houston Street on Avenue C where all the numbers
come up on street signs. There was no First Street. But there was Second,
Third, Fourth, and so on. I was surprised to see almost as many pushcarts on
Avenue C as there were near my block on Willett and Rivington. Some of
these pushcarts rested on wooden sticks in a holder that was like a table leg;
some were on wheels. Some of the men alongside wore caps and some only
yarmulkes even though it was pretty cold. Some of them had beards, some
not. The not-beards were not so religious, but they also yelled in Yiddish and
said Hebrew words like *Rachmono litslun*—God save us—when a customer
wanted a lower price. My father said those were Aramaic Hebrew words
from the Talmud, but that didn't help much anyway if the customer was too
poor to pay more.

The yelling and screaming floated above our heads and mixed, as always,
with the same smells of food and leather and other things that reminded me
of Clinton Street, where my father had his synagogue. I could hear all the
yelling even though I was wearing a heavy cap with ear muffs. Vigdor wasn't
wearing anything. He was a not-religious, and he was so strong that he never
felt cold.

After Fourth Street, came Fifth, then Sixth, then Seventh. Then we
walked sideways to the Avenues: from Avenue C to B to A, then to First Avenue and then to Second Avenue.

"Why is there a First Avenue," I asked Vigdor, "but not a First Street?"

"Because," he said, "if there would be a First Street, you wouldn't have
any more stupid questions to ask."

I didn't think the question was so stupid. Actually, Vigdor was a little bit
stupid himself because I could read better than he could and he was much
taller than I was and a lot older and would soon be graduating high school in

the stupid class. I never called him that because my father said to me that I should never call anybody stupid, not a son or a daughter or a student or a friend or an enemy. Vigdor didn't really call me stupid; he just said my question was stupid. So he wasn't disobeying my father's advice either. Anyway, a smart person can also ask a lot of stupid questions.

I gave myself answers. First Street was not wiped out by a hurricane. Otherwise there would have been a big empty hole between Houston Street and Second Street. But since Houston Street was really the first street on the other side of our park, it seemed to me that Houston Street was once upon a time called First Street. Then somebody named Houston changed the name to make himself famous, and abracadabra, First Street disappeared. Better that way. No street should be the first street in the world.

When we got to Avenue B and Seventh Street, we came to another park, just like the one in our neighborhood except maybe bigger. This one had more trees and looked like the country places I only saw in the movies but never for real. It was the Garden of Eden. In fact, since the other side of the park was Avenue A and since after Avenue A came First Avenue, I knew that this place was once the Garden of Eden.

"God created the world starting here," I said to Vigdor. He looked at me strangely. "When God began, He stood between First Avenue and Avenue A and said, *Let there be a world and a Garden of Eden for starters. This is the beginning,* He said. *On this side of Me begins Avenue A in one direction, and on this side of Me begins First Avenue in the other direction. This is the center of the world.*"

"Why did God put First Avenue on this side and not Avenue A?" Vigdor asked. That was really a smart question, which proves the opposite—that even stupid people can ask smart questions.

"If you take this side," I figured aloud, "First Avenue and onward goes all the way to California. Therefore, God needed a lot of streets, up to a million or a zillion. So He worked with numbers. But this other side goes straight to the Atlantic Ocean, which is pretty near since Ma once took me on a train to Coney Island and the ocean. So all God needed on this other side was a few streets until He got to the ocean. That meant He could use twenty-six letters in the alphabet. No need for a zillion numbers. Get it?"

I don't think Vigdor did. But it didn't matter. He liked me when I was smart because he couldn't be it. And I liked him when he was strong.

On First Avenue we saw our first parade. The men were carrying a statue of Jesus and some paintings of other people, and a priest was sprinkling holy water on everything and everybody. It was so cold I expected the water to turn to snow before it hit the ground.

"Why is Jesus hanging on a plus sign?" I asked Vigdor. I sometimes asked him silly questions, because he was older, and if I didn't ask such questions every now and then, he would know that I thought he was stupid.

"That's not a plus sign, you dope," he said to me. "A plus sign has the sideways thing in the middle. This one has it near the top, so it's a cross. Jesus is nailed on the cross."

"I feel sorry for him," I said. "When Ma wants to put a picture on the wall, she doesn't nail the picture to the wall at the two top ends. She puts a nail on the wall and then a cord behind the picture and then hangs the cord on the nail. Jesus wouldn't hurt so much if his mother had done it Ma's way."

"Yeah," scowled Vigdor. "Then the cord would have to go around his neck and he would be choked to death. What good is that?"

I thought a while without speaking, like my father often did.

"The cord could go around his chest," I said finally, "not his neck. The Christians are cruel to keep him nailed up like that. They don't have any *rachmoones*." I think Vigdor knew that meant pity, but I decided not to tell him. He hated a lot of people, and I didn't want him to hate the Christians for keeping Jesus nailed to the cross.

On Second Avenue we saw our second parade. This time it was a Jewish parade. A bunch of old men with long beards were carrying a Torah up the street, and many many boys with women in the rear were following along and singing and even dancing. That confused me because I thought that only Miss Morgenstern and the students in the Hebrew School including me did all that dancing.

"What are they carrying the Torah for?" Vigdor asked me. I never liked it when he asked me questions. That's not the way it was supposed to be. He was older.

"They're carrying it to a shul," I said. "They bought a new Torah, which takes a long time to write out by hand and costs a lot of money. So they're celebrating because they now will have a new holy Torah to read from. The parade is the celebration."

"I think," said Vigdor, "that it's part of a play. You see all them theaters there? They show Jewish plays, and this is a scene from one a them plays. If you like what you see, you pay money and go inside and see the whole shebang. All them people in the parade are really actors."

I didn't argue with Vigdor because I wanted him to be right. But I knew he was wrong. That was a real Torah, and those were real people, and those were not fake beards, and the dancing was not fake dancing—it was like the way King David danced in the streets of Jerusalem long ago, except that an older boy from my father's yeshiva told me that David was almost naked when he danced, which is why his wife Michal got angry at him, while all these Jews on Second Avenue were dressed in heavy coats against the cold, cold weather.

I joined the parade and danced with them, and Vigdor walked alongside and laughed and laughed at me. I didn't mind at all.

"You're not such a sick kid," he said. "You been faking it. You can dance! You can sing!"

"The Torah makes me strong and healthy," I sang out.

"Bullshit," Vigdor said. "My walking exercise makes you strong and healthy. Soon you'll be as big and strong as me, and we'll both go in the army and kick the shit outa that bastard Hitler."

On Third Avenue, called, I think, the Bowery, we saw our third parade that was not really a parade because nobody marched. Near every doorstep, some guy was stretched out on the ground and sleeping. Sometimes, if the man was not curled up into a ball, I could see a red face, pock-marked, stubbles of hair on the chin and cheeks, sores on the nose, blood on the eyebrows. Sometimes, I saw a hand out of the pocket of a torn coat, holding a bottle. And sometimes, a hand was missing, or a foot. There were so many of them on both side of the street on the sidewalks along the line of houses and stores that they looked like a grim parade without movement of a dying army.

"They're Bowery bums," Vigdor said. "They're useless."

I started to cry.

Vigdor grabbed me. "Let's go to the next Avenue, maybe Fourth Avenue."

An elevated train came roaring by above us that drowned out his words and covered my sniffles. It gave me time to think. We didn't go yet to Fourth Avenue. We walked up Third Avenue between the shadows from the rails above us and the cold sun that peeked through every other girder. I looked at all the sleeping men. I looked for a sign. I looked for troubles that would change them suddenly, like my father said, and make them give up foreign gods. I looked for Nazi storm troopers who must have stacked them all here and put the bruises on their broken faces. I wondered why they hadn't learned the right things from their mother and father and teachers and had to wait for troubles on the street in the shadows of the elevated subway.

Then I saw one of them sitting up. He broke the line of sleepers and the parade of stretched-out bodies that hardly moved. The man smiled at me when I came up to him. He was black, and he had a yarmulke on his head.

"You wanna come with me?" I asked him. "I'll take you to Mr. Slomowitz who's the janitor of the Hebrew School on Houston Street. He grabs kids off the street who never learned Hebrew and don't go anywhere, and he teaches them for nothing to *davn*—that means to say prayers in Hebrew—and to read the Torah and the Haftorah. Come with me. It won't cost you a cent."

"What are you doin'?" Vigdor screamed at me. "The guy ain't even Jewish."

I paid no attention to Vigdor even though I liked him. It was clear that the man with troubles had a yarmulke on and was a black Jewish prince from Africa. I once read about Ethiopian Jews who were sons of King Solomon, a king who kept to the teachings of his father David for at least fifty-two years. So what did Vigdor know? He still didn't know how to read Hebrew too well after all the time Mr. Slomowitz spent with him.

"I'm hungry," the black man said.

I opened the bag my mother provided for me and gave him my sandwich. I kept the cookies for myself.

Vigdor yelled again at me. "You can't do that, you idiot! You gotta eat that sandwich yourself. You're a sick child. At least, give him only half. Your mother cut the sandwiches in half."

The man took both halves of my lettuce-and-tomato sandwich. I let him. He ate them both up pretty fast.

"I'm cold," he said.

Vigdor jumped in front of me. "You're not givin' him your coat," he said.

I was wearing a long heavy coat that my mother had gotten from her brother, Uncle Oosher, who was Aunt Geety's father and who brought me chocolate candy bars whenever he visited us. Sometimes he brought clothing. The coat was a little too big on me and too long, but it didn't touch the ground if I didn't bend my knees, and it sure did keep me very warm. I could have given the man my coat because even though he was sitting on the ground with his legs folded in front of him, I could tell that he wasn't so tall. Maybe my coat would have gone to his knees and not all the way around his belly missing the buttons, but my coat had a long belt which he could have used to tie it up and hold it tight, and that would have made the coat good enough to keep him warm. But Vigdor didn't let me.

"Maybe Mr. Slomowitz will find you a coat while you're learning to *davn*," I said. "Come with me."

The black man jumped to his feet as if he wasn't sick or drunk or anything like that. I guessed right. He was pretty short and could have used my coat successfully. I even think he was skinny enough to button it and would not have had to rely on the belt to keep it around him. We walked down Seventh Street back to Second Avenue, the two of us next to each other, with Vigdor, twice as tall as both of us, trailing behind. Vigdor was grumbling all the way.

"Eat at least one of my sandwiches. Your mother'll kill me."

I didn't eat. I hated peanut butter and jelly.

We turned right and continued walking on the numbered streets in backward order—Seventh, Sixth, Fifth, Fourth—down Second Avenue past all the Jewish theaters. The Torah parade had long since gone. The sound of feet tramping and dancing and voices raised in song had long since vanished. Just the three of us in cold weather, with other people walking by silently, blowing on their hands, not even looking at the three of us. They must have thought we were tough and kept their distance.

At Houston we turned left and walked all the way on a fairly straight line to the park and the yeshiva and the library and the Hebrew School. I wasn't tired. I ran down the steps to the boiler room and called Mr. Slomowitz. I presented the black man to him.

"We found him on the street—a black Jew from the Queen of Sheba. He needs to learn to *davn* and he needs a coat for the cold weather and he doesn't have any money."

Mr. Slomowitz looked at him cross-eyed.

"*Du bist a Yid?*" he asked.

"He's not from Europe," I said. "He doesn't speak Yiddish. He's from Africa. Mr. Slomowitz wants to know if you're a Jew."

"I'm from the lost ten tribes," the black man said. "The tribe of Dan."

"Did you hear that, Mr. Slomowitz?" I said gleefully.

Vigdor turned to Mr. Slomowitz. "Don't blame me," he said. "This kid does what he wants. He picks up people. He gave him his sandwich to eat."

At that moment, Dr. Shulman came down the stairs to go to the basement bathroom. He didn't go into the boiler room; he just peeked in.

"What are you doing now, Slomowitz?" he bellowed. "You're picking up Bowery bums from the street? What are you going to teach them? *Borey pree ha-gawfen?* The blessing for wine? Don't forget *sheh-ha-kol,* the blessing for whiskey. This school is going to become a den of drunkards and thieves."

Mr. Slomowitz waved his hand in derision. "I need a goy to help me clean in my old age. I need a *Shabes goy* to put on the lights in the shul on *Shabes.* Don't worry. I'll pay him out of my own pocket. It won't cost you a penny."

Dr. Shulman went into the bathroom.

"These modern Jews," Mr. Slomowitz said, "they learn a lot of holy books, but they're not holy themselves. You wait here and see if that principal says the prayer he's supposed to when he gets out of you-know-where. He should be praising God for keeping the holes open for number one and number two, but he won't say a word. I guarantee. Teach the children to sing and dance and speak Hebrew and to go live in Eretz Yisroel with socialists and Arabs—that's what these modern Jewish teachers believe. But to say a prayer with the whole heart and soul—that's not for them. Come, *shvartser goy,* I know your tricks. You're from *Sheyvet Dan* like I'm the son of Tsar Nicolai. I'll give you a job helping me, and I'll even find you a coat maybe. Friday and Sunday you'll have off during the day so that you can go to a mosque or church, whatever you want. You can drink one drink a day in the morning after we finish *davnen* every day and a little bit cake with it and three drinks on *Shabes* that has three holy meals. No more. Not a drop more. If you drink more than that and you become a *shiker,* you can go back and freeze on the Bowery. You got a family?"

The black man was frightened by all this talk, but he summoned up enough strength to shake his head meaning no.

"Then if you want, you can sleep here in a room behind the boiler where there's a mattress on the floor. And I'll give you five dollars a week from the twenty dollars they pay me. So it's settled?"

The black man started to cry. "Settled," he said between tears.

I didn't cry. Vigdor didn't cry. Dr. Shulman came out of the bathroom and walked past all of us silently. He didn't say any prayers. His mind was somewhere else, like my father's, but my father said all the prayers.

"So I'm not a Jew?" the black prince asked me when it was all settled.

"Don't worry," I told him. "The lost ten tribes will be Jews again when the messiah comes. It says so in the holy books."

That seemed to satisfy him, so he went with Mr. Slomowitz to look at his bed and maybe to find a coat.

❦

"Let's go back on our walk," I said to Vigdor.

"Not on your life," he said. "First of all, I'm too tired. Second of all, I can't trust you. Next time you'll pick up John Dillinger or Bugsy Siegel and bring them back to Mr. Slomowitz and tell the dopey old man that they're all Jews. Why do you love everybody so much when the world out there wants to kill us all, like Hitler?"

Vigdor wasn't so dumb after all. He also knew about the world. He knew about my uncle in occupied Poland. He knew about the Bowery bums not only on the Bowery but all over. He must have walked to many places before he started taking me. Maybe my father told him too.

"Why do I love everybody so much?" I said. "Ask Miss Morgenstern in the Hebrew School. She taught me what comes first and what comes second. And love comes first. She taught me everything, more than my father and mother even. That's the way it's supposed to be. A teacher gives me my share in the-world-to-come. It says so in the Talmudic tractate *Sanhedrin,* page 101, three lines from the bottom."

But Vigdor wasn't much of a student. He wasn't interested in books or tractates. He wanted to fight Hitler like his oldest brother, and he ended up in the Pacific fighting Japan where he got killed in Okinawa or some other place soon after he left me, or maybe a little later. The world was hard to understand. Vigdor found his death far, far away, while our black prince came to life in the Hebrew School around the corner.

Life and death were both on my mind a lot in those days, tied together like Siamese twins. O my black prince! O my friend Vigdor, brother of beautiful Feygy who had also disappeared, but without living and without dying.

THE SURVEY

I CAME DOWN with a heavy bronchial cough one year to the day after my Bar Mitzvah and on the very day that my mother went to the hospital to give birth to her third child, a baby girl, my little sister. My father tended to me in her absence. When on the third day of my illness the cough hadn't disappeared in spite of my taking medicine prescribed by a doctor, my father took matters into his own hands. He put together a concoction that his own parents had given him when he was a child: the yellow of eggs, one squeezed lemon, one spoon of honey, and two or three teaspoons of sugar, all mixed together and taken down as if I were drinking a milkshake or an egg cream in the candy store downstairs. Unlike all other medicines, this tasted fine. In fact, I made note of the ingredients so that I could put all that stuff together for myself secretly, even when I didn't have a cold.

"What is it called?" I asked my father.

"In our shtetl in Galitsya and in Russia, an *ogl-mogl,*" he said. "In Rumania, a *gogl-mogl.* In France, a *chateau,* but what do assimilated French Jews know about Yiddish."

"What is it supposed to do?" I asked hoarsely.

"With God's help," my father said, "it's supposed to break up the phlegm and clean your throat out."

But my father didn't rely on the *ogl-mogl* alone. He also went to shul on the fourth day of my illness, which was the Sabbath, and said special prayers at the Torah for my recovery and for the good health of my mother and the new baby sister whom he named after his own departed mother.

The prayers did only part of the job. I recovered almost immediately, but my mother came home from the hospital one week after giving birth without the baby. The baby, apparently very sickly, remained behind, lingered for another week, and died.

My mother's grief was deep and anguishing. I could see it all the time even though, despite her physical weakness and her sorrow, she tried mightily to minister to me in order to make sure that I did not have a relapse after my illness. My father comforted her at every moment and tried to persuade her to let him do things for me. I myself told her that I was okay and didn't need such close attention, but she drove herself, as if being busy all the time would help her fight off despairing thoughts.

We did not sit shiva. Pa said that a baby less than a month old that passes away is not yet a *bar kayama,* a fully assured life according to religious law, and that therefore there is no official mourning period. But I could see that my mother and father would mourn forever.

◆

About two or three months later, when my father and I were alone in our kitchen, my mother out of earshot two rooms away in the bedroom with the door closed, I dared interrupt my father from his intense study of a Talmudic tractate.

"Why did the baby die?" I asked hesitantly.

My father did not look up immediately. He finished a passage, studied the Rashi commentary and *Tosafos,* then spoke without looking at me.

"*Ha-Shem nosan v'Ha-Shem lokach, y'hi shaym Ha-Shem m'voyruch,*" he said.

I knew what that meant in Hebrew. "God has given and God has taken away, may God's name be blessed." It didn't satisfy me. She was my only sister.

"But why?" I asked. "Why?"

My father must have realized that I wasn't a kid anymore and that he would have to deal with me.

"In the *Toyreh* in *D'vurim* it says that we know the things that are revealed but that the hidden things are God's."

I would not be trifled with. I almost leaped at him from the other side of

the table, knocking over my science book and the written homework I had
been doing for school.

"But if we never tried to find out the hidden things, we wouldn't have a
radio or cars or airplanes or telescopes to see the stars and the planets or
medicines to heal the sick. We wouldn't have an Einstein. We must know
what's hidden."

My father rose from the table. He marched back and forth, his head bent
forward so that he was shorter than usual, his hands clasped behind his back.
He did not speak.

I did. "And if there is no good reason," I asked brazenly, "then what's the
difference between God killing an innocent child and Hitler and the Nazis
killing innocent children?"

My father stopped in his tracks. I could not tell if he was shocked, angry,
distraught, annoyed, or anything else. His face was a mask, a mystery, a hidden thing like God's motives. He stood his ground for an unbelievable
amount of time, like a tree rooted to its spot for generations, unmoving in
the windless room. His eyes were dead though open. I knew he was thinking
of my mother and her lost baby daughter and of his brother, the *shoychet,* the
ritual slaughterer in Poland or in Russia or in God-knows-where who
hadn't been heard from with his family since the end of the war, the defeat of
the Germans and the Japanese, and the liberation of the concentration camps
in Europe.

Finally, he sank into a seat much closer to me, away from his Talmudic
tractate, and spoke softly.

"It is time you should know that your father, the *melamed,* the teacher,
does not know everything. I don't know. I don't know. Ask other people
smarter than me. Ask your Hebrew teachers. Ask your English teachers. Ask
goyim. Ask the world for an answer. I don't have any answers."

❧

Big Red was the first guy I asked. He came by to visit us the following Sunday with his wife Aunt Geety who was not really my aunt but my cousin.

She was much younger than my mother, who was her real aunt. In spite of the difference in their ages, Aunt Geety had given birth to her first child, a girl, almost at the same time that my mother had given birth to her ill-fated baby daughter. Aunt Geety and Big Red came visiting without their baby. Big Red's mother was taking care of the baby elsewhere for the hour or two of the visit.

"Why didn't you bring the baby?" my mother asked.

Aunt Geety caressed my mother who had brought her up during her teen years when she lived at our house. She said nothing.

"You didn't wanna hurt me," my mother said.

Aunt Geety nodded.

"Next time," my mother said, "bring the child."

Big Red winked to me, and I followed him out the door just as he was telling the others that he and I would be taking a stroll. I went willingly because I didn't really care to hang around in our apartment. Aunt Geety didn't look like Aunt Geety anymore. She looked like she was still pregnant and hadn't as yet given birth. She was very fat and lumpy, and her face was blubbery with many chins and a disappearing neck. She just wasn't the beautiful Aunt Geety whom I once loved when I was a kid. And she hardly looked at me, as if she didn't recognize me, or maybe because I had grown so much and had become a man.

"Why does God let children and babies die?" I asked Big Red as we pounded down the four flights of stairs to the candy store below.

Big Red took off the yarmulke that he wore whenever he came to visit my parents. I kept mine on my head. Big Red looked inside the candy store and waved to Vinnie who came out from behind the counter to slap him on the back. Big Red was too tall for fat little Vinnie, and the owner's slaps on the back almost hit Big Red in the tush. Nobody else was in the store, none of Big Red's old friends from his hanging-around days, so after Vinnie and Big Red had talked about this and that, we moved on toward Avenue C and the Sunday morning pushcarts that stretched all along on both sides of the street as far as the eye could see.

"Why does God kill little babies? " I asked again.

Big Red shrugged. "Those are the breaks a the game," he said.

"That's no answer," I said.

"Sure it's an answer," he said. "You want everything in life to happen just the way you want it? Who are you? Who am I? I married the best-lookin' broad on the block. For her sake I quit the mob and only do a little loan-sharkin' on the side in Brooklyn to make a decent living, and now we got a kid, and I hafta get a regular nine-to-five job that'll kill me, and my wife looks like a tub. That's the way the cookie crumbles. I'm a man and I gotta take it. You a man?"

I knew there was no sense arguing with Big Red. He had his mind made up. But it didn't satisfy me one bit. Big Red bought a bat from a pushcart peddler and also a used indoor baseball, a softball that is, which was bigger than the hardball major-leaguers played with. We headed back to the park and went to the basketball courts that were set up in the dry swimming pool every winter. Big Red talked a bunch of guys into a softball game. He already had the bat and the ball, and he volunteered to be the umpire. Most of the guys willing to play baseball were Puerto Ricans who had recently arrived and settled on the Lower East Side of New York and spoke almost no English. Big Red didn't speak any Spanish except to imitate the words *mira, mira,* which we heard all the time around us. But he wanted a game—I think a game for me—or maybe a game to remind himself of old times when he hung out at the candy store and played ball with Vigdor Grossman and Mugger Wojehowicz and other guys who weren't on an errand for the mob. So he communicated with the Spanish guys in one way or another and got them to come with him. We all marched out of the pool area into the baseball field. Big Red made me play with them. I didn't want to, not because I didn't like the guys, but because they were too good for me. Boy, could the Puerto Ricans field! I was an amateur compared to them. But I played anyway to please Big Red.

It was only a three-inning game, but since each side scored quite a few runs, almost everybody got to bat at least twice. In fact, I came up for the third time in the bottom half of the last inning with two outs and the bases loaded and our team a run behind. Big Red was the umpire for our side except when he was at bat, and he called a ball on me that should have been a strike. It gave me extra time to settle down at the plate. Then I managed to hit a dinky ground ball between second and third. The nifty Puerto Rican shortstop moved to his right and should have easily tossed out the runner at third on a forced play to end the game. He had done that twice before. He was the only player on both teams to use a major-league glove that he carried around with him all the time. The other guys fielded with bare hands. The glove should have made it even easier for him to make the routine play. But in his haste to get to the ball, the glove suddenly dropped from his hand down to the concrete. My high-bouncing grounder hit the leathery glove on the ground and skittered off without another bounce under the shortstop's straining hand into the left-field corner. The guy on third scored easily, and the guy on second came prancing in with the winning run, and I was credited with a game-winning single, my only hit. The other players on my team mobbed me as if I had hit the ball over the fence and broken a window on the second floor of the school across the street from the park.

"Happy, kiddo?" Big Red asked me on our way home. I didn't say anything.

"Sure you're happy," he added. "When the breaks a the game go your way, you're happy. And you don't even question it. Why did the breaks come your way? You don't ask. You take what you can get. That's life. You only question it when the breaks go against you. I don't question it either way. So be happy, and forget everything else."

"I'm not so happy," I said. "That shortstop got a rotten break. He's a much better ballplayer than I am. He didn't deserve to be the goat. It's unfair."

Big Red stopped in his tracks at the base of the stairs leading up to our fourth-floor apartment.

"I can't believe this kid. He got the weight a the whole world on his shoulders. You think Johnny Mize and Ralph Kiner who each hit fifty-one homers last year cried into their beer when the wind suddenly picked up a routine fly ball a theirs and pulled it into the stands? Not on your life."

"God should have cried," I said. "If God kills innocent baby children, then He's acting just like a Hitler who killed a million and a half children in the Holocaust."

Big Red's face suddenly became deathly pale. "Don't talk that way," he said. "Maybe I ain't religious and I don't know how to *davn,* but you don't see me talkin' that way. God is God and the bastard Hitler was Hitler. Don't put them two together in the same sentence. You should be ashamed a your-self. Pfui, pfui, pfui."

And he actually spit at the bottom of the stairs.

When Aunt Geety came to kiss me goodbye, I drew back a little, and she seemed to be disturbed by my resistance. As for Big Red, he didn't even want to shake my hand. My quest for the truth was pushing me into making ene-mies, even among my very own relatives, which I didn't really intend to do. Who could understand all of the consequences in this world?

Mr. Spring, my ninth-grade English and French teacher in school, was the second person not counting my father that I asked. He was a tiny man with three strands of jet black hair that he brushed sideways on his head to cover up the center baldness, and he also wore a skimpy mustache over buck teeth that made him look, not like Hitler, but like a Japanese diplomat.

Once, after seeing a rerun at a local movie theater of *How Green Was My Valley,* I had asked Mr. Spring what he thought of the film.

"Sentimental slush," he said, which shocked me. I had rather liked the movie, especially Maureen O'Hara. I thought perhaps Mr. Spring was put off by the mushy parts involving love and the women in the movie. Not so.

"The minister gets the crippled little boy to walk," he sneered. "Tear-jerking baloney, that's what it was. Stay away from the movies."

He sounded like the rabbis and even like my father, who hated all the movies, but for a different reason.

"Don't addle your brain with that pap," Mr. Spring said. "Read, read. Read good stuff. You want to read about a boy growing up? Forget Wales

and *How Green Was My Valley.* Read Joyce's *Portrait of the Artist.* Read
Rolland's *Jean Christophe.* You're a musician, aren't you? You play the piano.
That novel is really about Beethoven. Read books like that by great writers
who are also touched by music."

Mr. Spring's opinions seemed so very daring to me. He was a real cynic. I
wondered if there was anything that he liked. For a while, I wanted to have
opinions just like him, but I hadn't read enough to know what I liked and
what I disliked or why. But since Mr. Spring mentioned the minister in *How
Green Was My Valley,* I decided that my teacher was the one to be asked the
question.

"Why does God allow babies and innocent little children to die?" I asked
him one rainy afternoon after school. Mr. Spring didn't like the rain. He
didn't have a car and went home every afternoon by subway. And since it was
a long walk to the subway station on Second Avenue even if he took the First
Avenue entrance, he normally hung around school after class and dawdled
with books and things until the heavy rain stopped. That's when I collared
him after school hours.

"Are you sure," he said slowly, "that God is responsible for these things?"

"God is responsible for everything."

"Is He responsible," Mr. Spring asked slowly, measuring his words, "for
your asking me this question?"

I said yes.

"Then if God is responsible for your asking me this question, then God is
responsible for whatever answer I give you."

"So?"

"So, consider the inevitable consequence. If God is responsible for my
answer, then He undoubtedly won't put an answer into my brain and mouth
that casts doubt upon God's goodness. So how can you trust my answer? I'm
God's mouthpiece. I defend Him like a crooked lawyer who knows his client
is guilty but can't say it. In other words, there's no sense asking me or anybody else this question. You're going to get God's defensive answer, not
mine. I'm a corrupt witness."

My head was swimming. I tried to follow Mr. Spring's words. They were complicated and twisting. His face was wreathed in a smile, his buck teeth protruding between thin lips under his black mustache, as if he had won a contest.

"Let's go back," I said. "I changed my mind. My answer is no to your first question. God is not responsible for every question I ask. He gives human beings the right to think for themselves and to do good or bad by themselves. Rabbi Akiva said that everything is in the hands of heaven except the fear of heaven. That means that we make the choices. You can choose what answer to give, to defend God or to condemn God. You alone."

Mr. Spring was clearly taken aback by my passion. His smile narrowed, his buck teeth disappearing over lips that grew and grew and covered them completely. The contest was not yet over.

"Your rabbi teachers in afternoon Hebrew School and probably your father have really fortified you with the goods," he said. "I don't want to contradict them. That's dangerous stuff for me. I'm a public junior-high-school teacher. There are limits to what I can say to students. Go home and read everything. Read Spinoza, read Bergson, read T. S. Eliot, read André Gide."

"You can say anything you want to me, Mr. Spring," I said boldly. "I won't tell anybody."

At that moment Mr. Yochnowitz, the social studies teacher, walked into the room. He looked at the two of us and cleared his throat.

"Tell the kid to get lost," he said. "My wife just came by in the car. We'll give you a ride to the subway."

Mr. Spring hesitated.

"What gives here?" Mr. Yochnowitz growled. He wasn't much taller than Mr. Spring, but he was twice as wide, like a football tackle. His neck seemed wider than Mr. Spring's chest from shoulder to shoulder. "Are you molesting this snotnose? Is Mr. Spring molesting you, Sonny?"

"No, sir," I said. "We're discussing literature and—and religion."

"Just as I thought!" Mr. Yochnowitz howled. "That's molestation. Nothing less. Leave the kid alone. Sonny, don't listen to this atheist over here. How the Inquisition ever missed him I'll never figure out. He should have been burned at the stake long ago."

Mr. Yochnowitz guffawed with such power that he blew some pencils off Mr. Spring's desk. Mr. Spring bent down to pick them up at the same time that I did from my seat near the desk. He spoke to me quickly and softly from underneath the table.

"If God is not responsible for your question or for my answer," he whispered, "then maybe He has given up responsibility for a lot of other things in this world—like the death of little children."

"I heard that! I heard that!" Mr. Yochnowitz screamed. "God is responsible for everything in this world except your miserable sophistry. Stop taking advantage of a little kid, you pederast!"

"He's not a little kid anymore," Mr. Spring said as he followed Mr. Yochnowitz out the door. "Read Keats. Listen to Beethoven's *Eroica,* to Stravinsky's *Sacre du Printemps.* Look at Picasso's *Guernica.* You're not a little kid anymore."

Actually, I was taller than he was. He pinched my cheek as he passed by. Ordinarily, I would have been annoyed because my mother's friends pinched my cheek pretty often when I was a kid, but not this time. Not this time.

♥

I was at the point of losing my childish high alto voice that had put me into Berel Braverman's liturgical choir, and Berel made it clear to me that I would not be singing anymore for the High Holidays. But every now and then, he did call on me to sing alto at a Saturday night or Sunday evening wedding because it was harder and harder for him to get kid singers on those nights.

When I started, he had paid my mother fifty cents per wedding for my services and a dollar if I sang a solo, compared to a big twenty-five bucks for the two days of Rosh ha-Shanah and the one day of Yom Kippur. By the time I was losing my voice, I was getting only a dollar a wedding without singing a solo, which wasn't much of an inducement to the other kids.

But it was different for our family. We were still living on the Lower East Side in a tenement apartment walk-up on the fourth floor. My father was still a teacher of Talmud in the local yeshiva and earned a very low salary. The yeshiva teachers had gone on strike on three different occasions during the Depression before the war—not for higher pay, but to *get* paid. The yeshiva had delayed paying salaries for months, but the strikes didn't succeed because the money simply wasn't there.

My mother, meanwhile, had given up being the janitor of our building because she wasn't strong enough anymore for the exhausting job the land-lord expected her to do, maybe because of the difficult pregnancy that led to the ill-fated birth. This meant that my parents now had to pay full rent for our apartment, and it wasn't easy. So I sang at two or three weddings each week and delivered *Women's Wear Daily* during the summer months to the doors of garment-industry firms and did some other odd jobs for local mer-chants that brought a few extra bucks into the house. My newspaper-delivery job took place long before that particular paper began to be sent by mail, making delivery boys a thing of the past.

There was no sense asking my question of anybody in the choir. Every one of the older men—the four male sopranos, the bass, and the tenor—were only interested in copping a few free drinks and some food at the smor-gasbord that preceded our participation in the wedding ceremony. The boy altos—three, sometimes four others besides myself—who were almost my age, went chasing around the floor sneaking looks at the girls with real low décolletage and sometimes befriending teenage kids by claiming they were sixteen or seventeen years old. On several occasions, they even sneaked off with a few girls to an empty ballroom in another part of the wedding-hall building and played kissing games with them and felt them up. I didn't join them in these escapades though I sometimes wanted to. My father would have frowned on such behavior. He often assured me that the parents of all these kids had not brought them up correctly and had not taught them Torah and *tsnies,* which meant modesty and proper moral behavior.

But I did ask Mrs. Braverman, who had long since stopped fooling around with me and touching me. I think she was having an affair with the tenor in our choir, who wasn't a religious man. In fact, nobody in our choir was religious except me. They sang sacred texts at Jewish weddings and in shuls all over the city on holidays and special Sabbaths, but it was only a job to them. I don't think they really loved music. They considered me a double nut because I was still religious and because I took lessons in classical piano.

One Sunday evening on the way to a wedding hall, Berel Braverman got into a conversation with a seated passenger on the subway train who was studying a musical score. Berel called me over from my seat and introduced me to the stranger.

"This kid here," he said to the stranger, "is my prize alto soloist and the music expert in our choir. He knows every piece of classical music. Try him out. Show him your score."

The man showed me the sheet music. It was a vocal score of some songs by Mahler.

"I don't know Mahler's music," I said. Berel was clearly disappointed in me. "I don't think he wrote piano music, and I play the piano."

"Do you play Chopin?" the stranger asked.

"Yes, I do. I've played some études, especially Opus 10, #3, and some waltzes, but not the Minute Waltz. I'm now working on one of the scherzos. It's very hard."

Berel Braverman beamed at me and at the old man with his score.

"Chopin was Polish, you know," the old man said.

I nodded.

"And Mahler was Jewish," the old man continued.

I nodded again, though I really didn't know for sure even though the composer's name Mahler sounded very much like mine which was Mehler.

"The Jews in Germany," the stranger proceeded, "and the Jews in Austria, Vienna, like Mahler, produced great music. They were cultured people. I'm not Jewish, but I'm the first to admit it. But the Jews in Poland were only religious fanatics and finagling people, very dirty. They spit in their beards. They didn't produce anything worthwhile. There was no Jewish Chopin among those kinds of people. They're gone now. Good riddance. No great loss to the world. They were not cultured like you, my young man."

I turned away from the stranger and went back to my seat next to Mrs. Braverman. She and Mr. Braverman still shepherded me everywhere, just as they had promised my parents they would do when they had hired me for the first time when I was eight years old. They persisted in never letting me go alone even though I was traveling alone to all other places for a long time now. It bothered me a little as I got older, but I tolerated it because Mr. and Mrs. Braverman had no children—the choir was their whole life—and I was like their substitute child. This time I didn't feel like a child. I turned to Mrs. Braverman in anger.

"The sonofabitch!" I said. It shocked her. She had never heard me use such language before. "The war is long over, but it never ends," I added. "The murderers are still around. So why did God let little children die in the death camps built by the Nazis in Poland and other places? Why did He let the bastards do their dirty work? Why little children?"

Mrs. Braverman began to cry. She never gave me an answer. She just cried and cried, and I put my arm around her big fat body and comforted her.

I didn't go to any of my Hebrew teachers with the question because they were modern teachers, secular Zionists all of them, and they weren't really interested in religion. They preferred to talk about the United Nations Partition Resolution, which gave the Jewish community in Palestine the right to proclaim an independent Jewish state. They had been dreaming about this all their lives, and they had been teaching us Hebrew, the modern living language, to prepare us kids for life in the Jewish state that had just miraculously come to pass. They were nationalists, most of them socialists, not really religious, in some cases antireligious, and they grew impatient with questions about God and religion.

So I became very courageous and went to the old *rebby* in the street-level store on Stanton Street who years before had given me a beating with a *kantshik*, a multi-strapped rod, and to whom my mother refused to send me anymore for religious studies whether my father liked it or not.

The old rabbi was still plying his trade, teaching those youngsters who would not go to my father's yeshiva because it was a school that took up the full day until seven in the evening or to the local Zionist Hebrew School because some of the religious folk in the area said it wasn't religious enough. He looked just as old as he had looked when I was his student—a hundred years at least. Or so it seemed. I froze when I saw the *kantshik* on the wall— that hadn't changed either—but I was older now, taller, stronger, and I think smarter. I was not afraid. If I could stand toe to toe with Mr. Spring, I could do the same with *Reb* Duvidl. I was also old enough to call him, as others did, by his title and first name, but I didn't.

I came after his last class and reintroduced myself. *Reb* Duvidl made as if he didn't recognize me and as if he didn't remember who I was. But when I mentioned my father's name, he rose in respect for my father's scholarship and bade me to continue speaking.

"I have a question that's been bothering me," I said. "My mother gave birth to a little baby girl that died within two weeks after birth in the hospital. I want to know why God allows little babies to die. God is just. Hitler was evil. God cannot do Hitler's work. Why did my little sister die?"

Reb Duvidl opened a holy book on his side of the desk. Then he opened another. Then he began to sing a wordless tune. "Deedl, deedl, dai. Deedl, deedl, dai." He opened another book without closing the others. His eyes roamed from book to book to book, singing all the time, humming when he stopped singing.

"Do you mean older children or just your sister?" he asked.

"I mean all babies who couldn't have sinned. I'm not asking about older people because everybody who is older commits sins and because of our sins we were exiled from our land, it says in the *yontev Misef* prayer, so there's no sense asking about sinful people because you're gonna say that if they suffer they should examine their own actions to see where they sinned and why God brought the suffering on them, and if they get killed in a hurricane or an airplane crash then their relatives have to ask the same question, but I'm asking about little babies and children who never sinned. Why do they die before their time? Why does God kill them?"

I was breathless—I had to get it out fast. *Reb* Duvidl closed all four books. He spoke slowly.

"The *Medrish Tanchuma* brings that when The-Holy-One-Blessèd-Be-He was about to give the holy *Toyreh* to the Jewish people, He asked for a guarantee that the people would obey the laws of the *Toyreh* and not do sins. The Jewish people offered their forefathers as the guarantee, the pledge. But *Der Aybershter,* the Eternal One, said that even the forefathers could not be a fit guarantee because they sinned and sometimes showed lack of faith. So the people offered the prophets of Israel, but the *Reboy-nesheloylem,* the Lord of the World, would not take the prophets either. They also were sinners in their time. Then the people of Israel offered their children. They brought their babies to the mountain, even those who were not yet born, and the *Boyre Nefushes* gave all the babies the power of speech. 'I'm ready to give the *Toyreh* to your parents now and in the distant future till the *moshiach* comes,' the Creator said to all the children who would be born from then to eternity. 'Will you pledge that your parents will keep all the laws and do nothing but good in this world and be repentant when they make a mistake and beg forgiveness and not do evil ever again?' The children of all generations then and in the future made such a pledge on their lives. So when Israel violates the *Toyreh,* the Lord of Justice demands return of the pledge. The prophet *Hoyshaye* says so in *Sayfer Tray-Ooser,* the Book of Minor Prophets: 'Seeing that you have forgotten the law of your God, I also will forget your children.' That's what's written in the holy books."

I didn't say a word. I kept quiet for a long, long time.

"I beg of you, I beg of you," *Reb* Duvidl said all of a sudden, "*sleecheh* and *m'cheeleh* for—for hitting you that time. I beg of you a third time for forgiveness. All these year, I have not been able to sleep."

I nodded my head vigorously to show that it was okay, and I said that I hadn't even thought about it for a long time. But it wasn't enough. *Reb* Duvidl wanted me to say the words.

"*Ich bin aych moychl,*" I finally said. "I forgive you."

Reb Duvidl sighed in relief. "*Danken Got,*" he said. "Now my little grandchildren, born and unborn, will live and be well."

I met a girl in the library on Houston Street whom I had seen both in public school and in Hebrew School without ever saying a word to her. She had strands of hair over her forehead that I think they called bangs and bright red cheeks as if she had just come from the park and a game of paddle tennis. Somehow we got to talking. I guess she began talking to me in the literature section of the library when she saw that I had taken a book of poetry by Keats off the shelf.

"Boys don't read poems," she said.

And that got it started. Her name was Sarah and she was a grade below me in both schools. She said that she had seen me before too.

"I saw you talking to Mr. Spring and to Mr. Yochnowitz after school the other day," she said. "Are you the teacher's pet?"

"Mr. Spring is my favorite teacher," I said. "I was asking him a question about religion."

"What question?"

"A question. I ask him a lot of things. He's a smart man."

"Did he give you an answer?"

"Not really."

I liked the way she looked at me on the other side of the library table without raising her head from her book. She just raised her eyes. They were very, very big and bright. I would have wanted her to raise her head a little so I could see some more of her, but I settled for her big eyes.

"What question?" she asked again. Her voice was low.

"A question about things like the Holocaust and Hitler and stuff like that."

"Oh," she said. She finally raised her head as if she now understood it all. "That's why Mr. Yochnowitz was there. He's a good history teacher, and the Holocaust and Hitler are in history."

"Mr. Yochnowitz wasn't involved in the discussion," I said.

"So it wasn't a history question. Look," she said, "if you don't wanna tell, then you don't have to." And she turned back to her book.

"I asked why God lets little children die during childbirth or in accidents when they didn't do anything. If God is just, God shouldn't have allowed a Hitler to make a Holocaust of children."

Sarah screwed up her lips in a way that showed she was thinking.

"Then you don't believe in God. If there is no God, then there doesn't have to be a reason for children dying. They just die by accident, like many other people."

"I didn't say I didn't believe in God." I was disturbed by her snap conclusion, but I couldn't take my eyes off her. She wore a blouse with a V neck and a Star of David hanging down. No earrings, no makeup. She didn't need any.

"I didn't say that," I repeated.

"So what you really mean is if there is a God and if God is good, then how come little children die?"

"Yeah, that's it," I said. "You got it right."

A librarian came by and told us to be quiet. The old lady looked like a witch, and I didn't want to tussle with her. I put the Keats book back on the shelf. Sarah put her book back too. I walked out of the library and sat on the concrete slabs that framed the library steps. Sarah came along. I told her that I felt like taking a walk to the East River Drive to look at the water below the Williamsburg Bridge. She nodded. We walked together, saying nothing at all to each other. When we got there, the lights were on, I mean the field lights in the dance area, and older people were doing folk dancing with music on loudspeakers from a record player. They were dancing a Neapolitan tarantella. It was lively. We walked pretty far away from the music and the dancing and the lights. In the shadows near the bridge, we could see couple after couple sitting on the benches opposite the river in the dark and necking. We sneaked looks at them as the couples coiled into each other. They were older than we were. We were too young for that. We just hung over the railing at riverside and followed the ripples in the water from distant boats that occasionally cruised by. It almost reminded me of *Tashlich* on the first day of Rosh ha-Shanah when my mother and father and kid brother Noosn and I would come to the same spot in the afternoon and say prayers of repentance and throw crumbs of bread into the river to symbolize throwing our sins away. I wondered if kissing and hugging Sarah and feeling her up was a sin. It's a question I wouldn't ask *Reb* Duvidl or my father or even Mr. Spring. There was no point asking Big Red because he used to do that stuff all the time with Aunt Geety before he married her when they took me along with them to Central Park or Prospect Park. He once used to be a hoodlum, a mob member, and he did everything. So I would have to answer that question for myself some day.

"So let's say just for argument's sake," Sarah said, "that there is a God and that God is just and God is good. Let's also say that God decided to give us human beings the choice of believing in God or not believing in God, a kind of test. Is that okay with you? Nothing terribly wrong with that even though it may seem funny that God needs to have believers, but that's His business. Okay?"

"Okay," I said, my astonishment growing.

"Now let's say," she continued, the large whites of her eyes and her flaming cheeks lighting up the dark river edge, "that because God is just and God is good, He makes it that no child ever dies. All the children live. An airplane crashes—only the bad people die. All the children on the plane live. A car crashes. The little children live. Only sinful adults die. No child can ever die. They all live until they grow up and do wrong things. Then maybe they die. Is that a problem?"

I didn't know what to say. I couldn't believe that this girl who was one grade below me in public school and in Hebrew School was saying all these complicated things.

"Yes, it's a big problem," Sarah said without really waiting for me to answer, which I wasn't going to do anyway. "If little children never died, everybody in the world would automatically know that there is a good God in the universe and that they have to be good. So there's no more test. No more choices for human beings to believe in God or not to believe in God, to follow the rules to be good or not to follow. There can't be a test anymore if all of us know that all the little children always live."

I had never heard anybody speak like that, not even Mr. Spring or the principal of the Hebrew School, not any guy or girl my age or even older. I would have liked to kiss her, but I hadn't yet decided if fooling around was a sin or not, and I certainly wasn't going to ask her that question.

***

"Why did our baby sister die?" my kid brother Noosn asked me one day. We were in the local park, and I was watching him for my mother. He was already in school, and he even knew how to read. I didn't answer.

"Will I die also?" Noosn asked.

"Not soon," I said. "Only when you're a very old man."

Noosn began tracing the foul lines on the softball field where nobody was playing at the time. I was on the parallel bars that were in foul territory along the first-base line. Noosn crawled on his hands and knees down the foul line all the way to the right field fence and then all the way back to me. He strolled over to me, his bare knees below his short pants scuffed and even a little bloody, the palms of his hands very dirty. My mother would be very angry with me for letting Noosn mess himself up though she wouldn't raise her voice in anger. Noosn walked up to my chest just as I dropped down from doing dips on the parallel bars.

"How do you know I'll die only when I'm an old man?" he said. "You're not God."

***

"I'm not interested in any answers," said my piano teacher, Mr. Edelstein. "I don't want to know the answers to the death of children. No answer, no matter how smart, will satisfy me. I ran away from Berlin in 1933 soon after conducting my first performance at the *Deutschen Oper.* My career in Germany ended almost when it began. The family I left behind I never saw again—my parents, grandparents, brothers, sisters, cousins, old people, little children. Who wants answers? God has to answer to God. He doesn't have to answer to me. Human beings will have to answer to human beings. And human beings of good will can react only as human beings do—through art. Gustav Mahler, who was a Jew for part of his life, read and loved the poetry of Friedrich Rückert. Two of Rückert's children died in childhood from scarlet fever, and Rückert wrote hundreds of poems in his sorrow. Mahler, who lived much later, had about a dozen brothers and sisters, and seven of them died in infancy, some also from scarlet fever. One brother, whom he loved very much, died at age fourteen. It crushed him."

I stirred in my seat at the piano, where I wasn't playing a note.

"Did I mention that Gustav Mahler set five of Rückert's memorial poems to music? He called the work *Kindertotenlieder, Songs on the Death of Children,* written for a singer and orchestra. The words give the impression that a bereaved father is speaking even though a woman can also sing the song cycle. In one of them, the father sees the child's beautiful eyes, which upon death will be *nur Sterne,* only stars in the sky to him. In another song, the father says that when the child's mother comes into the room, he doesn't look first on his dear wife's face but on the place where the little child's face used to be when the child was alive and following the mother into the room, where the child used to enter *Wie sonst, mein Töchterlein,* as usual, my little daughter. If a brother like you was the writer of the poem, not the father, the singer would sing, *my little sister.* The death of children can never wither from the memory. The death of children can never be explained by God to human beings in an explanation that we could accept. The death of children can only be absorbed through the consolation of art, through the words of a poet like Rückert and through the divine music of a Mahler. Make art, young man. Make music. Make poetry. Make stories. Don't look so much for logical answers. Art is the only answer."

❦

Big Red and Aunt Geety came to visit us again on the Sunday after the Sunday of my baseball game with Big Red's pickup team. This time they brought along the new baby girl, my new cousin.

"Feel a little better this week, Uncle?" Big Red asked my father, adjusting the yarmulke to his own shock of red hair at the same time. When my father didn't answer, Big Red added: "Not that anybody can feel good these days. You and Auntie suffered enough."

My father turned his remark aside with a wave of his hand. "*Eeyiv hot geliten mer fin mir,*" he said.

"What did he say?" Big Red whispered to me.

"He said that Job in the Jewish Bible suffered more than he did."

"Is that Hebrew he said?" Big Red asked.

"No, Yiddish."

My father turned to us both. "What are you two whispering about? If it's worth saying, it's worth hearing by everybody."

That was my father's teaching voice, I'm sure—words he probably used frequently to students in his classes. But in this case, Big Red jumped in, ostensibly to protect me. "The kid is makin' a survey of what people think about God and—and—good people sufferin'. Is God doin' the right thing? I mean to little children, when they suffer, or when they—when they suffer the—the most."

My father turned to me and cleared out his ear with the index finger of his left hand. That meant that he was suspicious. I knew the signs. We were sitting in the kitchen drinking coffee and tea and for me milk, and the two women, my mother and my Aunt Geety and the baby, were in the living room. The light streamed in from a corner window that faced an empty lot. Sometimes, in the spring, we cleaned out all the garbage from the lot, set up bases, and played punchball. It was easier than playing stickball in the street among the parked cars and traffic that moved briskly much of the time.

"So you're makin' a survey, *tachshitl.*" My father didn't sound like he liked the idea that he himself had set in motion. "Who did you ask?" he continued. "What did they say? Did they reveal to you the unrevealable? Who gave you wisdom?"

"I asked *Reb* Duvidl," I said. I didn't intend telling him about anyone else because everyone else would have made a bad impression on him. I certainly didn't want to tell my father that I even talked to my kid brother Noosn about it even though it was Noosn who really brought up the subject. My father seemed quite surprised by my mentioning the name of the elderly teacher.

"*Reb* Duvidl? He's a *misnaged*. He doesn't like *Chaseedim*. He's too rigid. Once he—he—" my father broke off in mid-sentence. Perhaps he didn't want to remind me of the old beating with the *kantshik*. Perhaps he didn't want to speak ill of a man behind his back so many years later. That was *looshn-hore,* the language of evil gossip, and my father tried to fight such compulsions most of the time.

"What did he say?" my father asked again.

I told my father the *Medrish Tanchuma* that *Reb* Duvidl quoted almost by heart—God's refusal to accept the patriarchs and the prophets as guarantees for giving the Torah to Israel, His acceptance of the offer of the children as pledges because they were sinless, and His demand of the penalty when the people of Israel violate the Torah, as written in the prophecy of Hosea.

My father jumped to his feet and almost knocked over his glass of tea and Big Red's coffee mug. My father screamed in a way I had never heard him scream before. He was a wounded animal, at once a bleating sheep and a roaring lion.

"*Chilul Ha-Shem!*" he screamed. "Desecration of God's Name! God isn't cruel. What do these *rebelech* know? They are half-learned and half-ignorant. They latch on to a *medrish,* they leave out the last lines of the *medrish,* they—they—you know what the last lines are in the *medrish?* You know what? That God then says that He also is so unhappy for the little children because the parents did not teach them *Toyreh.* This shows that the *medrish* was not speaking about newly born babies who cannot as yet learn, but about big boys and girls a little below Bar Mitzvah age who are not taught *Toyreh* and the right way of living. Then the children suffer because of the sins of the parents. That's an entirely different thing. Isn't that true in life? If the parents don't bring up the children properly, the children suffer. What does a *dardeke-melamed,* a teacher of 'A-B-C,' know except to twist a *medrish* upside down and to be rigid and cruel in his interpretation, as if *medrish* is law. He knows only to hurt the *uvel,* the mourner, instead of to comfort. He knows only *Elokim,* the God of justice, but he doesn't know *Ha-Shem Yisborach* of *rachamim,* the God of mercy."

My father repeated the word *rachamim,* which also meant "pity" in Hebrew, over and over again, his voice cracking, close, very close to tears. The only other time I had ever seen my father close to tears was when the Joint Distribution Committee told him three years after the war that there was no living record of his brother, the *shoychet* of Radom, and his brother's wife and children, among the remnant that had escaped the gas chambers in Europe and the Holocaust of the Jews or even among the holy dead.

My father's words were so loud in the beginning and he seemed so distraught that even Big Red jumped out of his seat. The big guy's yarmulke fell to the floor, and he picked it up quickly and reset it on his head. Then he moved to my father's side and shushed him, trying hard to quiet him down.

"*Reb* Mehler, Uncle," Big Red said to my father, "don't yell so much. Cry, but don't yell. Think of the ladies out there. Those are the breaks a the game. You can cry, you can cry. The kid tells me that God is cryin' too. It's permitted to cry."

Then Big Red turned to me. I had retreated to the far reaches of the kitchen. I had never seen my father this way.

"Run to the ladies!" the big guy with the flaming red hair called out to me desperately. "They'll be terrified by all the yelling. See if they're okay."

My father wasn't actually yelling anymore. His last few words had frittered away into breathless gulps and gasps as if he were sobbing. First I also worried along with Big Red that my mother and Aunt Geety who was really my mother's niece and my cousin would be shocked by all the screaming. But then I worried that my mother in the living room would hear my father crying and would become disturbed for him and maybe disturbed herself.

I ran into the living room in our railroad flat, but I did not see the two women. I looked around for a moment or two, foolishly wondering where they could be. Then I moved straight through the room to the door of the bedroom. I entered the bedroom without knocking, something I never did with my parents. Aunt Geety was there, sitting on the bed, her heavy body down on the spring mattress, her legs dangling over the side facing my mother, apparently not conscious at all of the yelling and crying that had been going on two rooms away. My mother was seated in the adjoining chair—a sofa-like upholstered chair and a very comfortable one too—a look of almost joyful acceptance upon her face as she caressed the tiny little baby, holding her beautiful grandniece close, close to her motherly breast.

INCOGNITO

BIG RED barged in on us one Sunday evening when we least expected him, or anyone else for that matter. Normally, Aunt Geety would come with the baby on alternate Sundays, and my mother looked forward to these visits with undiminished joy. Her pleasure was tempered a little bit by the fact that Big Red had stopped accompanying his wife to our house for some months now. Mama began to worry that something was up between the two of them. She even mentioned it to me, but she hadn't pursued the matter with Aunt Geety, apart from asking about Big Red's health every now and then.

Not only did Big Red show up by himself without Aunt Geety on that Sunday night, but he came one week after her visit with the baby when we didn't expect either of them, and he came, not at a reasonable hour in the afternoon, but quite late at night when we were almost ready to go to bed. I had attended the Hebrew High School early that morning and had followed it up with a heavy game of touch football that afternoon in the public park opposite our tenement house. Though I came home somewhat beat up—I hadn't fared too well in the game even though we merely touched and didn't tackle, I had enough energy to spend the evening with my girlfriend Sarah at her house working out a problem in math that had stumped us both. When I got home, I was really pooped and willing to hit the sack. My growing kid brother Noosn was already asleep on the couch in the living room that opened into a bed and that I shared with him. My father and mother were in the kitchen of our three-room apartment, as they always were, when they were still up and either Noosn or I had already gone to bed on the living-room couch. My mother was at the sink rinsing a dish, and my father was

164

seated at the kitchen table bent over a large volume of the Talmud. He had spent the day with some advanced students who wanted to study a different tractate of the Talmud from the one they were learning in my father's yeshiva. So my father accommodated them, as he always did, and after they left, he finished off the day with more study on his own.

My mother tried to get him to eat something. Apparently, he hadn't touched a morsel of food all day. And now at a late hour of the evening, she was afraid to serve him heavy stuff that would upset his short night's sleep. He hadn't been feeling well recently, and my mother was clearly worried about him.

"I have to look after you like you was a baby," my mother said. "You're worse than a baby. Geetele's baby cries when she wants food. And she wants food regular. You don't cry. You don't even speak. You don't ask. If I didn't ask, every day would be Yom Kippur to you."

There was rarely any sharpness in her voice, only a wistful annoyance that one might feel in the presence of inevitable foolishness. My mother's jet black hair had grayed perceptibly in the year following the death of her newly born baby girl, my little sister. Her voice, which had never been strong, had grown even weaker in the days since then. But she was doggedly intent upon lecturing my father, voice or no voice, tragedy or no tragedy.

So we were all of us ready to call it quits when Big Red walked in. We hadn't seen him in months, perhaps since Aunt Geety's and his first visit with *their* newly born daughter almost a year earlier, when Big Red and I went out to play some softball with the neighborhood guys. Big Red was almost unrecognizable. He hadn't shaved for days, and the stubble of a beard coming in gray was clearly visible. His brow was wrinkled and blanched white, as if the normal red color of his light complexion had fled the skin in a panic. He didn't even stand up straight to his full height as he had always done in the past. His shoulders were rounded, and he stooped forward as if he was suffering from some disease of the bones.

"Uncle, Auntie, I'm in trouble," he said bluntly.

My mother jumped up to push a seat under him. "Where is Geetele?

How is the baby? Are they all right?" she asked, a rising tide of agitation in her weakened voice.

"Okay," Big Red said. "They're okay. They're all okay. *I'm* not okay. I'm the one that's in trouble. *Reb* Moyshe, you gotta do somethin' to help me. You're a wise scholar. You're a religious man. You gotta figure out what to do."

My mother sighed in relief. No trouble she could think of would be equal to that of danger to her niece and the baby. Everything else in this wicked world was manageable. She turned to the stove and began to heat some *pirogn* that she had been preparing for my father.

"Potato *pirogn*," she said to Big Red. "You'll have some too. They'll settle the stomach."

"It's not my stomach that needs settling," Big Red responded. "It's my wallet. I owe a ton of money, and the mob is after me. If they find me, they'll maybe kill me. I'm scared."

My father's eyes were fixed again on a page of the Talmud. He began to sway back and forth in the learning mode. His voice whispered a song, the sacred words of the text coming out in strands of melody. My mother covered and uncovered the pot on the stove to see if the food was ready. She did this three or four times, and the plop of the metal cover on the pot was like an accompanying rimshot of a drum to my father's music.

"Uncle, Auntie," Big Red almost shouted. "You're not takin' me seriously. Do you know what the mob is? Do you understand what I'm sayin'? I owe big money. I don't have it to pay. The mob is after me. If they don't find me—and they will, they will—meanwhile they'll maybe find Geety and the baby, and who knows what they'll do."

My mother jumped. The cover of the pot fell to the floor. My father stopped learning. The sweet melisma came to a sudden end.

"They'll maybe hurt Geetele and the little one?" my mother asked, said. "They'll hurt you too?" She bent to the floor to pick up the cover. Her hand trembled. I held her hand and helped her to her feet. I cleaned the cover and replaced it on the pot at the stove.

"Me they'll first break my legs, then maybe my arms, then maybe they'll gouge out my eyes, and if I don't ante up by then, they'll kill me. Remember the guy who was shot in front of the house here? He owed money a little too long also."

I certainly remembered. I remembered the neighborhood idiot Moysh, not my father with the same name, God forbid, on whom the wounded hood planted his own gun even while he was lying prostrate on the sidewalk in front of our tenement house bleeding to death. I remembered as a kid skipping over the prone body that was bloodying up the sidewalk. I remembered my childhood friend Chaim and his blue gun that he gave me as a gift, and the Passover with chicken that I would not eat because my uncle in Poland was a *shochet* who slaughtered them cruelly even though he had temporarily escaped the wrath of the oppressor, and my return of the gun to dead Chaim by burying it underground in the park across the street among the live, scurrying squirrels. I could not forget.

My father actually closed the large volume of the Talmud. It was as if Big Red's words had finally registered, and he did not want the big guy's profane talk to sully the exposed sacred book.

"You got money from loan sharks?" he asked. "Gangsters? Murderers?"

Big Red nodded.

My father rose from his seat. He walked from one end of the kitchen to the other several times. His hands were clasped behind his back. His eyes were gleaming.

He turned to me. "Go sleep," he said. "First go say *Krishma,* and then go to bed."

I stirred but I didn't really move. I looked toward my mother.

"Let the boy stay," she said. "He's old enough. *Der Royter's narishkaytn* won't hurt him. He's smart enough to know good from bad. Let him stay. Maybe he can help."

My mother continued calling Big Red *der Royter,* the Redhead in Yiddish, even though he was more gray than red by this time. His *narishkaytn* were his acts of foolishness. Soft-spoken as she was, she minced no words. And to my father, her word was law. So I stayed.

"My wise brother in Poland was right," my father mumbled almost to himself. "This country is a free country and lets us live like no other country.

But it also kills us. It lets us do what we want, and what we want to do is kill ourselves. We kill the good human being that the Almighty created in us a little lower than the angels, and we kill the Jew in us. We don't act like religious Jews no more. We act like heathens. My brother in Poland did not want to come here. I tried. I tried to get him. I was ready to sponsor him and his family. But he said that America is *a trayfene medine,* a not-kosher country. It would make his children go away from *Yiddishkayt,* from obeying and doing the 613 commandments. He was right. *Royter,* do you ever say *Krishma* before you go to sleep every night?"

"Uncle, you ain't dealin' with my problem. You're hung up on nonsense. What the hell is *Krishma?*"

I couldn't believe it. I had once explained *Krishma* to Big Red long ago when he was courting Aunt Geety. Apparently this kind of knowledge didn't stick in his head that was concerned with other things.

"'What the hell,' he says," my father almost shouted. "'What the hell.' That's the way you talk about sacred things? No wonder you're in such trouble. *Krishma* is the prayer you say before you go to sleep to put your soul in God's hands for the night. It shows that you know that a human being is only a human being, not so almighty as he thinks. And the *Krishma* includes the *Shma Yisrool,* the holiest prayer in Judaism. You probably don't say the *Shma* in the morning and evening prayer, so why should you say it in the *Krishma.*"

I had rarely heard my father resort to sarcasm, but this time he was not himself. Perhaps his not having eaten much accounted for it. Perhaps it was Big Red's brazenness in coming so late at night with tales of the mob and gangsters. Perhaps the danger in which Big Red had put himself and our beloved Geety and the baby had set him off.

"I barely know how to read Hebrew," Big Red said sheepishly. "You know that, Uncle. Your son taught me when I got married so I could say the proper words at the marriage ceremony. But I don't hardly remember anything. It ain't my fault."

"Are you in trouble with the government?" my father asked suddenly.

"What government?" Big Red asked.

"The government. The government. Is it only the loan sharks? Or are you also a gangster like the others, and the government, the police are looking for you?"

Big Red smiled wanly for the first time. "My record is clean, Uncle. I got nothin' to do with the government. It's private parties that are after me. I got a clean record. Except for maybe a traffic ticket or two or three. And one time in Prohibition long ago, they caught me with some booze. I got a suspended sentence. That ain't considered a record. I'm a good upstanding citizen."

"Some citizen!" my father scowled, continuing in his sarcastic vein. "What do you owe so much money for? You gave *tsedukeh* contributions to the Lubavitcher *Rebbe* maybe? Are you maybe a Zionist, and you give to the *trayfe* kibbutzim in Israel so they can work on Yom Kippur and call themselves cultural Jews? How much do you owe? And why?"

"You know I gamble a lot, Uncle. It ain't no secret. I just got unlucky. I got stuck with a string of losses, and every time I tried to recoup by doubling up, I lost more. That's the story. No government, no Lubavitcher *Rebbe,* no kibbutzes in Israel. I'm an American."

"How much do you owe?" my father persisted.

Big Red didn't flinch this time. A strange note of defiance seemed to enter his voice. He had come in whimpering, but now he spoke up with gusto.

"Ten grand. I'm a big roller, ain't I? That's your nephew-in-law, Auntie."

"Grand what?" my father asked. "What's so grand about owing money to anybody, but especially to crooks? Why do you hang around with people like that? In *Tehillim* it says that the man is happy who doesn't sit in the habitation of scoundrels. So what's so grand?"

Big Red grew impatient. "Grand means a thousand dollars. It don't mean grand grand."

My mother turned from the stove. "You mean ten thousand dollars you owe? That can't be." While saying this, she set three plates on the table, one for each of us, but not one for herself. She filled them with potato *pirogn* that sent a warm smoke into the air. "That's maybe more than three years' pay," she added.

"That's about it, Auntie."

"Hey Red," I said, jumping in for the first time. "You know Ma and Pa don't have that kind of money. You didn't come here for a loan, did you? You're not that stupid."

Both my parents looked at me peculiarly and, perhaps, with a little bit of annoyance. Big Red also looked at me, then dropped his chin to his chest. He must have felt betrayed. He probably never expected the kid with whom he had played softball to talk back to him and put him in his place, the kid to whom he had once said, in reference to God's allowing innocent children to die and good people to be cruelly murdered, you gotta roll with the punches.

"Nah," he said. "I didn't come for your money. I know Uncle is only a scholar, a teacher of holy books, and don't make much loot. I know Auntie works pretty hard as the janitor, the super that is, of this building to pay for the rent. I didn't—I really didn't just come for the green stuff. I—I came—I came to find any other way out. I came for a wise word of advice. I came for a blessing."

My mother draped her arm around Big Red's neck while he was seated. She hugged him to her side. My father exploded.

"I don't give blessings!" he yelled. "I'm not a priest. I'm not the pope. We Jews don't give blessings. We *say* blessings. We bless God when we eat, when we exit from the toilet, when we hear thunder, when we escape danger, when we get up from bed, when we go to sleep. Say blessings; don't ask for blessings."

"*Sha,* Itsik," my mother said. "*Sha, sha,* not so loud. You'll wake up Noosn. *Der Royter* ain't such a bad fellow. He's Geetele's husband. He's family. He needs our help."

Big Red swiveled his head in confusion, as if he didn't know who was being addressed. He apparently wasn't used to my mother calling my father by his middle name Itsik.

"What help?" my father yelled, his voice just a tiny bit softer than before, but not by much. "Whose help? Help from me he won't get. God helps them who help themselves. Let him become an observant Jew and then God will help him. I don't help those people who spit on our traditions of four thousand years and then come for help when they're in trouble they made themselves by straying from the right path."

Big Red looked at his watch. It seemed as if he was becoming bored with all the haggling. Apparently, he hadn't expected such resistance. He would have to look for other avenues of escape. His beady eyes scoured the bare walls, the ceiling, the oilcloth on the floor. He tried to straighten out a bulging crack in the cloth with his big foot, but the tough material wouldn't move. The smoke from the food had risen and evaporated. The soft smell of the potatoes mixing gently with fried onions inside the crisp dough of the *pirogn* filtered through the room and lent an otherworldly air to the evening. We were in an opium den, and from a distance, we heard the clear sound of a radio blaring midnight band music from some hotel dining room in Jersey. It almost seemed as if Noosn had turned on the radio in our living room, but when we adjusted our ears to the direction of the music, we realized that it was coming from another venue far away, not from us, not from our world.

Now it was my mother's turn to raise her voice. "I'm ashamed of you, Itsik," she said to my father. "What kind of talk is that from an observing Jew? You're gonna abandon your own people? You're not gonna try to help *der Royter?* When God wanted to destroy all the evil people of the city of S'dom, Avroo'um Uveenee began to argue with God Himself. Then God wanted to destroy all the complaining Jews in the desert and make a new nation from Moyshe Rabbaynee, but Moses our leader said no. Forgive, forgive, he said. Avroo'um is concerned with helping *goyim* and don't want them destroyed if there's some good among them, and Moyshe in the *Toyreh* speaks up for all the sinning Jews. And you? And you? You're gonna neglect your own flesh and blood? I can't believe I hear this from my own husband sitting over a book of the Talmud near him."

It was perhaps the longest speech I had ever heard my mother make in a public situation. It was amazing. My father sat down next to the closed Talmudic tractate but did not say a word in response. Nor did he eat. The plate of *pirogn,* cold by now, remained untouched. Big Red was digging into his plate with appetite. He did not seem to concern himself with the debate that had been taking place on his account.

There was nothing more to say. My mother had spoken herself out, my father would not respond to her attack, and Big Red was busy eating. The music from beyond the window had ceased. The usual street noises faded out. The streets below were strangely silent. The guys who ordinarily hung out at the candy store on the ground floor must have gone home early. To-morrow was a working day. Ordinarily, if one listened long enough and with patience, one would ultimately hear a siren in the distance representing a po-lice car on the prowl or an ambulance speeding in desperation or a fire en-gine or two racing to a fire. But nothing was burning this time, no one was desperate, no living thing in palpable danger. Only the four of us in a cramped kitchen, looking for a redeeming word.

"I got an idea," I said finally. My mother turned to me. My father did not avert his eyes from the closed Talmudic tractate. Big Red swallowed and wiped his mouth with a towel that had been draped over an adjoining chair.

"I got a real good idea," I said. "Harry Frimmer and Celia and their kids just moved out from the apartment in the rear. Why can't Big Red move in? You got the keys, Ma, and the landlady asked you to find a tenant, didn't she? So now you found somebody. Make up a phony name for Big Red, and move him in. He can sleep on the empty floor there until he gets a bed. The rent is pretty low in this area. He can make it. Aunt Geety can come with the baby every week, instead of every other week, to see him. At least until it all blows over."

"Who is Aunt Geety?" my father asked.

My mother's impatience with my father was growing by leaps and bounds. "I can't believe it. Itsik, you don't live in this world, it looks like. Your mind is in another world, not with real people. Your *zindele,* your son here, has been calling his cousin Geetele by the name Aunt Geety forever, ever since he was still almost a baby and she was living with us and helping me take care of him. Don't you know that? *Im ayn kemach, ayn Toyreh*—if there is no flour, there is no Toyreh learning, it says somewhere. You gotta live in both worlds, in the world of *Toyreh* and in the world of people and making a living and eating on time and sleeping and even getting into trouble some-times. You can't live in one world only."

"*Mahn vabele* has been become a real *rebbetsin,*" my father said. "She quotes the holy books."

"It won't help," Big Red piped up. "The mob is all over. They'll find me here too, and they'll recognize me. I can't escape."

"Yes, you can," I said. "How long will it take to grow a real beard from that stubble on your face?"

Big Red was taken aback. He scratched his chin, not as if it itched, but as if to locate the point under discussion. "Two weeks," he said. "Three maybe."

"That's it," I said. "You grow a gray beard, let your sideburns grow long too, the *peyes* that is, and we'll get you a white shirt and a black satin coat and a black hat, and you'll look like one of the *Chaseedim* in the area, the very religious types. You'll even look a little like my father! You'll be unrecognizable, especially in this part of the city that's filled with very religious guys like that. The mob won't touch you."

My mother clapped her hands in glee. "*Royter,* you'll even be able to go around anywheres in the street wherever you like. Nobody'll know you. You'll be an unknown. You'll be free."

"Yeah, I'll be free," Big Red scowled.

"You'll be free," I added, "because you'll be able to move about your business incognito."

"What the hell is *incognito?*" Big Red asked.

"*Incognito?*" I responded. "That means with a concealed identity. *Incognito.* Good word." I was proud of myself. So was my mother.

My father spoke without turning toward us. His eyes were still glued to the closed volume in front of him. "*Incognito,*" my father repeated. "Identity concealed. We hide from the world who we are. We always try to be one of them. We gamble, we run around with other women, we join mobs and deal with loan sharks, we listen to their music and read their books and watch their movies and even get drunk on their whiskey and wine. We're one of them. Incognito. Our own identity always concealed. We worship their golden calf. And then we hide from them by being *incognito* in a costume like one of us. *A mishige velt.* A crazy world. And the two tablets remain broken. Who is going to pick up the pieces and put them together again in this *gold-*

ene medine, this golden land? I ask you who? My brother, the *shoychet* in Poland, was right. He was wrong not to come here to save his life and his family. Maybe he's still alive in Shanghai or somewhere like that where the Nazis didn't reach. But he was right about America."

We sat in silence. We could not interrupt my father's harangue. He was focused on one idea only and could not escape his thoughts. At such times, we knew not to interrupt. At last my father turned and faced Big Red squarely.

"In the fourth book of the *Toyreh,* in chapter 19, in the portion called *Chukas,* there is the strange law of the Red Heifer. When a person touches a dead person, the living one becomes ritually unclean, defiled. That does not mean dirty. It's just a ritual matter. He cannot touch holy things until he removes the defilement. In comes the law of the Red Heifer. A red cow without a blemish is sacrificed and burned. Its ashes are mixed with other ingredients and with water by the *kohen,* the priest from the Holy Temple, and the mixture is sprinkled on the defiled person. This makes him ritually clean, and he can approach Godly things with the proper respect. Why is this procedure so strange, even in ancient times when they had ritual sacrifices all the time? Because the *kohen* who prepared the mixture from the Red Heifer becomes unclean himself, defiled by handling the remedy that makes a person clean. In other words, the Red Heifer makes the unclean clean and the clean unclean! Did you ever hear of such a thing? It perplexed the rabbis of the Talmud. Not the fact that the cow has to be red—a rarity among animals. This did not bother them. But how could something so sacred as the remedy of the Red Heifer do a good thing and also its opposite at the same time—make those who are unclean clean and make those who are clean unclean?"

My father almost sang the last words, as if he were again studying a page of the Talmud with all his pupils, this time with his pupil Big Red.

"All my life, I never understood this law. Neither did King Solomon, they say. But I accepted it because it's in the *Toyreh.* It is God's law to the Jewish people. *Chazal,* our sages of blessed memory, said it is one of the most important laws and that a Red Heifer was chosen for this ritual of cleansing, a red cow, as a symbol of atonement for the terrible sin of the Golden Calf, the *eygel,* at the foot of Mount Sinai.

But why this contradiction of good and evil in the same Godly remedy? And now I think I finally understand what this law is trying to teach us, even though it's a sin to think one can understand everything that comes from the Almighty. The Red Heifer is a *moshol,* a comparison. And a great and good country like America is the *nimshol,* the thing it is being compared to. From the Red Heifer we learn about things and places in this world that are good and even appointed from God to do good but end up sometimes doing the opposite. Just as the Red Heifer makes the unclean clean, a free democratic country like America teaches all sorts of people who would otherwise be bad to respect other people, to let everybody make a decent living, to allow every religion and every book and every song and every foolishness to exist and to prosper. Everything is permissible. The black man and the yellow man and the Jew and the gentile are free to do what they want. But handling the Red Heifer also makes the clean unclean. The Jew now is free to run after strange gods, to become one of them, to become *incognito* as a Jew, unrecognizable from all the others. He even becomes *incognito* to himself."

My father put his hand out and touched Big Red's shoulder. His steely eyes peered through Big Red, the point of a metal bullet entering a resisting body.

"You will do as my son says," my father said with sudden finality. "My wife will take you tonight to the apartment in the back and give you the keys. You will sleep on the floor for the time being. You will not go outside until your beard is grown to your neck and your *payes,* those sideburns, are long enough to twist and twirl. We'll bring you all your meals. We'll pay your rent until you can walk out unharmed and make a living. We'll buy you all the *Chaseedish* clothing my son mentioned. Geetele and the baby will come every week to see you. Geetele will sleep with you when she wants."

Big Red smiled through morsels of food. My father did not relent.

"But you will also have to live up to my side of the bargain. You will *not* go through this life *incognito.* You will *not* be lost to the Jewish people. You will *not* play a game with the beard and the *payes* and the traditional clothing.

When you are bearded appropriately and fully dressed, you will go every day, every night if you work during the day, to the neighborhood *shteebl,* the prayer-room and house of study run by the *Chaseedim,* and I'll get them to teach you how to be a Jew. That's the bargain with us and with God. Shake your head if you agree. If you don't, you're free to leave here tonight and seek another *incognito.* Do you understand what I'm saying?"

Big Red froze for a moment, but he managed to shake his head wearily up and down.

"Do you agree to the plan a hundred per cent with no reservations, as long as it takes to save your life and Geetele's life and the baby's life and make you a recognizable Jew in this free country?"

Big Red shook his head again up and down, up and down. He did not smile anymore.

❤

Later that very night, my mother went with Big Red through the darkened hall to the modest apartment in the rear and opened the door for him to his new hideout, perhaps to his prison, perhaps to his redeeming place. When they were gone from our kitchen, my father turned to me coldly.

"Past time for you to go to bed. Don't forget to say *Krishma.*"

I spoke sharply to my father. "My uncle, your beloved younger brother— the pious, gentle *shochet* in Poland—*davned* three times a day and said *Krishma* every night of his life. It didn't help him or his family one bit when the Nazis came. He was not *incognito* to them. He was *cognito.* They knew who he was. They hadn't forgotten who he was. God had forgotten."

I turned with some resentment to the living room in our three-room railroad flat where I slept on a couch next to Noosn that opened into a bed and left but a narrow path to my parents' bedroom. From the corner of my eye, through the doorless opening between the two rooms, I watched my father, bent over his sacred tome of the Talmud, and for the first time in my life, in my presence, I think I saw him really cry.

THE RED HEIFER

I BEGAN to talk to my mother more and more about final things and less and less to my father. And also more and more to Sarah—not only about math and other school subjects, but about things that mattered.

I told Sarah about the Red Heifer that my father conceded was one of the oddest laws in the Torah—the sacrificing and burning of a red cow without blemish, the mixing of the ashes with other ingredients and with water, and the sprinkling of the concoction by the priest in ancient times on whoever had come in contact with a dead person.

Sarah wanted to know if the sprinkled recipe made the person who got sprinkled on holy.

"Sort of," I said. "It removed his ritual uncleanness gotten from contact with the dead, and it made him ritually pure and ready for holy service."

"Catholic priests," she said, "do a sprinkling on the dead man's casket. I saw that in a movie. So Jewish priests sprinkled the living human being in ancient times. Interesting. Is that why a married Jewish woman has to go to the ritual bath after menstruation? To remove the ritual uncleanness and make herself holy for sex with her husband again?"

I got embarrassed listening to Sarah say such things. First of all, I wasn't used to girls talking openly about sex. Sure, the guys in school kidded each other and told dirty jokes all the time, but it was private talk, away from the girls, like in the locker room after the phys-ed class. And the older guys who hung out at the candy store on the ground floor of our tenement talked about girls and sex all the time. Definitely the guys who played pool or gambled on baseball at the poolroom not far from the neighborhood Chasidic *shteebl* where the bearded men in black coats prayed and studied the Talmud. The pool sharks cursed in the filthiest language, especially when they lost a bet, which was often, or when they missed an easy shot on the pool table, which happened even more frequently.

One evening, two women moved into a neighboring building that had been abandoned, and the guys at the candy store took turns visiting the place. Afterward, they made fun of one of their buddies who was soon to be married and hounded him mercilessly because he refused to go to the women. I heard it myself while sipping an egg cream at the candy-store counter.

But I wasn't used to girl-talk about such things. Second, I wasn't sure I understood everything Sarah said. I really didn't know much about menstruation, and what is more, I wasn't sure I wanted to know too much about it.

Nor was it the kind of subject I could bring up to my mother. Though I began discussing deep ideas with her more and more, there were certain aspects of things that I completely avoided. I would sometimes make mention to my father of our relatives who had been killed in Europe, a subject I couldn't get out of my mind, but I almost never mentioned them to my mother because I was afraid she would cry. My father's face tightened up at the neck when I asked him to tell me about his brother and his brother's wife and their two sons who were close to my age, all of whom probably died in the camps. My father stiffened, but he never completely lost his composure. I couldn't count on that as far as my mother was concerned.

I certainly never talked to her about sexual matters, definitely not about the sexual nature of girls, women that is. The only time I recall the subject of sex coming up almost inadvertently was when I asked my mother rather innocently, with no particular agenda in mind, how old she was when she married my father.

My mother laughed that bashful giggle that always made me smile and think this is the way she looked when she was young. "How old?" she repeated after me. "Not old enough. I was maybe nineteen, and I still didn't know anything."

The last part of her sentence perplexed me. What was there to know? I wondered. Was she referring to the Jewish laws of marriage that my father studied in the tractate of the Talmud entitled *Kiddushin?* Or did she simply mean that she hadn't as yet learned how to keep house and how to cook meals when she was nineteen? On the Lower East Side of Manhattan where we lived, a woman who was very capable in this sphere was referred to as a *balebuste,* an expert house-manager, actually a female owner of the house-hold. Women who honored such a neighbor would say that you could see your reflection in her furniture, so shiny and clean were the surfaces. My mother was surely in this category, but when she continued speaking with-out any additional urging from me, it became quite clear that she was talking about a wholly different matter.

"A half year before I was married," she persisted at some length, to my surprise, "when I was still living in that one-room little house with my mother, who was a widow and very sick, the tsar's soldiers entered our home town. It was the time of the First World War, and the Russians were our en-emies. We lived in Poland and spoke Polish in addition to Yiddish, but we were really under Kaiser Franz Yozef of Austria/Hungary. The two coun-tries were together at that time. Franz Yozef was a good and wise king, good to the Jews. Our area didn't become a country by itself called Poland until after the First World War. So we also spoke a little German and some Hun-garian and even Ukrainian Russian. But that's not what I was talking about."

My mother stopped talking, ostensibly to spread sheets of newspaper on the kitchen floor that she had just washed and scrubbed clean for the Sab-bath, but in retrospect, I think she was debating with herself whether or not to continue her story.

"So?" I said.

"So I was working as a serving girl in town in a tavern owned by our only rich relative, a grand uncle of yours who had pity on my mother and gave me a job so I could support her a little. One night, I had to stay much later than usual, and when I left to go home to my mother, nobody came with me. Your father was already sneaking out from his house to see me frequently and to walk me home all by himself. That was something! It was unheard of in those days among us Jews to do a thing like that before you got married. But your father did it to protect me, except this time, I didn't expect to stay so late, and there was no way for me to call him and tell him I was ready to go home. We didn't yet have telephones in those days."

My mother laughed her giggle again, this time because she realized how funny her last statement really was. We didn't even have a telephone now, in our New York apartment. Other neighbors had gotten telephones long before, but we couldn't afford it. My mother, in an emergency, used Harry Frimmer's phone in the rear apartment when he still lived there or the public phone in Vinnie's candy store downstairs. In my younger days, I got a few pennies from neighbors for getting them to come to Vinnie's phone in the store when somebody else was calling them up. Naturally, if I had to call my own mother to the phone, I didn't expect anything in return. But she always managed to give me something for the service. If it wasn't a nickel for an egg cream at Vinnie's fountain, when I was a kid, it was a special treat like letting me lick up the sides of the almost scalding pot that had just been emptied of newly cooked, delicious chocolate pudding.

I thought she would never finish her story and get to the point. Maybe she was still debating with herself.

"So," she finally said, "so I had to go home from the tavern by myself on that night. It was cold. There was snow on the ground. I think there was a lot of snow. I remember shivering. And when the soldier, the Russian soldier, came from behind a tree, I didn't see him until he put his hand on my shoulder. He grabbed my shoulder. I won't say what he said. I won't repeat those words. He was drunk. They drink a lot, the Russians, and the tsar's soldiers in particular. But I was lucky he was a *shiker,* a drunkard, this Russian soldier with a big spoon stuck in his boot. The spoon was for eating if he came into your house and found some food you didn't show him in the first place. So I pulled hard, and his arm fell off my shoulder, thank God, and I think he fell down to the ground. I'm not sure because I ran so fast and didn't look back even once. I came in crying to my mother's house. We had a small house just outside of the town with a small garden and one cow to give milk. That's all we had. We didn't have bottles of milk as much as you want in a grocery store like here, especially during the war when we didn't have anything. We ate mainly potatoes for four years during the First World War."

"Was the cow a red cow?" I asked.

My mother scowled. "What are you talking about?" she said. She must have thought that, as usual, I hadn't been paying attention. "A red cow? I never saw a red cow in my life."

"What happened to your mother's cow?" I asked.

She waved her hand as if giving up. "That's a different story."

"Tell me this one too," I begged.

My mother lowered her head. She would not look at me as she told me this part of the story. Her eyes were vacant. "The Russians told us to leave the village for just one week because the German and Austrian army was going to attack to try to win it back. They promised to protect our village, and after the week of fighting, after the Russians would win the battle, we would all go back. So we all left very quickly with just a few clothes. Then the Russians suddenly burned our village down to the ground. Our cow was still there in our small garden. When my mother saw the fire from far, she wanted to go back to save the cow. She saw the flames from a distance. But she was too weak, and it was too late, and I wouldn't let her. I loved that poor scrawny cow. It was black and white, not red, you foolish boy."

"Go on with the first story, Ma."

My mother acted surprised at my continuing interest. She turned away from me again. "I told your grandma, my mother," she said, "may she rest in peace, and this was while I was still crying because I was so frightened—I told her what happened to me with the Russian soldier. Then I asked her if that meant I was going to have a baby because a man touched my shoulder with his hand. So that's how much I knew when I got married six months later to your father. I didn't know anything."

"What did your mother say?"

"My mother? What could she say? She probably didn't know too much herself. Jewish ladies in those days, especially the ones from nice religious families, didn't know about such things. There was no radio, no movies, and we didn't read *goyish* books."

"But what did she say, Ma?"

"What did she say? My mother, your grandmother, laughed and laughed and told me I was a foolish girl. How many times, she asked me, had my uncles put their hands around my shoulder. Many times. And they were all men, and I didn't have a baby. 'But they're relatives,' I said to her, 'not strange men.' 'So what's the difference when it comes to having a baby?' she answered. 'Touching a shoulder don't do anything.' And then she told me again that I was a foolish girl, which I was."

"You're not foolish, Ma," I said.

"Maybe now I'm not foolish," she said without assurance. "I suppose you live and learn. You'll learn too. In time you'll learn. In America, the children learn too soon. It's a learning country, but sometimes they learn the wrong things too early in life. You take your time. This Sarah, this little friend of yours, she's a nice girl, isn't she? I know her parents. Good people. You don't do anything except go for walks with her, right?"

"Right, Ma."

"And you study together for public school, for high school. Is that right, my little *zindele?*"

"I'm not little anymore, Ma."

"That's what I'm afraid of," my mother said.

I told all this to Sarah a few days later.

She laughed too, not exactly like my mother's laugh—which must have been the way my grandmother laughed at my mother if laughter is hereditary—but a laugh that was also very nice to listen to.

"Touch my shoulder," Sarah said to me.

I jumped back a little afraid, just like my mother.

We were walking hand in hand along the East River at night on newly paved ground with many benches alongside, not too far from the bridge. The air was sweet, heavy and sweet. Across the river, on the Brooklyn bank, there was a giant sign advertising the Domino Sugar Company. Perhaps some of the product had oozed out of the pores of their factory walls and had filtered across the river to saturate the air all around us with this inescapable sweetness. Perhaps sailing people all along the river were smoking sweet weeds as they lazied it on their summer boats, and that particular sweetness was the cause of it all. The hot heavy air formed a kind of weighty mist, not a fog of rainwater, just a mist of heat, a haze in the night air that made it even harder to see onto the decks of boats. We only imagined that we saw sailors and their girls and their pipes and their special lives of indolence and sweet pleasure.

"So tell me more about the Red Heifer," Sarah said suddenly.

We were hanging over the railing facing the river and the Williamsburg Bridge and were watching the bridge lights sparkling in the dark. The bridge traffic on the outer roadway looked like a thin string of kiddie cars that you could hold in your hand. I was so close to Sarah that I could smell the waves of her auburn hair fluffed alongside my face. It had its own sweetness, a fragrance beyond all imagining.

"My father is hung up on the Red Heifer," I said.

"He's a very learned man," Sarah said. "It must be a very important law."

"Yes and no," I said. "The law has been out of circulation for maybe two thousand years, at least since the destruction of the Second Temple in the year 70 C.E. But you know how it is. To religious Jews, every law of the Torah and Talmud is of equal importance. They study about animal sacrifices, for example, as if they were still taking place on a daily basis in the Holy Temple in Jerusalem. But what bugs my father is that the law of the Red Heifer is so strange, unlike any other law in the Torah. It's one of those called *chukim,* meaning laws for which no reason is given, ones that don't have a clearly logical explanation. But the strangest thing about it to my father is that the mixture made from the ashes of the Red Heifer and water purifies an unclean person who has come in contact with the dead, but at the very same time, it defiles the person who administers the mixture. The priest becomes temporarily unclean himself by doing the cleansing ritual and can't participate in other holy duties until the evening. The impure become pure through contact with the Red Heifer, and the pure become impure. That combination of good and bad in God's remedy perplexes my father. It makes no logical or religious sense. So he mulls it over and over and over again. He won't let it go."

"So there's good and bad in this world at the same time," Sarah said. "So what's new?"

"In this world, yeah," I responded. "But it's not supposed to be in God's remedies. They should be all good, not bad. At least to a religious person."

"So what's your father's answer?"

I told her about my father's amazing analogy—his comparison of the Red Heifer to America. "The law of the Red Heifer, according to him, is supposed to teach us to understand the double nature of a good and democratic country like America. It purifies its citizens by giving them freedom, and at the same time, it gives them the opportunity to contaminate themselves, to destroy themselves through the same freedom. Especially the Jews."

Sarah wrinkled her nose. "You mean we take advantage of the freedom and mess up?"

"My father says that Jews stop being Jews in a free country. He also says that my uncle, who probably died with his whole family in a concentration camp, refused to come to America before the war because he was afraid that his children wouldn't remain Jews here. So he stayed in Europe and got slaughtered by the Nazis either in Poland or in Russia. My father spends a lot of time these days trying to find out what exactly happened to his brother and his brother's family. We haven't heard from them in years, since the war ended. Even longer. Since the first year of the war."

I stiffened for a moment, just like my father did when he spoke of these things. I looked at Sarah—her face was drawn, then at the bridge lights as we hung over the railing at the river's edge.

"The Red Heifer," Sarah said again.

"Yes, the Red Heifer, " I said. "Anyway, that's my father's reason for the strange law of the Red Heifer. The power of the Red Heifer to make pure and to make impure is supposed to teach us about the advantages we have and the dangers we face. We're free to do what we want in America. We can be ourselves or we can run after the majority culture and give up our identity. My father's not too happy about me playing baseball all the time or practicing so much on our neighbor's piano or going to so many movies or listening to comedy shows on the radio or even running around with you." I turned away.

"Your father knows?"

I hesitated. "Could be. My mother knows. She mentioned you to me. She wanted to makes sure we don't fool around."

Sarah laughed. Not a giggle, this time. A full-throated laugh.

"I don't agree with your father's analogy," she said abruptly.

"Come again?"

"The ashes of the Red Heifer purify and contaminate at the same time. American freedom may purify people, but if people get contaminated by misusing that freedom, that's their problem. It's not America that did it. But in the Red Heifer business, it's the ashes of the Red Heifer mixed in water, it's the drink that does both good and bad no matter what the giving person or the receiving person does."

I was amazed by her comment. "You could be a Talmudic scholar," I exclaimed.

"Maybe I will be," she said. "It's about time they let girls in on the deal. Your mother is smart too, but all she does is hang around the house and take care of her three little boys, you and your kid brother Noosn and your father. That's boring."

"My mother says that my father in Poland used to come to where she worked when she was a teenager to take her home in the evening. And that was before they were married, which is unbelievable. I can't imagine my religious father doing such a thing."

"It's love, love, love," Sarah sang out.

"Oh, shut up," I said.

I grabbed her and kissed her. My hands were on her shoulder and waist. I pressed her breasts to my chest. I could feel them. I was dizzy. She let me, and then two strange things happened. I suddenly thought of my uncle who probably got killed in Europe. That is, I thought of his two sons—he also had two sons—my first cousins. I would never see them or play ball with them.

They would never come to America and would never have a girlfriend here. I loosened my hands from Sarah's shoulder.

Then something crazy happened. We had left the railing at the river's edge to sit down on one of the wooden benches some twenty feet away from the river. The benches stretched in a long straight line for as far as the eye could see in the semidark, and on almost every bench a guy and a girl were seated and locked in a close embrace. Noise of the rippling current from passing boats only yards away meshed with soft but intense sounds of passion that came from the benches in either direction up and down. We were lucky to find an empty bench where the two of us could sit and be alone with each other. Suddenly, we heard shouting that drowned out the heavy breathing and the ripple of waves up against the embankment. This intrusive, unloving sound was followed by another—a tidal rush of hissing noise like a giant waterfall coming down from a Niagara up high. In a split second we were drenched by a powerful stream of water that ricocheted off our bench and made us both wince more in shock than pain. We jumped up excitedly, our bodies dripping from the sudden flow, and we saw a wild man standing some forty feet away on the grass behind our swath of benches with a nozzle in his hand at the end of a long hose coming between his thighs that was attached to a water spout in the ground some ten feet behind him. He was waving the nozzle wildly in every direction and spraying all the couples who were seated on the other benches on either side of us.

"Whores of Babylon!" he yelled at the top of his lungs. "Wicked minions of Satan! I give you the punishment of water, but fire and brimstone will be your fate. It is the judgment of our Lord Jesus. Repent before it's too late. Whores, prostitutes, pimps, contaminated libertines! I purify and punish with water!"

When his relentless spray got as far as it could go down the line, he swung the hose back in our direction. The volume of water seemed suddenly greater, a raging torrent by now. We ran. We took off together in the opposite direction, our clothes dripping wet. I pushed Sarah in front of me to protect her from the maniac, but I got a direct hit from the returning blast of water in the hollow of my thigh. It was painful. It felt like a pulled hamstring muscle that I had often heard about in the school gym but had never actually experienced myself. Even though I was limping on my thigh from the powerful stream of water, I held on to Sarah, and we ran as fast as we could before the loony guy could aim the hose at us a third time. The sound of his voice rang in our ears, the exact syllables of imprecation indistinct but raging. We could only make out a word or two or three. "Sodom and Gomorrah. Filth and purification." We ran and ran until we were on city streets and safely away from the river edge and the religious lunatic on the grass with the terrible hose.

Sarah stopped to catch her breath. We found ourselves at the door of the Hebrew School that we still attended on Sundays and weekday evenings even though we were public high-school students full-time with other obligations. The Hebrew School was closed at this late hour and the hallways dark. I looked inside through the glass door and squinted to see a sign of one of our teachers or of the old man, Mr. Slomowitz, who functioned as the janitor of the building with the help of the black prince and might be cleaning the classrooms at this time of night. I thought they might let us in to dry up in the bathroom since they knew us well enough from years back. The stairs up to the classrooms were unlit. The staircase on the left, which led down to the shul, the sanctuary with the Holy Ark and the Torah scrolls and also to the boiler and the small room that was home to the black prince, was also dark—no sign of life.

I turned back to Sarah. She pushed me up against the door of the Hebrew School and threw her arms around my shoulder. She kissed me again and pressed her body closer. I could not breathe.

"That lunatic won't like this," I gasped.

"Too bad," Sarah said.

"My mother won't like this," I added.

"I know more than she does," Sarah replied.

"My father—"

"Tell your father that if you get contaminated, I'll sprinkle ashes from a Red Heifer on you. You won't need the water for the mixture. We already got the water from the fire-and-brimstone evangelist."

"The Red Heifer may help me get clean, but it won't help you," I barely mumbled. "You'll become contaminated just by handling the ashes of the Red Heifer."

Her hands dropped from my shoulders and flew. "I'm contaminated already," she said. "Nothing'll help me. I'm in America, the greatest country in the whole wide world. It frees and it contaminates, but at least I won't die in some inhuman Nazi concentration camp."

I held her close and thought of my grandmother's abandoned black-and-white cow, not a Red Heifer, and of my uncle's two sons, pure, innocent sacrificial victims both of them in a distant hell, cousins I would never see, robust boys who would not ever play ball with me or have girlfriends, and this time I would not let go.

SAMSON

I HADN'T PAID much attention to my kid brother Noosn until he was seven or eight years old. At that time, a disturbing thing happened. I began to notice that he was reading very poorly, both in English and in Hebrew. I checked him out one day by asking him to read one of his storybooks to me. He seemed to be so glad that I was paying some attention to him that he jumped at the opportunity. But he didn't read well. He always mumbled his Hebrew prayers, so at first I thought that only his English skills had been neglected in the yeshiva he was attending. But when I asked him to read a Rosh ha-Shanah prayer that was not part of his daily and weekly repetitive routine, he again stumbled very badly. I brought this, reluctantly, to the attention of my parents.

They were disturbed. My father had continued testing me every Friday night on the Torah portion of the week, but somehow, Noosn had escaped his notice. My mother—well, I wasn't sure what my mother thought or suspected. So long as Noosn was healthy and thriving, she did not look for trouble elsewhere. Both my parents insisted that they hadn't heard a word of complaint from Noosn's teachers at the yeshiva, neither in the sacred nor in the secular subjects. Consequently, they were surprised by the intensity of my concern. After a good deal of urging from me, they visited with his teachers in school—my father with the *rabbeyim* in the religious sector and my mother with the English teacher and others in the other half of the school.

After a while, it became clear to them that there was a problem and that the teachers and the administrators had preferred to keep it to themselves in the hope that Noosn would grow out of it. The administrators especially had been reluctant to disturb my parents. One of the rabbis even said that he could not believe that a son of so revered a scholar as my father would not himself be a potential scholar of the first rank. The Baal Shem Tov who founded Chasidism also gave the impression in his younger days of perhaps being retarded. He would run off to the woods during school hours and commune with the trees and the clouds, and he was not much of a student. Time would reveal everything, Noosn's rabbinic teachers thought, and the truly elevated soul soaked in holy wisdom would ultimately come to the fore. But in Noosn's case, it never did.

Three or four years passed, and Noosn grew and grew physically, but his brain did not follow suit. By the time he was approaching his Bar Mitzvah at age thirteen, he was already a head taller than I, broad-shouldered like a football lineman or a professional wrestler. I never saw him go to the neighborhood park and work out on the parallel bars, but his biceps bulged in spite of this. After all, he was a yeshiva boy. He followed rabbinic dictates to a tee, outdid my father in traditional stances. He wore very long *peyes*—curled sideburns—down to his chin, a black, broad-brimmed fedora hat, a white shirt without a tie, and ritual fringes—*arba kanfos*—sticking out of his black pants and floating in the wind as he walked. I had never gone that far. In any case, it would have looked rather strange to see this kid on the bars in the park with all the bare-chested tough kids from adjoining neighborhoods and the few Jewish kids dressed conventionally who emulated them. But the muscles were there. I think that at age thirteen, Noosn looked eighteen or twenty. He was also fearless.

It was during this period of time that I did two things that were out of the ordinary. I joined a Puerto Rican softball team that played every Sunday in the park in a pickup league. Since my days with Big Red, who always took me to the park on Aunt Geety's visits to my mother and always organized a baseball game for my pleasure, I had improved my skills in the sport. I could hit quite well under Big Red's coaching in spite of my poor eyesight that wasn't wholly corrected by glasses, and I even learned to field reasonably well at first base. I never could make a good throw to second on a ground ball, since I was a right-handed fielder and had to turn forty-five degrees to make the throw, but that sort of play rarely took place. Most of the batters were also right-handed, and they hit ground balls to short and third almost all the time. On occasion, they punched the ball to second, better yet, to the mound or over second base, but very rarely to first. So it didn't matter much that I was merely an average fielder with a mediocre arm. The Puerto Rican guys who had migrated to the neighborhood after the war were terrific fielders, the very best. But they needed a few good hitters to support their deft but light-hitting fielders, and one of the teams asked me to join them. So I began a career at first base on a Spanish-speaking or -yelling team, and my classmates in the Hebrew School joked that I had jumped to the Puerto Rican League at the very same time that some major leaguers had actually jumped to the Mexican League. It didn't bother me because Sarah was proud of my newly found skills and of my open-mindedness.

"You're coming out of your shell," she said. "You're exploring the world." She hugged me at the waist, and that was enough for me.

The second thing I did that was out of the ordinary was to begin taking Noosn places in the city. I thought that if I widened *his* horizons, he might possibly ease out of his mental funk. It was not a scientifically based nostrum, but then again, nobody knew everything yet about the human mind and soul. It was worth a try. Maybe I also felt a little guilty for neglecting him for so long. Had I involved him since his babyhood in more demanding maturer activities, who knows how he might have developed.

First I took him to the top of the Empire State Building, and he seemed to enjoy the panoramic view of the city from on high. He squealed and giggled like a six-year-old, but I was pleased. From 34th Street, it was an easy stroll to Times Square at 42nd Street, but the daytime view of the Square without the brilliant, neon-lit signs of the evening made less of an impression on Noosn.

We continued our stroll northward and somehow, without a plan on my part, we found ourselves in several art galleries on West 57th Street and on Madison Avenue. We surely must have looked like a strange couple in those surroundings—I bareheaded and dressed in light-brown slacks and my brother, towering over me, dressed in black religious garb with long sideburns and ritual fringes swinging in tandem as he walked. People turned and stared. We paid them no heed.

Surprisingly, Noosn liked the abstract art he saw in some of the avant-garde galleries. Consequently, on another day, I took him to the Metropolitan Museum of Art, but he recoiled in horror when he saw traditional representational paintings of human beings in realistic scenes.

"It's against the *Toyreh*," Noosn said. "You're not allowed to make any idols or pictures of people. God don't like it."

I was about to tell him that these weren't religious objects or idols, but it wasn't long before we came to paintings of the Christ child and Mary, and I decided not to try to explain these things to him. The Greek statues of nude men with everything showing fascinated him. He averted his eyes in shame, but he peeked through his spread fingers.

We went to a baseball game at the Polo Grounds and sat in the bleachers some 480 or 500 feet from home plate. It was too far for him. His eyesight was very sharp, unlike mine, but Noosn was confused by the fact that a batter swung the bat, and the sound of the bat hitting the ball came to us in the bleachers a second or two later. He would look in all directions to find the ball. He rarely succeeded. Since we were kosher, we couldn't buy any of the hot dogs sold in the stands. This didn't help at all. Noosn got hungry pretty fast and simply couldn't concentrate on the game.

I used to worry in those days that my parents would not be able to afford his appetite. He ate everything placed before him, and my mother, as to be expected, encouraged him to eat more and more, as if he would otherwise starve to death.

One summer day, I took Noosn on the subway across Brooklyn to Coney Island. We first went on the Steeplechase ride. Noosn roared with uncontrolled excitement up and down the rails. I was scared stiff. Not he. He wanted to go again and again, and I managed to escape this agony by enticing him into the kiddie-car rides on a flat surface with him at the steering wheel bumping into other drivers to his undiminished delight.

The sea fascinated him, the ocean that is. We stood on the boardwalk, leaning over the railing, and watched the tons of people squished together on the sand and cavorting about in the ocean water beyond. This time he seemed not to mind the semiclad people. His eyes were not on them. They were riveted on the blue-gray waters beyond and the bobbing bodies of swimmers and the distant ships cruising somewhere or other beyond our vision.

"Where do all those ships on the ocean go?" I asked Noosn on the Coney Island boardwalk.

"They go looking," he said. "They go in search of the River Sambatyon. If they cross that dangerous river safely, they will find the Lost Ten Tribes of Israel. That's where they go."

I tried to see the world through his eyes. The silly remarks that people made had no impact on him. He probably didn't understand them. And when I bumped into one of my friends from school and talked about some extraordinarily beautiful solution to a math problem that had stumped us for so long, Noosn only twiddled his thumbs. He didn't really. He had a tendency to grab at the ends of the *tsitses*—the sacred fringes—that stuck out from under his shirt and twirl them around his forefinger as he waited for us to finish our intense discussion. Then he would stare at my friend and look him up and down. As we walked away, he would say to me, "A nice man. Is he a man or a boy? He talks like a man like you do, but he scratches one foot with the other one like a little boy."

On another occasion, in the summer when all of us were wearing short-sleeved shirts, I met one of my black friends very early in the morning while I was taking my kid brother to the yeshiva. Later Noosn asked, "Is the black man a Jew or ain't he?" I wondered what put the question into his mind. Then he added, "In the morning, right after he puts on *tefillin* and *davns* the prayers, I should be able to see the marks from the straps on his left arm before they wear off. But his skin is dark so I couldn't tell."

My only problem in arranging these jaunts with Noosn was when Sarah came along. I persuaded her because I wanted to see her more often. She held back—I think her instinct was surer than mine, and she foresaw trouble more instinctively than I. Not real trouble. Noosn, after all, was a kid, a giant of a kid to be sure, but a kid nevertheless and under my control. He listened to me most of the time. But he was not about to give up griping or pouting like a kid when things happened that he didn't particularly like.

And he didn't like Sarah. To be fair, I should say that he didn't like Sarah coming along on these trips. Maybe he wanted me all to himself, although I would insist that he couldn't really give expression to a motive of this kind. Maybe he felt embarrassed in the close presence of a girl. Whatever the state of his intelligence, he was still a maturing boy, advanced in size beyond his years, and possibly equally advanced in his inner turmoil and the stirring inside. Maybe he sensed that she was becoming more important in my life than anybody else. I'm resorting to all the "maybes" of my childhood, none ever resolved.

Noosn didn't look Sarah in the face. He spoke to me with his eyes looking straight ahead and sometimes turned sideways in the other direction. He frequently raised his voice, ostensibly because he wasn't speaking in my direction, perhaps out of an inner anger that was beyond his control. If Sarah said let's go to the Statue of Liberty, Noosn said he didn't want to and would prefer to go in the other direction to the Bronx Zoo. If Sarah said let's go to Harlem and walk down 125th Street and maybe buy a wig or a bebop jazz record, Noosn said let's go to Poland and try to find the graves of all our family. Sarah tried hard to say nice things to him, but he paid little attention. One time he said to her—perhaps the only words he ever spoke directly to her—that Sarah in the Torah stayed in the tent when Abraham went out to greet the three angel/guests, and this Sarah should learn to do the same thing.

"He's a stupid golem," Sarah said to me angrily when we saw each other alone that very night, and though I could understand her resentment, I yelled at her that he was only a kid and couldn't be blamed for what he said and that she was being cruel and self-centered. The result was that we didn't see each other for two weeks, and I suppose, I blamed Noosn for the temporary breakup and let it out on him during that difficult period of time.

The *golem* word disturbed me. According to legend, the famous Rabbi Loew of Prague some centuries before had made a giant mechanical man that came to life in a mystical way through the affixing of the holy letters of God's name to the robot's forehead. This golem, this automaton, served the rabbi and protected the endangered Jewish community. But then it turned upon its benefactors and ultimately had to be destroyed. Since that time, the word *golem* had become a Yiddish synonym for a stupid, even dangerous person, and I could not abide the use of the word in reference to my kid brother.

Eventually, I relented and Sarah relented. I apologized and Sarah apologized. But she didn't join us again on the trips. We both agreed that she would wait until Noosn was older and perhaps more amenable to her presence.

Two incidents brought the trips to a halt. I had taken Noosn on a tour of the used-book stores on Lower Broadway and Fourth Avenue below 14th Street. I tried to introduce him to the pleasures of browsing among musty old books. Then we sat down in Union Square Park to eat some sandwiches that Ma had packed for us. At the end of the meal, I gave Noosn five dimes and told him that I was organizing a contest. I would give him a half hour on the clock in Union Square to go back to the book stores and buy some books with his fifty cents. There were tables filled with books for a dime apiece. I tried hard to explain to him that I wasn't interested in quantity, only quality. If he brought back one special fine book that he had bought for fifty cents, he could win the contest. But I made the mistake of adding that if he brought back five good books for the fifty cents, he would surely win.

A half hour went by and Noosn didn't return. I was sure it wasn't a matter of telling time. He was pretty good at that. When an hour went by and he still didn't show up, I decided to investigate myself. I went from book store to book store asking about a big kid dressed as he was. In one of them, I was told the story. Noosn had apparently come in and had gathered up in his massive arms a dozen or so new books with fancy dust jackets costing several dollars each, a hefty price in those days. Then he dropped his five dimes on the table near the cash register and ran out of the store full steam ahead. The proprietor called the cops who caught him almost immediately down the street and took him to the station house.

I chased after him to the police station and spent the rest of the afternoon explaining to the officers in charge that Noosn had meant no harm. I explained the contest and his mental condition and a lot of other things that I probably made up in my anxiety and desperation. It finally worked, and they let him go home with me without writing up a charge against him. I never told my parents or even Sarah about this incident.

The second and last incident could not be withheld from my parents because all of the Lower East Side heard about it. It was a Friday night near the end of the year. We had eaten our Sabbath meal at home, had sung the *zmires* and the prayers after the meal, and had even reviewed the Torah portion of the week with much of the evening still left to us. Snow had begun to fall that morning, and at evening time, it had not stopped. It was a blizzard. We had trudged our way to the synagogue through a foot and a half of snow, and we managed it back home after the services in at least two feet of snow. To my parents' consternation, I decided to meet some of my friends from the Hebrew School after the meal in spite of the mounds of snow that covered all the streets of the city. It was surely a sight to behold, and I didn't want to miss it. I took Noosn with me.

Four other guys showed up at the door of the Hebrew School on Houston Street next to the public library, all dressed in their finest Sabbath suits and overcoats in spite of the weather. The wind was surprisingly quiescent. It was a silent ton of snow glowing white on the ground, covering parked cars completely, almost blotting out the contours of the cars. The streets, block after block, were unsullied by human footsteps or even moving vehicles. It didn't really seem so cold because it was a windless night, but it provoked eerie feelings because of the white glare of the snow surfaces reflecting in the beams of light from every corner lamppost. The guys wore yarmulkes attached to their pompadour hair styles by bobby pins from their mother's or sisters' collection. Noosn alone wore his wide-brimmed black hat.

We walked down Sheriff Street to Rivington in two groups of three—three of my friends in front of us on the sidewalk and the other one alongside Noosn and me. Unlike the situation with Sarah, Noosn did not react adversely to sharing me with another guy. We gabbed about nonsense—from a college basketball game of the night before at Madison Square Garden, to a boxing match that was on every television set in every bar we passed, to a Talmudic passage that had stumped a yeshiva friend that week. My walking buddy even began to tell a dirty joke, but I stopped him in his tracks. Not because I didn't want to hear it but because I didn't want Noosn to hear it.

The other three guys, somehow or other, got almost a block ahead of us. We three would stop for a moment when a debating point got hot and heavy, but the other three apparently moved ahead in the deep snow without missing a step. They turned the corner to the right on Rivington Street, and for a few good minutes we lost sight of them totally. But just as we turned the corner of the same street, we heard shouts and screams that shook us to the core. In the distance we saw that our three friends were actually in the middle of the snow-filled gutter at the next corner without a moving vehicle in sight. They were surrounded by at least a dozen other guys who pounced upon them and slammed them up against the cars and buried punches into their heads and midriffs. We froze in our tracks for a moment. It was Noosn who did not hesitate. He took off with incredible speed and raced toward the melee with no regard for the consequences. We had no choice but to follow in his footsteps. The screams and the yells were in several languages as we approached, and it didn't take long for me to realize that almost all the attackers were members of my softball team.

"Hey guys!" I yelled at the top of my lungs. "They're my friends, *mi amigos!* Leave them alone. It's me! It's me!"

It seemed like a stupid thing to say, but it worked. There were about four guys beating up on every one of ours, and when they all looked and caught sight of me, they dropped their battered victims into a snowbank and sheepishly inched toward me and my two colleagues. They began to apologize, half in English, half in Spanish.

At that moment, Noosn dropped his coat and jacket behind us, picked up the first attacker who reached me, and held him high above his head. For a single moment, I was speechless, and in that moment, he hurled the attacker over the line of parked cars into a set of trash cans that were barely visible on the sidewalk over the snow surface.

"No, Noosn," I yelled, "No."

He didn't listen. He punched the second guy square in the gut, and when he doubled over, Noosn kicked him in the chin as if he had studied martial arts all his life. The other members of the Spanish team could not let this go by. But they did not attack Noosn en masse. They came at him two at time, as if they were gladiators circling an animal. I screamed some more, to both sides, that this was my brother, and that he didn't understand, and that this was my team. It didn't help. The bloody fight continued, with Noosn smashing into two of them at a time and either crushing them against cars or felling them on the spot as if they had been hit by a sudden bullet in the groin. Not a sound issued from his mouth. His eyes were intent on his prey. His beardless chin thrust forward with a determination I had never seen before. Out of the corner of my eye I saw curtains being parted in all the windows, seemingly on every floor. The last two guys who came at Noosn drew knives, and I jumped between them and Noosn. My kid brother shoved me aside as if I were an annoying mosquito. He jumped in front of one of the knife-wielders and pushed his chest out for the intended cut in a wild act of bravado. And when it came, he pulled his own black hat off with the quickest motion—it hadn't fallen off in all of the previous fighting—and received the blade through the thick felt. This gave him the momentary opportunity to grab at his assailant's hand and break it against the elbow. The poor guy went down squealing in pain. Noosn picked him up and hurtled him into the second knife-wielder. Both went down. Noosn dived at them, the yarmulke that had been under his hat finally flying off. He bashed their heads together until they lost consciousness in the white, sinless snow.

We thought we heard sirens in the distance. This sound Noosn understood, and he began to run. We followed him, my wounded friends limping along. I ran because I was afraid that reinforcements for my teammates would soon show up, something that I knew from past hearsay about other street fights. But I also ran because I did not want Noosn to face the cops again.

For a week, perhaps a month, I was in a frenzied state, not afraid of going out, but afraid that the police would show up at the door and take Noosn away. It never happened. Though the neighbors on every street seemed to know all the details of the battle, they passed the information around only to each other but not to the authorities. My softball teammates recovered, but they too would not say anything to the cops. Though I never played for them again, they treated me with a strange respect in the park and on the streets. They even looked for me when I was with Noosn, not to gain revenge on him in any way, but to stand from afar and admire this unbelievable Superman.

As I mentioned before, my parents did hear about it, down to the final detail. My mother cried, perhaps in relief, perhaps with joy. My father stormed up and down the three rooms of our apartment in unappeasable despair.

"Who does he think he is?" my father wailed. "Shimshen *ha-Giber?*"

His reference was to the hero Samson in the Book of Judges.

"Shimshen *ha-Giber* was an ignoramus, a fool, a showoff. He never understood the *Toyreh* and any of its laws. He was a stupid man. And in our own family? What have I spawned here? A breaker of idolatrous temple pillars, a blind child with the strength of lions and the understanding of a just-born baby. Do we need another Shimshen to bring down the wrath of God and man upon us, to provoke our enemies? *Vay iz mir.*"

◆

Less than six months later, my father came back from his shul on Clinton Street with unusual news. One of the society members at Sabbath services had heard from a friend that an escapee from the Soviet Union had turned up in New York who claimed to have met my father's brother during the war in the Russian-occupied zone of Poland. My father waited until after the final Sabbath service in the evening to copy down the address of an

American relative of the Soviet émigré. This American gentleman, who lived on Central Park West, would be willing to arrange a meeting between my father and the man from the Soviet Union.

A week later at Sabbath services, my father was told that the meeting at the Central Park West address would take place the following Tuesday evening, and he was assured that the American relative spoke both English and the Russian of his guest. My father asked me to come along to help him out in English in the event that he did not understand the Russian language. My father's English was improving every year, and he did speak Polish and Ukrainian tolerably well, but Russian was apparently somewhat different from the other Slavic languages. The best he could hope for was that the newcomer spoke Yiddish, but he took no chances and invited me along in case all the talk turned out to be in English.

Not a year had gone by since the end of the war without my father re-doubling his efforts to ferret out news about his brother and his brother's family. He contacted the International Red Cross, the Polish Consulate in New York, various Jewish organizations like HIAS and the Jewish Joint Distribution Committee in the city and others in Israel; he even wrote letters to Soviet delegates at the United Nations and to the American State Department—all to no avail. His own local society of former residents of his shtetl on the Polish/Ukrainian border was his best bet. These were the *landslayt*—hometown neighbors who had dozens and dozens of relatives of their own to track down, and whenever they came up with a lead, they contacted my father. But nothing worked. When Hitler's army invaded Poland, my uncle was not living in the shtetl where he and my father were born. He had been living for years in Radom, a Polish city where he served as *shochet* for the Jewish community. Consequently, *landslayt* from the shtetl who ended up in the Soviet zone or who were caught and transported to concentration camps from which they ultimately escaped to tell their story had nothing to say about my uncle. Once my uncle whom I had never seen had written a letter that got through to my father a half year after the beginning of the war to say that he had escaped the fury of the destroyer. My elated father read into this message that his brother was safe in the Soviet zone. But the trail abruptly ended there.

That is, until this message from a *landsman* at services who had heard from a friend about the defector from the Soviet Union and who had arranged a Central Park West meeting.

"It gives me hope," my father said to me as we sat together on the subway train. He had brought along with him a small copy of rabbinic responsa literature for study on the train ride, but this time he looked up at me to make the comment. "If a Jewish man can escape from Hitler and from the Soviet Union and turn up in New York so many years after the war, then maybe my brother can too."

I said nothing. We hadn't actually been told that the man was Jewish; nor did we hear that he had been living previously in Poland in the vicinity of my uncle or that he had ever been in the clutches of the Nazis. But I kept silent.

"I should've brought a *Tilliml* along to say on the train," my father said. He was referring to the Book of Psalms, which always served as a prayer book in a moment of danger.

It was probably the first time that my father had ever been to midtown Manhattan and beyond. He seemed astonished by the figure of the doorman of the apartment building dressed in a vaguely military uniform who opened the door for us and rang us up.

"*Ameyrike gonif,*" my father exclaimed. "He could be a general in Kaiser Franz Yozef's army the way he looks."

It was the only bit of levity on this trip. We were ushered into a very large apartment with several bathrooms, but this did not impress my father. He was intent upon questioning the Russian escapee. After a round of introductions and a maid's service of tea in cups rather than in glasses, the discussion began. My father fiddled with the teacups nervously, but he did not drink.

It turned out that the Russian fellow *was* Jewish but had never been caught in Nazi territory. He was a classical musician, a second violinist in a string quartet in the Ukraine at the beginning of the war, and he and his three mates had been mustered out of the Soviet army because of a variety of medical problems, his an arrhythmia of the heart that had little to no effect on his music making. He had subsequently incurred the wrath of the local commissars by not getting approval for the various musical programs the group was playing, a thankless job of ass kissing that the other quartet members had thrust upon him. His group played Shostakovich quartets when that composer had finally made himself acceptable to the central government, but the news of the composer's "reformation" apparently hadn't reached the local commissars. Worse yet, the Russian violinist had written a quartet of his own based on Chasidic themes, and when his group performed it without approval at two successive concerts in the Ukraine the year after the war began, someone reported the incident to the authorities. He was questioned and finally separated from his group and his profession and sent to a temporary Soviet detention camp in the area. It was there that he met up with my father's brother and family.

The news he had for us was limited and unsatisfying. He simply said that my uncle was the revered scholar of the detention camp, and that my uncle had expressed his resolution to some inmates to get out of the camp and return to the Nazi-occupied part of Poland. Our guest recalled how astonished he was by this comment, which he could hardly believe—to be intent upon going from the frying pan into the fire. He asked around and found out the reason. My uncle was not willing to live in a communist country that would not allow him to practice his religion and would actively prevent him from preparing kosher food for his Jewish community. He preferred to take his chances to the west under the Nazis who might kill him but would not pay attention to kosher food and its preparation within the Jewish ghettos.

That was it. The musician ultimately got out of that Russian detention area and returned to his own town and to music. He ingratiated himself with the commissars for the next several years by doing their cultural bidding until his group was permitted to go on a concert tour outside the country. And then he defected and came to America. He never found out if my father's brother had managed to make his way back to serve the Jewish community in Radom or elsewhere in Nazi-occupied Poland. He certainly didn't know the details of what undoubtedly would have happened to him there. Or did my uncle change his mind and decide to stay in the Soviet Union in spite of its proscriptions against religious practice? And if he did change his mind and stay, did he finally fall into Hitler's net with the invasion of the Soviet Union by Nazi forces later that year? The stranger did not know. Our hopeful inquiry led nowhere.

On our subway ride back home, my father bent his crumbling form over the sacred text he had brought with him. On the trip to the meeting, he had hardly looked at the text, had preferred to converse with me. This time, on the way back, he buried his head in his *sefer,* his holy book. Only once did he look up as before and make a remark to me.

"Poor poor Jews," he said. "*Imglikleche Yidn,* unlucky Jews." My father thought for a moment more without as yet lowering his head to the text that commanded his life. "Oh how we could have used a Shimshen *ha-Giber* in all the Nazi death camps to tear the pillars down."

THE FALSE MESSIAH

MY FATHER'S best friend for one whole year when I was a senior in high school was *Reb* Yussl Davidson, a friendship that lasted until the latter announced in shul one day that he was the messiah.

"Best friend" is not an accurate description since my father didn't really have friends in the way we normally use the word. Sarah and I had friends. We met a bunch of guys and girls almost every Friday evening after Sabbath dinner all of whom were hanging around the steps of the local library long after closing hours. We laughed together, told jokes to each other, took walks along the river edge in one extended straggling group, paired off occasionally into petting couples, and on Sunday morning we played paddle tennis together in the neighborhood park that was once my childhood haven. In the winter, the guys split off from the girls every Sunday for touch football in the empty pool in the middle of the park, and the girls retreated to the inside of the bathhouse that wasn't in use for extended games of jacks, their childhood diversion indoors.

But my father almost never indulged in idle talk or idle games with anyone. Not even with my mother, at least not in my presence. He adhered faithfully to the Talmudic dictum not to multiply chatter with women, even with one's own wife, lest it steal valuable time from Torah study. On Friday evenings, after the *zmires* and after our review of the Torah portion of the week, I would get up to leave and join my friends and Sarah, but my father would continue his own regimen of Talmud study in my absence. He did not look kindly on my leaving the *Shabes* table for the pursuit of frivolous things,

204

but he did not say a word of reproach. He would not disturb my mother with angry words on the Sabbath.

My father rarely laughed, though once I watched him when he was listening to the comic Yiddish rhymester on Sunday-morning radio whose gift of satirizing the week's news in verse did bring forth a furtive smile to my father's face. He also smiled when my mother showered him with too much attention, usually with remonstrations about his neglect of vital food on the table in favor of his sacred books.

So the word "friend" is a loose approximation. *Reb* Yussl Davidson was not really a friend of my father's; he was my father's "project." My father had noticed him for the first time at a *kiddush* given by the wealthiest man in the congregation one Saturday. This was a festive ritual spread of food laid out after the *Musaf* service close to noon on the Jewish Sabbath. The word itself referred to the sanctification of the wine, so this minor meal, usually donated by a congregation member in respect of some personal commemoration, began with wine and shots of whiskey undiluted in small jigger-glasses. Along with the drinks came slices of honey cake, followed by plates of herring, and on the most special of occasions, plates of steaming *tshulnt,* a meat-and-bean concoction that filled an empty stomach thoroughly and sometimes lay there for days on end. In truth, the *kiddush* was a rarity in my father's congregation because very few members could afford to sponsor such a spread. But when it did take place one rare Sabbath morning, my father noticed that a stranger had come up the steps from Clinton Street to the second-floor synagogue, just as the prayers had come to an end, as if drawn inexorably by the aroma of free food.

This didn't disturb my father. He had, in fact, expected it. It was common for the poor of the district to wander into synagogues when the rumor reached them that a *kiddush* was in process. This man—soon to be known as *Reb* Yussl—was a typical *shnorrer,* a moocher of food come a-begging. His black suit was frayed at the edges, his collar askew, his felt hat crushed and discolored from exposure to days and days of adverse weather. *Reb* Yussl's beard was scraggly, uncombed, his brow furrowed with lines of unrelenting care, as if a blunt scalpel had scraped them across his head. He walked with a distinct lean to the left, his head always forward and bent. He seemed a permanent menial, a slave to life without recourse. Only his eyes betrayed his true age. They were marvelously giant orbs, round, glowingly white, the pupils dark and darting from side to side, beams of iron light ready to hypnotize one and all who managed to wander into *Reb* Yussl's wavering path. He was not really an old man.

My father did not speak to him that first time. It was not appropriate. If a *shnorrer* came in for a half decent meal that he might not get again until the next Sabbath, so be it. One did not embarrass the poor under duress. Or to be exact, the poor did not embarrass the very poor lest God punish them with a similar fate. After all, my father had reminded me often enough that a corner of every agricultural field had to be set aside for the indigent in ancient Israel, according to Torah law. Why not a portion of a *kiddush* too in this country where Jews did not till the land?

Three months later, another *kiddush* at our shul and another sighting of *Reb* Yussl. This time I watched him eat, and oddly enough, he did not devour his food with outward show of appetite or a recurring history of hunger. He ate daintily, almost handling the food in the way my mother would eat a piece of rich cake—reluctantly, barely picking up the tiniest of pieces, slowly, drawing it near to her mouth, escaping notice. I can't say if my mother ate everything that way because I rarely saw her eat. Either she ate a full meal only when I was not looking or she actually lived her adult life on cups of coffee and an occasional small chunk of *mandlbroyt* or a rare slice of cake.

Three months after that, another *kiddush* and the third visit from the man with the darting eyes. After the last morsel had been consumed by congregants and interlopers, my father suddenly turned to me with a gleam in his normally half-closed eyes.

"Let's go quickly to the *Nufuk Strit Sheel*. They're still *davning* there because they engaged a professional *chazn* for today to *bentsh Rosh-Choidesh,* and a *chazn* draws out every note and takes a year and a day to finish. I'd like to hear him. You once sang in a choir with *groyse chazoonim* yourself. You should be interested too."

I jumped at the chance. My father was inviting me to accompany him to another synagogue to hear the great cantor Zavl Kwartin chant the special prayers for the new month on the Hebrew calendar. I had three good reasons for taking advantage of the opportunity. First of all, despite Kwartin's advanced age, he was still regarded as one of the titans of the art. Second, there weren't too many first-rate cantors around anymore. So many of them had been murdered in the concentration camps in eastern Europe by the Nazis and their followers during the war. Kwartin was a rare survivor of these vocal superstars. And third, and perhaps most important, my father almost never invited me to go with him anywhere. To his shuls, yes. But elsewhere to hear a cantor? Even this, a seemingly devout activity, was next to useless and almost unworthy in his own eyes. The words of prayer did not need florid, self-serving virtuoso singing to give them meaning and emotion to my father. In fact, he once assured me that this kind of singing could actually deter a person from true devotion, and he cited the oft-repeated rumor that many of the well-known cantors were not faithful followers of Jewish law.

"Then why did you let me sing in a liturgical choir with great cantors when I was a kid until my voice changed?" I asked my father. It almost sounded like a brazen question, but he did not react angrily to the oblique note of challenge in my voice.

"You were a child then," he said, "in a country of wandering children. I thought maybe this would make you love the synagogue and the prayers and keep you on a straight path."

And so we went to hear Cantor Kwartin *bentsh Rosh-Chodesh* and *davn* the *Musaf* service. My mother excused herself and returned home with my younger brother Noosn, the giant in the family, to rest a while and later to prepare a simple, delayed, second Sabbath meal. Cantors did not interest her or Noosn, but for other reasons.

♥

The Norfolk Street Shul gave a fine *kiddush* after the service. My father had intended for us to leave discreetly before the festive meal began; after all, one *kiddush* on any given Sabbath was more than enough for any man. But the rabbi of the shul caught up with us at the door and insisted that we stay. My father had often enough served as the rabbi's encyclopedia or reference book, furnishing him with the source of Talmudic quotations including exact page numbers that the latter would want to cite in his weekly sermon in the *dvar-Torah,* the speech made up of a learned exegesis of Torah and Talmud passages. So it was not surprising that the rabbi delayed his entrance to the room filled with food and a swarming crowd of hungry people to urge my father to accompany him as a special guest.

And there was *Reb* Yussl who had also been at our *kiddush* in our shul on the very same day an hour or so earlier. Unlike us, he had not come for the cantor. We knew this because my father actually asked him for his opinion of Cantor Kwartin, a question whose very formulation by one like my father who despised religious "performances" I could not have ever foreseen in my most daring of fantasies.

"I don't come to listen to cantors or even to pray," *Reb* Yussl said. "I come to eat."

His voice, his accent astonished me. My world was narrow. I had always expected bearded Jewish men in black caftans to speak English with an eastern European Yiddish accent—"com" for "come" and a guttural "r" for the distinctively sharp American front roll of the consonant. And most assuredly, they all said "*chazoonim*" for "cantors" and "*davn*" for "pray." But this man, this *Reb* Yussl spoke with a southern drawl that outdid the characters in *Gone with the Wind.* It was amazing. The thin ascetic mouth between the scraggly hairs of mustache and beard said "Ah" for "*I,*" a "liquid *l*" in "listen," and something like "caintuhs" for "cantors." Who was this man?

My father would not let him go. Something in the man drew my father—normally a standoffish person—to *Reb* Yussl. Within days, the man was coming twice a week to our home for an hour or two of study of sacred texts with my father. My father had taken this wayward soul under his wing.

"Sacred texts" is another exaggeration. It would be weeks before my father could put a sacred text of substance before our guest. "*Er iz an am ho-orets gumer,*" my father said to my mother in the first days of the relationship. He was telling her that our *Reb* Yussl was a complete ignoramus in regard to sacred texts. He didn't even know how to read the Hebrew prayers. How could this be? How could a bearded Jewish man dressed in traditional black, and a bright fellow at that, be totally unfamiliar with a single letter in the Hebrew alphabet?

"Is he really Jewish?" my mother asked one day. "Russian priests also wore beards, I remember."

My father was taken aback by this remark. But he could do nothing himself to learn the truth. It wasn't easy for my father, who almost never indulged in gratuitous gossip, to ask a personal question. He delegated the job to me.

On my mother's insistence, *Reb* Yussl was invited to our table for a festive Friday night dinner. My father didn't really like the idea. Friday nights were for family—for my parents and for me and for my kid brother Noosn. Friday nights were for singing *zmires* and for review of the weekly Torah portion with the commentaries. My father and I were the reviewers. Noosn, who was slightly retarded and could not master the sacred texts though he had learned how to read and how to *davn* with some difficulty, listened in to our scholarly discussions. It was a family affair. But if my mother insisted on something, it was done. So *Reb* Yussl came to our table from wherever he lived—still a mystery to us—and ate a good meal even if he could not sing the sacred hymns and could not understand the Hebrew texts.

When we had completed the course of Torah review after the meal, I arose and invited *Reb* Yussl to accompany me to the neighborhood library where my friends and my girlfriend Sarah were gathering. My father was almost relieved to see him go with me. For one thing, he cherished his own time at the table with his Talmud volume and with my mother hovering in the background. For another, I think he sensed that I would exploit the opportunity to delve into the history of our new friend.

"My father wants to know if you're Jewish," I said bluntly to *Reb* Yussl as we descended the stairs of our tenement.

"Your mama's a good woman," *Reb* Yussl said. "I can still savor the chicken soup and the chicken and the fruit dessert and the steaming glass of tea with generous slices of nut cake that she baked in the afternoon just for me."

"Where do you come from, and who were your parents?" I persisted in the darkened and somewhat deserted streets. I was pleased by my own bluntness. Sarah would be proud of me. She wanted a guy with guts and a forceful personality. I tried to act the part.

"I was born in Brooklyn," *Reb* Yussl finally said in his characteristic Southern drawl. "I" was "Ah," and "born" was "bone." I had to restrain myself from audible laughter—not a very kindly reaction on my part had I given in to it.

"When I was two," he continued, "my parents moved to Mobile, Alabama, to open a clothing store there. Both my parents were Jewish. My father was born in Smyrna and my mother in Salonika. They came to Brooklyn as a young married couple just before immigration was suspended in the early '20s, but they couldn't make it in New York."

"Then you're a Sephardic Jew," I said, "not an Ashkenazic Jew, whose parents came from central or eastern Europe. Your parents' cities are in southern Europe, I think somewhere in Yugoslavia or Turkey."

"I suppose so," he mumbled. He really didn't know. "In Alabama I didn't get a Jewish education. My parents tried to be like everybody else."

At the library, I introduced him to my friends, half a dozen guys and as many girls who had gathered for no activity in particular. They looked at him as if he were an intruder from Mars. It dawned on me that we were all dressed in conventional suits of varied shades, the girls in colorful Sabbath dresses, and that *Reb* Yussl was the only one in traditional garb. I introduced him to Sarah.

He looked her up and down. The faint traces of a smile creased his face between the fuzzy hair of his mustache and beard. "Sarah, nice name," he said. "I'm Abraham," he added.

"I thought your name was Yussl, Joseph," I said.

"My name is whatever it has to be," he replied promptly. His eyes were still on Sarah.

"Where did you come up with this character?" Sarah whispered to me.

"Be nice," I said to her softly. "He's a guest at my parents. My father wanted me to invite him out for a stroll."

"I don't like it," she said firmly. "He's giving me the once-over."

I took *Reb* Yussl or *Reb* Abraham aside and led the march of our dozen friends toward the East River and the bridge. Sarah mingled with the others in the group and did not show up at our side.

"So go on with your story," I continued. "If you're a Sephardic Jew, how come the name Davidson? It should be something like Abulafia or Shabtai or whatever."

"Names can be changed," he said. "I already told you so. When I was fourteen, I ran away from home and hoboed it throughout the States. I finally came back to New York. Things were worse for me than they had been for my parents when they lived in Brooklyn. As a hobo, I could always find lodging and food. But in New York, I was sleeping on park benches and under bridges and I was starving."

We had come to the Williamsburg Bridge arching over the East River from Delancey Street to Brooklyn. The water was calm and dark. The winds were inert. The tramping feet behind us had rumbled to a stop at the water's edge. It was silent. I looked in both directions for the religious Christian fanatic who had turned a water hose on Sarah and me and had sent us flying the previous year when we had been messing around on a waterside bench. I still limped a little bit, the hollow of the thigh never having healed completely from that encounter with the devil. No sign of the lunatic, unless our *Reb* Yussl was the rabid evangelist in disguise.

"Then I found a pack of black clothes in a trash can on Essex Street. They fit me perfectly, and I've been wearing them ever since. I bought a black hat on a pushcart on Rivington Street for a quarter that I stole from a kid who was out to buy some ice cream. I grew a beard, adopted the name *Reb* Yussl Davidson, came to the Lower East Side among the religious Jews, and I was in business. So here I am."

I froze. The ridiculous thought came into my mind that *Reb* Yussl was the reincarnation of Big Red, my Aunt Geety's husband who had lived on our fourth floor for a time disguised in ultrareligious black garb. After some months of moving around like this in the neighborhood incognito, Big Red disappeared from view along with Aunt Geety and their child. He must have gotten tired of the charade imposed upon him by my father of learning to be an ultrareligious Jew and of hiding from the loan sharks. My mother was totally distressed by Aunt Geety's disappearance until she got a letter from her beloved niece from another state saying they were all okay and would someday return. But the stupid thought came to me that Big Red must have discarded his black clothing in a local trash can when he made his getaway with Aunt Geety and the baby, and maybe *Reb* Yussl picked up Big Red's clothes and assumed his position, or his life. They were, more or less, of equal height. I tried to knock this silly line of thought out of my mind to concentrate on my guest.

My friends paid no attention to us. They were too busy talking about the final days of the baseball season and the almost successful attempt of the New York Giants to overtake the league-leading Brooklyn Dodgers for the pennant. Willie Mays and Jackie Robinson were much more on their minds than my friend in black caftan. Even the girls seemed engrossed in the baseball discussions under the bridge a few feet away from the two of us, though Sarah stole a glance every now and then at me and at the man who troubled her.

"He's a Sephardic Jew from Smyrna," I told my father and mother the morning of the Sabbath as we prepared to go to shul. "I think he's telling the truth. He doesn't lie about himself. He's also a *gonif*." I meant a crook. My father's face clouded over—to this day I'm not sure over which part of the remarks that I made, but he continued to see *Reb* Yussl and he continued to persevere with him to teach him what the guest never knew and what I was sure he really did not want to learn.

♥

Life wasn't easy for us those days even though the economic depression and the terrible war were not-so-dim memories of an evil time gone by. My mother developed arthritic pains that diminished her ability to roam about the house and the neighborhood freely. They kept her from the tasks she treasured—if standing over a hot stove or seated for hours at a Singer sewing machine can be called treasurable. She spent more and more time in the rocker that my father had picked up for a pittance in a local thrift shop, reading the Yiddish newspaper or the book of biblical stories written in the same mother tongue.

My father was also suffering from a variety of illnesses far more serious than arthritis though perhaps not as painful. He was not an old man, but he was crumbling under his years. He coughed a lot and often scared me with his coughing spells. My mother tended to him as best she could. She also tried to reassure me about my father's health, but the phlegm and the occasional blood were there and not to be denied.

Reb Yussl came dutifully to the twice-weekly lessons with my father. I sometimes felt that he was doing so in order to assure his acceptance in the local synagogues on the Sabbaths on which they presented a *kiddush* to the congregation. I did not trust his motives. My father, on the other hand, was overwhelmed by the man's apparent intellectual abilities. *Reb* Yussl learned to read Hebrew fluently in less than a month. He even picked up a few Yiddish words from my parents for use in daily conversation. Within six months, he was able to study the Torah portions on his own, and within a year, he was studying the Mishnah. It would not be long before he would be applying himself to the Gemara, written in Hebrew letters but in the difficult Aramaic language. The Mishnah and the Gemara printed together on the same page in related successive units constituted the Talmud, that awesome multivolumed tome of intricate Jewish law and lore that was the staple of my father's learning and the summa of achievement. *Reb* Yussl was replacing me as my father's favorite student, and perhaps as my father's only friend.

I even met him once or twice in the local library that was my friends' hangout many an evening, particularly on Friday nights. *Reb* Yussl was rummaging among the books in the Judaica section, and he had half a dozen in hand. Several of them dealt with Cabbalah, the mystical studies in Judaism, and one of them was a discourse or a translation of the *Zohar,* the most well-known mystical work.

"How old are you?" I asked him facetiously. "You're not allowed to study this stuff according to Jewish tradition until you're at least thirty-five or forty."

"I'm twenty-eight," he said, "but I'm permitted to break all the laws. My physical years on earth are few, but my soul is far older than forty."

I laughed and didn't give it another thought.

Then the traumatic moment—not the messiah announcement in shul but something else. *Reb* Yussl began making it a practice of coming to our home on Friday nights in addition to the weekday lessons with my father, and I fell into the pattern of taking him with me to meet my friends after my father had completed the study of the Torah portion of the week with the three of us. I should say with the four of us because, by this time, even Noosn, however slow he was in study, was able to follow along in our traversal of the biblical tales in Genesis and parts of Exodus though the legal and ceremonial sections of Leviticus, for example, remained an eternal enigma to my giant kid brother with the crippled mind.

My friends also got used to *Reb* Yussl. He opened up and talked sports and movie stars and even had some things to say about music and art and current American literature, though I could not fathom where he had picked up all this stray knowledge. He knew a good deal about Hemingway and Steinbeck, and he talked as if Faulkner was not from Mississippi, but from his hometown in Mobile, Alabama. He also told me that he hated Vivien Leigh and thought that a real Southern gal should have gotten the lead role in *Gone with the Wind.* Absent that, he said, he would have settled for Betty Grable because she had nicer legs.

My friends laughed at these remarks and began to think that he was a regular guy. They didn't, in the final analysis, mind his strange dress because elders all about us dressed that way and because *Reb* Yussl's garb had become immaculate. I never found out if he worked for a living or where he got some money to live on. His clothing—always the same whenever he met with us—had suddenly been mended and cleaned and pressed to a turn. At whose expense, we didn't know, but we couldn't complain about his appearance, as some of us did about other elders in the community. *Reb* Yussl's black shoes were shined, his beard now prematurely gray was trimmed, and his oval eyes were as darting and as compelling as ever.

On this trek, the two of us, *Reb* Yussl and I, began to trail away from the bridge along the river edge. Several of my friends paired off with girlfriends and sat down on a string of benches alongside. Within four or five minutes, *Reb* Yussl and I, Sarah bringing up the rear, were far ahead of our friends and alone bestriding the metal railing that overlooked the river. We stood side by side, our eyes focused on the opposite Brooklyn shore. Sarah's light tread was behind us. *Reb* Yussl turned around to face her. I continued examining the not-so-still waters and the neon lights on the other shore and the twinkling bridge lights in the distance to the right.

"Get your filthy hands off me!" Sarah screamed.

I turned quickly. There was no one behind her. Only myself and *Reb* Yussl were facing her. I looked around as if I couldn't understand what was happening. But *Reb* Yussl made it quite clear. He lunged for Sarah and grabbed her in an iron embrace. His legs straddled hers, and his hands were all over her body. She screamed again, this time a choking scream that had no heft to it and seemed to be caught in her strangled throat.

It took me a second or two to react to this unlikely scene. I jumped forward and put my hands on *Reb* Yussl's back and pulled as hard as I could. He didn't budge; he was taller and stronger than I had imagined. Sarah began to whimper. I then jumped to the side and tried to pry them apart, but the two seemed locked together as if in a vise. I had no choice. I lashed out with a fist that caught *Reb* Yussl on the temple just below his black hat, which came flying off. He was bald—not a hair on his head. His knees buckled, but he did not go down. I drove a fist into the side of his ribs, and I could hear a gasp of pain. And still, he had one hand behind Sarah's back, pressing her to his side, and one hand all over her breasts. His free hand suddenly darted to her crotch. For inexplicable reasons, I was frozen for more than a moment. The helpless thought entered my mind that I would have wanted at this time to have at my side my kid brother Noosn, whose powerful physique would have saved us all. There was space between the two bodies for a split second, and I kicked him hard in the balls. He fell to the ground screeching in pain, and I grabbed Sarah who started to run.

"She's mine! She's mine!" *Reb* Yussl yelled from the ground. "She's my Sarah!"

"We can't leave him here," I said to her. "He'll be mugged by somebody or other if we leave him here on the ground with those clothes on."

"Her name is Sarah. She's mine, she's mine!"

"If you stay here," Sarah gasped, "you stay here alone. I'm running home."

"Sarah, my fated consort," he wailed in apparent pain. "My *basherte.* It is written." He was writhing on the ground, holding his crotch.

I had no choice. I could either abandon this miserable man or abandon my beloved. I ran home with Sarah.

"What does *basherte* mean?" Sarah asked at the door of her apartment after we had managed several blocks in total silence. She did not know much Yiddish.

"It means *your intended one,* in Yiddish," I said in a faint voice devoid of emotion or strength, "the one chosen for you by God Who spends His days pairing off lovers. That sonofabitch Yussl has learned a lot this year."

❤

Things were not the same for a while between Sarah and me. She seemed distant and cold. I didn't know if she was angry with me for taking so long to protect her or if she was simply traumatized by the bastard's assault. I would guess that the whole event took no more than ten or fifteen seconds, maybe twenty, maybe thirty, but I suppose to her it seemed like an hour, and in a manner of speaking, to me too.

Sarah and I continued to meet, we continued to go places together, but we didn't hold hands, and we didn't kiss. I didn't really try, but the negative signals were there. I was young, and I was scared, more scared of losing her than of being beaten up by her attacker.

It wasn't my only worry. *Reb* Yussl disappeared from view. He didn't come to the twice-weekly lessons with my father, and he didn't show up on

Friday nights. Perhaps more worrisome, he didn't make a sudden appearance for *kiddush* in any of the local synagogues. I checked up on that. My friends attended a variety of shuls—all orthodox; there were no Conservative or Reform Temples in our neighborhood, as far as I knew—and they were my informers. Not a one of them saw the tallish young man with the graying beard and the black garb, leaning to the left as he walked, his vital eyes staring down everyone, in any of the synagogues in the whole neighborhood of our youth. I dreaded the thought that I had either left him for dead or that somebody else found him on the ground, abandoned, a ready target for violent robbery even though he ostensibly owned nothing worth robbing.

My parents never once inquired about him. Just as he came so suddenly, like a spiraling tornado in the distance out of nowhere, so he disappeared with equal suddenness, and my mother and my father acted as if this was to be expected in life. People come, people go. The bad times, and the good times. The Pharaoh who knew Joseph, and the Pharaoh who did not know Joseph.

I could not keep my mind on my studies. Baseball scores and heroes—or was it football at that time of the year? —were a frivolity to me. All the news in the newspapers seemed a side issue to me. This included the terrible war in Korea, the maniacal activities of Senator Joe McCarthy, the much more comforting exploits of the newly created State of Israel after two thousand years of Jewish exile, with its miraculously revived Hebrew language, and even the giddy fanfare preceding the coming American presidential election. Even music, my beloved music, my inept piano playing and the teacher who had once conducted the Berlin Opera before escaping from the Nazis and whom I had abandoned so cavalierly, was a distracting irrelevancy. I listened to Rubinstein's Chopin on an old shellac record in the apartment of Sarah's parents when they were not there and even brought along a joyful romp on Bachian themes by Alec Templeton that I had bought on Second Avenue to cheer her up, but none of these gladdened her heart or mine.

One Friday evening, I sneaked away from our friends at the library and took Sarah to a club on 52nd Street to hear the blind jazz pianist Art Tatum. Listening to him and his two-handed improvisations would have been enough for me to give up any thought of a career at piano playing. I, for one, couldn't keep my eyes off the keys when I played. I marveled that though Tatum saw nothing, he seemed to see everything. For a few minutes, I was separated from my concern for the whereabouts of *Reb* Yussl or from my fears about Sarah and our relationship. I was afraid to mention either of these things to her again. I did not know how she would react.

The last word in my thoughts popped into her conversation as if by magic. "How would your parents react," she asked, "or mine, if they knew we were here, on a Sabbath no less?"

"We're not eating anything unkosher," I said. We had ordered soft drinks and were nursing them for half the evening.

Sarah flipped her hair sideways as she always did when she thought I had spoken some foolishness. "Okay," she said. "You're kosher. But we've traveled up here by subway, and you've gone out into the world and read their books and studied their science and listened to their music. What next? Soon you'll be thinking their thoughts, drinking their drinks, and ditching me for a blond chick who does things."

I froze. "Never," I said, after a moment. "Maybe all the other stuff, but I'll never be a drinker." I tried to laugh. Sarah smiled. I was distraught. Nothing was working.

"I can't get my mind off *Reb* Yussl Davidson," I said finally. "He's disappeared. Whatever he did, I'm responsible for him. I knocked him down. Where is he? Is he alive? Did somebody kill him out there? All Israel is responsible for one another."

Sarah stretched out her hand and enveloped mine. We turned to listen to Tatum playing Dvořák's "Humoresque." There were no answers, but there were consolations.

♥

In the month of August, at the hottest time of the year, when my father was thoroughly depleted by the undiminished heat, he came upon a crisis in his synagogue that threatened to double his obligations beyond his waning strength. Some weeks before, he had risen in the morning with the left side of his face paralyzed, and we all thought that he had suffered a stroke. My father calmed us down and assured us that this was not so; he had complete use of his arms and legs. It turned out to be an attack of Bell's palsy, which froze his face into an uncharacteristic sneer and even slurred his speech for a time. Luckily, an elder physician from the old country who was also a family friend was quite familiar with modern treatment. He sent my father immediately to a physical therapist, who insisted upon certain facial exercises that my father was not prone to do. I prevailed upon him every day with my mother's help to do the exercises, even at the cost of valuable time that he might have devoted to his books, and after two weeks of this rigorous regimen, the sneer disappeared, and his face, always wreathed in sorrow, returned to its natural look. But, somehow, he was not the same again. He seemed much more exhausted than usual, coughed more, and consistently walked with a hunched shoulder staring at the ground, his eyes vacant and unseeing.

The Sabbath in August before Tisha B'Av, the most mournful fast-day of the Jewish calendar, is the Sabbath wherein the first *sedra,* the first section of the final Book of Deuteronomy is read in shul and the first chapter of Isaiah is chanted at the end of the Torah reading. It is a momentous Sabbath called *Shabes Chazon,* the Sabbath of Prophetic Vision, the Vision being Isaiah's. And just at this time, in the year of my father's increasing illness, the congregant who normally led the *Shacharis* and M*usaf* prayers and the young Torah reader who had been hired six months before to read the long Torah portions each week, both in place of my father, became ill and did not attend services. My father had relegated himself to one tiny job. He was the *gabbay,* the religious sexton who doled out the honors in the shul—calling men to the Torah to say the blessings over each subdivision of the reading and others to lift and tie the Torah at the end of the reading and still others to open the Holy Ark at various intervals. He also stood alongside the reader of the Torah to help him with difficult passages, and he recited the preliminary Hebrew formula before each honored congregant said his blessing and the closing "*Mi sheh-beyrach*" formula that ended each sequence.

Now, with the two others absent from shul because of their illness, the members of the congregation expected my father to lead both the *Shacharis* and *Musaf* services, each at least a half hour to an hour long, and also to read the Torah portion in the sacred scroll that required a good deal of prior review. My father certainly knew how to do all of these things, but I sensed that he was not physically up to the arduous tasks involved. I insisted that other members of the congregation take up the slack, but in truth, there was no one in attendance capable of doing the Torah reading, which differed each week and required a good measure of preparation and expertise.

The two services were the same from week to week, and regulars at the service knew the prayers well enough even if they could not sing. My father pleaded with other members to fill in for him, but they resisted, unsure of their own abilities. Then he asked me to do the Torah reading. I was stunned, not because I hadn't prepared the reading—and I hadn't, but because he asked *me* to do it. For once, I looked my father in the eye.

"I'm not religious enough," I said, "to *leyn* the Torah in shul."

My father did not say a word.

"And I haven't gone over the *trop,*" I added. I was referring to the melodic notation in the Torah texts in book form that had to be memorized because they were never written into the holy scrolls used in the synagogue.

My father looked at me with a determination that I had seen only in his younger days and was now generally lacking. My mother was behind the partition in the women's section. I could see her peeking out through a separation in the cloth.

"You're permitted to make up the notes," my father said. "The *trop* isn't important. All that's important is that you pronounce the holy words accurately and end a phrase and a sentence where it should end. You'll do it." My father was referring to the fact that the scroll text did not contain vowels or punctuation either, and that this required a solid knowledge of the Torah text itself in order to pronounce everything correctly, all of which he expected me to do.

"Now we have to find a *sheliech-tsiber,* a cantor," my father added with a wearied tone of finality, "to *davn Shachris* and *Misef.*"

THE FALSE MESSIAH | 221

At that moment, *Reb* Yussl entered the synagogue. I couldn't believe my eyes. I couldn't even respond to my father, to dispute him, or to fuss anymore.

Reb Yussl looked the same. In fact, he looked even younger. He didn't walk anymore with a lean to the left. His back was more than straight; it arched slightly backward, as if he was displaying medals on his chest. I never realized how tall he really was. His forehead wrinkles seemed to have disappeared. He looked regal, a veritable young King David loping along in dance among the populace.

My father did not display any overt reaction. "*Git* Shabes, *Reb* Yussl," my father said as if he had seen him the week before and the week before that. Then he brightened a bit. "You're a *nes min ha-shomayim*, a miracle from heaven. We need a *Ba'al-Shachris* and also a *Ba'al-Misef*. You'll *davn* for us."

Reb Yussl nodded. I was glad to see that he was alive, but what was he doing here? We had not planned a *kiddush* on the Sabbath before the fast day of the Ninth of Av. Why did he come? And how much of the prayers did he really know? And had he ever performed in public? I looked at his blazing eyes and knew immediately that he was trying to tell me something. I looked away.

One of the elders did volunteer for the *P'sukey d'Zimrah*, a set of preliminary prayers, and when *Reb* Yussl began with the *Shocheyn Ad*, the initial recitation by the cantor of the *Shacharis*, the walls trembled. His voice was stentorian, the sound a clear outpouring of lyrical emotion. By the time he got to the *Kedushah* in the cantor's repetition of the *Shemoneh Esreh*, also called the *Amidah*, the synagogue was filled to the rafters. The news had traveled to neighboring early-morning *minyans*, and their votaries came running to our shul to hear the new phenomenon. I say "cantor" because that's what he was, not a common *Ba'al-Tefillah*, lay leader of the service, but a world-renowned cantor, a veritable opera star.

Congregants had tears in their eyes. Even Noosn seemed excited. My father's eyes were closed. I walked past my mother in the women's section and nodded to her.

"He is your father's *talmid*, your father's student," she whispered to me across the curtain.

I tried to steal a few moments in order to practice the Torah-reading chant, but I was distracted. I thought of Sarah. A pity she wasn't in the women's section to hear her assailant sounding like an angel apostrophizing God with, "Holy, holy, holy." But I could not in my heart forgive him.

My chanting of the Torah portion went fairly well. My father standing alongside did not have to correct me more than three or four times. When it came to the sixth honor of going up to the Torah to say the blessing, my father motioned to *Reb* Yussl, who was seated a few yards away, resting from his labors. *Reb* Yussl mounted the *bima,* the elevated platform.

"Your Hebrew name?" my father asked, as he did of every honoree so that he could announce the person's elevation to the Torah in the traditional formula.

"*Reb* Yeyshu," *Reb* Yussl said.

"I thought your name is Yusef," my father countered.

"No, a mistake. That's my father's name. I'm *Reb* Yeyshu ben Yoseyf."

My father, hesitant, his eyes narrowing, began to recite. 'Ya'amoid, Yeyshu ben . . ."

"Ben Yoseyf," *Reb* Yussl urged him on, "*ha-melech ha-moshiach* ben Dovid."

My father stopped in mid-chant. His face went white, drained of all blood. "Are you going out of your mind? *Di machst choyzek farn Oorn Koy-desh?*" He was challenging *Reb* Yussl, asking him in Yiddish if he was making insulting jests in front of the Holy Ark.

Did *Reb* Yussl understand the Yiddish? Did the congregants understand that *Reb* Yussl wanted himself announced in Hebrew as Jesus, son of Joseph, the King Messiah son of David?

Reb Yussl raced around the table on which the Torah scroll was resting and planted his feet in front of the *Aron Kodesh,* the Holy Ark holding all the other Torah scrolls. He turned and faced the whole congregation, throwing up his long hands so that they almost reached the ceiling.

"I am the anointed one of God!" he shouted, his voice no more the lyrical instrument under lovely control. "Of God, of *Yehovah,* of *Yud, Hey, Vav, Hey,* of the *Sheym ha-Meforush.* I have been so informed by a *bas kol min ha-shomayim,* a heavenly voice. I was born in Smyrna, not Brooklyn, on Tisha B'Av, on the Ninth Day of the holy month of Av. I have the power to abolish all fasts. The law is hereby abrogated. This week's coming Tisha B'Av fast commemorating the destruction of the two ancient temples is now transformed into a joyous celebration of my return. No more fasting! Celebrate with me and with my future wife whose name is Sarah. I—"

My father, weak as he was, did not let him continue. "You are an *oycher Yisrool,* a troubler of Israel!" he shouted at *Reb* Yussl. "Descend from the *bima.* There is no *aliya* for you. Grass will grow over your head before the *moshiach* comes. You are an ignoramus and a misleader of Israel. You are also an *oysvurf,* a criminal, and a violator of women. No respectable Jewish woman named Sarah or any other name will lie down with you. Be gone! You are henceforth separated from the community of Israel!"

I was stunned. How did he know? My father pronounced these words with an audible tremor in his voice. I had never heard him pass stern judgment on any man except a Hitler or a Stalin.

The congregation was in turmoil. They shouted, mouthing incomprehensible words, and began moving toward the *bima* menacingly. I subsequently learned that it was *Reb* Yussl's pronunciation of the Ineffable Name of the Almighty in front of the Holy Ark and the sacred four letters of that name that provoked them to near-violence. Nothing else. *Reb* Yussl, terrified, descended quickly from the *bima* and ran out a side door. He was trying to save himself from a situation of physical danger I considered nonexistent since I couldn't envision all these bumbling elders resorting to their fists at any time and especially on the holy Sabbath.

My father had not budged from the *bima.* His voice suddenly rang out, louder and clearer than before, as if in the act of excommunication, he had gained a godly strength. "Return to your seats!" he bellowed. "Follow the reading in the holy *Toyreh.*" And then he announced my name in Hebrew as the substitute sixth *aliya* for *Reb* Yussl, his other errant son.

I said the blessing, chanted the Torah portion, and said the second blessing. My father called up another elder for the seventh *aliya.* Then he asked me to announce his own name for the final *Maftir aliya.* I did so hesitantly.

The congregant chosen for this *aliya* was expected to recite the *Haftarah,* a chapter from the Prophets, and I feared for my father's well-being after the previous ordeal. Nevertheless, I did as he asked.

My father's voice retained its newly found strength as he chanted the preliminary blessings for the *Maftir* and then for the *Haftarah.* Then he began the chanting of the first chapter of the Book of Isaiah, always read on the "Sabbath of the Vision" that preceded the Tisha B'Av fast later in the week. This *Haftarah* reading required a special melody, not the usual one used on other Sabbaths. This one imitated the mournful chant of the Book of Lamentations recited on Tisha B'Av. My father's voice rose in intensity and in bizarre beauty as he began the words, "The vision of Isaiah, son of Amots . . ."

He came to a passage where his voice broke and returned suddenly to its former weakness. "*Bunim gidalti v'roimamti v'haym pawsh'oo vi.*"

"Sons have I raised and elevated and they have betrayed me." The words of Isaiah were God's words speaking through the prophet, lamenting the betrayal of God's law by his Jewish people, but I think that my father's lament shattered in his throat for other reasons.

♥

I told Sarah all about these strange events, but she found it hard to believe the story. A week or two later, my mother invited her to our table for a Friday-night Sabbath meal by asking permission of her parents who had gone away to a hotel in the mountains and who were happy to see their only daughter looked after on the Sabbath by respectable people. Not that we were engaged or anything; we were too young. But the two sets of parents knew each other fairly well enough to help each other out in an emergency, and her parents leaving the city fell into this category. Sarah came, but she was a little bit uncomfortable about it all.

"A *shnorrer* is a *shnorrer,*" my mother said with a shrug in Sarah's direction, referring to *Reb* Yussl. "He thinks he can get food without working for it, and he thinks he can become a *moshiach* without becoming a righteous man and a religious one too." I laughed.

My father shook his head. "It is nothing to laugh at," he said, in a rare show of pique. "Our people have been ruined throughout the ages by false messiahs. They lead us astray with false hopes and abrogation of the law that is our life. Even Akiva, the great Akiva, thought that Shimon Bar Koziba, named Bar Kochba, the Jewish revolutionary against Rome, was the messiah. As if a murderous general of an army, no matter how just the cause, can be the *moshiach*."

My father gasped for breath. I lowered my eyes. I would not look at him in his agony, and I would not look at Sarah. I turned to my mother.

"All the messiahs come after the Jewish people have suffered a great tragedy," my father continued. "Jesus after the conquest of Judea by Rome, Bar Kochba after the destruction of our Holy Temple in Jerusalem, Shobse Tsvi after the Chmielnitzky pogroms of 1648 and 1649, and this fool after the Holocaust. Why don't they come before and prevent the calamity? Why after when the tragedy is done? Why? Tell me why?"

I never expected my father to ask such questions of us. I asked such questions, but not he.

"Who was Shobse Tsvi?" Sarah asked.

"The most awful of the false messiahs in Europe," my father said. His voice seemed to perk up for a moment, perhaps because Sarah had asked him the question. "In the seventeenth century. He came from Smyrna and misled thousands upon thousands of poor, persecuted Jewish people. They sold their homes and their stores to follow him to Palestine where he would oust the Turkish sultan and reestablish God's kingdom for the Jewish people. When the Turks arrested him and gave him a choice of conversion or death, he chose to convert to Islam."

"Do you think," my mother asked, "that our Yussl was imitating Shobse Tsvi? Was Yussl really born in Smyrna? He once said he was born in Brooklyn."

"Who knows?" my father said. "What we should all know is that we must work to bring the *moshiach* by multiplying good deeds, mitzvahs, but we should never say that *moshiach* has come. That's *avoyde zure,* idolatrous worship."

My mother could not put the subject to rest. "Is there a *medrish* maybe that says the *moshiach's* wife will be named Sarah?"

My father looked Sarah directly in the eye. For the first time in a long time, a very distinct smile broadened on his face. His eyes opened wider than usual. His brow creased in wonder. In a few seconds, he had shaken off many troubled years and looked almost young again.

"No, my dear *vabele.* No such tradition. But Shobse Tsvi did marry a woman named Sarah."

My father stretched a hand out toward my Sarah. He did not touch her. "Don't get any fancy ideas now," he growled at her. "My wandering son here is not religious enough."

"Not religious enough to believe in such things?" Sarah asked bravely. "Or not religious enough to be worthy of *being* the messiah?"

Silence for a moment or two.

"Both." my father answered after some thought. He stretched his hand farther across the table and still did not touch Sarah's fingers. "Both faults for all of us in our world today," he added, this time with a bitter note of resignation in his voice.

SISTER SARAH

MY FRIEND SARAH did not know she was beautiful. She wore no makeup whatsoever and no earrings or any other gaudy ornaments. In fact, she had never pierced her ears. Her dresses were plain and unassuming, and she wore bobby sox and loafers day in and day out, changing colors occasionally. She never fussed with her long auburn hair, but her cheeks were permanently inflamed as if she had just come in from a game of paddle tennis under the hot sun in the park. Her high forehead was nevertheless cool, but her lips were red-blooded and moist. When she smiled from ear to ear, she was irresistible.

Not long after I had met her in the library stacks and after I had found out that she was also a student at the Hebrew School next door in a class immediately below mine, I began to take her home almost every evening. Home meant her father's grocery store on the corner of Avenue C and Second Street since her family lived in an apartment immediately above the store. That's when I met her father, who worked at least fourteen hours a day from six in the morning to ten at night, a sixteen-hour stretch minus two hours from four to six in the evening when Sarah and her cousin Mickey came by after school to spell her father and give him a rest. The store was actually open twenty-four hours a day. Her father had hired an assistant for the night shift from 10:00 P.M. to 6:00 in the morning. Since Sarah's father was ostensibly an observant man, he also did not attend upon the store from before sundown on Friday to an hour or more after sunset on the Jewish Sabbath. Still, the store remained open. Another man, a local gentile, took over during that twenty-six hour period. This was grudgingly accepted by the local pietists who nevertheless groused about the fact that the grocery man seemed to be profiting from sales on the Sabbath. My father, who occasionally stepped into the store to buy a few items for my mother on his way home from the yeshiva and who therefore had a casual acquaintanceship with Sarah's father, never said a word of criticism.

Her father was a driven man and sometimes very blunt.

"So you're the kid who's running around with my daughter," he said, one evening, early on in my bringing Sarah home from Hebrew School or the library. "You think just because your father is a famous *tzaddik,* and a big scholar, unlike me, that you can get anything you want. Don't be so sure, kiddo."

"Please, Daddy," Sarah said, somewhat embarrassed by his remarks. I had rarely heard anyone my age call her father Daddy. My father was Pa or Papa. But her father was more of an American, which, I suppose, demanded the more sophisticated title. He spoke English with hardly the trace of an accent, unlike my parents or the parents of most of my friends. Sarah had told me that he came to America with his parents at a very young age, four or five, and that he had gone to grade school in the United States. He wore a skullcap in the store like most religious men, but his beard was not long. It was short and well-trimmed, what some of the boys called a Vandyke, and when he put on a fancy suit late Friday afternoon, he looked like a dandy.

"Don't Daddy me," he growled at his daughter. "In America you think you can say anything to your father. If I protested to my father, I would get a good crack in the face, but here, anything goes. This is my store, and I'll say anything I want to anybody. You got that?"

Sarah pouted at the reply. Even when she screwed her lips together unsmilingly, she looked great.

"Your father, the rabbi, lets you fool around with strange girls?" her father asked, a glint in his eye.

"Daddy, that's too much," Sarah yelled.

"My father isn't a rabbi," I said calmly. "He's a teacher, just as his father was a teacher."

The grocery-store man jumped on my words. "A teacher, a rabbi, what difference does it make? You come from a dynasty, a long line of learned men who know everything. Same difference. Don't put on any airs in front of me. It won't work. And watch out for my little girl. She's smarter than you think. You won't fool her either."

"Oh, Daddy!"

Sarah must have thought that I would be offended by her father's snide remarks, but I didn't care. He led a tough life. He had a right to grumble every now and then. And after all, I wasn't interested in *him*.

But something that began with what her father said a few days later did lead to our first real breakup, except that it was Sarah who broke with me.

We had spent a longer time in the library than usual because there was no school the next day and no homework to prepare. So Sarah and I stayed among the stacks until closing time at 9:00 P.M., leafing through scores of books to find the dirty parts to read together. It was great fun. But when I got her home, close to the time the night assistant would be coming in, her father started up again, as if the long ordeal of waiting for his replacement had unnerved him.

"Now here's my heir apparent," he said. "So you think that one day you'll inherit all my wealth and that I'm a rich man. What do they say all around? They say I made tons of money in the war by getting *shtipped* under the table from people who wanted more of this and more of that during the rationing period. Sugar, butter. Well, sonny, let me tell you. It's all a lie. I'm a poor man, and if you marry my daughter, you'll be stuck with a losing proposition in this store. You'll work day and night, and you'll have *bupkes* to show for it. Remember that, sonny. You didn't fall into a *shmaltsgrib*."

I think his last word meant a bed of fat or something like that. My father and mother never used such common language in Yiddish, but I had heard it out in the street. Sarah didn't react this time to her father's peroration. She simply lowered her head and covered her darting eyes.

A day or two later, a friend of mine in school, Mendy Wright, who lived on 3rd Street near Avenue C and next to the Boys' Brotherhood Republic, a settlement house, told me things. His parents shopped regularly in the grocery store, and he was the kind of guy who knew everybody else's business and didn't mind talking about it. He told me that Sarah's father was unhappy in his marriage, that the mother almost never came into the store, and that the grocery-store man was really the poor man he always claimed to be, but not for the reasons he gave. Then Mendy whispered to me out of the side of his mouth. He had a habit of putting his hand up across his eyes and lowering his head when he was about to tell a secret. It always looked like he was ready to recite the *Sh'ma* prayer with eyes shaded and closed. He said that Sarah's father was poor because he kept another woman in a fancy apartment on Second Avenue in the Yiddish theater district and that he spent all the money he had gotten during the war under the table on this broad. I must have looked astonished and disbelieving at this news because Mendy Wright began to insist that he was telling the truth and that he had all the evidence. His own old man had seen Sarah's father with the woman countless times in cafeterias on Second Avenue where they were lovey-dovey all the time. She was an actress of some sort, and Mendy confided with a knowing smile that actresses are hot stuff and play around all the time, even actresses in the Yiddish theater, but they cost a lot of money.

I don't know what got into me. I had been taught countless times by my father never to repeat gossip of this sort or of any other kind to anybody, that it was the worst of sins. But something in me compelled me to allude to this story to Sarah herself. I must have thought that by doing this stupid thing, I was being a frank and honest individual, keeping no secrets from a friend, or maybe I thought that I would impress Sarah all the more by telling her that I didn't believe a word of it. The results were disastrous. She pounced on me like a tigress.

"You have no right telling me this!" she screamed out in the street in front of the library and near the Hebrew School where both of us were students. The guys playing cards on the steps of the library did not look up for a moment. "You have no right to meddle! To spread rumors! My father was right after all. You think you can say anything to anybody. Well, you can't."

She stomped off in a huff, her face preternaturally white without a glint of red reflection from her auburn hair, and when I followed her, she told me to freeze. She marched home all by herself. For the next month, she did not step into the library—she must have gone to another branch for homework—and she avoided me at every turn in both schools, in the park, and in all our other haunts. I was devastated, and I did not know what to do.

❖

The summer vacation period, soon upon us, was agonizing in its slow crawl through tedious hot days and nights. I worked for a few weeks in the garment center hauling racks of clothing through the busy streets to make a few dollars for the piano lessons in the fall that I wasn't sure I was going to continue and to help out at home. The full day's activity kept me busy, but it didn't occupy my mind to any extent. I thought only of Sarah and what I had foolishly said to her. On weekends I buried myself in books and even tried some scientific experiments at home and in open spaces at the East River Drive. Einstein had come to America. I had seen him on the one day my mother had taken me years before to the World's Fair in Queens. I would follow in Einstein's path; then Sarah would come back to me with a look of awe and contrition in her misty eyes. But it did no good. The torrid air of summer that sat heavily on every living thing day in and day out had surely addled my brain. I was conjuring up stupid fantasies. And so I sweated out the days and lay awake in the muggy nights assured of the fact that I had messed up my whole life with a mere inadvertent sentence or two.

Then things happened that turned it all around. In the second week of September when I was still going to work every day in the garment center, I met Mr. Spring again on my way to the subway in the morning. My old junior high teacher dug into my ribs.

"Just the chap I've been looking for," he said. And without hesitation, he handed me two tickets to a Broadway production of Euripides' *Medea* starring Judith Anderson. "I can't use them. You take them. They're on the house. Maybe it'll restore you to sanity, and you'll see the glory of Greek drama and classical culture, and you'll give up all that obscurantist *drek* that you study in your Hebrew School."

I couldn't even argue with him. He raced off before I could resist taking the tickets or give him my own opinions about Hellenism and Hebraism and all that stuff. It was only later that I noticed that the tickets were not for that very night, but for a performance in November. I could not understand why Mr. Spring wasn't able to clear his calendar so far in advance and attend the performance himself. Maybe he was getting married on that night. Perhaps he was being knighted in London during that week. I thought of a dozen other sillier scenarios, but in the end it was totally incomprehensible. I had long since passed the time when I would read mystical significance into each passing senseless event, but I could still remember that once, long ago, I would surely have been assured of the fact that this bizarre turn of events was a foreboding of miraculous things to come.

I asked myself no more questions and put the two tickets away, not knowing at that moment that this would be the first of three events in a sequence leading to a redemption.

The second was the coming of the Jewish New Year in the third week of September, the two days of Rosh ha-Shanah spent in the synagogue reciting prayers of repentance. The first day was a Saturday, and on the Jewish Sabbath, the blowing of the shofar, the ancient ram's horn, is omitted from the service. The second day of the holiday, a Sunday, included the shofar-blowing sequence that was considered central to the service. The obligation to hear thirty blasts of the shofar calling to repentance was so important that my father arranged to dispatch the young man hired to blow the shofar to the homes of the seriously ill members of the congregation who could not attend the service. The fellow would perform the thirty blasts in the privacy of each home. My father had also arranged for an outside cantor to lead the prayers, both before and after the Torah reading. He felt strong enough this time to read the Torah portion himself, and he asked me to prepare the reading of the *Haftarah,* which he pronounced *Haftoyreh.* This always was a chapter from the prophets in the *Tanach,* the Jewish Bible, in this case, almost all of chapter 31 from the Book of Jeremiah.

I hadn't done much preparation since I felt I could sight-read the text and the musical notes called *trop* without too much trouble. It was, in a way, my father's favorite chapter in the prophets, containing lines very meaningful to him that were to be repeated in the final Rosh ha-Shanah prayer of

Musaf a bit later in the day. Speaking of the northern kingdom of Israel, sometimes called Ephraim after the leading tribe in Israel and after the name of Joseph's son mentioned in Genesis, the prophet promises God's restoration of the destroyed Jewish kingdom and asks: "*Ha-veyn yakir lee Efrayim im yeled sha'ashooim?* Isn' my son Ephraim most dear to me because he is my beloved child?" The passage continues to say: "As often as I speak of him, I will yet remember him, since my insides yearn for him. I will have pity on him, says the Lord." My father changed the spelling of one letter in one word in the sacred text to make the first line refer to two children: "Isn't my son Ephraim most most dear to me along with my other beloved child?" Then he would say that the line from Jeremiah refers to both Jewish kingdoms of the time, Ephraim and Judah, and by extension, to two Jewish children, his two children, to me and to my brother Noosn.

As old as I was, I still enjoyed these virtuosic variations on a biblical theme that my father and his scholar colleagues loved to play. And so his assignment of this, his favorite reading, to me on the second day of Rosh ha-Shanah in that significant year was not taken lightly by me.

About a half hour before I would be called to the Torah to say the blessings and do the prophetic reading, I left the synagogue on Clinton Street to go to the bathroom on the second floor. I wanted to avoid all problems during my reading. And then on impulse, I went down two flights to the street and stood alongside the Yiddish theater that had replaced the shoe store and offices on the first floor. It was closed on the Jewish holiday. I stood outside, pleased to take in a breath of fresh air. The synagogue had been a bit stuffy, even with almost all the windows open. I breathed in deeply. Clinton Street was ordinarily a major shopping center with stores lining both sides of the street for at least two blocks in each direction. But most of the stores were also closed, and the human traffic on the sidewalks on either side was sparse. Down the block to the right and across the street was another movie theater with the odd name of the "Palestine," this one open on the holiday. The moviehouse had nothing to do with the name. It never showed any films about the Jewish Zionist pioneers in the kibbutzim of Palestine or about the Arab inhabitants of the ancient Jewish homeland. In fact, rumor had it that it was owned by Chinese Buddhists from Mott Street who couldn't care less about the Holy Land. But I was sick of rumors, of hearing them, of letting myself even think of them.

I looked across the street and saw Sarah marching along. I couldn't believe my eyes. She walked right past the Palestine movie theater and began to cross the gutter in the middle of the block to my side of the street. For a split second, I wanted to shout to her to go back and to cross at the corner the way my mother used to warm me when I was a kid, but I resisted since no cars were coming and since I did not want her to notice me. She got closer and closer as I slithered along the doorways of the closed stores in the airy intoxication of the autumn sun in the late morning hours. She was dressed for the holiday— a dark blue suit, double-breasted jacket and pleated skirt, stockings, and low heels, her flushed face reflecting the blue suit and the red tint in her brown hair and the golden sun. She was beautiful. And she was coming toward me.

I dodged into one store that was thankfully open, and she passed by without turning her head right or left. I sneaked a look outside and saw her enter the door alongside the theater that led to our second-floor synagogue and to other businesses on upper floors of the same building. I was astounded. I raced ahead to return to my father's synagogue and heard the light clatter of her heels on the stairs above me. When she reached the second floor, I strained my head along the metal banister and looked up the stairwell. Sarah opened the door to the women's section of my father's shul and went inside. My heart pounded. I was beside myself with joy and trepidation.

I ran back upstairs. My father had just begun reading the first Torah portion. Normally, I would stand beside him and follow his reading in the Torah scroll with my own copy of the printed text that contained vowels and musical *trop,* but this time I sat in my seat and reviewed my own chanting of the chapter from Jeremiah over and over again. My father looked down at me and scowled because I was not at his side.

Why did she leave the shul her parents attended and come to ours on this second day of the holiday? My head was in a whirl. It was lucky that there were empty seats in the women's section of our shul that she could occupy. Or maybe it was unlucky, because then she would have had to stand throughout the service, and I would have been able to see her better from the *bima,* the raised platform, when I would join my father and the cantor up front. The lights from the two brilliant chandeliers hanging along the ceiling danced into my eyes.

I was called to the Torah and ascended the *bima.* I sneaked a look in her direction. She was clearly visible beyond the *mechitsah,* the curtain that separated the women's section from the men. Her head was lowered, and her eyes were cast down upon the sacred text. She would follow every word. I chanted the blessings for the final Torah portion in a bleating voice, and when the Torah scroll was raised up high and carried away, I stood aside, actually facing the congregation, and stole another look in her direction. She stared into my dazzled eyes, and I turned away in shame. Then, alone, not even my father at my side, I summoned reserves of untapped strength for the chanting of the passionate words from the prophet. I hoped that some vestige of my beautiful kid's voice from my days in the liturgical choir had remained with me.

When I was done, I descended and returned to my seat. My father suddenly rose from his and ascended the *bima* before the blowing of the shofar. He began to speak to the congregation, which was very unusual for him. I simply hadn't expected him to speak because he normally hated to function like a rabbi in his own shul that had no rabbi. He was a teacher of the sacred texts, not a sermonizer. This is what he said:

The words of the prophet Jeremiah chanted so beautifully by my son contain two of the most well-known passages in all of *Nach,* the sacred books after the *Toyreh,* the Five Books of Moses. Both passages speak of the tragic exiles of the Jewish people, especially the kingdom of ancient Israel, frequently called Ephraim, from the name of the son of Yusef ha-Tzaddik, Yankev's favorite son whose mother was the matriarch Rachel. The first passage reads as follows: "Thus says the Lord: A voice is heard in Ramah—lamentation, bitter weeping. It is Rachel weeping for her children. She refuses to be comforted about her children because they have gone away." The second passage presents God's promise to reverse his stern decree and ends with the glorious words given to God by the prophet Jeremiah: "*Ha-*

vayn yakir lee Efrayim im yeled sha'asheeim? Is it because Ephraim is my favorite son along with Yehudah, my playful child? . . . My heart yearns for them; I will have pity on them, God says."

These words are read on the second day of *Roshishooneh* just before the blowing of the shofar, the ancient call to repentance. Is it at all possible that not only are men and women called to repent their actions, but also God repents at this moment on *Roshishooneh?* Can we consider such a sacrilegious thought—God Himself repenting His destruction of the Jewish homeland and His exile of the Jewish people? And if this is so, is it not unusual that God would do so upon hearing the sound of Mother Rachel's voice crying for her lost children? Abraham prayed to God to keep His promise of making the Jewish people as numerous as the stars in the heavens and the sand particles on the face of the earth, but God did not listen. Moses begged God not to destroy His people, but generations later God did not listen. Rachel, our mother, cries, and God listens. Why?

I have mulled over this mystery for many years. Is it because Jacob loved her so much that he would work seven years and more to become her husband? Does love between man and woman command such respect from God? Is it because Rachel never embarrassed her sister Leah who was Jacob's unwanted, unloved wife? She never threw it up to her in a fit of anger or a desire to hurt? Or is it because Rachel died young in giving birth to her second child Benjamin and never lived to get *naches,* parental joy from her two children? Or is it because of all of these things put together?

We do not know. What we do know is that the shofar calls for repentance from man and God, for regret, and for forgiveness. If we have wronged another man or woman, we must ask them for forgiveness in this season, not once but three times if they resist. We must ultimately forgive each other and achieve reconciliation. Rachel crying for her lost children. Mother-love demands this. Now let us rise to say the preliminary prayers and hear the blessings that precede the blowing of the shofar.

At the end of the service, when all the congregation filtered out to the street wishing each other a good year and standing about in front of the theater area as if they had seen a spectacular play and were waiting for the actors to emerge from the stage door, Sarah came directly up to me and said, "I'm sorry. I'm sorry. Three times I'm sorry."

I mumbled, "I'm sorry too." We did not dare touch each other. We looked into each other's eyes and knew that the exile was over.

◆

But this was only the first time we almost broke up for good. The second time, which came very soon after, was again my fault. I wanted to take Sarah out somewhere special to make up for all past slights, but I had forgotten about the tickets to Euripides' *Medea* lying snugly in my drawer. Our school had decided to celebrate Columbus Day with a block-party dance in the roped-off street on the south side of the school on the eve of the holiday. The school had contracted with residents across the street to allow for the party and to string banners and gaudy decorations from the top floor of the school across to the upper floors of the apartment houses. It was almost like the block parties that took place during the war, except that most of those events collected money from participants for contribution to USOs abroad that entertained servicemen, and this one was a school party with a distinctly Italian slant in honor of Columbus, all the money going to extracurricular school activities. I bought two tickets and took Sarah to the block-party dance even though I wasn't much of a dancer.

We had once done Neapolitan tarantellas together at night below floodlights in the outdoor theater on the FDR Drive under the bridge, and I hoped that that experience would stand us in good stead. There weren't any live musicians for most of the evening though the school band did perform two or three rousing numbers that did not encourage dancing. When a contingent of Italian kids came along from Mulberry Street, the guy who manned the Victrola and the speakers switched to Italian music and to group and circle dances. I recognized Vito Tantilli among the Italian kids since he was the star fullback on the school football team. A kid he wasn't. People said he was twenty years old and that he had succeeded in retaining eligibility for six football seasons in spite of all the academic rules.

In one of the partnered dances that Sarah and I participated in, Tantilli ended up dancing with her on a switch. In two subsequent dances, even though he was at the far corner of a line, he somehow managed to end up with her again. How this happened, I couldn't figure out. I guessed that he must have been helped out by his Italian pals on the football team to whom he was king and whose bidding they would unquestionably obey.

Halfway through the evening, when the disc jockey had switched to social dancing—fox trots, lindies, and all kinds of jitterbugging, Tantilli and three other guys came over to us.

"Sarah," he said. "Nice name. Ain't as nice as Sophia or Gina, but good enough." He shook his head back to front on almost every word. He seemed sure of himself. He towered over us. His tongue sometimes came out and licked his upper lip. He turned to me.

"Can I dance with your girlfriend?" he asked.

I shrugged my shoulders. "She's not my girlfriend," I said. "She's my sister."

He jumped back on limber feet. "Oh, yeah!" He looked at his three football-pals with a knowing smile. "So can I dance with your sister?"

"That's for her to say," I said.

Sarah went off with him to the dance floor. A few minutes later, a girl from the Italian group came up to me and pulled me into the line of dancers. I was clumsy and very nervous. I stepped on her feet countless times, but she didn't seem to mind. In the middle of the dance, Tantilli and his three bodyguards came by again with Sarah trailing in their wake.

"Sarah wants to go home," Tantilli said to me. "I see you finally got yourself a great girlfriend to dance with that don't wanna be disappointed."

I came to a dead stop, but my new partner held on to me with an iron grip.

"Tell you what," Tantilli continued. "I got a nice new car. I'll take Sarah home for you, brother. You won't hafta worry about sis. She's in good hands. I won't fumble the ball."

And in what must have been not more than five minutes from the time I first set eyes on Vito Tantilli at the block-party dance, he was gone. And along with him disappeared my Sarah.

A second or two later, my new dance partner let go of me completely.

"You're a fuckin' asshole. Chickenshit, that's what you are. You can't even dance. I wonder if you can get it up." And she shoved me away with enough strength to have made the football team herself.

I went home desolate. What did I do this time? How come I screwed it all up again? Why couldn't I say the right words? What was I afraid of at a school party? What would Sarah think of me? No more perhapses. Only questions.

She let me know soon enough.

"What happened?" I asked when I saw Sarah again the next night coming out of the library. She hadn't gone off this time to another branch.

"What happened? What happened?" she said, mimicking me mercilessly. "Is that all you're interested in? What happened? What happened to *you?* What got into your Talmudic head that compelled you to say I was your sister? Did you go nuts suddenly?"

The truth was the only way out. "I was afraid of him and his bunch," I said simply. "I'm not a fighter. I was afraid that if he thought you were my girlfriend and that, in his way of thinking, you belonged to me, he would catch me in a dark alley and beat the hell out of me until I gave you up. So I said sister to get him off my back and allow you to decide what to do."

Sarah turned this way and that, a movement of frustration and unbelief. "I'm not your sister," she said sharply. "I'm not just your friend. I am your girlfriend, for better or for worse, for winning fights or losing fights, whether you like it or not."

I stumbled into her arms along the wall of the machine-tool shop several doors down from the library and into its recessed doorway. I was totally ashamed and could not look my Sarah in the face. I buried my head in her breast.

"So what happened?" I asked softly, fearfully, without moving my head one inch to look into her eyes.

She thrust me away with both her arms with strength almost equal to that of the Italian girl at the dance. "What the hell do you think happened? I was deflowered or something? God protects the Sarahs of the world. Tantilli took me on a circuitous route with his three pals in the back seat, and before I could get my bearings, he lost control of the car over an open manhole in the street and banged into a lamppost. Nobody was hurt, but then Tantilli gets out of the disabled car, cursing all the way, and falls into the open manhole himself. Can you believe that?"

Sarah began laughing as she told the story, and I tried to laugh along, but it didn't come out right.

"His guys go off to call emergency, and when they come back, Tantilli tells them from down in the hole in water up to his you-know-what to scatter, and me too. He didn't want any of us around when the cops would come. He would handle it himself and say he was alone. The other guys disappeared fast at the order of the king, but I bent over the hole and told Tantilli that I would tell the cops that he abducted me. He threatened me for a while, but then a bee stung him. I'm not kidding. A bee! He screamed in pain, maybe in fear, and yelled at me, 'You and your effin' brother are a curse!' I said, 'He's not my brother. He's my boyfriend. And if you promise never to come near us, you or your goombahs, I'll take off and never say a word.' I made him promise on his mother's life. Then I went home."

Tantilli didn't come to school for a week and missed playing in that Saturday's football game. When he finally returned, he went looking for me in the cafeteria. When he couldn't find me since I brought my own lunch every day and ate in the science lab, he waited for me outside school grounds at the end of the school day.

"Why didn't you tell me she was your girlfriend?" he said. "I wouldn't a touched her if you told me that. Why did you say she was your sister?" When there was no answer, he continued: "Hey, man, that bee sting still hurts like hell. I hear you're the rabbi's son. Say a hail Mary for me that I should get better and be able to play football this Saturday, and we'll call it even."

♥

The final act took place when I remembered the theater tickets for Euripides' *Medea* just in time to take Sarah with me to the Broadway play on that November date. Judith Anderson lived up to everything that Mr. Spring had promised. It goes without saying that Euripides didn't fall short of the mark either. Both of us sat transfixed in the darkened theater, the rest of the audience equally breathless, as Medea, the repudiated wife of the great warrior Jason, master of the Argonauts, ranted and raved her way across the stage in righteous anger against her hero-husband who had deserted her for a younger woman. And when Medea kills her children to spite her husband and to destroy him, all of us gasped in awe and disbelief, as if we had never heard the story before or never reconciled ourselves to hearing it.

We walked out of the theater in total silence. We had intended going to the ice cream parlor on Avenue A for sodas, but Sarah simply asked to go directly home. On the subway train downtown, in a deserted car, she broke down and started to cry bitterly. I had never seen her cry.

"She should have done the same," she gulped between sobs. "She should have done the same."

I was completely confused. I did not know what Sarah was talking about. She sounded almost delirious, and I couldn't figure out how to comfort her.

"She should have killed me like Medea did," Sarah wept. "She should have punished him for betraying us with that woman."

I was aghast. "Sarah, you're too distraught to know what you're saying," I whispered.

"I know what I'm saying!" she said sternly. The one drunk in a corner of the car did not move a muscle. "I know what I'm saying!"

"Sarah, please, pull yourself together." The tears were rushing down her flushed cheeks liberally and staining her winter cloth coat. Her lips were contorted. "Dry your tears, and smile. Look beautiful again."

"I'm not beautiful!" she yelled, stamping her slim foot. The drunk in the corner stirred. "I'm not beautiful. I'm ugly. I have ugly thoughts. Medea killed Jason's children. He deserved nothing less. My mother should have done the same to me." And she broke down again.

I grew impatient with her. "Sarah, you're being ridiculous. It's not our way. We don't kill innocent children to spite a husband or for any other reason." Then I said something that unhinged her completely. "Rachel crying for her children. That's our way. Crying for her lost children, praying from the grave for God to repent for punishing her children."

She turned to me, her lower lip jutting out the way I had never seen before, and hissed in my direction. The words came out soft, but sharp and clear and unmistakable.

"I am not Rachel. I am Sarah. And you, like all men, are another Abraham, denying his beloved and calling her his sister to save his own ass while he fools around with concubines and fathers children with other women. I am Sarah, not Rachel."

She suddenly stopped crying, as if strengthened by the bluntness of her own words, and was resolutely silent all the rest of the way home.

THE DREAM

WE CONTINUED going out together, and I tried all sorts of ways in the following months to break the unmentioned barrier between us. Late one Friday night, I told Sarah about my recurring dream while we were seated in the ice cream parlor on Avenue A after having seen the rerun of a creepy movie called *The Lost Weekend*. I didn't want to talk about the movie, and neither did Sarah. The waiter wanted to gab about a young basketball player named Bob Cousy who, he assured us, was going to be the greatest. We had gotten friendly with the waiter on past visits, but this time we must have annoyed him by our phlegmatic reaction.

"Wassa matter?" he griped. "Cousy don't sound Jewish enough for you guys? You think it's a sin if I don't talk about Sid Tanenbaum or Max Zaslofsky all the time? Or maybe you want me to go for the black kid from Seward, Sonny Jameson."

We looked down into our banana splits.

"Okay, okay," the waiter finally said. He was short, young, and already balding on top. He spoke with his hands even when he was holding a tray filled with dishes. The tray went in and out, toward us and away from us, with every phrase. As his voice grew louder, the tray traveled faster. We were transfixed by it, expecting at any moment that its contents would hurtle down upon our Sabbath clothes and betray our sin against the sacred day to our parents with an indelible stain.

"Okay, okay," he repeated. "I'll leave you alone tonight, lovebirds. But you don't fool me with all that stuff about the great Jewish basketball players. You don't got no beanie cap on when you eat, and I don't hear you say *brachas*, all them blessings when you eat. So get off the Jewish jag. Maybe you don't know it, but you got off it already. I know it. I'm a goy and still I can tell."

I wanted to talk about my dream.

"It's during the war," I said to Sarah, "and I'm still a kid, maybe eight, maybe nine, maybe ten. I don't know. My parents bring me to a monastery— I think it's in France—and they try to leave me there. I yell and I scream, but the nuns grab me away. I know it's France because all the kids call me by a new name—Jean Jacques Arouet de Daudet. I scream that it's not my real name, but the nuns tell me that if I want to save my life, I have to accept it. They also say that if I want to save my soul, I have to accept Jesus in my heart. That's the brunt of the dream. Sometimes it begins at the beginning, and sometimes it begins in the middle with the other kids. They laugh at me and scorn me. In fact, they make me their slave. They say that if I don't do every-thing they ask—like give them half of my food or shine their shoes or kiss their ass—they'll betray me to the Nazi commandant who visits all the time and even goes to confession in the monastery. Sometimes I see my parents in the dream, and sometimes I see another face of a bearded man and a woman, and they look like the picture we have at home of my uncle and his wife in the Polish city of Radom. Last night, there was a new twist. I came upon a ladder in my monastery bedroom, and dozens of people, phantom shapes, were going up and down the ladder. I thought of escaping to the sky with the ones going up, but I was afraid to try it since the Nazis could be outside in the street, on the ground, or in airplanes in the sky, and they would catch me. I woke up in a sweat. Or maybe I was still dreaming because my waking thought was not that this was all a dream and unreal and unthreatening, but that I had to stay in the monastery and not use the escape ladder, if I was to survive. Worse yet, not only were the nuns forcing me to accept Jesus if I didn't want to be handed over to the Nazis, but they also insisted that I study to become a priest. I screamed, asleep or awake."

"So what are you going to do now?" Sarah asked. "Make another survey of everybody you know like you once did when you were younger to get various interpretations of the dream?"

I shrugged my shoulders. "First I'm asking you," I said.

She looked at me and then away. She sucked on a spoon empty of ice cream as if there were hidden granules of joy to assemble and to imbibe.

"I'm not Joseph in the Bible," she said, "or Freud. Why don't you ask your father? He studies all the sacred books like the Cabbalah, and maybe he has the power to interpret dreams."

"No way," I said. "I can't tell this dream to my father. Living in a monastery? Studying to be a priest in the church, even if it's against my will? If I'm shocked by it, what sort of reaction would you expect from my father? Anyway, my father isn't really into Cabbalah or any mystical interpretation of dreams. He's a rationalist even though he was born into Chasidic circles in Galicia in Poland when it was Austria."

Sarah was taken with my dream. "Stuff like that happened during the war," she said. "It was maybe the only way to save little Jewish kids. If parents were trying to escape to places like Switzerland, they had to give their babies to Christians so they could be sure of the kids' safety and so they could travel unimpeded. With a family on the road and in hiding, a crying child was a dangerous thing. It could give them away."

"I know of a case just like yours," she added. My mother told me about it, monastery and all, and the kid wanting to become a priest after a while because he was baptized and brainwashed by Christian people who agreed to hide him. Did you ever speak to my mother? Maybe she planted the idea into your dream."

I did not really know her mother. I wasn't even sure I knew Sarah. We finished up, and I left a bigger-than-usual tip for our Cousy waiter. I probably felt guilty for disregarding him, and I didn't want him to hate Jews. We walked outside. It suddenly started raining, but we didn't feel a single drop on us. We saw the raindrops in puddles on the other side of the street, but our side was dry. It was unusual, a miracle maybe, a sign. I vaguely remembered such things from my childhood and my mother's reassurances that that's the way the world goes. It rains sometimes on this side of the street and sometimes on that, sometimes on other people, and sometimes on us.

"Why didn't you tell your dream to Mr. Edelstein?" Sarah suddenly asked on another evening.

Mr. Edelstein, my piano teacher, had given me two free tickets to an all-Bach concert at Town Hall played by James Friskin, a pianist friend of his, even though I had decided to stop taking lessons. I took Sarah to the concert. We went backstage afterward to see my teacher and to thank him for the tickets. Mr. Friskin had not yet come out from his dressing room to greet his public, so we had lots of time to talk to Mr. Edelstein. I introduced Sarah to him, and he asked her if she played an instrument. She said that she was taking jazz piano lessons at another settlement house, and Mr. Edelstein frowned. But I never told him about the dream.

"How could I?" I said to Sarah on the dry sidewalk in front of the ice-cream parlor. "I've decided to give up piano lessons, and I feel funny now about telling Mr. Edelstein anything personal."

Sarah wasn't shocked at all. "So you're giving up piano lessons. If you told that to Mr. Edelstein and then told him your dream, he would probably say that the dream is a mystical representation of betrayal. Just as you're betraying him and music and Bach and all that in real life, in your dream you're betraying your religion and becoming a priest. You're crossing over and becoming one of them. One of the jazz players."

I pushed her away with both hands. "Go on. That's ridiculous. You just can't get over the fact that he thinks jazz is for the birds. I once played a Charlie Parker record for Mr. Edelstein, and he screamed, 'Stop it! Stop it!' It hurt his ears. He refused to consider the complicated chord changes and the amazing improvisation. Mr. Edelstein had made his debut at the Berlin Opera as a conductor, believe it or not, before Hitler came to power in 1933. Then he had to get out. In the first two months of the Nazi regime, they kicked out the Jewish artists. They started with Jewish artists—musicians, writers, painters—before anybody else. So Mr. Edelstein came to America ultimately to scuffle for a living and teach untalented people like me. It's been raining on his side of the street for a long time."

"Jazz is the for the bird. Charlie Parker is called Bird."

"Smartass remark," I said. "I know that. And Dizzy Gillespie is called Diz. And Lester Young is called Pres. And Coleman Hawkins is called Hawk—another bird."

"You're a showoff yourself!" She kicked me. I didn't kick her back. I suddenly hugged her to protect her from the rain that had finally arrived on our safe side of the street. She let me.

"Is she still a religious girl?" my father asked.

"Who?" I asked.

"Who, who. Who do you think I mean? How many girls do you see after school? What are you, *Shloyme ha-Maylech,* King Solomon with a thousand wives? Since the Middle Ages and the *takune* of *Rabbaynee* Gershom we're allowed only one wife, *danken Got.* So is she still religious or not?"

"She goes to Hebrew High School with me," I said sheepishly.

"Hebrew High School, Hebrew High School. Another *gedille.* What does Hebrew High School mean? Instead of spending day and night in the sea of the Talmud and the *meforshim,* they sing and they dance and they put money in boxes for socialist farms in Israel that work on Yom Kippur, and they read books in Hebrew that are worse than the books in English."

I was brazen. "Maimonides—I mean Rambam—was a doctor, and the Vilna *Gaon* was a brilliant mathematician, and they say the son-in-law of the Lubavitcher *Rebbe* who may succeed him is a great scientist or engineer at the Sorbonne in Paris."

My father's tractate of the Talmud lay in front of him. He wiped the page down with the lapel of his black suit.

"A Lubavitcher in Paris," my father repeated. "*Herst azoins,* Rivkele?" he called to my mother who was seated opposite us in the kitchen and struggling with her arthritic hands to knit a sweater for Aunt Geety's youngest child. "Do you hear, my dear Rivke? A Lubavitcher in Paris. He better watch out. France is even worse than any other country for Jewish children."

I jumped back in astonishment, remembering my dream about France, and tried to pull the conversation in another direction. "You once told me that your brother the *shochet* in Poland, knew German and read Goethe and Schiller in the original, and also the great Polish writer Adam Mickiewicz in

Polish, and that just like your father in the shtetl, your brother was a public official who signed all the German documents for the Jews in the shtetl in the time of the Austro-Hungarian Empire. You said so yourself."

"We should all be the *tzaddik* my brother is . . . was . . . is. A precious soul. May you follow in his holy footsteps. And may your girl in his dear wife's footsteps. She even studied the Talmud in her day. Your mother knew her and can tell you that."

My mother was impatient with the whole discussion. I wasn't sure if she was out to protect me from my father or my father from me.

"Enough already!" she said, raising her voice a little to my father. "*Genig shoyn!* Itsik, why are you interrupting your studies with foolish questions about a girl? She's a nice girl, a Jewish girl. Her parents are fine people. We know them well enough. The girl studies Hebrew and even participates in the girls' service in the Hebrew School on *Shabes* in a separate room. What more do you want in America?"

"I don't want more," my father said wearily. "I'm afraid for much less."

He sank back into his Talmud page and I into my science homework. My mother continued knitting more warily, one eye upon the two of us. When I thought about this discussion afterwards, even when I told it to Sarah almost word for word, I had to confess that I wasn't sure if my mother meant for me not to interrupt my studies with useless talk about Sarah or for my father not to do so. Probably the latter because my mother knew that if my father remained immersed in the sacred books, he would not fall into discussions that might aggravate him. My father seemed frail in those days, and she, and I, feared for his health.

Ten minutes later, my mother took me aside out of earshot of my father. This could not be done in the same room in our small apartment. She motioned to me to follow her out of the kitchen where my father was seated at the table, not to eat but to study, and led me through the living room to the bedroom. There she put a hand on my shoulder, a motion I could not easily recall from the past.

"I hope you don't play with the girl," my mother said.

I was visibly annoyed by her bringing up a subject she had once before mentioned to me. But apparently, I misunderstood her this time. She hastily corrected herself.

"I mean—I hope you don't, as they say in America, play with her emotions."

Her words made me nervous. It was not so long ago that I, a school kid in junior high, had been teaching her English and American history to prepare her for her citizenship exam before a judge. Now she was using big words.

"Play with her emotions?" I repeated stupidly, but nevertheless entranced.

My mother sat down on the side of the bed, on the same side where once, long ago, she sat holding Aunt Geety's first baby daughter after the death of her own.

"It's a big sin," she said, "to disappoint a girl. My mother's older brother in Europe was a fine Talmud scholar. He sat all day in the yeshiva and learned. One day, my grandfather comes back from a trip to a neighboring town and says 'Mazel tov' to my uncle because my father found a girl for him in a very respectable family there. My uncle nodded in agreement as you would expect, and not much later, my father wrote out the t'nuim, the engagement articles, as they did in those days a few months before the wedding. What happened then? My mother's brother heard from another yeshiva bucher, a friend in the other town that the girl had a long nose. You see, they normally didn't see each other until the wedding. So what did my uncle do? He found the copy of the t'nuim and sent it back to the other family in the other town, which meant it was a rejection."

My mother lowered her head in shame for a moment before continuing her story. She nodded wearily, as if burdened by all the insensitivity in this world.

"It was a big sin, a big sin. That's what my mother told me. Later, much later, he chose his own wife who turned out to be a very nasty person. She was not a balebuste at all. She didn't take care of the house, she hit the children, and she didn't even take care of her husband no matter what he did for her. That's when my mother said that God punished her brother because he had sinned against the other girl."

I thought her story was over, her message delivered, and I started to retreat from the room. My mother did not raise her head to look up at me. When I was almost out of the room, she spoke up again.

"My mother was a *tzaddaykes,* a righteous woman. She never spoke bad about anyone, but she didn't have to say that about my uncle. She shouldn't have said that God punished him. They all died under Hitler. They didn't come to America or to Israel or any place else, and my uncle and his whole family were murdered by the beasts. Who knows God's will or purpose? My mother shouldn't have said that."

❦

In June of the following year, during the last week of exams when neither I nor Sarah had to go to school because we didn't have any remaining exams to contend with, we both set out each morning to look for summer jobs. With the "Help Wanted" section of the *Times* in hand, we walked together to the subway station in the early morning hours in order to get a leg up on job interviews. We also planned to visit firms in the garment district that were close by in the hope that we could land jobs not far apart from each other. In this way, we might meet each day for lunch and possibly go home together. Things were warming up again between us.

Sarah was looking for a secretarial job so that she could pay for the following year's jazz lessons and for a winter coat, and I was looking for anything, even pushing a rack of clothing through the streets, so that I could pay for concerts and plays and books and other stuff—for two tickets to each concert or play, that is—after ditching Mr. Edelstein and his free tickets that my parents couldn't possibly afford to replace.

One day, in the fourth week of June, just after I had picked up Sarah near her house and not far from the public school we had both attended, we bumped into Mr. Spring again, our old junior-high teacher of French and English, on his way to his school that ran to the very last day of June for both teachers and kids. It was pretty early for him, and he didn't seem to be in a hurry. He greeted us with the same quizzical look that was his approach to all of life.

The air was unusually cool for the beginning of summer. I wore a light coat and was bundled up to the neck. Sarah wasn't wearing a coat. I think she had two sweaters on that hugged her body, and Mr. Spring was taken with her.

"You look pretty good to me, but are you good enough for this guy here?"

He embarrassed me, but I wasn't about to say anything in protest. I had begun to stand up to my father, but I hadn't as yet learned to stand up to my teachers, even my former teachers.

Mr. Spring leaned back without moving his feet an inch. "I mean, this boyfriend of yours is a pain in the rear. He reads poetry and novels and plays Bach inventions and easy Beethoven sonatas, and when I debate him, he pulls a fast one on me by quoting the Talmud or some other esoteric Jewish text that is totally foreign and mumbo-jumbo to me. Are you going to stand for all that? I hope you have more gumption than I do."

Sarah didn't know what to say. Neither did I. You could never tell if Mr. Spring was serious or not. He knew more than he led on to.

"She reads more than I do," I said with a good deal of pride. "I gotta keep up with her, in English and in Hebrew."

"Halleluyah!" Mr. Spring exclaimed. "That's a girl for me. Not like the dumb broad that Joyce married who couldn't even figure out that her husband was a great writer. This is a new world, miss. You outdo this guy of yours and make your own way in life. It assures a happier marriage."

We really got embarrassed at this remark. Mr. Spring looked keenly at the both of us, at each of us one at a time, back and forth, and laughed. The thin wisp of a mustache that made him look like a comic Hitler vibrated up and down with his spastic giggles. We always thought he was a genius when we were in his class, and I still did, but whenever he laughed, he looked like a fool.

"Tell me," he said abruptly, turning to me and keeping his eyes centered on me. They were sharp arrows that pierced my skull and almost gave me the shakes. "What are you dreaming about these days? Tell me your dreams, and you reveal your soul. Let your old mentor know."

For a second time, I recoiled in astonishment. Sarah understood my reaction almost immediately. She even jumped to my side and held me tight, stopping me from bumping into an iron grating that fronted a small patch of green running up to the line of tenements.

She whispered into my ear. "Tell him," she said. "Tell him. Now's your chance. He may be the one. He may be Joseph or Freud."

Mr. Spring paled when he saw me almost fall. He must have thought I was epileptic or something. Sarah brushed off the back of my coat that had touched the rusty grating. An old woman with a kerchief around her head and paper bags in each hand came by and rummaged in the trash cans in front of the tenement buildings. She mumbled in Yiddish, cursing the world.

I told Mr. Spring my dream.

A stray dog raced up to us, sniffed, barked twice, and ran away. Three bearded men leaning forward against the wind, their hands on the brims of their wide hats to keep them from blowing away, headed toward the synagogue across the street. My father was not among them. For the first time in my memory, he had begun to say his morning prayers at home, forgoing the early morning *minyan* of ten or more in the synagogue. I think it was my mother who prevailed upon him to stay home and rest each morning even though it meant giving up the added mitzvah of praying with his fellow worshipers. That meant that he couldn't say certain prayers like the *Kedushah,* which required the *minyan* or respond with amens to the mourners' *Kaddish.* I scanned other late arrivals across the street for signs that my mother had relented. But her will was iron when it came to my father's health.

The ice wagon pulled up for those in the tenements who still had the old iceboxes and hadn't managed to buy the new refrigerators. My mother referred to the new ones as *Frigidaires,* as if the brand name was the generic name. She called down to Mendl the iceman to bring up a square piece. He was muscled and suntanned like no Jew that I had ever known, even including my brother Noosn. He also cursed in several languages—Polish I think, maybe Russian or Hungarian. His Yiddish curses sounded tame by comparison, even though I didn't really know all those expressions very well. I saw through to the soul of his words.

"So my French courses finally got to you," Mr. Spring blurted out. "It's pretty clear that Jean-Jacques in your dream refers to Rousseau and Arouet refers to Voltaire and Daudet refers to Daudet. How the devil did you come to Daudet? He's a third-rate writer compared to the other two. We never read any Daudet in our junior-high class, did we?"

"*Tartarin de Tarascon*," I said. "In the ninth grade, our last year in junior high. You sort of acted it out for us. You were the crazy southern Frenchman."

Mr. Spring smiled so broadly that his buck teeth showed. "The rest of the dream doesn't concern me," he added. "I don't put much credence in dreams. I'm not a Freudian, and all that stuff in the Bible about interpretations of dreams is a lot of hokum. Don't tell me you're still religious and in love with all that obscurantism? Are you now thinking of becoming a Catholic?".

"No," I said quickly. "I must have read about Jewish kids during the war being hidden in monasteries and being baptized secretly by their protectors."

"If you want to be a writer, a creative artist, you have to give up all that crap," Mr. Spring said. "I concede that there have been religious writers of note—T. S. Eliot and John Donne in his later life, but most of the great ones were naysayers, doubters, agnostics, atheists, challengers of the status quo. Joyce left Ireland and its rigid Catholicism to be a writer. That doesn't mean you can't write about your ancient culture. Joyce said at the end of *Portrait of the Artist* that he wanted to express in the smithy of his soul the collective unconscious of his race. You can do the same for the Jews, but not if you remain a naïve believer. Did you read *Portrait* as I had advised you to do?"

"I'm not going to be a writer," I said.

"Really." Mr. Spring seemed amazed. Even Sarah seemed surprised this time. She never expected me to be a musician—she had heard me play. But she had read my poems in the high-school magazine I had edited, and apparently she, like so many others, had no doubt that some day I would be a famous writer.

"So what are you going to be?" Mr. Spring persisted. "A Talmudic scholar like your father? A teacher in a yeshiva? A narrow, bigoted, ultrareligious fanatic?"

"No, not that either, and my father isn't narrow or bigoted or a fanatic. He lives in a different world."

"So did Torquemada," Mr. Spring said.

I always suspected that he knew more about Jewish history than he admitted to publicly. His reference to the leading inquisitor in medieval Spain, who burned Jews at the stake, proved it to me. But I wasn't pleased by his comparison. My old teacher-idol was crumbling.

He changed the subject. "Where are you two going so early in the morning?" he asked.

We told him. We also told him that we hadn't succeeded in landing any jobs.

"The trouble is," he said, "that you have this nasty habit of telling the truth. When they ask you if you're just looking for a summer job and intend to go back to school in September, say no. Tell them that you've graduated and you're starting on a working career. It's a white lie. But then they'll take you. And then in September you can say *au revoir,* or if you never expect to return to the exploiter, *adieu.* That's goodbye forever. They can't sue you. By then, when they find out how smart you guys are, they themselves will urge you to quit the job and go back to school. Take my advice."

We thanked him. We walked silently to the subway. When we were on the train uptown, I finally spoke up again. "Mr. Spring is smart, but he's not the deep thinker I took him for when I was younger. He's narrow himself."

I thought for a moment or two more, basking in the warmth of Sarah's meaningful silence, her hand in mine, the biting winds outside a memory.

"My dream is still inviolate," I said.

♥

"I think you're bullshitting me," Sarah said in the ice cream parlor after we had gone to a night game at the Polo Grounds that had ended badly with Larry Jansen losing 1–0 to Sal Maglie. "You probably made that whole dream up just to show me how sensitive and deep you are. You probably dream every night about that Feygy girl you once liked or your Aunt Geety when she was younger and slim and busty. Admit it. Admit the truth."

"No, I don't," I said. "I don't have to dream about them. I think about them when I'm awake."

The waiter Sal was seated at a corner table gulping down some liquid in a paper cup and studying the racing results in the nine o'clock edition of the *New York Mirror.*

"Where are they these days?" Sarah asked. She was sipping the remains of an ice cream soda through a straw. When her lips came together she looked like she was blowing a kiss in my direction.

I shrugged my shoulders. "Aunt Geety returned to Brooklyn with her three kids. Big Red, I heard, skipped town again some months ago, once more to avoid the loan sharks, but he sends money every now and then to support Aunt Geety and the kids. She comes around less and less. The kids are too much for her to handle, and my mother sometimes goes out there alone on a Sunday to help her with the housework. My mother doesn't eat there because she doesn't think Aunt Geety keeps kosher. She brings her own food and paper plates and plastic utensils with her. But it's getting harder and harder for my mother to go. She has arthritis and sciatica or something, and she can't walk distances. She also worries when she leaves my father. Still and all, it's her niece."

"And Feygy?"

"I lost track of her completely long ago. I don't think I ever saw her again since I was a kid, though one of her big brothers still runs the store on Pitt Street near the church. I sometimes go in there, but he doesn't talk about her. I haven't even seen her older sister Celia in years. Harry Frimmer, the husband, comes around whenever he hears that my father is sick. But he comes without his wife. They also live somewhere in Brooklyn, that is, if they live together. I think Harry Frimmer is also a big-time gambler, but unlike *der Royter,* Big Red, a successful one. Not to my father, naturally. Harry Frimmer, his sort-of adopted son, is in my father's soul another casualty of the

Red Heifer. Harry wears expensive clothes. My mother makes *pirogn* for him too whenever he comes. He likes that. But he never mentions his wife or Feygy."

"Maybe Feygy's in Argentina dancing the tango," Sarah said, "running her foot up the leg of her partner like I saw in a movie."

I was a little bit annoyed by Sarah's flippant remark about my Feygy. "Only escaped Nazis migrated secretly to Argentina," I said.

"You got Nazis on your mind all the time. Just like your father has his brother the *shochet* on his mind all the time."

"My dream," I said. "My dream."

Sal the waiter came by without the check. He just wanted to talk, this time not about Bob Cousy. He wore short sleeves on hot summer nights, and the ugly edges of a new tattoo on the biceps of his right arm stuck out from under his fraying sleeve.

"You're a smart Jewish kid," he said, "so explain this to me. Why is it, why is it you guys got no guts? You never fight. You don't use curse words. All you drink is malteds and ice cream sodas. What are you, a fuckin' angel or somethin'? You like sports. Hank Greenberg was a great hitter, I gotta admit, but a crappy fielder with a miserable arm, not like my Carl Furillo. Sid Luckman could throw that football and was a real brain at quarterback. City College got some pretty good Jewish basketball players even though none a them ain't anything like Cousy. But they're all exceptions. And you try to be hip and up on sports, but you probably throw a ball like the way a girl does. What gives with you people—one foot in the real world with regular guys like me and one foot in the sky? I don't get it."

When I didn't answer immediately, he turned his attention to Sarah.

"Hey babe, how can you like a guy like that? He ain't gonna protect you if somebody starts up with you. He'll run for cover the first thing. A guy like me is a different story. I'll make you happy every which way. How about it?"

"No deal," Sarah said quickly. "I like men with no guts. I can beat up on them whenever I want. I don't have to be afraid of them. It assures a happier marriage."

I almost cracked up in laughter. "What brought this on, Sal?" I asked.

"What brought it on, what brought it on. Somethin's gotta bring everything on? Wassa matter? I can't think about things by myself? Only you can be a philosopher? What brought it on is that your fuckin' goombahs in Israel, they give them Arabs a lickin'. The newspaper is full of this shit. How come? Ain't they like you and all the other little asshole Jewish kids I went to school with? And if they're so tough now, how come they weren't so tough a bunch a years ago with them Nazis in Germany? They hadda get killed six million times before they developed balls? Go figure."

"First the Jewish kids had to land up in a monastery," I said, "and get forced into being converted. Then they got balls."

"What? What monastery?"

"He's kidding you, Sal," Sarah interjected. "He had a dream."

Sal sat down opposite me next to Sarah. I think he was the nephew of the owner and could get away with things like that even though he was just a waiter. That's why he sat so much at tables when he wasn't serving.

"I had a dream last night too," he said. He moved his left hand backward over his balding scalp. " I was humpin' this broad who's wearin' big bracelets—your girlfriend should excuse me for the language—I mean, in my dream, not in real life, even though I get my share in real life you should know, and this completely naked Jewish guy comes in with a beard down to his balls and hair all over his body, but his thingie, a little one, sticks out between the hairs of the long beard, and I can tell he's Jewish since he's also wearin' a beanie and he sings when he talks, and he says to me, you're not doin' it right, the broad don't like it that way, and I says to him, what do you want me to do, read the Bible to her to get her hot, or maybe say a poem?"

"So?" I said.

"So nothin'," Sal said. "That's the dream. I woke up and jerked off. What else was I gonna do? You're so smart, tell me what my dream means."

There was a jukebox in the far corner of the room. A black couple strolled up to the box and put in some coins. Billie Holiday began to sing "Lover Man." The black couple held hands.

"My uncle don't want no trouble," Sal said. "We let everybody in here, even you Jews. Ha, ha, ha." His laugh was high-pitched, from the head, almost falsetto in sound, like the male sopranos I sang with as a kid in the liturgical choir. I thought of the choir leader's wife and how she once made me caress her. She was beautiful too, though fat, a little like Aunt Geety. I hadn't thought of her in a long time.

"The beautiful girl in your dream," I said impetuously, "was wearing seven bracelets that represent seven good years here in the ice cream parlor where you and your uncle are gonna make tons of money. The seven areas of hair that the old naked Jew showed you—his head, his nose, his ears, his beard, his chest, his scrotal area, and his legs—represent seven bad years here in the ice cream parlor where nobody is gonna come in on a Saturday night after the Giants lose at the Polo Grounds to the hated Dodgers and listen to your baloney about Carl Furillo or Bob Cousy or black people or the Jews in New York or Israel. This means, Sal, that you gotta save up a lot of moolah during the first seven good years to tide you over the next seven bad years. Don't spend everything on flashy cars and clothes and tattoos."

Sal was shook up. "You're a genius," he said. "The Jews are too smart for their own good. Can I spend a few bucks on whores?"

"No," I said. "They'll give you the clap, even during the seven good years."

"Aw, shit," he said. "Tell me *your* dream," he added.

I froze.

Sarah stood up. "I think it's time for me to go home," she said. She seemed tall though she wasn't, unsmiling this time, the faint trace of a frown at the corners of her mouth.

"I didn't insult you, babe, did I?" Sal asked.

"I wouldn't worry about it," Sarah said.

When we were at the register, Sal came by to make change. "My guess is you probably dream only Jewish dreams. You don't dream about broads like I do and all that stuff. You dream about goody-goody stuff. I don't see any sense in dreamin' if you dream only about that. There's enough of them rules and things in real life to drive you up the wall. But, I suppose, who can control their dreams?"

We did not go directly home. We must have walked miles on a very hot summer night that had not let go of its heat even with the sun in hiding. We hardly spoke. We held hands like the young black couple in the ice cream parlor, almost stumbling on the Bowery over a prostrate body, flimsily clothed, stretched out on the sidewalk in a drunken stupor, and we stopped to listen to three Hispanic street musicians accompanying each other on tin cans with wooden mallets and metal spoons. Then we impulsively doubled back to put a few coins into the upturned caps of the musicians and also into the paper cup that stood upright next to the crumpled body of the man in rags. The man was sleeping. Who can control their dreams?

"So you're not going to go to a great yeshiva and study *Toyreh* and Talmud day and night and be a rabbi and a *talmid chuchem,*" my father said one Friday evening after singing the Sabbath hymn "*Tsur Mishelo.*" He brushed the challah crumbs from off the tablecloth and dropped them into an empty plate. "So what are you gonna be? You're not gonna be a *chazn,* a cantor in a synagogue. They don't know much anyway and so many of them are not observant Jews. Anyway, you don't sing the way you did as a child. I think that choir ruined your voice. A child should be a child and rest the vocal cords at that young age so they could grow the right way. Otherwise, they get strained, and then when you're all grown up, they don't work so well. And you're not gonna be a *shoychet* like my brother in Poland who is not only a ritual slaughterer but also one of the greatest Talmudic minds in all of Galitsye. I hope the war didn't mix up his mind and put a big depression on him to stop him from learning the holy books the way he always did before the war. How can you be a *shoychet* like him? You can't stand the sight of blood, and you don't even eat chicken to this day. I always expected you to grow out of it. But things don't always happen the way we expect. The *Toyreh* says that man is to rule over all the animals, but you say it didn't mean kill them for food. So what can I do? The House of Hillel and the House of Shammai also disagreed about everything. Why not us? So what are you gonna be? A ballplayer? In baseball maybe? Not possible. You don't have good eyes, you don't run so fast, and you're a Jew. A Jew don't play children's games, even for a living. That's for *goyim*. What do you expect them to do? Learn *Toyreh* and *a blat Gemoore* all day and night? Thank God for the *goyim*. Without them, what would you listen to on the radio instead of the baseball games and the football? There'd be no sports in the world, and that's not so good. Even that giant of the Talmud, Raysh Lukish, lived in Rome for a while when he was young and made a living fighting with the lions in the big stadiums. Then he became sensible and began to study *Toyreh*. Or maybe he got older and couldn't fight so good and had to look for another profession. A man must work. Your mother tells me that once when she visited one of your teachers, the teacher in public school said you should be a writer. A writer of what? Of *bube manses?* Of foolish stories for old women? Or young? What good is that? The world never improved from *bube manses.* They only get people to think of wrong things. They don't bring people closer to the *Reboyne-sheloylem,* the Almighty. Still there was Goethe and Schiller that my brother in Poland says are great men and they were big writers. So how bad can it be? But they wrote in German and had respect for the sacred books. Heine was a Jew and he wrote beautiful poems in German even though he had to become a Christian for the sake of his career. What they did to the Jews, even long ago! But the writers today in America, in free America, don't have respect for anything. They write. They just write to make a fortune. They write what the lowest people wanna hear. *Shmuts,* dirt. The prophets wrote what people don't wanna hear. That's why Umis *ha-Nuvee* was persecuted for what he said, and that's why Yoyneh didn't want the obligation and ran away to go on a ship and into the belly of a big fish that the *goyim* call a whale. He also didn't want to save the people of Nineveh in another country. He only wanted the Jews to change and become better and their enemies destroyed. But God is God. If the enemies change and become good, why should He destroy them. God is God of the whole world. What kind of writer will you be? One like Umis and Yeshaye and Yirmiye and maybe Schiller and Lessing, *lehavdl,* or one like the writers of—of—of maybe burlesque shows and maybe murder and cowboys and Indians like in the foolish movies? The movies are the *malech ha-muves,* the angel of death. Maybe you could write about your own people. Writers should write about their own people. Shulem Alaychem wrote funny stories in Yiddish about plain Jews in the shtetl. So did Mendele. I don't read such things. I don't have time for *narishkayt,* for foolishness, but they were good writers with good hearts. It's possible. But a good heart is not enough. The socialists have good hearts. They want everybody to be equal and to have bread on the table, not only the rich. But they don't believe in anything else. The Jewish socialists don't wanna be Jews anymore. They're for every other nation in the world if they're socialist or under the foot of capitalists, but not the Jewish nation. It's a plague. The eleventh plague in Egypt was not on the Egyptians. It was on the Jews. And it was not from God. It was from the Jews themselves when they argued and fought with Moyshe Rabbaynee, with Moses himself, and tried to destroy their own people. It goes on till this day. It hasn't changed. And the Jewish socialist writers are the worst. If not a writer, then what will you be? A musician, a klezmer, with your piano and your Bach and Beethoven and boogie-woogie? Music is from God, but not musicians. They are low-class people mainly. They play cards in between jobs and gamble and stay with actresses and drink day and night at bars and taverns. It's a miracle they can still play. But at least music don't contaminate. It touches the heart and the soul. It don't curse with words, unless it's a song. It don't hate if it's only instruments. It's not like the Horst Wessel song of the Nazis, *yemach shemum v'zichrum.* But your mother tells me you stopped practicing the piano. She should have given you a violin when you were a child. A violin is more for a Jew. There's Heifetz and Hubermann and Elman. The best. They play so that it comes from the Jewish soul. But the piano—*feh!* It bangs and bangs and hurts the nerves sometimes. So there are strings in a piano, but it's not like the strings of a violin. It's a *goyish* instrument even though Rubinstein and Horowitz and Benny Goodman play the piano. No, I think he plays the clarinet. That's also a sweet Jewish instrument. A *chaleel,* a pipe from Judea like King David used to play. Still, a violin is the best. Only six generations after Cayin, which is Cain in English, Yuval invented the *kinnor* and the *ugov.* The world says that means a harp and an organ, but we know it means a violin and maybe a shepherd's pipe. That's how ancient these instruments are, so close to the time of creation, and therefore part of the creation by the *Reboynesheloylem.* But you don't play a violin or a clarinet. You don't sing, you don't dance, you don't play, you don't write, you don't study the holy books anymore. Maybe you'll go to the new State of Israel as a *chaluts,* a pioneer. The country needs educated Jews like you who know *Toyreh* and wordly wisdom together. The land is our ancient inheritance. If only my brother had gone there—in time. So, *mahn zindele,* what are you gonna be in this world where the Almighty decreed that man should labor all his grown-up life by the sweat of his brow?"

"I think I'll go into science."

"Science?"

"Science. Maybe physics."

"Like Einstein?"

"Nobody's like Einstein."

"I mean the same field like Einstein. You wanna find out what makes the universe tick? You wanna know what comes before the holy letter *Bays* of *Berayshis?* The *Toyreh* begins with a *B,* not an *A,* to tell us that we shouldn't look for beginnings. *Ha-Koodish Boorich Hee,* The-Holy-One-Blessèd-Be-He, is the beginning. We can't research Him. He is beyond our knowledge. We only know His deeds, His will for good. We don't know *Him.* So what are the physicists gonna find out from atoms and electrons and stars and planets? They'll only find the wonderful evidence of His work, but not Him. So you wanna be a physicist and find out where the feet grow from? You will be entering the *pardes,* my son, the mystical orange grove of knowledge of original things. It's a dangerous place. Three Talmudic scholars made that trip, and only Rabbi Akiva came out whole. Elisha ben Avuya called Acher came out a nonbeliever, his soul wounded, his life ruined. Which way will you go, my son, in physics? A writer can only destroy others, but a physicist who is also a philosopher can destroy himself. Watch out for the dangers, my son. It is the Red Heifer all over again. The study of science and physics cleanses and also contaminates. Which one will it be, my son, my dreamer?

Your mother and me, we also came here with a dream. Some dreams can be interpreted for good, like the dream of Pharaoh's chief butler in prison, and some for bad, like the dream of Pharaoh's chief baker in prison. Lord of the world, my God and God of my fathers, may it be Thy will that all the dreams that come to my *kaddishl,* my son the dreamer, be for good in this blessed country, thank God without Pharaohs."

THE BLESSING

HARRY FRIMMER came running up the four flights of the tenement at six in the morning when he heard that my father had suffered a stroke. The doctor was already there, and soon enough, he was joined by medics with emergency equipment from an ambulance stationed below. Harry insisted on helping the medics and my giant kid brother Noosn to carry my father down the perilous stairs and into the ambulance. He slipped a few bills into the hands of the medics. "Give him some extra help wherever you can," he said. "He's my father too."

My mother was tearless. Only her lined face betrayed some emotion. It seemed as if the creases grew deeper overnight, the lines longer and more wavering. She moved quickly into a seat alongside my father in the ambulance, her arthritis and sciatica notwithstanding. I was very nervous. I couldn't sit straight in the ambulance. My mother had insisted that my younger brother Noosn go to school as if nothing had happened, so I was left alone with my parents. I had to handle things by myself. My mother's English was good enough, but like my father, she often relied on me in public places. I normally would remove my skullcap when I got anywhere beyond the Lower East Side, but I did not, this time, in the company of my parents, even though the ambulance took us to 16th Street near Second Avenue and Beth Israel Hospital.

"Papa will live," I said to my mother. "Don't worry, Ma."

"I worry. I worry," my mother mumbled.

"Pa'll make it. He's got lots of years more to live. His mind is too active."

My father suddenly pushed off the metal covering on his mouth though

we thought he wasn't conscious and spoke up before the medic could replace it. "The days of our years are seventy. It says so in *Tehillim,* Psalm 90.
You should know. It's in the morning prayers every *Shabes.* Seventy years is
enough for any person."

The left side of my father's mouth was distorted as if he had been filled
with novocaine by a dentist, but he seemed able to speak, at least well enough
to be understood. His left hand hung limply at his side. I didn't think he
could move his left foot. I looked closely to see if his left eyelash responded
in tandem with his right, but I didn't notice anything unusual.

The medic made my father stop talking and replaced the breathing mech-
anism. I did remember the prayer my father referred to as if it were carved out
in hieroglyphs in my brain. "A Prayer for Moses, the Man of God." I thought
that my father might be delirious because I couldn't believe he was referring
to himself as seventy. My parents, like other pious Jews, never celebrated
birthdays. That was an American thing—not for them. But seventy seemed
to me to be a mistake, product of a fevered mind. I looked down at my prostrate father, half awake, half asleep, gravitating toward another world, no paper
cup at his side with a coin or two in it thrown in by wandering lovers.

"Pa, rest easy," I said. "The psalm doesn't end with seventy years. It also
says that with vigor, a person can reach eighty. And remember, Moses himself, your namesake, lived to a hundred and twenty."

I could not detect any reaction on my father's moist face. His left eye
seemed closed as if he was squinting. The gadgetry covered too much of the
rest of his face for me to tell. His thoughts, whatever they were, were his
own, unshared, hidden as with all other secrets. I did not quote the end of the
biblical passage that mentioned the seventy years and the eighty. "And the
majority are trouble and misfortune." I didn't have to complete the quotation for my father. He knew all these things without my help.

After a long silence, my father mumbled a reply. "I am not Moyshe. I am
Moyshe Yitschok." Then he turned to me with a suddenness of action that
made me shiver. Disobeying the medic, he added, "Did you bring my *tefillin*
along?" He directed the question to me.

"*Sha, Itsik, reyd nisht azoy fil,*" my mother cautioned, asking him not to talk so much. Once again I had forgotten that my mother called him Itsik in the rare instances when she mentioned his name at all. It was the familiar form of his Hebrew middle name, Yitschok, Isaac in English. As in past instances, it took me by surprise.

"Nu? Nu?" my father said or asked. The grunts were a substitute for speech, the sounds he used at table when he had already said the blessing for bread and could not find the saltshaker to complete the ritual in silence. But this time he added a mumbled "Rivkele," little Rebecca, as if begging her to leave him alone.

I showed my father the velvet pouch with his ritual phylacteries that I had not forgotten. I even brought along a prayer book—a *siddur*—though he knew all the prayers by heart. I did not include any of the Talmudic tractates because I knew that my mother would not want me to press them upon him at this early stage in his illness. He could not hold the phylacteries and the *siddur* in his limp hands, and perhaps, he could not see them since his eyesight had also deteriorated from macular degeneration that sometimes afflicts the retina of the elderly.

They wheeled the stretcher through the doors of the hospital with me alongside, my mother trailing behind. I steadied him with my hand, and my father took the opportunity to speak beyond the hearing of my mother.

"If I live," he said, "you'll come tomorrow morning and help me put on the *tefillin*."

"Pa, the ritual laws can be suspended when one is ill."

"Don't tell me what to do. I put on *tefillin* every day of my life since my Bar Mitzvah, I'm not gonna stop now."

As the stretcher sailed through the corridor, my father touched my fingers with his good right hand and continued. "The left hand is dead, and maybe the left part of the brain, but my memory of who I am is not dead. And who my brother is, and my father was, and his father before him. Remember to come early in the morning to help me with the *tefillin*. I don't ask for a lot."

When Harry Frimmer heard what I was doing each day, he volunteered to come every morning in my place so that I could prepare properly for school. He insisted that the hospital was on his way to work and that it wouldn't be an imposition at all on him. I always suspected that Harry didn't have a regular job, let alone a nine-to-five daily work-destination, since he made his money in secret ways. At first, I resisted his proposal and came to the hospital early every morning to help my father with the *tefillin,* but after a week, I acceded to Harry's request and let him come in my stead.

My father remained in the hospital for much longer—for six weeks. The doctors had diagnosed a rare disease that had brought on the stroke whose medical name eludes me at this time, and it required aggressive treatment that precluded his being sent home quickly. Every three hours on the dot for the full six weeks, the nurses came to my father and filled him with the new antibiotics by injection, first in his dead arm, then when that one was black and blue, in the other arm, then elsewhere, and finally intravenously.

One afternoon, when I came to visit, I told my father my dream. I left out the part about being forced to become a priest. I just mentioned the monastery in France and being abandoned there during the war by two adults—I didn't even say by parents or by an uncle and aunt—and I also mentioned the escape ladder in the monastery bedroom that sometimes appeared in my recurring dream.

"We'll talk some other time about it," my father said abruptly. His mouth had straightened a little, oozing back to its former self, though he still could not move anything else on the left side of his body. "First bring your friend Sarah with you to visit me."

"*Er redt fin hits,*" my mother said, referring to his request as feverish talk. But then she added, "Do as he says. I know you're very young and you and the girl are not serious yet, but do as he says anyway. *Tee im tsileeb.* Obey his wishes. Ask the girl if she's willing to come. Tell her it don't mean anything so she shouldn't get scared. When she ate in our house because her parents were away, that was one thing. But this is different, and she might be afraid or embarrassed."

Sarah was hesitant at first. "Do you think he's gonna make me promise to marry you when we get older?" she asked. "Or promise not to marry you?"

"I don't know what he wants to say."

"What made him ask such a thing suddenly? What were you two talking about?"

"I had just told him my dream. He put off talking about it."

"Your dream?"

"My dream."

"The one about the monastery in France during the war?"

"What other one is there?"

"Did you tell him about becoming a priest?"

"No."

"Did you tell him that sometimes your parents are not your parents in the dream but that two different older people—maybe your *shochet* uncle and aunt from Poland—act as your parents?"

"I just said two people without designating who they were."

"Maybe your father wants me to interpret the dream. Women are good that way outside of the Bible. Did you ever hear of a store on the Lower East Side with a male fortune-teller? Never. Always a woman. We can read the future because of our superior sensitivity. You guys are gross, by comparison."

I reintroduced Sarah to my father. My mother had already met her more than once outside in the street, after the one Friday night meal she ate in our house. But my father saw her only the one time she came for dinner, unless he had seen her on his own in her parents' grocery store on Avenue C when he occasionally shopped there. He did not seem to recognize her, or even to see her clearly this time. His eyes shifted this way and that. Though I was closer to him and Sarah at my far side, he managed to stretch out his dead left hand to touch mine while extending his right hand across to touch Sarah's fingers.

Sarah shuddered for a moment, then wished my father a complete recovery—a *refuah sheleymah*. He nodded his head in thanks. We were all silent in a sort of embarrassed way. My kid brother Noosn suddenly barged into the hospital room. He towered over everyone, his wide-brimmed black hat almost touching a high-lying intravenous contraption that was hanging loose.

My father turned to him. "Noosn, put me in a seat near the window. I want to sit up a little."

My father wasn't attached to anything at the moment. Noosn lifted him out of bed as if he were a very light bag of feathers and placed him in a chair. Then Noosn smiled at Sarah for the first time as if to say—see what I can do? —and winked at me.

"I knew I could count on Noosn when he got here," my father commented.

Noosn turned to my mother. "How's he doin', Ma?"

My mother nodded. "*Booruch Ha-Shem.*"

Her "Blessed Be God" meaning "thank God" was more an expression of hope than an objective statement of fact. My father had actually suffered some setbacks the previous day or two. In fact, I was not pleased by his being moved from bed to chair under these circumstances, but Noosn acted so quickly and I was so immobilized by the situation with my father and Sarah that I could not react in time. Once he was in his seat, I surmised that it was better that he not be moved back again to the bed for a while.

"When Pa eats from the machine into his veins, not into his mouth," Noosn asked nobody in particular, "does he have to say a *brooche?* And what *brooche* do you say over food that's like medicine? I think a *sheh-ha-kol* because it ain't bread and it ain't fruit and it ain't vegetables. It's nothing. And nothing is like everything else and everything is what the *brooche sheh-ha-kol* means. Am I right, Pa?"

"You're right, my strong and wise son," my father said. "Take special care of such children because out of their mouth will come *Toyreh.*"

My father suddenly motioned with the pinky of his good right hand for me and Sarah to return to his side. We obeyed, but we came to a stop two or three feet away.

"The ladder is the important thing," he said. "A ladder goes up and down, up and down. Angels go up and down a ladder, down and up in a never-ending stream. Ladders can lead you to high altars where in Bible times people worshiped idols and did evil things like sacrificing children to their gods or forcing women to do you-know-what in public in front of the statues of the gods or a ladder can lead you beyond evil to heaven itself. Ladders can lie sideways down on the ground. Then a ladder can be a ladder to the past. What past? A ladder can lead you to a time when people were ignorant and did not understand science and did not read or study the deepest thoughts of human beings in poems and philosophy or a ladder can lead you back to a holier time when our people were closest to God at Sinai. A ladder can be an escape from something, from a jail, from a fire, from a home where the parents keep the child like a prisoner or a ladder can be an entrance into something, into a beloved's bedroom, into a high tree to save a wounded animal, into a new world of study and understanding of God and man. Which ladder was your ladder?"

Neither Sarah nor I could say a word.

Noosn spoke up. "I like the ladder up to the top of the tree," he said. "But I really don't need a ladder most of the time. I can reach Ma's top shelf in the kitchen easy. But if a sick little bird fell out of a nest and got caught in a branch high, high up to the sky almost, even I would need a ladder. Then after I reached the first strong branch, I would be able to climb up myself to the bird without the ladder."

My mother patted Noosn on the back. Her hand actually reached the small of his back. Then she tried to steer him in another direction. She pointed to the patient in the adjoining bed and suggested to Noosn that the poor man could use some cheering up.

"Teach him some holy words," my mother said. "Your father comforts him when nobody is over there to visit him and the curtain is open. You do the same. You be like your father."

Noosn gladly obliged. He disappeared behind the curtain enclosing the other man's bed, and from our side of the curtain we could hear him babbling away in English laced with Yiddish and with references to Hebrew prayers and biblical quotations. It didn't seem to concern him that the sick man was a Korean who spoke some English but certainly no Yiddish or Hebrew at all.

"My younger brother the *shoychet* was right," I heard Noosn orate, as if he were my father. His voice was partially muffled from behind the curtain. "If you don't keep the law, it says in *Dvoorim,* you will have a trembling heart and failing eyes and a hurt soul. Yirmiye says: *Thou hast chastised me, I have been punished, like an untrained calf.* You too, Mr. Korea? Moyshe also says there on *Har Eyvawl* that your sons and your daughters will be given to another nation, and your eyes will fail with longing for them all day, but your hand will be powerless. *Ich bin geshtruft.* I am punished. The hand, the dimming eyes. Where is Hershl? Where is *der Royter* and Geetele and Feygele and Joe and Shmeel and *Reb* Elya and *Reb* Yussl? I can't see them anymore. I can't see Avigdor. They are lost. *Ha-vayn yakir lee Efrayim im yeled sha'asheem.* Where are my beloved sons, my playful children? Where? Where? Rachel is crying again for all her children."

The babbling of Noosn as background noise was all the sound we heard for a few more moments. Afternoon sun rays pierced the window and illuminated half my father's face as he sat alongside the windowsill. Both his wounded eyes were closed at this time. His sparse gray hair fluttered above his black yarmulke as if a wisp of wind had also charged through the windows on the back of the brilliant rays. His graying beard seemed longer than usual and less thick, the strands apart revealing a wrinkled neck and almost a hole where his goiter had been. The dead hand rested on the arm of the upholstered chair, graceful in its weakness, surprisingly wrinkle-free and pink in complexion like the poised hand of a virtuoso child-pianist. He seemed so small.

My mother moved to the left, then to the rear of the chair and straightened his head by cupping her hands over my father's ears and swinging gently side to side until the battered face maintained an upright position. I envisioned a puppeteer working on the artist's creation. My mother's hands slid down from his ears to his shoulders and rested there. I could not recall seeing her ever touch my father before or lean on his shoulder or even hold his hand.

Sarah drifted closer to my father's chair without being asked. An invisible magnet seemed to draw her to him, while I trailed behind Sarah as if in a trance. I moved with her, small step by small step, the two of us inching our way to the front of his chair. My mother hadn't stirred from his side. We huddled close together in a narrow space as if protecting each other from a blast of cold Arctic wind. Then we all stood still. We formed a tableau of four, bleached by the decaying sun working its way through the blinds of the adjacent window, distant from the hubbub and frolic several floors below in the street and from the hustle-bustle out in the hall of nurses and orderlies scooting around in every direction, and even distant from babbling Noosn and his comatose patient a few paces away beyond the closed curtain. We drifted into shadow. Time stopped—the planets motionless, the rampant diseases arrested in flight, the aging-process frozen, a daguerreotype in amber, black, and gray.

My father reversed his hands again to touch mine and Sarah's. He whispered to us. "The God that my fathers walked with Who shepherded me safely until this day and His angel who redeemed me from all evil, may He bless you and your children and let my name be named in them, and let them grow into a multitude in the middle of this land."

Then he suddenly added, "Let my name be named in them later, much later." I looked at Sarah. She avoided my eyes. Her eyes were riveted on my father.

His head not now controlled anymore by my mother's gentle hands, he turned his face slowly to the window and away from us, taking the red rays of the sinking sun directly on his closed eyes. This time he spoke without looking at any of us, in a much louder voice that had gathered unusual strength from unknown sources. He stared to a distant horizon.

"If you marry," he said, "I mean in the future, and if I am gone . . ." He hesitated for a moment or two, perhaps because of his illness, perhaps for other reasons, then continued without completing the sentence.

"It is the traditional right of the wife to choose the name for the first child after her own departed relative. But even if it is a son and Sarah has chosen the first name and allows you to choose a middle name for your first child, do not rush to name the child after me. Even to honor my memory right away. Name him after my brother."

We did not respond. We touched silently. The waning light from the window streaked my father's half-hidden face.

Soon enough, seven or eight bearded men broke the silence. They hurried into the hospital room to *davn* the *Mincheh* and *Maariv* prayers in the presence of my father. Noosn and I joined them to complete the *minyan,* the quorum of ten. Sarah and my mother stepped out into the hallway to whisper to each other. Through the partially open door I saw them embrace.

My father did not stand up from his chair with all the other men during the silent *Amidah* and the *Kedushah* prayer that was chanted aloud. He couldn't. When the prayers were completed, the elders wished him well and left immediately. My mother and Sarah reentered, and after some inconsequential chatter, Sarah and I left too.

There were more comings and goings for me in that hospital and many more arrivals and departures to and from home after my father returned to convalesce within the walls of our own small Lower East Side apartment. But my leaving with Sarah on that night from that hospital room where my father had been propped up in a chair by my giant kid brother Noosn with my tiny mother hovering over him in the background seemed like a once-in-a-lifetime departure for me. It was like the leaving of a wandering Jew ages ago from the town of his birth for a voyage to a new land and a new life, with the clear but unspoken understanding that he would never be back again, though he would always speak of his childhood shtetl as *di haym*—the home—however few years he had spent there in distant times past, more dream than real, and however many many more years he would subsequently spend elsewhere in alien surroundings.

GLOSSARY

GLOSSARY

a bintl kinder: a bunch of children; literally, a bundle of children

a blat Gemoore: a page of the Talmud. See also **Gemoore**

a mishige velt: a crazy world

a nechtiker tug (tog): an impossibility; "no way"; literally, a day that happened yesterday

a refiye shelayme (a refuah sheleymah): a complete recovery

a shlok zol es trefn: a curse on it; literally, may something evil (or a stroke) find it

a trayfene medine: a country whose culture entices Jews to abandon Judaism; literally, a nonkosher country

Ahavas N'ooray: love of my youth (a Hebrew expression not ordinarily used in Yiddish)

aliya: the honor of being called up to a Torah reading to recite the blessings; also ascent or immigration to Israel *(aliyah)*

Ameyrike gonif: thieving America; "What a country!"

am ho-orets gumer: a complete ignoramus

apikoyres: heretic, atheist

arba kanfos: ritual four-fringed undergarment worn by very devout men (Hebrew for the Yiddish *laptsedekl)*

arbes: chickpeas, frequently eaten at the third Sabbath meal; also green peas

Aron Kodesh: the Holy Ark in a synagogue

avoyde zure: idolatrous worship

aydle mentshn: high-class people who are learned, sensitive, and well-spoken

Ayshes Chayil: "a Woman of Valor or Virtue" (referring to any woman but usually a reference to one's wife; a Hebrew quotation from chapter 31, verse 10, of the Book of Proverbs)

Ba'al-Shachris (Shacharis), Ba'al Misef (Musaf), Ba'al Tefillah: titles respectively for the leaders of the two morning services on the Sabbath and holidays; the third is the overall title for a prayer leader

balebuste: expert female house-manager

bandit (pl. *banditn):* thief; little rascal, when used in reference to a child

bar kayama: a fully assured life a month after birth (an Aramaic expression not ordinarily used in Yiddish)

basherte: one's divinely intended or destined bride

bas kol: echo, voice from heaven

Bays (Beys, Bet): the second letter in the Hebrew alphabet, the letter "B," and the first letter of the first word in the Torah

ben: son of

bentsh Rosh-Choidesh (Rosh-Chodesh): chant the special prayers ushering in the new month on the Jewish calendar

Berayshis (Bereyshis): the Book of Genesis, the first book of the Torah

bestid: bastard (not a standard Yiddish word—merely a mispronunciation of the English word by some eastern European Yiddish speakers)

b'feyresh: clearly, explicitly

bima: raised platform or pulpit in a synagogue; also, a stage in a theater

bituchn: hope (noun)

booky b'Toyreh v'Shas: expert in Torah and Mishnah. See also *Shas*

booruch Ha-Shem (boruch): Blessed Be God

Borey pree ha-gawfen: "Who created the fruit of the vine"; the ending of the Hebrew blessing over wine

boychik: young boy (an Americanism not standard in Yiddish)

Boyre Nefushes: the Creator of All Humanity; God

brooche: blessing

bube manses (bobe mayses): foolish or untrue stories; literally, grandmother stories

bucher: young unmarried man *(yeshiva bucher:* a yeshiva boy)

bupkes: nothing, zilch; literally, beans

B'vakashah g'veret: please, Miss or Madam (a Hebrew expression not ordinarily used in Yiddish)

chaleel: flute, shepherd's musical pipe

chaluts: pioneer

chamas ha-maytsik: "the wrath of the oppressor"; a Hebrew quotation from the Book of Isaiah, chapter 51, verse 13

chas ve-cholile: God forbid

chaver: friend, comrade

Chazal: our scholars of sacred memory (an acronym)

chazn: cantor

chilul Ha-Shem: desecration of God's Name

chimish (chumash): The Pentateuch (Five Books of Moses) in book form, not in the scroll form of the Torah

chipe (chupe): wedding canopy

chukim: laws

chumets: leavened bread

Daf keef-alef (kuf-alef): Page 101 (a typical reference in Hebrew to a specific page in the Talmud)

Danken Got: Thank God

dardeke-melamed: a Hebrew teacher of the youngest beginners in an elementary Jewish school or cheder

davn: pray

davnen farn umed: to lead the prayers before the lectern on the *bima*

davner: one who prays

dayan: a judge

Der Aybershter: The Eternal One, God

Di bist a Yid (Du): You are a Jew

dictatoor: dictatorship

drek: manure (a vulgarism frequently used to mean worthless nonsense)

dvar-Torah: a speech containing a learned exegesis of Torah texts; literally, a word of Torah

D'vurim (D'vorim): the Book of Deuteronomy, the fifth and final book of the Torah

Elokim: God (when not praying, the "k" is pronounced by a pious Jewish speaker instead of the written Hebrew "h" in order not to use a sacred reference to God cavalierly or in vain)

emeeneh (emunah): faith, trust

Eretz Yisrool (Yisroel, Yisrael): the Land of Israel

Erev Shabes: Sabbath Eve; actually, all day Friday

erliche Yidn: upright, righteous Jews

Er redt fin hits: He's speaking out of fever

eygel: calf (usually a reference to the Golden Calf worshiped by the Children of Israel at Mount Sinai as described in the Book of Exodus, chapter 32)

gabbay: sexton of a synagogue; occasionally, treasurer

gaon: genius (frequently, a rabbinic title or honorific, as in the Gaon of Vilna)

gedille (gedulah): big deal (said sarcastically); literally, a heroic act or event of greatness

Gemoore (Gemara): the major section of the Talmud written in Aramaic that evolved circa 200 C.E. to 500 C.E. in Babylonia and that contains rabbinic commentary and legal debate on the laws of the *Mishnah,* the earlier section of the Talmud written in Hebrew; by synecdoche, the term *Gemara* is used frequently to refer to the whole Talmud made up of both *Mishnah* and *Gemara*

Genig shoyn (Genug): Enough already!

ge'ulo: redemption

Git Shabes: Good Sabbath (a greeting)

goldene medine: a golden land

gonif: thief

Gots bashefenish: God's creation

Got vet helfn: God will help

goyim (sing. *goy):* gentiles

groyse chazoonim (chazonim): great cantors

Haftoireh (Haftorah, Haftarah): passages from the Prophets chanted after the Torah reading in the synagogue on Sabbaths and holidays

ha-Koodish Boorich Hee (ha-Kodosh Boruch Hu): The-Holy-One-Blessèd-Be-He

ha-melech: the king

Haray Ot (Harey): "Behold thou art"; the first two Hebrew words of the formula of consecration and acceptance that a groom says to his bride at a traditional Jewish wedding

Har Eyvawl: Mount Eyval (Ebal) mentioned in chapter 27 of the Book of

Deuteronomy; the mountain upon which six of the Israelite tribes stood to re-
ceive pronouncements of doom from the Levites and, subsequently, warnings
from Moses about the consequences of betraying God and doing evil

Ha-Shem Yisborach: The Name (God) Be Blessèd, Blessèd God

haym: home; one's place of birth and childhood

herst azoins: Do you hear this? Have you ever heard anything like this? (an expression of astonishment and even annoyance)

heyratn: to marry

Ich bin aych moychl: I forgive you

Ich bin geshtruft: I am punished; I've been punished

Ich chalish avek: I'm fainting away

Imglikleche Yidn: Unlucky Jews! Ill-fated Jews!

Im yirtse Ha-Shem: God willing

kaddishl: a young son; literally, one's child who will recite the mourner's prayer
called **Kaddish** upon the death of the parent

kanehore: no evil eye (usually said after praising someone in order to ward off evil
consequences that may arise from the hubris of praise)

kantshik: a rod with straps (once used by some teachers of an earlier era to punish
students)

k'das v'k'din (u-ch'din): according to the strict law

Kedushah: a prayer of holiness inserted in the cantor's repetition of the *Amidah;* see:
Shemoneh Esreh

Keren Kayemes: Jewish National Fund (JNF)

kiddush: the prayer of sanctification over wine recited on Sabbaths and holidays; by
extension, also the festive spread of food served at the end of Sabbath morning
prayer following recitation of the *kiddush*

kinnor: in the Jewish Bible, a harp, as in Samuel I, chapter 16, verse 23); in modern
Hebrew, a violin

klutz kashes: stupid questions

knubl: garlic

kohen: priest in Judaism

koosher (kosher, kasher): ritually correct or pure

Krishma: the prayers recited before going to sleep at night that contain the *Sh'ma* prayer—"Hear, O Israel!"

kurves: prostitutes

landslayt (sing. *landsman*)*:* hometown neighbors and friends

laptsedekl: ritual four-fringed undergarment worn by very devout men (Yiddish for the Hebrew *arba kanfos*)

Lebn zul Ameyrike: Long Live America!

lehavdl (lehavdil): to differentiate (said when mentioning something sacred and something profane or secular in the same breath)

lekech: sweet cake

leyn: recite or sing the Torah portion in the synagogue

lidl: a little song (usually, a secular song)

looshn-hore: evil gossip; literally, language of evil

loy-yitsluch: an unsuccessful person

Maariv: the evening prayer service recited daily

machloykes: controversy, usually a rabbinic disagreement in the Talmud or in other comparable works on a matter of Jewish law or legend

Maftir: the final Torah reading on Sabbaths and holidays; a reference to the person given the final *aliya* who will subsequently chant the *Haftarah*

malech ha-muves: the angel of death

mamzeyrim (sing. *mamzer*)*:* bastards (the word, especially in the singular, is frequently used vis-à-vis a child as a term of criticism or even endearment meaning, "the little rascal")

mandlbroyt: almond bread

m'cheeleh: forgiveness

mechitzah: the partition or curtain separating the women's section from the men's section in an orthodox synagogue

medrish: a homiletical story or commentary; legendary material in the Talmud and in other writings ancient and even modern, usually embroidering on biblical events and characters; also the corpus of such literature

meforshim: commentators; exegetes of religious texts

melamed: teacher

mentshn (sing. *mentsh*): men (frequently used in the singular to mean a decent human being, a good man)

meziza (mezuzah): small encasement attached to the doorpost of a Jewish home containing the *Sh'ma* prayer and other Torah passages

mileh: circumcision

Mincheh: the afternoon prayer service recited daily

minyan: a quorum of ten required for public prayer in a synagogue

Misef (Musaf): the additional prayer service chanted after the *Shacharis* service on the Sabbath and holidays

Mishnah: the rabbinic commentary discussing and interpreting the laws of the Torah, written in Hebrew, and codified circa. 200 C.E. in the Land of Israel; forms the first part of the Talmud when printed together with the *Gemara*. See **Shas**

misnaged: an opponent of the Chasidic movement

mit Gots hilf: with God's help

moshiach: messiah

moshol: parable or fable; also used to mean a resemblance or comparison

moyhl: person who performs the ritual circumcision

m'sader k'dishin: one who performs the Jewish ritual ceremony of marriage

naches: joy (a Hebrew word emphasizing spiritual joy, but used in Yiddish to mean parental joy at the achievements of their children, especially in marriage and parenthood)

narishkayt (narishkeyt) (pl.: *narishkaytn):* foolishness; acts of foolishness

N'eeleh: the final, climactic prayer service on Yom Kippur

neshume: soul, human being

nes min ha-shomayim: a miracle from heaven

nigun: melody, tune (usually, a religious melody)

nimshol: a maxim, usually the second part of a comparison

noch: additionally, also, yet, "of all things!"

Oorn Koydesh (Aron Kodesh): the Holy Ark in a synagogue containing the scrolled Torahs

oyker hurim: a genius of Torah learning and Talmudic analysis, literally, an uprooter of mountains

oycher Yisrool (ocher Yisroel, Yisrael): disturber of Israel; one who troubles the Jewish people (usually said of another Jew; a phrase found in Kings I, chapter 17, verse 17)

oylem-habe (eylem habaw, olam haba): the-world-to-come

oysvurf: a contemptible, unscrupulous person; a scoundrel

pardes: orchard, orange grove (metaphorically extended by interpreting the Hebrew word as an acronym that refers to the four traditional methods of Biblical analysis leading the scholar to the grove of philosophical study of the deepest religious mysteries)

payes (peyes): lengthy, curled sideburns worn by very devout Jewish males in observance of a Torah text

Paysach (Peysach, Pesach): the holiday of Passover

pirogn: pies, dumplings (from the Polish *pierogi*)

poosik (posuk): a verse in the Jewish Bible, a sentence

prost: unlearned, common, even vulgar

P'sukey d'Zimrah: preliminary prayers of the morning *Shacharis* service made up of psalms

purits: lord of the manor

Rabbaynee (Rabbeynu): title meaning "our rabbi"; *Rav:* rabbi; *rebbe:* rabbi, frequently a Chasidic rabbi; *rebby:* designation for one's teacher of sacred subjects, used especially by American students; *Reb* or *Rab:* honorific for an elder, not necessarily a rabbi

rabbeyim: rabbis (frequently used in this plural form to refer to rabbis who teach in a yeshiva)

rachamim: pity, mercy (Hebrew for the Yiddish *rachmoones*)

Rachmono litslun: God save us

rachmoones: pity, mercy (used more often in Yiddish)

Rashi: the name, in the form of an acronym, standing for Rabbi Shlomo Yitschaki (ben Isaac), one of the greatest commentators on the Torah and other sacred writings, who lived in the south of France in the eleventh century; by extension, a common reference to his Torah commentary that is frequently printed below the Torah text in a *chumash* and studied together as one unit; his annotations also appear on the pages of the Talmud

Rebbetsin: the rabbi's wife, an honorific title

rebelach: another plural for "rabbi"; sometimes derisive in tone: little rabbis

Reboynesheloylem: Lord of the World; God

reyd nisht azoy fil: Don't talk so much

Roshishooneh (Rosh ha-Shawnaw, Rosh ha-Shanah): the Jewish New Year holiday

sedra: the weekly portion of the Torah read in the synagogue

sefurim (seforim, sefarim sing. *sefer):* books, frequently a reference to a holy book

Shabes (Shabbos, Shabbat): Sabbath

Shachris (Shacharis): the morning prayer service recited daily

shadchn: marriage broker

Shalesheedes: the third and last festive ritual meal of the Sabbath

Shas: another name for the *Mishnah;* actually, an acronym in Hebrew for the six orders or books of the *Mishnah* that are sometimes printed in separate volumes and without the *Gemara* commentary; when copies of the Talmud were burned in Paris and Rome (from the thirteenth to sixteenth centuries) and the church forbade even saying the word "Talmud," *Shas* came into use among Jews, by synecdoche, to refer secretly to the whole Talmud

shaydim: evil spirits or sprites (mentioned in Deuteronomy, chapter 32, verse 17, as false gods)

sheel (shul): synagogue

sheh-ha-kol: a single word in Hebrew from the blessing said over miscellaneous items (including whiskey) by which name this blessing is frequently identified

sheliech-tsiber: leader of the service; literally, messenger of the community in prayer; usually, a lay person, but also a professional cantor

Shemoneh Esreh: the Hebrew number 18, the name of a major prayer sequence in every service, originally composed of eighteen blessings; also called *Amidah,* the standing prayer

Sheym ha-Meforush: the four sacred Hebrew letters of God's name, tetragrammaton

sheyner boychik: nice boy, pretty boy

Sheyvet Dan: the ancient tribe of Dan

Sh'foch chamaws'chaw . . . : "Pour out Thy wrath"; the opening words of a prayer said in the second half of the Passover Seder beseeching God to punish those who do not know God and are evil enemies intent upon destroying the Jewish people; the initial verses of the prayer come from the Book of Psalms, chapter

79, verses 6 & 7, with a similar version containing slight variations in Jeremiah, chapter 10, verse 25

shidduch: marital arrangement suggested by a professional *shadchn* or even by friends and neighbors

shiker: drunkard

shikse: a gentile girl

Shimshen ha-Giber: the hero Samson in the Book of Judges

Shloyme ha-Maylech (ha-Melech): King Solomon

Shma Yisrool . . . (Sh'ma Yisroel, Yisrael): the initial words—"Hear, O Israel!"—of what is generally considered to be the central prayer of Jewish worship:"Hear, O Israel! The Lord, our God, the Lord is One" ("is the One Eternal Being"): Deuteronomy, chapter 6, verse 4

shmaltsgrib: sudden wealth or good fortune; literally, a hole or ditch filled with chicken fat

shmates: rags, tattered clothing

shmuts: dirt, filth

shnorrer: moocher, beggar

shoychet (sheychet, shochet): ritual slaughterer of chickens

shteebl: small Chasidic prayer and study room, in contrast to a larger synagogue

shtikl: a tiny piece

shtill: quiet

shtipped: thrust, paid off, bribed; also a vulgarism

shvag: Be quiet!

shvartser goy: black gentile

siddur: prayer book

Sikkes (Succos, Sukkot): the holiday of Tabernacles

Si shtayt geshribn b'fayresh: It is written explicitly

sleecheh: forgiveness

tachshitl: precious little son or boy, sometimes said sarcastically; literally, little jewel

takune: a rabbinic amendment to the law

talmid: student

talmid chuchem: scholar, sometimes said sarcastically to mean a smart aleck; literally, a wise student

Talmud: multivolumed tome of Jewish law and lore made up of the *Mishnah* and the *Gemara,* containing rabbinic discussion and controversy spanning a lengthy period from circa. 200 B.C.E. to 500 C.E.; sometimes referred to as the Babylonian Talmud; a parallel version, codified circa 400 C.E. in the Land of Israel and less frequently studied, is referred to as the Jerusalem Talmud

Talyener: an Italian, a common mispronunciation by Jewish immigrants where standard Yiddish requires "Italyaner"

Tanach: the Jewish Bible, a Hebrew acronym made up of Torah, Prophets, and (Miscellaneous) Writings; *Nach:* the Hebrew acronym for the last two sections of the Jewish Bible

tante: aunt

Tashlich: Rosh ha-Shanah afternoon ritual wherein Jews pray for forgiveness on the banks of a body of water and symbolically cast away their sins into the water, frequently in the form of pieces of bread

Tateh: Father, Dad

techiyas ha-maysim: revival of the dead

Tee im tsileeb: Do as he says; Obey him

t'filleh (tefillah): prayer

tefillin: phylacteries or leather boxes containing major prayers strapped on the left arm and head by worshipers (of Bar Mitzvah age) at the beginning of morning services on weekdays

tereetsim: answers to questions or explanations given in the form of an excuse

Tilliml: a tiny book containing all the psalms; the Book of *Tehillim* in the Jewish Bible

t'nuim: formally signed engagement articles preceding marriage

Toyreh (Teyreh, Torah): Pentateuch, the Five Books of Moses; specifically, the handwritten scrolled parchment properly covered and kept in the Holy Ark in the synagogue; the word is also used to refer to all of divine teaching

Toysefes (Tosefos, Tosafot): additional annotations or commentary on the Talmud by rabbis called Tosafists (twelfth to fourteenth centuries) who lived in France and Germany that are printed in the outer column opposite Rashi's commentary on each page of the Talmud

trayfe (treyf): not kosher

trop: the musical notes of cantillation used to recite or sing the Torah portion or the *Haftarah* passage from the Prophets in the synagogue service *tsedukeh:* charity

Tsenerene (Tzena u-Re'ena): title, derived from The Song of Songs in the Jewish Bible, of a book written in Yiddish by Jacob Ashkenazi (died 1626) containing rabbinic commentary and legends on each weekly reading of the Torah; very popular among women in Poland and elsewhere throughout the centuries who read and studied it devoutly, especially on Sabbath afternoons

tsheeva (teshuva): repentance

tshulnt: a stew of meat, beans, and potatoes (with regional variations); this delicacy served in honor of the Sabbath

tsi lange yoorn: to or for many years (usually, a wish for longevity)

tsitses: ritual fringes on a prayer shawl or on the *arba kanfos*

tsnies: modesty, proper moral behavior

tzaddaykes: a very righteous woman

tzaddikl: little righteous child (sometimes used affectionately and sometimes sarcastically)

uf der elter: in old age

ugov: in the Jewish Bible, perhaps a shepherd's musical pipe; in modern Hebrew, an organ

ulev ha-shulem: Peace be upon him (said of the dead)

umed: one side of a page of the Talmud; also a lectern or table on the *bima* in a synagogue where the cantor stands to lead the service

Umis ha-Nuvee: the prophet Amos

uvel: one who is in mourning

vabele: little wife (usually, a term of endearment)

Vay iz mir (Vey): Woe is me!

vos mir: What do you mean? What is it to me? (an expression of contempt about the matter being mentioned)

Ya'amoid: Let him stand; the first word in Hebrew introducing a person by name receiving an *aliya* to the Torah

Yasher koyech! (Yishar kochachaw!): Congratulations! (usually said to someone who has completed an honorable deed or service in the synagogue like leading the prayers, opening the Ark, being called up to the Torah for an *aliya,* or delivering a learned speech; may be used as a congratulatory greeting in other more secular circumstances; literally, May your strength be straight and just!

yaytser-hore: the evil inclination

yemach shemoy (shemo) (pl. *yemach shemum):* May his name be erased (used in reference to an evil tyrant or an oppressor); when **v'zichroy (v'zichro)** is added (pl. **v'zichrum**), the phrase is extended to mean, May his name and his memory be erased

yichusdik: of exalted pedigree

Yiddishkayt: Judaism, Jewish tradition

yingele: little boy

yiseerim (yisoorim): troubles, suffering

yishuv: the Jewish settlement in pre-state Israel

Yontev: any Jewish holiday besides the Sabbath

yoymum vaw-loylaw: day and night (a common Hebrew expression in the Jewish Bible, as in the Book of Psalms, chapter 1, verse 2)

zindele: little son

zindik nisht: Don't sin

zmires: Sabbath or holiday songs usually sung at table

zoynes: prostitutes